THE EYE OF THE LEOPARD

Henning Mankell is the prize-winning and internationally acclaimed author of the Inspector Wallander Mysteries, now dominating bestseller lists throughout Europe. He devotes much of his time to working with Aids charities in Africa, where he is also director of the Teatro Avenida in Maputo.

Steven T. Murray has translated numerous works from the Scandinavian languages, including the Pelle the Conqueror series by Martin Andersen Nexø and three of Henning Mankell's Kurt Wallander novels. He is Editor-in-Chief of Fjord Press in Seattle.

HENNING MANKELL

The Eye of the Leopard

TRANSLATED FROM THE SWEDISH BY
Steven T. Murray

VINTAGE BOOKS
London

Published by Vintage 2009

Copyright © Henning Mankell 1990

English translation copyright © Steven T Murray, 2008

Henning Mankell has asserted his right under the Copyright, Designs
and Patents Act 1988 to be identified as the author of this work

This book is sold subject to the condition that it shall not,
by way of trade or otherwise, be lent, resold, hired out,
or otherwise circulated without the publisher's prior
consent in any form of binding or cover other than that
in which it is published and without a similar condition,
including this condition, being imposed on the
subsequent purchaser

First published with the title *Leopardens Öga* in 1990 by
Ordfronts Förlag, Stockholm

First published in Great Britain in 2008 by Harvill Secker

Vintage
Random House, 20 Vauxhall Bridge Road,
London SW1V 2SA

www.vintage-books.co.uk

Addresses for companies within The Random House Group Limited
can be found at: www.randomhouse.co.uk/offices.htm

The Random House Group Limited Reg. No. 954009

A CIP catalogue record for this book
is available from the British Library

ISBN 9781784708900

Penguin Random House is committed to a sustainable future for
our business, our readers and our planet. This book is made from
Forest Stewardship Council® certified paper.

Printed and bound in Great Britain by Clays Ltd, St Ives plc

PART I

MUTSHATSHA

Chapter One

He wakes in the African night, convinced that his body has split in two. Cracked open, as if his guts had exploded, with the blood running down his face and chest.

In the darkness he fumbles in terror for the light switch, but when he flips it there is no light, and he thinks the electricity must be out again. His hand searches under the bed for a torch, but the batteries are dead and so he lies there in the dark.

It's not blood, he tells himself. It's malaria. I've got the fever, the sweat is being squeezed out of my body. I'm having nightmares, fever dreams. Time and space are dissolving, I don't know where I am, I don't even know if I'm still alive . . .

Insects are crawling across his face, enticed by the moisture that is oozing from his pores. He thinks he ought to get out of bed and find a towel. But he knows he wouldn't be able to stand upright, he would have to crawl, and maybe he wouldn't even be able to make it back to bed. If I die now at least I'll be in my own bed, he thinks, as he feels the next attack of fever coming on.

I don't want to die on the floor. Naked, with cockroaches crawling across my face.

His fingers clutch at the wet sheet as he prepares himself for an attack that will be more violent than the ones before. Feebly, in a voice that is hardly audible, he cries out in the darkness for Luka, but there is only silence and the chirping cicadas of the African night.

Maybe he's sitting right outside the door, he thinks in desperation. Maybe he's sitting there waiting for me to die.

The fever comes rolling through his body in waves, like sudden storm swells. His head burns as if thousands of insects were stinging and boring into his forehead and temples. Slowly he is dragged away from consciousness, sucked down into the underground corridors of the fever attack, where he glimpses the distorted faces of nightmares among the shadows.

I can't die now, he thinks, gripping the sheet to keep himself alive.

But the suction draught of the malaria attack is stronger than his will. Reality is chopped up, sawed into pieces that fit nowhere. He believes he is sitting in the back seat of an old Saab that is racing through the endless forests of Norrland in Sweden. He can't see who is sitting in front of him: only a black back, no neck, no head.

It's the fever, he thinks again. I have to hold on, keep thinking that it's only the fever, nothing more.

He notices that it has started to snow in the room. White flakes are falling on his face and instantly it's cold all around him.

Now it's snowing in Africa, he thinks. That's odd, it really shouldn't be doing that. I have to get hold of a spade. I have to get up and start shovelling, otherwise I'll be buried in here.

Again he calls for Luka, but no one answers, no one comes. He decides to fire Luka, that's the first thing he'll do if he survives this fever.

Bandits, he thinks in confusion. Of course, that's who cut the electrical line.

He listens and seems to hear the patter of their feet outside the walls of the house. With one hand he grips the revolver under his pillow, forces himself up to a sitting position, and points the gun at the front door. He has to use both hands just to lift it, and in desperation he fears he doesn't have enough strength in his finger to pull the trigger.

I'm going to give Luka the sack, he thinks in a rage. He's the one who cut the electrical line, he's the one who lured the bandits here. I have to remember to fire him in the morning.

He tries to catch some snowflakes in the barrel of the revolver, but they melt before his eyes.

I have to put on my shoes, he thinks. Otherwise I'll freeze to death.

With all his might he leans over the edge of the bed and searches with one hand, but finds only the dead torch.

The bandits, he thinks groggily. They've stolen my shoes. They've already been inside while I was asleep. Maybe they're still here . . .

He fires the pistol out into the room. The shot roars in the dark and he falls back against the pillows with the recoil, feeling calm, almost content.

Luka is behind it all, naturally. It was he who plotted with the bandits, he who cut the electrical line. But now he's been unmasked, so he has no more power. He will be sacked, chased off the farm.

They won't get me, he thinks. I'm stronger than all of them.

The insects continue boring into his forehead and he is very tired. He wonders whether dawn is far off, and he thinks that he must sleep. The malaria comes and goes, that's what is giving him the nightmares. He has to force himself to distinguish what he's imagining from what's real.

It can't snow here, he thinks. And I'm not sitting in the back seat of an old Saab racing through the bright summer forests of Norrland. I'm in Africa, not in Härjedal. I've been here for eighteen years. I have to keep my mind together. The fever is compelling me to stir up old memories, bring them to the surface, and to fool myself that they're real.

Memories are dead things, albums and archives that have to be kept cold and under lock and key. Reality requires my consciousness. To have a fever is to lose one's internal directions. I mustn't forget that. I'm in Africa and I've been here for eighteen years. It was never my intention, but that's how it turned out.

I've lost count of how many times I've had malaria. Sometimes the attacks are violent, like now; other times milder, a shadow of fever that quickly passes across my face. The fever is seductive, it wants to lure me away, creating snow even though it's over thirty degrees Celsius. But I'm still here in Africa, I've always been here, ever since I landed and stepped off the plane in Lusaka. I was going to stay a few weeks, but I've been here a long time, and that is the truth. It is not snowing.

His breathing is heavy and he feels the fever dancing inside him. Dancing him back to the beginning, to that early morning eighteen years ago when for the first time he felt the African sun on his face.

From the mists of the fever an instant of great clarity emerges, a landscape in which the contours are sharp and washed clean. He brushes off a large cockroach that is feeling his nostril with its antennae and sees himself standing in the doorway of the big jet at the top of the mobile staircase they have brought out.

He recalls that his first impression of Africa was how the sunshine turned the concrete of the airport completely white. Then a smell, something bitter, like an unknown spice or a charcoal fire.

That's how it was, he thinks. I will be able to reproduce that moment exactly, for as long as I live. It was eighteen years ago. Much of what happened later I've forgotten. For me Africa became a habit. A realisation that I can never feel completely calm when faced with this wounded and lacerated continent . . . I, Hans Olofson, have grown used to the fact that it's impossible for me to comprehend anything but fractions of this continent. But despite this perpetual disadvantage I have persevered, I have stayed on, learned one of the many languages that exist here, become the employer of over 200 Africans.

I've learned to endure this peculiar life, that involves being both loved and hated at the same time. Each day I stand face to face with 200 black human beings who would gladly murder me, slit my throat, offer up my genitals in sacrifice, eat my heart.

Every morning when I awake I am still, after eighteen years, surprised to be alive. Every evening I check my revolver, rotate the magazine with my fingers, make sure that no one has replaced the cartridges with empty ones.

I, Hans Olofson, have taught myself to endure the greatest loneliness. Never before had I been surrounded by so many people who demand my attention, my decisions, but who at the same time watch over me in the dark; invisible eyes that follow me expectantly, waiting.

But my most vivid memory is still that moment when I descended from the plane at Lusaka International Airport eighteen years ago. I keep returning to that moment, to gather courage, the power to survive; back to a time when I still knew my own intentions . . .

Today my life is a journey through days coloured by unreality. I live a life that belongs neither to me nor to anyone else. I am neither successful nor unsuccessful in what I set out to accomplish.

What possesses me is a constant amazement at what actually did happen. What was it that really brought me here, made me take that long journey from the remote interior of Norrland, still covered in snow, to an Africa that had not summoned me? What is it in my life that I have never understood?

The most curious thing is that I've been here for so long. I was twenty-five when I left Sweden, and now I'm forty-three. My hair began turning grey long ago; my beard, which I never manage to

7

shave off, is already completely white. I've lost three teeth, two in the lower jaw and one in the top left. The tip of my ring finger on my right hand is severed at the first knuckle, and sometimes I suffer from pain in my kidneys. I regularly dig out white worms that have bored underneath the skin on the soles of my feet. In the first few years I could scarcely bring myself to carry out these operations using sterilised tweezers and nail scissors. Now I grab a rusty nail or a knife that's lying about and carve out the parasites living in my heels.

Sometimes I try to view all these years in Africa as a wrinkle in my life, one which will some day turn out to never have happened. Maybe it's an insane dream that will be smashed apart when I finally manage to extricate myself from the life I'm living here. Someday this wrinkle in my life will have to be smoothed out . . .

In his attacks of fever, Olofson is flung against invisible reefs that tear his body apart. For brief moments the storm subsides, and he rocks on the waves and feels himself quickly turning into a block of ice. But just when he thinks the cold has reached his heart and frozen his last heartbeat to stillness, the storm returns and the fever slings him once more against the burning reefs.

In the restless, shredded dreams that rage like demons in his mind he keeps returning to the day he came to Africa. The white sun, the long journey that brought him to Kalulushi, and to this night, eighteen years later.

Like a malevolent figure, with no head or neck, the fever attack stands before him. With one hand he clutches his revolver, as if it were his last salvation.

The malaria attacks come and go.

Hans Olofson, once raised in a grim wooden house on the banks of the Ljusna River, shakes and shivers under his wet sheet.

From his dreams the past emerges, a reflection of the story he has still not given up hope of someday understanding . . .

Chapter Two

Through the swirling snow he returns to his childhood. It is midwinter 1956. It's four in the morning and the cold whines and prises at the beams of the old wooden house. That's not the sound that wakes him, but rather a stubborn scraping and muttering from the kitchen. He wakes as abruptly as only a child can, and he knows at once that his father has started scrubbing again. Dressed in his blue-trimmed pyjamas with their permanent snuff stains, with thick rag socks on his feet that are already soaked through from all the hot water he is madly sloshing across the floor, his father chases his demons through the winter night. He has chained up the two grey elkhounds out by the woodshed, hauling on the frozen chains as he stands half-naked in the freezing cold, while the water slowly comes to a boil on the stove.

And now he scrubs, a raging assault on the dirt that is visible to no one but himself. He throws the boiling water on cobwebs that suddenly flare up on the walls, then dumps a whole bucket over the hood of the stove because he's convinced that a knot of filthy snakes is hiding there.

All this the son lies in bed and watches, a twelve-year-old with the woollen blanket pulled up over his chin. He doesn't need to get up and tiptoe across the cold planks of the floor to watch it happen. He knows all about it. And through the door he hears his father's muttering and nervous laughter and desperate outbursts of rage.

It always occurs at night.

The first time he woke up and padded out to the kitchen he was five or six years old. In the pale light from the kitchen lamp with its misty shade he saw his father squelching around in the water, with his brown hair in wild disarray. And he understood, without putting it into words, that he was invisible. It was another kind of vision that occupied his father as he raced about with his scrubbing brush. His father was looking at something that only he could see. It terrified the boy, more so than if his father had suddenly raised an axe over his head.

Now, as he lies in bed listening, he knows that the coming days will be calm. His father will lie motionless in his bed before he finally gets up, pulls on his rough work clothes, and heads out into the forest again, where he cuts trees for Iggesund or Marma Långrör.

Neither father nor son will utter a word about the night-time scrubbing. For the boy in the bed it will fade like a malevolent apparition, until he again awakes in the night to the sound of his father scrubbing away his demons.

But now it is February 1956. Hans Olofson is twelve years old, and in a few hours he will get dressed, munch a few slices of rye bread, take his knapsack and head out into the cold on his way to school.

The darkness of night is a split personality, both friend and foe. From the blackness he can haul up nightmares and inconceivable horrors. The spasms of the roof beams in the hard frost are transformed into fingers that reach out for him. But the darkness can also be a friend, a time in which to weave thoughts about what will come, what people call the future.

He imagines how he will leave this lonely wooden house by

the river for the last time, how he will run across the bridge, disappear past the arches of the bridge, out into the world, almost all the way to Orsa Finnmark.

Why am I who I am? he thinks. Why me and not somebody else?

He knows precisely the first time that he had this crucial thought. It was a bright summer evening, and he was playing in the abandoned brickworks behind the hospital. They had divided themselves into friends and enemies, hadn't defined the game any more than that, and they alternately attacked and defended the windowless, half-razed factory building. They often played there, not just because it was forbidden, but because the building provided endlessly adaptable stage sets for their games. Its identity was forgotten, and with their games they lent constantly changing faces to the ruin. The dilapidated brickworks was defenceless; the shadows of the people who had once worked there were no longer present to protect it. Those who played there ruled. Only seldom did a bellowing father come and drag his child away from the wild game. There were shafts to plunge into, rotten steps to fall through, rusty kiln doors that could slam shut on hands and feet. But the boys playing there knew the dangers, avoided them, and had explored the safe paths through the endless building.

And it was there on that bright summer evening, as he was lying hidden behind a rusty, collapsed brick kiln, waiting to be discovered and captured, that he had asked himself for the first time why he was who he was and not someone else. The thought had made him both excited and upset. It was as if an unknown being had crept into his head and whispered to him the password to the future. After that, all his thoughts, the very process of thinking, seemed to come from a voice that was external, that had crept into his head, left its message, and then disappeared.

On that occasion he left the game, sneaked away from the others, vanished among the fir trees surrounding the dead brickworks, and went down to the river.

The forest was quiet; the swarms of mosquitoes had not yet taken over the town, which lay where the river made a bend on its long journey to the sea. A crow squawked its loneliness at the top of a crooked fir and then flapped away over the ridge where Hedevägen wound its way to the west. The moss under his feet was spongy. He had grown tired of the game, and on his way to the river everything changed. For as long as he had not established his own identity, was just *somebody* among all the others, he had possessed a timeless immortality, the privilege of childhood, the most profound manifestation of childishness. At the very moment that the unfamiliar question of why he was who he was crept into his head, he became a definite person and thus mortal. Now he had defined himself; he was who he was and would never be anyone else. He realised the futility of defending himself. Now he had a life ahead of him, in which he would have to be who he was.

By the river he sat down on a rock and looked at the brown water slowly making its way towards the sea. A rowboat lay chafing at its cable and he realised how simple it would be to disappear. From the town, but never from himself.

For a long time he sat by the river, becoming a human being. Everything had acquired limits. He would play again, but never the same way as before. Playing had become a game, nothing more.

Now he clambers over the rocks on the riverbank until he can see the house where he lives. He sits down on an uprooted tree that smells of rain and dirt and looks at the smoke curling out of the chimney.

Who can he tell about his great discovery? Who can be his confidant?

He looks at the house again. Should he knock on the draughty door to the ground floor flat and ask to speak with Egg-Karlsson? Ask to be admitted to the kitchen where it always smells of rancid fat, wet wool, and cat piss? He can't talk to Egg-Karlsson, who doesn't speak to anyone, just shuts his door as if he's closing an eggshell of iron around himself. All Hans knows about him is that he's a misanthrope and bull-headed. He rides his bicycle to the farmhouses outside town and buys up eggs, which he then delivers to various grocers. He does all his business in the early morning, and for the rest of the day he lives behind his closed door.

Egg-Karlsson's silence pervades the house. It hovers like a mist over the neglected currant bushes and the shared potato patch, the front steps, and the stairs to the top floor where Hans lives with his father.

Nor does he consider confiding in old lady Westlund who lives across from Egg-Karlsson. She would sweep him up in her embroidery and her Free Church evangelism, never listening to him, but proceeding at once to fling her holy words at him.

All that remains is the little attic flat he shares with his father. All he can do is go home and talk to his father, Erik Olofson, who was born in Åmsele, far from this cold hole in the interior of melancholy southern Norrland, this town that lies hidden away in the heart of Härjedal. Hans knows how much it hurts his father to have to live so far from the sea, to have to make do with a sluggish river. With a child's intuition he can see that a man who has been to sea can never thrive where the dense, frozen grey forest conceals the open horizons. He thinks of the sea chart that hangs on the kitchen wall, showing the waters around Mauritius and Réunion, with a glimpse of the east coast of Madagascar on the fading edge of the chart, and the sea floor indicated in places, its inconceivable depth 4,000 metres. It's a constant reminder of a sailor who wound up in the utterly wrong place, who managed to make landfall where there wasn't any sea.

On the shelf over the stove sits a full-rigger in a glass case, brought home decades ago from a dim Indian shop in Mombasa, purchased for a single English pound. In this frigid part of the world, inhabited by ice crystals instead of jacarandas, people have moose skulls and fox tails as wall decorations. Here it should smell of sour rubber boots and lingonberries, not the distant odour of the salty monsoon sea and burned-out charcoal fires. But the full-rigger sits there on the stove shelf, with its dreamy name *Célestine*. Long ago Hans decided that he would never marry a woman who wasn't named Célestine. It would be a form of betrayal; to his father, to the ship, to himself.

He also senses a murky connection between the full-rigger in its dusty case and the recurring nights when his father scrubs out his fury. A sailor finds himself driven ashore in a primeval Norrland forest, where no bearings can be taken, no ocean depths sounded. The boy senses that the sailor lives with a stifled cry of lamentation inside. And it's when the longing grows too strong that the bottles end up on the table, the sea charts are taken out of the chest in the hall, the seven seas are sailed once more, and the sailor metamorphoses into a wreck who is forced to scrub away his longing, transformed into hallucinations dissolved in alcohol.

The answers are always found in the past.

His mother disappeared, was simply gone one day. Hans was so little then that he has no memory either of her or of her departure. The photographs that lie behind the radio in father's unfinished logbook, and her name, Mary, are all he knows.

The two photographs instil in him a sense of dawn and cold. A round face with brown hair, her head tilted a little, maybe a hint of a smile. On the back of the photographs it says *Atelier Strandmark, Sundsvall*.

Sometimes he imagines her as a figurehead on a ship that was wrecked in a heavy storm in the southern seas and has since lain on the bottom in a watery grave 4,000 metres down. He imagines that her invisible mausoleum lies somewhere on the sea chart that hangs on the kitchen wall. Maybe outside Port Louis, or in the vicinity of the reef off the east coast of Madagascar.

She didn't want to leave. That's the explanation he gets. On the rare occasions that his father talks about her departure, he always uses the same words.

Someone who doesn't want to leave. Quickly, unexpectedly she disappeared, that much he understands. One day she's gone, with a suitcase. Someone saw her get on the train, towards Orsa and Mora. The vastness of Finnmark closed in around her disappearance.

For this disappearance he can manage only a wordless despair. And he assumes that they share the guilt, he and his father. They didn't die. They were left behind, never to receive a sign of life.

He's not sure whether he misses her, either. His mother is two photographs, not a person of flesh and blood who laughs, washes clothes, and tucks the covers under his chin when the winter cold penetrates the walls of the building. The feeling he bears is a kind of fear. And the shame of having been found unworthy.

He decides early on to share the contempt that the decent town has hung like shackles around his runaway mother. He goes along with the decent people, the grown-ups. Enclosed in an iron grip of constancy they pass their life together in the building where the beams scream out their distress during the long drawn-out winters. Sometimes Hans imagines that their house is a ship that has dropped anchor and is waiting for the wind to come up. The chains of the elkhounds out by the woodshed are actually anchor chains, the river a bay of the open sea. The attic flat is the captain's cabin, while the lower flat belongs to the crew. Waiting for the wind takes a long time, but occasionally the anchors are hauled up from the deep. And then the house sets off under full sail to race down the river, saluting one last time where the river bends at the People's Park, before the wind carries them away. Towards an Away that doesn't entail a return.

In an attempt to understand, he creates for himself the only rational explanation for why his father remains in this parched town, every day grabbing his tools and heading out into the forest that prevents him from seeing the ocean, or taking a bearing, or gazing at distant horizons.

Out there, he chops down the forest. Plodding through the heavy snow, chopping down tree after tree, stripping the bark from the trunks and slowly opening the landscape to the endless horizon. The sailor driven ashore has set himself a task – to clear a path back to a distant shoreline.

But Hans Olofson's life is more than just melancholy mother-lessness and a woodcutter's bouts of alcoholism. Together they study his father's detailed world maps and sea charts, go ashore in ports his father has visited, and explore in their imagination places that still await their arrival. The sea charts are taken down from the wall, rolled out, and weighted down with ashtrays and chipped cups. The evenings can be long, because Erik Olofson is a good storyteller. By the age of twelve Hans possesses an exhaustive knowledge of places as distant as Pamplemousse and Bogamaio; he has glimpsed the innermost secrets of seafaring, mysterious ships that vanished in their own enigma, pirate captains and sailors of the utmost benevolence. The secret world and the construct of regulations, so difficult to grasp, with which trading companies and private shippers have to live and comply, he has stratified in his mind without fully understanding them; yet it is as though he has touched on a great and decisive source of wisdom. He knows the smell of soot in Bristol, the indescribable sludge in the Hudson

River, the Indian Ocean's variable monsoons, the threatening beauty of icebergs, and the rattle of palm fronds.

'Here the wind murmurs in the trees,' says Erik Olofson. 'But in the tropics there is no murmuring. The palm leaves rattle.'

He tries to imagine the difference, striking his fork against a glass, but the palms simply refuse to clatter or rattle. They still murmur in his ears, like the firs he is surrounded by.

But when he tells his teacher that palms clatter and that there are water lilies as big as the centre circle on the ice-hockey rink outside the elementary school, he is ridiculed and called a liar. Red in the face, Headmaster Gottfried comes storming out of the musty office where he quells his distaste for teaching by imbibing vermouth assiduously. He grabs Hans by the hair and threatens him with what happens to anyone who is on an excursion to the land of lies.

Afterwards, alone in the schoolyard in the spotlight of derision, he decides never again to share any of his exotic knowledge. In this hellhole of filthy snow and wooden houses, no one understands a thing about the truths that must be sought at sea.

His eyes red and swollen, he comes home, boils potatoes, and waits for his father. Maybe this is when he makes his decision. That his life will be an unbroken journey. Standing over the pot of potatoes, the holy spirit of his journey takes possession of him. His father's smelly rag socks hang on the stove.

Sails, he thinks. Patched, mended sails . . .

That night, as he lies in bed, he asks his father to tell him one more time about the water lilies on Mauritius. And he falls asleep, assured that Headmaster Gottfried will burn in hell for not believing a sailor's report.

Later that evening, Erik Olofson drinks his coffee, sunk in the rickety chair next to the radio. He lets the waves of the ether hiss softly, as if he doesn't really want to listen. As if the hissing is message enough. The breathing of the sea, far away. The photographs burn in the logbook. All alone, he must guide his son. And no matter how much he reveals to the boy, the forest still seems to tighten around him. Sometimes he thinks that this is the true great defeat of his life, that despite everything he endures.

But for how long? When will he splinter, like a glass that has been heated for too long?

The ether waves hiss and he thinks again about why she left him, left their son. Why did she act like a man? he wonders. Fathers are the ones who leave and disappear. Not mothers. Least of all after conceiving a precise and premeditated plan of escape. How much about another person can you ever understand? Especially someone who lives close to you, in the inner circle of your own life.

In the pale light of the radio Erik Olofson tries to comprehend.

But the questions return, and the next evening are still hanging on their hooks. Erik Olofson tries to force his way into the core of a lie. Tries to understand, tries to endure.

Finally both of them are asleep, the sailor from Åmsele and his twelve-year-old son. The beams writhe in the midwinter darkness. A lone dog runs along the river in the moonlight. The two elkhounds lie curled up next to the stove in the kitchen, shaggy, with ears that prick up and fall again as the beams scrape and complain.

The house by the river sleeps. The dawn is far off on this night in Sweden in 1956.

Chapter Three

He can recall his departure for Africa like a dim shadow play.

He imagines the memories he bears to be a forest which was once open and clean, but which has become more and more overgrown. He has no tools for clearing the brush and scrub in this landscape. The growth of his memories is constant, the landscape harder and harder to take in.

Still, something does remain of that early morning in September 1969 when he left all his horizons behind and flew out into the world.

The Swedish sky was heavy that morning. An endless carpet of rain clouds hung over his head as he boarded an aeroplane for the first time. As he walked across the tarmac the damp seeped through his shoes.

I'm leaving Sweden with wet socks, he thought. If I ever make it to Africa I might bring along an autumn greeting in the form of a cold.

On the way to the plane he had turned around, as if someone might be there after all, waving goodbye to him. But the shadowy grey figures on the roof terrace of Arlanda didn't belong to him. His departure was noticed by no one.

As he checked in he suddenly felt an urge to snatch the ticket back, yell that it was all a mistake, and leave the airport. But he said thank you when they handed the ticket back to him, along with his boarding card and the wish for a pleasant trip.

His first stop on the way to foreign horizons was London. Then Cairo, Nairobi, and finally Lusaka.

He imagined that he might just as well be on his way to a distant constellation, the Lyre or one of the faintly glowing fixed stars in Orion's Belt.

All he knew about Lusaka was that the city was named after an African elephant hunter.

My objective is as unreasonable as it is ridiculous, he thought. Who in the world but me is on his way to a strange mission station deep in the bush of northwest Zambia, far beyond the roads to Kinshasa and Chingola? Who travels to Africa with a fleeting impulse as his only carry-on luggage? I have no detailed itinerary, nobody accompanied me to the airport, nobody will be meeting me. This journey I am about to begin is merely an escape . . .

He remembers that this is what he thought, and then there are only the vague shadows of memory. The way he sat in the plane holding on to himself with a cramplike grip. The vibrating fuselage, the whine of the jet engines, the machine gathering speed.

With a slight bow Hans Olofson made the climb into the air.

Twenty-seven hours later, precisely according to the schedule, he landed at Lusaka International Airport.

Naturally there was no one there to meet him.

Chapter Four

There is nothing remarkable about Hans Olofson's first encounter with the African continent, nothing unusual. He is the European visitor, the white man with his pride and his fear, who defends himself against what is foreign by instantly condemning it.

At the airport, disorder and chaos reign: incredibly complicated entry documents to fill out, badly spelled instructions, African immigration officers who seem unfazed by anything as mundane as time or organisation. Hans Olofson stands in a queue for a long time, only to be brusquely shunted to another queue when he finally reaches the brown counter on which black ants are hauling invisible particles of food. He realises that he has joined the queue intended for returning residents, those with Zambian passports or residence permits. Sweat pours out, strange foreign smells fill his nose, and the stamp he finally obtains in his passport is upside down, and he sees that the date of his arrival is wrong. He is handed a new form by an unbelievably beautiful African woman, brushes her hand quickly, and then truthfully fills in the amount of foreign cash he is bringing in.

At customs there is seemingly insurmountable chaos; suitcases are tossed off noisy carts pushed along by excited Africans. Among the pile of cardboard boxes he finally finds his suitcase, half squashed, and when he bends down to pull it out someone bumps into him and sends him sprawling. When he turns around there is no one apologising, no one seems to have noticed that he fell, only a billowing mass of people pushing towards the customs agents who are angrily ordering everyone to open their bags. He is sucked into this human surge, shoved back and forth like a pawn in some game, and then suddenly all the customs agents vanish and no one asks him to open his battered suitcase. A soldier with a submachine gun and a frayed uniform scratches his forehead with the muzzle of his weapon, and Olofson sees that he is hardly more than seventeen. A creaky swinging door opens and he steps out on to African soil in earnest. But there is no time for reflection; porters grab at his suitcase and his arms, taxi drivers yell out offers of their services. He is dragged off to an indescribably dilapidated car on which someone has painted the word TAXI on one of the doors in sloppy, garish letters. His bag is stuffed into a baggage compartment which already contains two hens with their feet tied together, and the boot lid is held in place by an ingeniously bound steel wire. He tumbles into a back seat with no springs at all, so that it feels as if he is sitting right on the floor. A leaky plastic container of petrol is leaning against one knee, and when the taxi driver climbs into the driver's seat with a burning cigarette in his mouth, Olofson for the first time begins to hate Africa.

This car will never start, he thinks in desperation. Before we even get out of the airport it will explode . . . He watches the driver, who can't be more than fifteen years old, join two loose wires next to the steering wheel; the engine responds reluctantly, and the driver turns to him with a smile and asks where he wants to go.

Home, he wants to answer. Or at least away, away from this

continent that makes him feel totally helpless, that has ripped from him all the survival tools he had acquired during his previous life . . .

His thoughts are interrupted by a hand groping at his face, stuck in through the window which has no glass in it. He gives a start, turns around, and looks straight into two dead eyes, a blind woman who is feeling his face with her hand and wants money.

The driver shouts something in a language that Olofson doesn't understand, the woman replies by starting to screech and wail, and Olofson sits on the floor of the car unable to do a thing. With a screech of tyres the driver leaves the begging woman behind, and Olofson hears himself yelling that he wants to be taken to a hotel in the city.

'But not too expensive!' he shouts.

He never hears the driver's reply. A bus with stinking exhaust and a violently racing engine squeezes past and drowns out the driver's voice.

His shirt is sticky with sweat, his back already aches from the uncomfortable sitting position, and he thinks he should have settled on the price before he let himself be forced into the car.

The incredibly hot air, filled with mysterious smells, blows into his face. A landscape drenched with sun as if it were an over-exposed photograph rushes past his eyes.

I'll never survive this, he thinks. I'm going to be killed in a car crash before I've even understood that I'm really in Africa. As if he had unconsciously made a prophecy, the car loses one of its front wheels at that instant and careens off the road into a ditch. Olofson strikes his head against the steel edge of the front seat and then heaves himself out of the car, afraid that it's going to explode.

The driver gives him a surprised look and then squats down

in front of the car and looks at the axle, which is bereft and gaping. From the roof of the car he then takes a spare tyre, patched and completely bald. Olofson leans over the red dirt and watches the driver put on the spare tyre as if in slow motion. Ants are crawling on his legs and the sun is so sharp that the world turns white before his eyes.

In order to hold on, regain an inner balance, he searches for something he can recognise. Something that reminds him of Sweden and the life he is used to. But he finds nothing. Only when he closes his eyes are the foreign African odours mixed with vague memories.

The spare tyre is put on and the journey continues. With wobbly movements of the steering wheel the driver pilots the car towards Lusaka, which will be the next stage in the nightmare that Olofson's first meeting with African soil has become. The city is a clamorous chaos of broken-down cars, swerving cyclists, and peddlers who seem to have laid out their wares in the middle of the street. There's a stench of oil and exhaust, and at a traffic light Olofson's taxi stops next to a lorry piled high with flayed animal carcasses. Black and green flies instantly swarm into the taxi, and Olofson wonders if he will ever find a hotel room, a door to close behind him.

But finally there is a hotel. The taxi comes to a stop under blooming jacaranda trees; an African in an outgrown, frayed uniform succeeds in prising open the door and helping Olofson to his feet. He pays the driver what he asks, even though he realises the amount is preposterous. Inside he has to wait for a long time at the front desk before they can work out whether there are any vacant rooms. He fills out an endless registration form and thinks that he'd better learn his passport number by heart, since this is already the fourth time he has had to repeat it. He keeps his suitcase between his legs, certain that thieves are lurking everywhere. Then he waits for half an hour in a queue to exchange money, and fills out another form with the feeling that he has seen it before.

A rickety lift transports him upwards and a porter in worn-out shoes carries his suitcase. Room 212 at the Ridgeway Hotel at last becomes his first breathing space on this new continent, and in impotent rebellion he strips off his clothes and crawls naked between the sheets.

The world traveller, he thinks. Nothing but a scared rabbit.

There's a knock at the door and he jumps up as if he had committed a crime by getting into bed. He wraps the bedspread around him and opens the door.

An old, shrunken African woman in a cleaning smock asks if he has any laundry to be done. He shakes his head, replies with exaggerated politeness, and suddenly realises he has no idea how he is expected to behave towards an African.

He lies down in bed again after drawing the curtains. An air-conditioning unit rattles and all of a sudden he begins to sneeze.

My wet socks in Sweden, he thinks. The wetness I brought with me. I'm nothing but an endless string of weaknesses. Anxiety is hereditary in my life. From the snowstorm a figure has emerged, someone who is continually threatened by his lack of inner direction.

In order to shake off his dejection he takes action, picking up the phone to call Room Service. An incomprehensible voice answers just as he's about to give up. He orders tea and chicken sandwiches. The mumbled voice repeats his order and says it will be brought to his room at once.

After an almost two-hour wait, a waiter appears at his door with a tray. During these two hours he was incapable of doing anything but waiting – with a crushing sense of being someone who does not exist, not even to the person who takes the Room Service orders.

Hans Olofson sees that the waiter has a pair of shoes that are almost falling apart. One heel is missing, and the sole of the other is gaping like a fish gill. Unsure how much to tip, he gives far too much, and the waiter gives him a quizzical look before vanishing silently from the room.

After the meal he takes a nap, and when he awakes it is already evening. He opens the window and looks out into the darkness, surprised that the heat is just as intense as it was that morning, although the white sun is no longer visible.

A few street lamps cast a faint light. Black shadows flit past, a laugh comes from an invisible throat in a car park just below his window.

He looks at the clothes in his suitcase, uncertain what would be proper for the dining room of an African hotel. Without actually choosing, he gets dressed and then hides half of his money in a hole in the cement behind the toilet bowl.

In the bar he sees to his surprise that almost all the guests are white, surrounded by black waiters, all wearing bad shoes. He sits down at a solitary table, sinks down into a chair that reminds him of the seat in the taxi, and is at once surrounded by dark waiters waiting for his order.

'Gin and tonic,' he says politely.

One of the waiters replies in a worried voice that there isn't any tonic.

'Is there anything else you can mix it with?' asks Olofson.

'We have orange juice,' says the waiter.

'That will be fine,' says Olofson.

'Unfortunately there is no gin,' says the waiter.

Olofson can feel himself starting to sweat. 'What do you have then?' he asks patiently.

'They don't have anything,' a voice replies from a nearby table, and Olofson turns to see a bloated man with a red face, dressed in a worn khaki suit.

'The beer ran out a week ago,' the man continues. 'Today there is cognac and sherry. For a couple of hours yet. Then that'll be gone too. Rumour has it that there may be whisky tomorrow. Who knows?'

The man finishes his speech by giving the waiter a dirty look and then leaning back in his chair.

Olofson orders cognac. He has the feeling that Africa is a place where everything is just about to run out.

By his third glass of cognac an African woman suddenly sits down in the chair next to him and gives him an inviting smile.

'Company?' she asks.

He is flattered, although he realises that the woman is a prostitute. But she arrived too early, he thinks. I'm not ready yet. He shakes his head.

'No thanks. Not tonight.'

Unfazed and still smiling, she gazes at him.

'Tomorrow?'

'Perhaps,' he says. 'But I may be leaving tomorrow.'

The woman gets up and disappears in the darkness by the bar.

'Whores,' says the man at the next table, who seems to be watching over Olofson like a guardian angel. 'They're cheap here. But they're better at the other hotels.'

'I see,' replies Olofson politely.

'Here they're either too old or too young,' the man goes on. 'There was a better arrangement before.'

Olofson never finds out what the prior arrangement consisted of, since the man again breaks off the conversation, leans back in his chair, and closes his eyes.

In the restaurant he is surrounded by new waiters, and he sees that they too all have worn-out shoes. One waiter who sets a carafe of water on his table has no shoes at all, and Olofson stares at his bare feet.

After much hesitation he orders beef. Just as the food is set on the table he feels an attack of severe diarrhoea coming on. One of the waiters notices that he has put down his fork.

'It doesn't taste good?' he asks anxiously.

'I'm sure it tastes excellent,' says Olofson. 'It's just that my stomach is acting up.'

Helplessly he sees the waiters flocking around his table.

'There's nothing wrong with the food,' he says. 'It's just my stomach.' Then he can't hold out any longer. Astonished guests watch his hasty flight from the table, and he fears he won't make it to his room in time.

Outside the lift he sees to his surprise that the woman who had previously offered him her company is leaving the hotel with the bloated man in the khaki suit who claimed that the prostitutes weren't any good at this hotel.

In the lift he shits his pants. A terrible stench begins to spread and the shit runs down his legs. With infinite slowness the lift takes him to his floor. As he stumbles down the corridor he hears a man laughing behind a closed door.

In the bathroom he studies his wretchedness. Then he lies down in his bed and thinks that the assignment he has given himself is either impossible or meaningless. What was he thinking?

In his wallet he has the smudged address of a mission station on the upper reaches of the Kafue. How he's going to get there he has no idea. He checked that there was a train to Copperbelt before he left. But from there, another 270 kilometres straight out into a pathless, desiccated landscape?

At the library back in his home town he had read about the country where he now found himself. Large parts of it are inaccessible during the rainy season. But when is the rainy season?

As usual, I'm ill-equipped, he thinks. My preparation was cursory, just throwing a few things into a suitcase. Only when it's too late do I try to make a plan.

I wanted to see the mission station that Janine didn't have a chance to visit before she died. I took over her dream instead of creating my own . . .

Hans Olofson falls asleep, sleeps restlessly, and rises at dawn. Out of the hotel window he sees the sun rise like a huge ball of fire over the horizon. Black shadows appear on the street below him. The fragrance of the jacaranda trees blends with the stifling smoke of the charcoal fires. Women with bulging bundles on their heads and children tied on to their backs walk towards goals he cannot fathom.

Without consciously making a decision, he vows to continue, towards Mutshatsha, towards the goal that Janine never reached . . .

Chapter Five

When Hans Olofson awakes in the cold winter morning, and his father lies collapsed over the kitchen table, asleep after a long night's struggle with his invisible demons, he knows that he is not completely alone in the world. He has a confidant, a warrior with whose help he torments the life out of the Noseless One who lives in Ulvkälla, a cluster of shacks on the south bank of the river. The two of them go searching for the adventure that must exist even in this frozen community.

The wooden house where Hans's accomplice lives has a mighty fir tree. Fenced in by stone posts and well-polished steel wire stands the district court and courthouse, a white building with a columned portico and wide double doors. The ground floor is the courtroom, and the judge lives upstairs. For over a year the building stood empty, after old Judge Turesson died. Then one day a fully packed Chevrolet drove into the courtyard of the courthouse, and the town peeked expectantly through its curtains. From the gleaming car poured the family of the new district judge. One of the children running around in the yard was named Sture. He became Hans Olofson's friend.

One afternoon, when Hans is wandering aimlessly down by

the river, he sees a boy he doesn't know sitting on one of his special boulders, a look-out over the steel bridge and the south bank of the river. He hides behind a bush and watches the interloper, who seems to be busy fishing.

The boy is the son of the new judge. Pleased, he summons up all the contempt he can muster. Only an idiot or a stranger from another parish would think it possible to catch fish in the river at this time of year.

Von Croona. That's the family's name. A noble name, he has heard. A family, a name. Not ordinary, like Olofson. The new judge has ancestors reaching back into the mists of historical battlefields.

Hans decides that because of this the judge's son must be a really unpleasant devil. He steps out of the bushes and shows himself.

The boy on the rock regards him with curiosity.

'Are there any fish here?' he asks.

Hans shakes his head and decides he ought to hit him. Chase him away from his private rock. But he stops short, because the nobleman is looking him straight in the eye, with absolutely no sign of embarrassment. He reels in his fishing line, pulls the piece of worm off the hook, and stands up.

'Are you the one who lives in the wooden house?' he asks, and Hans nods.

And as if it were the most natural thing in the world, they fall in together along the path. Hans leads the way, and the nobleman follows a few steps behind. Hans directs and points out things; he knows the paths, the ditches, the rocks. Finally they reach the pontoon bridge that leads over to the People's Park and then take a short cut across the common until they come to Kyrkogatan. Outside Leander Nilsson's bakery they stop to watch two dogs mating. At the water tower Hans shows him the spot where Rudin the madman set fire to himself a few years earlier, in protest at Head Physician Torstenson's refusal to admit him to the hospital for his stomach troubles.

With undisguised pride Hans tries to recount the most hair-raising events that he knows in the town's history. Rudin wasn't the only madman.

He directs their steps towards the church and points out the hollow space in the masonry of the south wall. As recently as the previous year one of the trusted deacons, in a fit of acute crisis of faith, tried to demolish the church one late January evening. With a pick and sledgehammer he resolutely set to work on the thick wall. The commotion naturally prompted the police to be called in, and Constable Bergstrand was forced to button up his winter coat and venture out into the snowstorm to arrest the man.

Hans tells the story and the nobleman listens.

From that day on a friendship grows between this ill-matched pair, the nobleman and the son of a woodcutter. Together they surmount the vast differences between them. Not all of them, of course; there is always a no-man's-land they can never enter together, but they grow as close to each other as possible.

Sture has his own room up in the attic of the courthouse. A large, bright room, with an abundance of curious equipment, maps, Meccano constructions, and chemicals. There are no toys, only two model aeroplanes hanging from the ceiling.

Sture points to a picture hanging on the wall. Hans sees a bearded man who reminds him of one of the portraits of the old pastors that hang in the church. But Sture explains that this is Leonardo, and he wants to be just like him someday. Inventing new things, creating what people never even imagined they needed . . .

Hans listens without fully understanding. But he senses the passion in what he hears, and thinks he recognises in it his own obsessive dream of getting the miserable wooden house to cut its moorings and float away down the river towards the sea he has never yet seen.

In this attic room they act out their mysterious games. Sture seldom visits Hans at home. The stuffy smell of elkhounds and wet woollens bothers him. He says nothing of this to Hans. Sture has been brought up not to offend anyone unnecessarily; he knows where he belongs and he's glad he doesn't have to live in Hans's world.

Early that first summer they begin to go on nightly excursions. A ladder raised towards the attic window enables Sture to escape without anyone hearing him, and Hans bribes the elkhounds with bones he has saved and sneaks out the door. In the summer night they stroll through the sleeping town, investing all their pride in never being discovered. Cautious shadows in the beginning, they develop a less and less restrained audacity. They slip through hedges and broken fences, listen at open windows, climb up on each other's shoulders and press their faces against the windows where the few night-time lamps in the town are still burning. They see drunken men in filthy underwear sleeping in musty flats; on one golden but sadly never repeated occasion they witness a railway worker cavorting with Oscaria the shoe salesgirl in her bed.

They rule the deserted streets and courtyards.

One night in July they commit a ritual break-in. They enter the bicycle shop near the chemist's, the Monarch Specialist, and move some bicycles around in the display window. Then they hastily leave the shop without taking anything. It's the break-in itself that tempts them, pulling off a bewildering mystery. Wiberg the bicycle dealer will never figure out what happened.

But they steal things too, of course. One night, from an unlocked car outside the Tourist Hotel, they snatch an unopened bottle of booze and ramble through their first bout of drunkenness, sitting on the boulder down by the river.

They follow each other, first one leading, then the other. They never fight, but they don't share all their secrets. For Hans it's a constant source of humiliation that Sture has so much money. When the feeling of subordination grows too strong, Hans decides that his own father is a good-for-nothing who never had enough sense to secure himself a real income.

For Sture the secret is the reverse. In Hans he sees a capable warrior, but he's also thankful that he doesn't have to be him.

Perhaps they both have an inkling that their friendship is an impossibility. How long can the camaraderie be stretched before it snaps? The abyss is there, they both sense how close it is, but neither wants to confront the catastrophe.

A streak of malice develops in their friendship. Where it comes from neither of them knows; suddenly it's just there. And it's towards the Noseless One in Ulvkälla that they direct their dark weapons.

In her youth the Noseless One was struck by a thyroid fever which necessitated an operation on her nose. But the accident and emergency surgeon at the time, Dr Stierna, was having a bad day. The woman's nose disappeared completely under his knife and fumbling fingers, and she had to return home with a hole between her eyes. She was seventeen at the time and twice tried to drown herself, but both times she floated to shore. She lived alone with her mother, a seamstress, who died less than a year after the disastrous operation.

If Pastor Harry Persson of the Free Church, nicknamed Hurrapelle, hadn't taken pity on her, she would certainly have succeeded in taking her own life. But Hurrapelle brought her to the wooden pews in the Baptist church, which lay between the town's two dominant dens of iniquity, the beer café and the People's Hall. At the church she was surrounded by a community she hadn't known existed. In the congregation there were two elderly nurses who weren't scared off by the Noseless One and her hole between the eyes, into which she stuck a handkerchief. They had served as missionaries in Africa for many years, mostly in the basin of the Belgian Congo, and there they experienced horrors far worse than a missing nose. They bore with them the memories of bodies rotted with leprosy and the grotesquely swollen scrotums of elephantiasis. For them the Noseless One was a grateful reminder that Christian mercy could work wonders even in such a godless land as Sweden.

Hurrapelle sent the Noseless One out on endless door-to-door rounds with the congregation's magazines in her hand, and no one refused to buy what she had to sell. Soon she had become a goldmine for Hurrapelle, and within six months he could even afford to trade in his rusty old Vauxhall on a brand-new Ford.

The Noseless One lived in a secluded house in Ulvkälla. One night Sture and Hans stood outside her darkened window. They listened in silence before they went home across the river bridge.

The next night they returned and nailed a dead rat to her front door. Her deformity led them to torment her for a few intense weeks that summer.

One night they threw an anthill they had dug up through her open kitchen window. Another night they splashed varnish all over her currant bushes and finished by putting a crow with its head cut off in her letterbox, along with some pages torn out of a well-thumbed and sticky issue of *Cocktail* that they had found in a dustbin. Two nights later they came back, this time equipped with a pair of Nyman, the courthouse caretaker's, hedge clippers. Their plan was to butcher her flowers.

While Hans stood watch by the corner of the house, Sture attacked one of the well-tended flower beds. Then the front door opened and the Noseless One stood there in a light-coloured bathrobe and asked them, quite calmly, without being sad or angry, why they were doing these things.

They had an escape route planned. But instead of disappearing like two hares in a hunt they just stood there as though struck by a sight they couldn't escape.

An angel, thinks Hans Olofson much later, many years after vanishing into the tropical night of Africa. He remembers her like an angel descended from heaven, now that she is dead and he has set out on the journey to fulfil her dream that he has taken as his own.

In the summer night the Noseless One stands in the doorway, her white bathrobe gleaming in the early grey light of dawn. She waits for their answer, which never comes.

Then she moves aside and asks them to come in. Her gesture is not to be refused. With bowed heads they pad past her, into her freshly scrubbed kitchen. Hans recognises at once the odour of soap, from his father's furious scrubbing, and he has a fleeting thought that maybe the Noseless One also scrubs her way through sleepless, haunted nights.

Her kindness makes them weak, defenceless. If fire and fuming sulphur had spewed out of the hole where her nose used to be, they could have dealt with the situation more easily. A dragon can be more easily conquered than an angel.

The smell of soap is mixed with the scent of bird cherry trees from outside her open kitchen window. A clock ticks softly on the wall. The marauders crouch down with their gaze fixed firmly on the linoleum. There in the kitchen, it is as quiet as if a prayer service were in progress. And perhaps the Noseless One is silently appealing to Hurrapelle's God to counsel her on how she can make the two shipwrecked vandals explain why one morning she came out to a kitchen crawling with angry ants.

In the minds of the two warrior brothers there is a great emptiness. Their thoughts are locked like frozen gears. What is there to explain? Their impetuous desire to torment her has no tangible cause. The roots of evil grow in the dark subterranean soil that can scarcely be viewed, let alone explained.

They crouch in the kitchen of the Noseless One, and after they sit in silence long enough, she lets them go. To the end she holds them there with her kindness, and she asks them to come back when they think they can explain their actions.

The meeting with the Noseless One becomes a turning point. They return to her kitchen often, and slowly a great intimacy develops among the three. That year Hans turns thirteen and Sture fifteen. They are always welcome at her house. As if by silent agreement, they don't talk about the crow with its throat cut or the crawling ants. A wordless apology is given, forgiveness is received, and life turns the other cheek.

Their first discovery is that the Noseless One has a name. It isn't just any old name, either; it's Janine, a name that emanates a foreign, mysterious fragrance.

She has a name, a voice, a body. She hasn't yet turned thirty. She is still young. They begin to sense the vague shimmer of beauty when they succeed in looking past and beyond the gaping hole below her eyes. They sense a heartbeat and lively thoughts, desires and dreams. And as if it were the most natural thing in the world she pilots them through her life story, lets them accompany her to the appalling moment when she realises that the surgeon has carved off her entire nose, follow her twice into the black water of the river and feel the ropes from the weights snap just at the instant her lungs are about to burst. They follow her like invisible shadows to Hurrapelle's penitent bench, listen to the mysterious embrace of salvation, and finally stand next to her when she discovers the ants crawling across the kitchen floor.

That year a strange love blooms among those three. A wildflower in the house just south of the river . . .

Chapter Six

On a dirty map Hans Olofson puts his finger on the name Mutshatsha.

'How do I get there?' he asks.

It is his second morning in Africa, his stomach is unsettled, and the sweat is running down inside his shirt.

He is standing at the front desk of the Ridgeway Hotel. Behind the desk is an elderly African with white hair and tired eyes. His shirt collar is frayed and his uniform unwashed. Olofson can't resist the temptation of leaning over the counter to see what the man has on his feet.

On the way down in the lift he'd thought, if the condition of the African continent is the same as the shoes of its inhabitants, the future is already over and all is irretrievably lost. He senses a vague unrest growing inside him from all the worn-out shoes he has seen.

The old man is barefoot. 'Maybe there's a bus,' he says. 'Maybe a lorry. Sooner or later a car will come by, I'm sure.'

'How do I find the bus?' asks Olofson.

'You stand by the side of the road.'

'At a bus stop?'

'If there is a bus stop. Sometimes there is. But usually not.'

Olofson realises that the vague answer is the most detailed one he will get. He senses something tentative, ephemeral in the lives of the blacks, so distant and foreign from the world he comes from.

I'm afraid, he thinks. Africa scares me, with its heat, its odours, its people with bad shoes. I'm much too visible here. My skin colour shines as if I were a burning candle in the dark. If I leave the hotel I'll be swallowed up, vanish without leaving a trace . . .

The train to Kitwe is supposed to depart in the evening. Olofson spends the day in his room. He stands at the window for long stretches. He sees a man in ragged clothes cutting grass around a big wooden cross with a long, broad-bladed knife. People pass by with shapeless bundles on their heads.

At seven in the evening he leaves his room and has to pay for the night he won't be spending in it. When he emerges from the hotel screaming taxi drivers fall upon him.

Why do they make such a damned racket? he thinks, and the first wave of contempt washes over him.

He walks towards the car that seems the least dilapidated and puts his suitcase in the back seat with him. He has hidden his money in his shoes and underwear. When he sits down in the back seat he immediately regrets his choice of hiding places. The banknotes are sticky and cling to his body.

At the railway station there is, if possible, even greater chaos than at the airport. The taxi lets him off in the midst of a surging sea of humanity, bundles of clothes, chickens and goats, water sellers, fires, and rusted cars. The station is almost completely dark. What few lightbulbs there are have burned out or have been stolen.

He barely manages to pay the taxi driver before he is surrounded by filthy children offering their services as porters or begging for money. Without knowing what direction he should take, he hurries off, his feet already hurting from the wads of notes. He discovers a gaping hole in a wall above which a rickety sign says Ticket Counter. The waiting room is packed with people, it smells of urine and manure, and he gets into something that appears to be a queue. A man with no legs comes sliding along on a board and tries to sell him a dirty ticket to Livingstone, but Olofson shakes his head, turns away, and retreats within himself.

I hate this chaos, he thinks. It's impossible to get an overview. Here I am at the mercy of chance and people sliding along on boards.

He buys a ticket to Kitwe and walks out on the platform. A train with a diesel locomotive is waiting, and he looks despondently at what awaits him: run-down carriages, already overfilled, like bursting cardboard boxes with toy figures in them, and broken windowpanes.

He notices two white people climbing into the carriage behind the locomotive. As if all white people were his friends in this black world, he hurries after them and almost falls on his face when he trips over a man lying stretched out on the platform asleep.

He hopes he has bought a ticket that gives him access to this carriage. He makes his way forward to the compartment where the white people he has been following are busy stowing their bags on the baggage racks.

Entering a compartment on a train in Sweden can often feel like intruding in someone's private living room, but in this compartment he is met by friendly smiles and nods. He imagines that with his presence he is reinforcing a disintegrating and ever-diminishing white army.

Before him are an older man and a young woman. Father and daughter, he guesses. He stows his suitcase and sits down, drenched in sweat. The young woman gives him an encouraging look as she takes out a book and a pocket torch.

'I come from Sweden,' he says, with a sudden urge to talk to someone. 'I assume that this is the train for Kitwe?'

'Sweden,' says the woman. 'How nice.'

The man has lit his pipe and leans back in his corner.

'Masterton,' he says. 'My name is Werner, and this is my wife Ruth.'

Olofson introduces himself and feels a boundless gratitude at finding himself together with people who have decent shoes on their feet.

The train starts up with a jolt and the uproar in the station increases in a violent crescendo. A pair of legs is visible outside the window as a man climbs up on to the roof. After him come a basket of chickens and a sack of dried fish which rips open and spreads a smell of decay and salt.

Werner Masterton looks at his watch.

'Ten minutes too early,' he says. 'Either the driver is drunk or he's in a hurry to get home.'

Diesel fumes waft by, fires are burning along the tracks, and the lights of Lusaka slowly fall behind.

'We never take the train,' says Masterton from the depths of his corner. 'About once every ten years. But in a few years there will hardly be any trains left in this country. Since independence everything has fallen apart. In five years almost everything has been destroyed. Everything is stolen. If this train suddenly stops tonight, which it most certainly will do, it means that the driver is trying to sell fuel from the locomotive. The Africans come with their oil cans. The green glass in the traffic lights has disappeared. Children steal them and try to palm them off on tourists as emeralds. But soon there won't be any tourists left either. The wild animals have been shot, wiped out. I haven't heard of anyone seeing a leopard in more than two years.' He gestures out into the darkness.

'There were lions here,' he says. 'Elephants wandered free in huge herds. Today there is nothing left.'

The Mastertons have a large farm outside Chingola, Olofson learns during the long night's journey to Kitwe. Werner Masterton's parents came from South Africa in the early 1950s. Ruth was the daughter of a teacher who moved back to England in 1964. They met while visiting friends in Ndola and married despite the great age difference.

'Independence was a catastrophe,' says Masterton, offering whisky from his pocket flask. 'For the Africans, freedom meant that nobody had to work any more. No one gave orders, no one considered they might have to do something that wasn't demanded of them. Now the country survives on its income from copper mining. But what happens when prices drop on the world market? No investment has been made in any alternatives. This is an agricultural country. It could be one of the world's best, since the soil is fertile and there is water available. But no efforts are being made. The Africans have grasped nothing, learned nothing. When the British flag was struck and they raised their own, it was the beginning of a funeral procession that is still going on.'

'I know almost nothing about Africa,' says Olofson. 'What little I do know I've already begun to doubt. And I've only been here two days.'

They give him an inquisitive look and he suddenly wishes he could have offered a different reply.

'I'm supposed to visit a mission station in Mutshatsha,' he says. 'But I don't really know how to get there.'

To his surprise, the Mastertons immediately take up the question of how he can complete his expedition. He quickly surmises that perhaps he has presented a problem that can be solved, in contrast to the one Werner Masterton has just laid out. Perhaps black problems have to be solved by the blacks, and the whites' problems by the whites?

'We have some friends in Kalulushi,' says Werner. 'I'll take you there in my car. They can help you to continue from there.'

'That's too much to ask,' replies Olofson.

'That's the way it is,' says Ruth. 'If the *mzunguz* don't help each other, no one will. Do you think that any of the blacks climbing on the roof of this train car would help you? If they could, they'd steal your trousers right off you.'

Ruth lays out a meal from her baggage and invites Hans to join them.

'Didn't you even bring water with you?' she asks. 'The train could be a day late. There's always something that breaks down, something missing, something they forgot.'

'I thought there would be water on the train.'

'It's so filthy that not even a *munto* will drink it,' says Werner, spitting into the darkness. 'This would be a good country to live in if it weren't for the blacks.'

Olofson decides that all whites in Africa probably espouse racist views just to survive. But is that true of missionaries too?

'Isn't there any conductor coming?' he asks, to avoid responding to this last remark.

'There may not be one,' replies Ruth. 'He may have missed his train. Or else some distant relative died and he went to the funeral without letting anyone know. The Africans spend a great deal of their lives going to and from funerals. But maybe he will come. Nothing is impossible.'

These people are the remnants of something utterly lost, thinks Olofson. Colonialism is completely buried today, with the exception of South Africa and the Portuguese colonies. But the people remain. A historical epoch always leaves behind a handful of people for the following period. They keep looking backwards,

43

dreaming, aggrieved. They look at their empty hands and wonder where the instruments of power have gone. Then they discover these instruments in the hands of the people they previously only spoke to when giving out orders and reprimands. They live in the Epoch of Mortification, in the twilight land of ruin. The whites in Africa are a wandering remnant of a people that no one wants to think about. They have lost their foundation, what they thought was permanent for all eternity . . .

One question remains obvious. 'So things were better before?'

'What answer can we give to that?' says Ruth, looking at her husband.

'Answer with the truth,' says Werner.

A weak, flickering lamp casts the compartment in darkness. Hans sees a lampshade covered with dead insects. Werner follows his gaze.

'For a lampshade like that a cleaning woman would have been given the sack,' he says. 'Not the next day, not after a warning, but instantly, kicked out on the spot. A train as filthy as this one would have been an impossibility. In a few hours we'll be in Kabwe. Before, it was called Broken Hill. Even the old name was better. The truth, if you want to know, is that nothing has been maintained or become better. We're forced to live in the midst of a process of decay.'

'But –' says Olofson, before he is interrupted.

'Your "but" is premature,' says Ruth. 'I have a feeling that you want to ask whether the blacks' lives are better. Not even that is true. Who could take over from all the Europeans who left the country in 1964? There was no preparation, only a boundless arrogance. A bewitched cry for independence, their own flag, maybe soon their own currency.'

'Taking responsibility requires knowledge,' Werner continues. 'In 1964 there were six blacks with university degrees in this country.'

'A new era is created out of the preceding one,' Olofson counters. 'The education system must have been poor.'

'You're starting from the wrong assumptions,' says Ruth. 'No one was thinking about anything as dramatic as what you call a new era. Development would continue, everyone would be better off, not least the blacks. But without chaos taking over.'

'A new era doesn't create itself,' Olofson insists. 'What did actually happen?'

'Treachery,' says Ruth. 'The mother countries deceived us. All too late we realised we had been abandoned. In Southern Rhodesia they understood, and there everything has not gone to hell as it has here.'

'We've just been in Salisbury,' says Werner. 'There we could breathe. Maybe we'll move there. The trains ran on time, the lampshades weren't full of insects. The Africans did what they do best: follow orders.'

'Freedom,' says Olofson, and then has no idea what to say next.

'If freedom is starving to death, then the Africans are on the right track in this country,' says Ruth.

'It's hard to understand,' says Olofson. 'Hard to comprehend.'

'You'll see for yourself,' Ruth goes on, smiling at him. 'There's no reason for us not to tell you how things stand, because the truth will be revealed to you anyway.'

The train screeches to a stop, and then everything is quiet. Cicadas can be heard in the warm night and Olofson leans out into the darkness. The starry sky is close and he finds the brightly glowing constellation of the Southern Cross.

What was it he had thought when he left Sweden? That he was on his way to a distant, faintly gleaming star?

Ruth Masterton is engrossed in a book with the help of her shaded pocket torch, and Werner is sucking on his extinguished pipe. Olofson feels called upon to take stock of his situation.

Janine, he thinks. Janine is dead. My father drank himself into a wreck that will never again go to sea. My mother consists in her entirety of two photographs from Atelier Strandmark in Sundsvall. Two pictures that instil fear in me, a woman's face against a backdrop of merciless morning light. I live with an inheritance of the smell of elkhound, of winter nights and an unwavering sense of not being needed. The moment I chose not to conform to my heritage, to become a woodcutter like my father and marry one of the girls I danced with to Kringström's orchestra in the draughty People's Hall, I also rejected the only background I had. I passed the lower-school examination as a pupil none of the teachers would ever remember, I endured four terrible years in the county capital and passed a meaningless student examination so that I wouldn't be a failure. I did my military service in a tank regiment in Skövde, again as a person no one ever noticed. I nourished the hope of becoming a lawyer, the sworn defender of extenuating circumstances. I lived for over a year as a lodger in a dark flat in Uppsala, where a fool sat across from me every day at the breakfast table. The present confusion, indolence and fear within the Swedish working classes have found in me a perfect representative.

Still, I haven't given up. The failed law studies were only a temporary humiliation – I can survive that. But the fact that I have no dream? That I travel to Africa with someone else's dream, someone who is dead? Instead of grieving I set off on a journey of penance, as if I were actually to blame for Janine's death.

One winter night I crept across the cold iron spans of the river bridge. The moon hung like a cold wolf's eye in the sky, and I was utterly alone. I was fourteen years old and I didn't fall. But afterwards, when Sture was supposed to follow me . . .

His thoughts burst. From somewhere he hears a person snoring. He traces the sound to the roof of the train car.

In a sudden flare-up of rage, he gives himself two alternatives: either continue his law studies or return to the frozen landscape of his childhood.

The journey to Africa, to the mission station in Mutshatsha, will fade away. In every person's life there are ill-considered actions, trips that never needed to be taken. In two weeks he will return to Sweden and leave the Southern Cross behind. The parentheses will then be closed.

Suddenly Werner Masterton is standing by his side and looking out into the darkness.

'They're selling diesel fuel,' he says. 'I just hope they don't miscalculate, so we wind up stuck here. Within a year the wandering hunter ants will have transformed this train into a deformed steel skeleton . . .'

After an hour the train jolts to a start.

Later they stop for an inexplicably long time at Kapiri Mposhi. In the dawn light Olofson falls asleep in his corner. The conductor never appears. Just as the morning's heat breaks through, the train screeches into Kitwe.

'Come with us,' says Ruth. 'Then we'll drive you to Kalulushi.'

Chapter Seven

One day Janine teaches them to dance.

The rest of the town expects her to whine and complain, but she chooses to go in a completely different direction. In music she sees her salvation. She decides that the affliction so deeply incised in her body will be transformed into music. In Hamrin's music shop she purchases a slide trombone and begins to practise daily. Hurrapelle tries for the longest time to persuade her to choose a more pleasing instrument, like the guitar, mandolin, or possibly a small bass drum. But she persists, forgoing the possible joy of joining in the concerts of the Free Church, and practises by herself in her house by the river. She buys a Dux gramophone and searches often and eagerly through the record selection at the music shop. She is entranced by jazz, in which the trombone often has a prominent role. She listens, plays along, and she learns. On dark winter evenings, when the door-knocking with her magazines is over for the day, and the congregation doesn't have a prayer meeting or other fellowship, she loses herself in her music. 'Some of These Days', 'Creole Love Call', and not least 'A Night in Tunisia' flow from her trombone.

She plays for Sture and Hans. Astonished, they watch her the first time, barefoot on the kitchen floor, with the gramophone spinning in the background and the brass instrument pressed to her lips. Sometimes she deviates from the melody, but usually the notes are woven together with the orchestra that is pressed into the grooves of the record.

Janine with her trombone . . .

Janine with her noseless face and her incredible gesture of inviting them into her house instead of calling the police, transforms that year, 1957, into a fairy tale they doubt they will ever experience again.

For Sture the move from the cathedral and residence in a city in Småland to this market town had seemed a nightmare. In a desolate and snowed-in Norrland he would go under, he was convinced of that. But he found a warrior and together they found Janine . . .

Hans creates a huge dream for himself which he can crawl inside like a voluminous overcoat. He realises at once that he loves her; in his dreams he furnishes her with a nose and transforms her into his vicarious mother.

Even though Janine is their common property, separate walls close tightly around their experiences. One cannot share everything; secrets must be carefully kept to oneself. A piece of crucial wisdom on life's arduous path is to learn which dreams can be shared and which must be kept inside one's own secret rooms.

Janine watches, listens and senses. She sees Sture's tendency towards arrogance and bullying, she senses Hans's longing for his absent mother. She sees the chasms that exist there, the huge differences. But one evening she teaches them to dance.

Kringström's orchestra, which had played at every Saturday night dance since 1943, has testily accepted the challenge emanating from the increasingly discontented youth and has reluctantly begun to alter its repertoire. One Saturday in early spring they surprise everyone, not least themselves, by striking up a tune that might be related to the new music pouring in from the USA.

On this very evening Sture and Hans are hanging around outside the People's Hall. Impatiently they are waiting until they're big enough to buy their own tickets and step on to the crowded dance floor. The music comes through the walls, and Sture decides it's time they learned how to dance.

Later that evening, when they are frozen and stiff, they wander down by the river bridge, race each other and yell underneath the iron span, and they don't stop until they are standing outside Janine's door. Music is coming through the walls. She's playing tonight . . .

When she realises that they want to learn to dance, she is ready at once to teach them. Before the surgeon deformed her face, she had danced quite often. But she has not moved across a dance floor since. With a firm grip around the waist and simple repeated steps to the left and right, she leads them into the rhythmic stamping of the waltz and foxtrot. She keeps pressing them to her, one after the other, and sweeps around on the linoleum of the kitchen floor. Whoever is not dancing runs the gramophone, and soon the windows are fogged up from their efforts to follow and keep track of the steps.

From a kitchen cabinet she pulls out a bottle of homemade booze. When they ask where she got hold of it she just laughs. She offers each of them only a little glass, but keeps on drinking until she gets drunk. She lights a cigar and blows smoke out her nose hole, while claiming to be the world's only female locomotive. She tells them that sometimes she imagines how she will leave Hurrapelle's penitent bench and vanish into the world of carnival sideshows. She will never be a prima donna on the slack wire, but perhaps a freak who can elicit horror from the crowd. Exhibiting deformed people for money is a tradition that has been lost in the mists of time. She tells them about the Laughing Kid, who had the corners of his mouth sliced open to his ears and was then sold to a carnival troupe and made his owners rich.

From a kitchen drawer she takes out a red clown nose which she fastens with an elastic string around her head, and dumbstruck they watch this woman who radiates so many contradictory powers. What is hardest to understand but also most disturbing is how Janine can live this double life: the barefoot dance on the kitchen floor, the booze in the cupboard; the hard pews in Hurrapelle's church.

But her salvation is no fabrication. She has her God securely placed in her heart. Without the fellowship that the congregation once extended to her she would no longer be alive. This is not to say that she is attracted to or professes all the beliefs of the congregation. Raising money to send missionaries to distant Bantu tribes in Africa she considers not only meaningless but a serious violation of the decree that all faith must be voluntary. When the women of the congregation meet in sewing circles for the production of table runners to sell at fairs, she stays home and sews her own clothes. She is a restless element in the congregation's world, but as long as she can single-handedly collect the majority of its annual income by knocking on doors, she does not hesitate to indulge her freedoms. Hurrapelle makes regular attempts to coax her into the sewing circle, but she refuses. Since he's afraid she might begin to waver in her faith, or even worse, move her God to a competing congregation, he doesn't press the issue. When the members of the congregation complain about her self-indulgent behaviour, he deals sternly with the criticism.

'The least of my children,' he says. 'Think of her suffering. Think how much good she is doing for our congregation . . .'

The evenings with Janine during that year become an unbroken series of peculiar encounters. Against a background of 'Some of These Days' she holds her hand over the two vandals who in the malevolence of ignorance once decided to torment the life out of her.

Both of them, each in his own way, find in her something of the mystery they had previously sought in vain in the town. The house by the south bank of the river becomes a journey out into the world . . .

On the evening she starts teaching them to dance, they experience for the first time the exciting sensation of being close to a warm, sweaty female body.

And the thought occurs to her – maybe not just at that moment, but later – that she would like to take off her clothes and stand stark naked before them, to be seen just once, even if it's only by two skinny, half-grown boys.

At night come the dark powers that are never permitted to surface and burn. To cry out her distress and follow Hurrapelle's admonition always to surrender to God, who keeps His ear in constant readiness; that would be impossible. There the religious thread breaks, and then she has no one but herself to cling to. The greatest of all the sorrows she has to bear is that she has never had the chance to sink into an embrace, even in the dirty back seat of a car parked on a remote logging road.

But she refuses to complain. She has her trombone. In the dawn of winter mornings she stands in her kitchen and plays 'Creole Love Call'.

And the boys who brought the sack of ants – she always lets them in. When she teaches them to dance she feels happy that she could overcome their childish shyness . . .

During the late winter and early spring of 1957, Sture and Hans spend many evenings at her house. They often don't go home until the winter night has driven its frozen ship towards midnight.

Spring arrives again. One day the unassuming but eagerly awaited yellow crowns of the coltsfoot begin to glow in a dirty ditch. Hurrapelle stands one morning in the back room of the Baptist church and searches in a cardboard box for handbills announcing the Spring Meeting. Soon it will be time for even the sermon placards to change their skin.

But spring is deceptive, because its beauty barely conceals the fact that death is hiding in the eye of the coltsfoot blossom.

For Sture and Hans, death is an invisible insect that eats away at life and every event. Long evenings they sit on the boulder by the river or in Janine's kitchen and ponder how death actually ought to be understood and described. Sture suggests that death ought to be like Jönsson, the restaurant owner, who stands on the doorstep of the Grand Hotel and welcomes his guests in a black, greasy tuxedo. How easily he could then drip poison into the black soup or the sauce on the roast beef. He would lurk by the swinging doors to the kitchen and the tablecloths would be transformed into stained shrouds . . .

For Hans Olofson, death is much too complicated to be compared to a restaurant owner. Thinking of death as *a person* of flesh and blood, with a hat and coat and sniffling nose, is too simple. If death had a face, clothes and shoes, it wouldn't be any harder to conquer than one of the scarecrows that Under the horse dealer uses to protect his berry bushes. Death is more vague, a cool breeze that suddenly wafts across the river without rippling the water. He won't come any closer than that to death this spring, until the great catastrophe occurs and death blows its shrillest trumpet.

And yet it's something he will always remember. Much later, when the African night closes in on him, and his childhood is just as distant as the land he now inhabits, he remembers what they talked about, on the boulder by the river or in Janine's kitchen. As if in a fleeting dream, he remembers the year when Janine taught them to dance and they stood in the darkness outside her house and heard her playing 'A Night in Tunisia' . . .

Chapter Eight

In Kitwe a laughing African comes running to meet them. Hans Olofson sees that he has trainers on his feet, with no holes, and the heels have not been cut off.

'This is Robert,' says Ruth. 'Our chauffeur. The only one on the farm we can count on.'

'How many employees do you have?' asks Olofson.

'Two hundred and eighty,' replies Ruth.

Olofson crawls into the back seat of a Jeep that seems much the worse for wear.

'You have your passport, don't you?' asks Werner. 'We'll be going through several checkpoints.'

'What are they looking for?' Olofson asks.

'Smuggled goods headed for Zaire,' says Ruth, 'or South African spies. Weapons. But actually they just want to beg for food and cigarettes.'

They reach the first roadblock just north of Kitwe. Crossed logs, covered with barbed wire, cut off the lanes of the road. A dilapidated bus stops just before they arrive, and Olofson sees a young soldier with an automatic rifle chase the passengers out of it. There seems to be no end to the Africans who come pouring out, and he wonders how many can actually fit inside. While the passengers are forced to line up, a soldier climbs up on the roof of the bus and starts tearing apart the shapeless pile of bundles and mattresses. A goat that was tied up suddenly kicks its way loose, jumps down from the roof of the bus, and disappears bleating into the bush by the side of the road. An old woman begins to shriek and wail and a tremendous commotion breaks out. The soldier on the roof yells and raises his rifle. The old woman wants to chase her goat but is restrained by other soldiers who suddenly appear from a grass hut beside the road.

'Coming right after a bus is a nightmare,' says Ruth. 'Why didn't you overtake it?'

'I didn't see it, madame,' replies Robert.

'The next time you'll see the bus,' says Ruth, annoyed. 'Or you can look for a new job.'

'Yes, madame,' Robert answers.

The soldiers seem tired after searching the bus and wave the Jeep through without inspecting it. Olofson sees a moonscape spreading before them, high hills of slag alternating with deep mine pits and blasted crevices. He realises that now he is in the midst of the huge copper belt that stretches like a wedge into Katanga province in Zaire. At the same time he wonders what he would have done if he hadn't met the Mastertons. Would he have got off the train in Kitwe? Or would he have stayed in the compartment and returned with the train to Lusaka?

They pass through more roadblocks. Police and drunken soldiers compare his face to his passport photo, and he can feel terror rising inside him.

They hate the whites, he thinks. Just as much as the whites obviously hate the blacks . . .

They turn off the main road and suddenly the earth is quite red. A vast, undulating fenced landscape opens before the Jeep.

Two Africans open a wooden gate and offer hesitant salutes.

The Jeep pulls up to a white two-storey villa with colonnades and flowering bougainvillea. Olofson climbs out, thinking that the white palace reminds him of the courthouse in his distant home town.

'Tonight you'll be our guest,' says Werner. 'In the morning I'll drive you to Kalulushi.'

Ruth shows him to his room. They walk down cool corridors; tiled floors with deep rugs. An elderly man appears before them. Olofson sees that he is barefoot.

'Louis will take care of you while you're here,' says Ruth. 'When you leave you can give him a coin. But not too much. Don't upset him.'

Olofson is troubled by the man's ragged clothes. His trousers have two gaping holes in the knees, as if he has spent his life crawling on them. His faded shirt is frayed and patched.

Olofson looks out a window at a large park extending into the distance. White wicker chairs, a hammock in a giant tree. Somewhere outside he hears Ruth's excited voice, a door slamming. From the bathroom he hears water running.

'Your bath is ready, *Bwana*,' says Louis behind him. 'The towels are on the bed.'

Olofson is suddenly agitated. I have to say something, he thinks. So he understands that I'm not one of them, merely a temporary visitor, who is not used to being assigned a personal servant.

'Have you been here long?' he asks.

'Since I was born, *Bwana*,' Louis replies.

Then he vanishes from the room, and Olofson regrets his question. A master's question to a servant, he thinks. Even though I mean well I make myself look insincere and common.

He sinks down in the bathtub and asks himself what escape routes are still left to him. He feels like a conman who has grown tired of not being unmasked.

They're helping me carry out a meaningless assignment, he thinks. They're ready to drive me to Kalulushi and then help me find the last transport out to the mission station in the bush. They're going to a lot of trouble for something that's just an egocentric impulse, a tourist trip with an artificial dream as its motive.

The dream of Mutshatsha died with Janine. I'm plundering her corpse with this excursion to a world where I don't belong at all. How can I be jealous of a dead person? Of her will, of her stubborn dream, which she clung to despite the fact that she could never realise it? How can an atheistic, unbelieving person take over the dream of being a missionary, helping downtrodden and poverty-stricken people with a religious motive as the foremost incentive?

In the bathtub he decides to return, ask to be driven back to Kitwe. Come up with a credible explanation for why he has to change his plans.

He dresses and goes out into the large park. Under a tall tree that spreads a mighty shadow there is a bench that is carved out of a single block of stone. He scarcely manages to sit down before a servant brings him a cup of tea. All at once Werner Masterton stands before him, dressed in worn overalls.

'Would you like to see our farm?' he asks.

They climb into the Jeep, which has been newly washed. Werner puts his big hands on the wheel after pulling a worn sunhat down over his eyes. They drive past long rows of hen houses and fields. Now and then he brakes to a stop and black workers instantly come running. He barks out orders in a mixture of English and a language that is unknown to Olofson.

The whole time Olofson has a feeling that Werner is balancing on an ice floe beneath which an outbreak of rage might erupt at any moment.

'It's a big farm,' he says as they drive on.

'Not that big,' says Werner. 'If it were a different time I would

57

probably have expanded the acreage. Nowadays you never know what's going to happen next. Maybe they'll confiscate all the farms from the whites. Out of jealousy, or displeasure at the fact that we're so infinitely more skilled than the black farmers who started after independence. They hate us for our skill, our ability to organise, our ability to make things work. They hate us because we make money, because our health is better and we live longer. Envy is an African inheritance. But the reason they hate us most is that magic doesn't work on us.'

They drive by a peacock ruffling its gaudy feathers.

'Magic?' Olofson asks.

'An African who is successful always risks being the target of magic,' says Werner. 'The witchcraft that is practised here can be extremely effective. If there's one thing that the Africans can do, it's mixing up deadly poisons. Salves that are spread on a body, herbs that are camouflaged as common vegetables. An African spends more time cultivating his envy than cultivating his fields.'

'There's a lot I don't know,' says Olofson.

'In Africa knowledge does not increase,' says Werner. 'It decreases, the more you think you understand.'

Werner breaks off and furiously slams on the brakes.

A piece of fence has broken off, and when an African comes running, Olofson sees to his astonishment that Werner grabs him by the ear. This is a grown man, maybe fifty years old, but his ear is caught in Werner's rough hand.

'Why isn't this fixed?' he yells. 'How long has it been broken? Who broke it? Was it Nkuba? Is he drunk again? Who's responsible for this? It has to be fixed within the hour. And Nkuba must be here in an hour.'

Werner shoves the man aside and returns to the Jeep.

'I can be away for two weeks,' he says. 'More than two weeks, and the whole farm would fall apart, not just a bit of fence.'

They stop by a small rise in the midst of a vast grazing pasture, where Brahma cattle move in slow herds. On top of the small hill is a grave.

JOHN MCGREGOR, KILLED BY BANDITS 1967, Olofson reads on a flat gravestone.

Werner squats down and lights his pipe. 'The first thing a man thinks about when settling on a farm is to choose his gravesite,' he says. 'If I'm not chased out of the country I'll lie here one day too, along with Ruth. John McGregor was a young Irishman who worked for me. He was twenty-four years old. Outside Kitwe they had set up a fake roadblock. When he realised he had been stopped by bandits and not police, he tried to drive off. They shot him down with a submachine gun. If he had stopped they would only have taken the car and his clothes. He must have forgotten he was in Africa; you don't defend your car here.'

'Bandits?' Olofson asks.

Werner shrugs. 'The police came and said they had shot some suspects during an escape attempt. Who knows if they were the same people? The important thing for the police was that they could record somebody as the guilty party.'

A lizard stands motionless on the gravestone. From a distance Olofson sees a black woman moving with infinite slowness along a gravel road. She seems to be on her way directly into the sun.

'In Africa death is always close by,' says Werner. 'I don't know why that is. The heat, everything rotting, the African with his rage just beneath the skin. It doesn't take much to stir up a crowd of people. Then they'll kill anyone with a club or a stone.'

'And yet you live here,' says Olofson.

'Perhaps we'll move to Southern Rhodesia,' Werner replies. 'But I'm sixty-four years old. I'm tired, I have difficulty pissing and sleeping, but maybe we'll move on.'

'Who will buy the farm?'

'Maybe I'll burn it down.'

They return to the white house and out of nowhere a parrot flies and perches on Olofson's shoulder. Instead of announcing that his journey to Mutshatsha is no longer necessary, he looks at the parrot nipping at his shirt. Sometimes timidity is my main psychological asset, he thinks in resignation. I don't even dare speak the truth to people who don't know me.

The tropical night falls like a black cloth. Twilight is an ephemeral, hastily passing shadow. With the darkness he feels as though he is also taken back in time.

On the big terrace that stretches along the front of the house, he drinks whisky with Ruth and Werner. They have just sat down with their glasses when headlights begin to play over the grazing meadows, and he hears Ruth and Werner exchange guesses about who it might be.

A car comes to a stop before the terrace and a man of indeterminate age steps out. In the light from shaded kerosene lamps hanging from the ceiling, Olofson sees that the man has red burn marks on his face. His head is completely bald and he is dressed in a baggy suit. He introduces himself as Elvin Richardson, a farmer like the Mastertons.

Who am I? Olofson thinks. An accidental travelling companion on the night train from Lusaka?

'Cattle rustlers,' says Richardson, sitting down heavily with a glass in his hand.

Olofson listens as if he were a child engrossed in a story.

'Last night they cut the fence down near Ndongo,' says Richardson. 'They stole three calves from Ruben White. The animals were clubbed and slaughtered on the spot. The night watchmen didn't hear a thing, of course. If this goes on, we'll have to organise patrols. Shoot a couple of them so they know we mean business.'

Black servants appear in the shadows on the terrace. What are the blacks talking about? Olofson wonders. How does Louis describe me when he sits by the fire with his friends? Does he see my uncertainty? Is he whetting a knife intended expressly for me? There doesn't seem to be any dialogue between the blacks and the whites in this country. The world is split in two, with no mutual trust. Orders are shouted across the chasm, that's all.

He listens to the conversation, observing that Ruth is more aggressive than Werner. While Werner thinks that maybe they should wait and see, Ruth says they should take up arms at once.

He gives a start when one of the black servants bends over him and fills his glass. All at once he realises that he is afraid. The terrace, the rapidly falling darkness, the restless conversation; all of it fills him with insecurity, that same helplessness he felt as a child when the beams of the house by the river creaked in the cold.

There are preparations for war going on here, he thinks. What scares me is that Ruth and Werner and the stranger don't seem to notice it . . .

At the dinner table the conversation suddenly shifts character, and Olofson feels more at ease sitting in a room where lamps ward off the shadows, creating a light in which the black servants cannot hide. The conversation at the dinner table turns to the old days, to people who are no longer here.

'We are who we are,' says Richardson. 'Those of us who choose to stay on our farms are surely insane. After us comes nothing. We are the last.'

'No,' says Ruth. 'You're wrong. One day the blacks will be begging at our doors and asking us to stay. The new generation can see where everything is headed. Independence was a gaudy rag that was hung on a pole, a solemn proclamation of empty promises. Now the young people see that the only things that work in this country are still in our hands.'

The alcohol makes Olofson feel able to speak.

'Is everyone this hospitable?' he asks. 'I might be a hunted criminal. Anyone at all, with the darkest of pasts.'

'You're white,' says Werner. 'In this country that's enough of a guarantee.'

Elvin Richardson leaves when the meal is over, and Olofson realises that Ruth and Werner retire early. Doors with wrought-iron gates are carefully barred shut, German shepherds bark outside in the darkness, and Olofson is instructed how to turn off the alarm if he goes into the kitchen at night. By ten o'clock he is in bed.

I'm surrounded by a barrier, he thinks. A white prison in a black country. The padlock of fear around the whites' property. What do the blacks think, when they compare our shoes and their own rags? What do they think about the freedom they have gained?

He drifts off into a restless slumber.

He jumps awake when a sound pierces his consciousness. In the dark, he doesn't know for a moment where he is.

Africa, he thinks. I still know nothing about you. Perhaps this is exactly how Africa looked in Janine's dreams. I no longer recall what we talked about at her kitchen table. But I have a feeling that my normal judgements and thoughts are insufficient or perhaps not even valid out here. Another kind of seeing is required . . .

He listens to the darkness. He wonders whether it is the silence or the sound that is imagined. Again he is afraid.

There is a catastrophe enclosed within Ruth and Werner Masterton's friendliness, he thinks. This entire farm, this white house, is enclosed by an anxiety, an anger that has been dammed up for much too long.

He lies awake in the dark and imagines that Africa is a wounded beast of prey that still does not have the strength to get up. The breathing of the earth and the animals coincides, the bush where they hide is impenetrable. Wasn't that the way Janine imagined this wounded and mangled continent? Like a buffalo forced to its knees, but with just enough power left to keep the hunters at bay.

Maybe she with her empathy could probe more deeply into reality than I can, tramping about on the soil of this continent. Maybe she made a journey in her dreams that was just as real as my meaningless flight to the mission station in Mutshatsha.

There may be another truth as well. Is it true that I hope I'll meet another Janine at this mission station? A woman who can replace the one who is dead?

He lies awake until dawn suddenly breaks through the dark. Out the window he sees the sun rise like a red ball of fire over the horizon. Suddenly he notices Louis standing by a tree, watching him. Even though the morning is already quite warm, he shivers. What am I afraid of? he thinks. Myself or Africa? What is Africa telling me that I don't want to know?

At a quarter past seven he bids farewell to Ruth and takes his place next to Werner in the front seat of the Jeep.

'Come back again,' says Ruth. 'You're always welcome.'

As they drive out through the farm's big gate where the two Africans helplessly salute, Olofson notices an old man standing in the tall elephant grass next to the road, laughing. Half hidden, he flashes past. Many years later this image will resurface in his consciousness.

A man, half hidden, laughing soundlessly in the early morning . . .

Chapter Nine

Would the great Leonardo have wasted his time picking flowers?

They're sitting in the attic room of the courthouse, and suddenly the great silence is there between them. It's late spring in 1957 and school is almost over for the year.

For Sture, elementary school is at an end, and middle school awaits. Hans Olofson has another year before he has to make up his mind. He has toyed with the idea of continuing his studies. But why? No child wants to stay a child; they all want to be grown-ups as soon as possible. Yet what does the future actually have to offer him?

For Sture, the path already seems laid out. The great Leonardo hangs on his wall, urging him on. Ashamed, Hans crouches over his own hopeless dream, to see the wooden house cast off its moorings and drift away down the river. When Sture plies him with questions, he has no idea how to answer. Will he go out in the forest and chop his way to the horizon like his father? Hang up his wet rag socks to dry eternally over the stove? He doesn't know, and he feels envy and unrest as he sits with Sture in the attic room, and the late spring blows in through the open window. Hans has come to suggest that they pick flowers for the last day of school.

Sture sits leaning over an astronomical chart. He makes notes, and Hans knows that he has decided to discover an unknown star.

When Hans suggests flowers, the silence spreads. Leonardo didn't waste his time going out in the fields hunting for table decorations.

Hans wonders with suppressed fury how Sture can be so damned certain. But he doesn't say a word. He waits. Waiting for Sture to finish one of the important tasks he has set himself has become more and more common this spring.

Hans senses that the distance between them is growing. Soon the only thing left of their old familiar friendship will be the visits to Janine. He has a feeling that Sture is about to leave. Not the town, but their old friendship. It bothers him. Mostly because he doesn't understand why, what has happened.

Once he asks Sture straight out.

'What the hell is supposed to have happened?' Sture replies.

After that he doesn't ask again.

But Sture is also changeable. Now, he suddenly flings aside the astronomical chart impatiently and gets up.

'Shall we go then?' he says.

They slide down the riverbank and sit under the wide expanse of the river bridge's iron beams and stone caissons. The spring flood surges past their feet; the usual soft gurgle has been replaced by the roar of the river's whirlpools. Sture heaves a rotten tree stump into the river, and it floats away like a half-drowned troll.

Without knowing where it comes from, Hans is attacked by a sudden fury. The blood pounds in his temples and he feels that he has to make himself visible to the world.

He has often fantasised about completing a test of manhood, climbing across the river on one of the curved bridge spans that are only a couple of decimetres thick. Climbing up to a giddy height, knowing full well that a fall would mean his death.

Undiscovered stars, he thinks furiously. I'll climb closer to the stars than Sture ever will.

'I was thinking I'd climb across the bridge span,' he says.

Sture looks at the gigantic iron arches.

'It can't be done,' he says.

'The hell it can't,' says Hans. 'You just have to do it.'

Sture looks at the bridge span again.

'Only a child would be that stupid,' he says.

Hans's heart turns a somersault in his chest. Does he mean him? That climbing across bridge spans is for little children?

'You don't dare,' he says. 'God damn it, you don't dare.'

Sture looks at him in astonishment. Usually Hans's voice is almost soft. But now he's loud and talking in a harsh, brusque way, as if his tongue had been replaced by a piece of pine bark. And then the challenge, that he doesn't dare . . .

No, he wouldn't dare. To climb up on one of the bridge arches would be to risk his life for nothing. He wouldn't get dizzy; he can climb a tree like a monkey. But this is too high; there's no safety net if he should slip.

Of course he doesn't say this to Hans. Instead he starts to laugh and spits contemptuously into the river.

When Hans sees the gob of spit he decides. Sture's derisive accusation of childishness can only be countered on the iron beams.

'I'm going to climb it,' he says in a quavering voice. 'And damned if I won't stand up on the span and piss on your head.'

The words rattle around in his mouth, as if he were already in the utmost distress.

Sture looks at him incredulously. Is he serious? Even if the trembling Hans, on the verge of tears, looks nothing like a grown-up, an intrepid climber prepared to scale an impossible mountain face, there is something in his shaking obsession that makes Sture hesitate.

'Go ahead and do it,' he says. 'Then I'll do it after you.'

Now, of course, there's no turning back. Quitting now would expose Hans to boundless humiliation.

As though on his way to his execution, Hans scrambles up the riverbank until he reaches the bridge abutment. He takes off his jacket and climbs up on one of the iron spans. When he raises his eyes he sees the gigantic iron arch vanish into the distance, merging with the grey cloud cover. The distance is endless, as if he were on his way up to heaven. He tries to persuade himself to be calm, but it only makes him more agitated.

Desperately, he starts slithering upwards, and deep down in his gut he realises that he has no idea why he needs to climb across this damned bridge span. But now it's too late, and like a helpless frog he crawls up the iron arch.

It has finally dawned on Sture that Hans is serious, and he wants to yell to him to come down. But at the same time he feels the forbidden desire to wait and see. Maybe he will witness how somebody fails in attempting the impossible.

Hans closes his eyes and climbs further. The wind sings in his ears, the blood pounds in his temples, and he is utterly alone. The bridge span is cold against his body, the heads of the rivets scrape against his knees, and his arms and fingers have already gone completely numb. He forces himself not to think, just to keep climbing, as if it were one of his usual dreams. And yet he seems to be climbing up over the axis of the earth itself . . .

He feels the bridge span under him begin to flatten out, but this doesn't calm him, it only increases his terror. Now he sees in his mind's eye how high up he is, how far away in his great loneliness. If he falls now, nothing can save him.

Desperately he keeps crawling forward, clinging to the span, floundering his way metre by metre back towards the ground. His fingers grip the steel like claws, and for a dizzying second he thinks that he has been turned into a cat. He feels something warm but doesn't know what it is.

When he reaches the bridge abutment on the other side of the river and cautiously opens his eyes and realises that it's true, that he has survived, he hugs the bridge span as if it were his saviour. He lies there before jumping down to the ground.

He looks at the bridge and knows he has conquered it. Not as some external enemy, but as an enemy within himself. He wipes off his face, flexes his fingers to get the feeling back, and sees Sture come walking across the bridge with his jacket in his hand.

'You forgot to piss,' says Sture.

Did he? No, he didn't! Now he knows where the sudden warmth came from up on the cold steel span. It was his body giving way. He points at the dark patch on his trousers.

'I didn't forget,' he says. 'Look here! Or do you want to smell it?'

Then comes his revenge.

'It's your turn now,' he says, sitting down on his jacket.

But Sture has already prepared his escape. When he realised that Hans would make it down from the bridge span without falling into the river, he searched feverishly for a way to get out of it.

'I will,' he replies. 'But not now. I didn't say when.'

'When will you do it?' asks Hans.

'I'll let you know.'

They head home in the spring evening. Hans has forgotten all about the flowers. There are plenty of flowers, but only one bridge span . . .

The silence grows between them. Hans wants to say something, but Sture is lost in his own thoughts and impossible to reach. They part quickly outside the courthouse gate . . .

The last day of school comes with a light, hovering fog that rapidly thins and vanishes in the sunrise. The schoolrooms smell newly scrubbed, and Headmaster Gottfried has been sitting in his room since five in the morning preparing his commencement address for the pupils he will now be sending out into the world. He is cautious with the vermouth this morning, so filled is he with melancholy and reflection. The last day of the school year is a reminder of his own mortality in the midst of all the effervescent anticipation that his pupils feel . . .

At seven-thirty he walks out on the steps. He sincerely hopes he won't see a pupil arrive without a relative. Nothing makes him so upset as to see a child arrive alone on the last day of school.

At eight o'clock the school bell rings and the classrooms are brimming with expectant silence. Headmaster Gottfried walks down the corridor to visit all the classes. Schoolmaster Törnkvist appears before him and announces that a pupil is missing from the commencement class. Sture von Croona, the son of the district judge. Headmaster Gottfried looks at his watch and decides to ring the district judge.

But not until it's time to march over to the church does he hurry into his office and ring the district court. His hands are sweaty and no matter how he tries to tell himself that there will be an explanation, he feels very uneasy . . .

Sture left in plenty of time that morning. Unfortunately his mother couldn't go with him because she was struck by a bad migraine. Of course Sture went to school, says the judge over the telephone.

Headmaster Gottfried hurries to the church. The last children are already on their way into the vestibule with their parents and he stumbles and practically runs as he tries to understand what could have happened to Sture von Croona.

But it isn't until he is holding in his hand the prize book that is intended for Sture that he seriously begins to fear that something might have happened.

At the same moment he sees the doors to the vestibule cautiously being opened. Sture, he thinks, until he sees that the father is standing there, District Judge von Croona.

Headmaster Gottfried speaks about a deserved rest, the mustering of strength and preparation for the coming year of study; he calls on them to consider all of life's shifting situations, and then there is no more. In a few minutes the church is empty.

The district judge looks at him, but Headmaster Gottfried can only shake his head. Sture did not show up for graduation.

'Sture doesn't just disappear,' says the district judge. 'I'll contact the police.'

Headmaster Gottfried nods hesitantly and feels the torment increasing.

'Perhaps he still . . .'

He gets no further. The district judge is already leaving the church with determined steps.

But no search needs to be organised. Only an hour after the end of school, Hans Olofson finds his missing friend.

His father, who had attended the graduation, has already changed into his work clothes again and headed out to his logging. Hans is enjoying the great freedom that lies before him, and he strolls down to the river.

It occurs to him that he hasn't seen Sture today. Maybe he just played truant on the last day and devoted himself to coaxing an unknown star from the heavens.

He sits down on his usual boulder by the river and decides that he's pleased to be alone. The coming summer requires a good deal of reflection. Ever since he conquered the huge span of the iron bridge he feels that it's easier to be by himself.

His gaze is caught by something shining red underneath the

bridge. He squints, thinking that it's a scrap of paper caught on the branches along the bank.

But when he goes over to investigate what the shining red thing is, he finds Sture. It's his red summer jacket, and he is lying there at the edge of the river. He has fallen from one of the bridge spans and broken his back. Helpless, he has lain there since the early morning hours when he awoke and decided to conquer the bridge span in secret. He had wanted to explore any hidden difficulties in solitude, and once it was done he planned to accompany Hans to the bridge and show him that he too could conquer the iron beams.

He hurried down to the bridge in the damp dawn. For a long time he regarded the huge spans before he started to climb.

Somewhere along the way he was gripped by pride. Much too rashly he raised his upper body. A gust of wind came out of nowhere and he swayed, lost his grip, and plunged from the bridge. He hit the water hard, and one of the stones in the riverbed cracked his spine. Unconscious, he was carried by an eddy towards the shore, where his head lolled above the water surface. The cold water of the river gave him hypothermia, and when Hans found him he was almost dead.

Hans pulls him out of the water, calls to him without getting an answer, and then runs screeching up to the streets of town. As he runs along the riverbank, summer dies. The great adventure vanishes in a gigantic cloud passing before the sun. Howling, he reaches the town. Frightened people draw back as if he were a mad dog.

But Rönning the junk dealer, who was a volunteer in the Winter War in Finland and has experienced much worse situations than a wildly gesticulating young man, grabs hold of him and bellows at him to tell him what has happened. Then the townsfolk rush to the river.

The taxi that is also used as an ambulance comes skidding through the gravel down towards the iron bridge. The district judge and his wife are informed about what has happened, and at the hospital the lone and always weary doctor begins to examine Sture.

He's alive, he's breathing. The concussion will pass. But his spine is broken; he is paralysed from the neck down. The doctor stands for a moment at the window and looks across the ridges of the forest before he goes out to the waiting parents.

At the same time Hans Olofson is vomiting into the toilet of the police station. A policeman holds him by the shoulders, and when it's over, a cautious interview begins.

'The red jacket,' he keeps repeating over and over. 'I saw the jacket lying in the river.'

At long last his father comes hurrying from the forest. Rönning the junk dealer drives them home and Hans crawls into bed. Erik Olofson sits on the edge of his bed until long after midnight, when his son finally falls asleep.

All night long the lights are burning in the spacious upper floor of the courthouse.

A few days after the accident, Sture disappears from town.

Early one morning Sture is carried out on a stretcher to a waiting ambulance which quickly drives off to the south. The vehicle sprays gravel when it passes through Ulvkälla. But the hour is early, Janine is asleep, and the car disappears towards the endless forests of Orsa Finnmark.

Hans Olofson never gets a chance to visit his fallen brother in arms. At dusk on the day before Sture is driven away, he wanders restlessly around the hospital, trying to figure out which room Sture is lying in. But everything is secret, concealed, as if the broken spine were contagious.

He leaves the hospital and wanders down towards the river, drawn inexorably to the bridge, and inside he feels a great burden of guilt. The accident was his creation . . .

When he discovers that Sture has been driven out of town early one morning, to a hospital far away, he writes a letter that he stuffs into a bottle and flings into the river. He watches it float down towards the point at People's Park and then he runs across the river to the house where Janine lives.

There is A Joyous Spring Fellowship at her church that evening, but now that Hans is standing like a white shadow in her doorway, of course she stays home. He sits down on his usual chair in the kitchen. Janine sits down across from him and looks at him.

'Don't sit on that chair,' he says. 'That's Sture's.'

A God that fills the earth with meaningless suffering, she thinks. Breaking the back of a young boy just as summertime is bursting forth?

'Play something,' he says without raising his head to look at her.

She takes out her trombone and plays 'Creole Love Call' as beautifully as she can.

When she finishes and blows the saliva out of the instrument, Hans gets up, takes his jacket, and leaves.

Far too small a person in a far too large and incomprehensible world, she thinks. In a sudden flare-up of wrath she puts the mouthpiece to her lips and plays her lament, 'Siam Blues'. The notes bellow like tortured animals and she doesn't notice Hurrapelle step through the doorway and gaze at her in dismay as she rocks on her bare feet in time with her music. When she discovers him she stops playing and pounces on him with furious questions. He is forced to listen to her doubts in the God of reconciliation, and he has a sudden sense that the hole below her eyes is threatening to swallow him up.

He squats there in silence and lets her talk herself out. Then he carefully chooses his words and coaxes her back to the true path once again. Even though she doesn't put up any resistance, he's still not sure whether he has succeeded in infusing the powers of faith into her again. He decides at once to keep her under close observation for a while, and then asks her whether she isn't going to take part in the evening's Joyous Fellowship. But she is mute, just shakes her head and opens the door for him to go. He nods and vanishes out into the summertime.

Janine is far away in her own thoughts and it will be a long time before she comes back . . .

Hans plods homeward through the dandelions and moist grass. When he stands underneath the beams of the river bridge he clenches his fists.

'Why didn't you wait?' he yells.

The message in the bottle rocks towards the sea . . .

Chapter Ten

After a journey of two hours on his way to the mission station in Mutshatsha, the distributor of the car Hans is riding in becomes clogged with silt.

They have stopped in a forlorn and desiccated landscape. Olofson climbs out of the car, wipes his filthy, sweaty face, and lets his gaze wander along the endless horizon.

He senses something of the great loneliness that it is possible to experience on the dark continent. Harry Johanson must have seen this, he thinks. He came from the other direction, from the west, but the landscape must have been the same. Four years his journey took. By the time he arrived his entire family had perished. Death defined the distance in time and space. Four years, four dead . . .

In our time the journeys have ceased, he thinks. Like stones with passports we are flung in gigantic catapults across the world. The time allotted to us is no more than that of our fore-fathers, but we have augmented it with our technology. We live in an era when the mind is less and less often allowed to be amazed by distance and time . . . And yet that's not true, he laments. In spite of everything, it has been ten years since I heard Janine for the first time tell the story of Harry Johanson and his wife Emma, and their trek towards the mission station of Mutshatsha.

Now I'm almost there and Janine is dead. It was her dream, not mine. I'm a pilgrim in disguise, following someone else's tracks. Friendly people are helping me with lodging and transportation, as if my task were important.

Like this David Fischer, bent over the distributor of his car. Early that morning Werner Masterton had turned into David's courtyard. A couple of hours later they were on their way to Mutshatsha. David Fischer is about his own age, thin and balding. He reminds Olofson of a restless bird. He keeps looking around, as if he thinks he's being followed. But of course he will help Hans Olofson make it to Mutshatsha.

'To the missionaries at Mujimbeji,' he says. 'I've never been there, but I know the way.'

Why doesn't anybody ask me? Olofson wonders. Why does no one want to know what I'm going to do in Mutshatsha?

They travel through the bush in David Fischer's rusty military Jeep. The top has been put up, but the dust seeps in through the cracks. The Jeep pitches and skids in the deep sand.

'The distributor will probably silt up again,' yells Fischer over the roar of the engine.

The bush surrounds Hans Olofson. Now and then he glimpses people in the tall grass. Or maybe it's only shadows, he thinks. Maybe they're not really there.

Then the distributor silts up, and Olofson stands in the oppressive heat and listens to the African silence. Like a winter night in my home town, he thinks. Just as still and deserted. There it was the cold, here it's the heat. And yet they are so similar. I could live there, could have endured. So I can probably live here too. Having grown up in Norrland, in the interior of Sweden, seems to be an excellent background for living in Africa . . .

Fischer slams down the bonnet, casts a glance over his shoulder, and sets about taking a piss.

'What do Swedes know about Africa?' he asks out of the blue.

'Not a thing,' Olofson replies.

'Even those of us who live here don't understand it,' says Fischer. 'Europe's newly awakened interest in Africa, after you've already abandoned us once. Now you're coming back, with a guilty conscience, the saviours of the new age.'

All at once Olofson feels personally responsible. 'My visit is utterly futile,' he replies. 'I'm not here to save anyone.'

'Which country in Africa receives the most support from Europe?' asks Fischer. 'It's a riddle. If you guess right you'll be the first.'

'Tanzania,' Olofson suggests.

'Wrong,' says Fischer. 'It's Switzerland. Anonymous numbered accounts are filled with contributions that make only a quick round trip to Africa. And Switzerland is not an African country . . .'

The road plunges steeply down towards a river and a ramshackle wooden bridge. Groups of children are swimming in the green water, and women are kneeling and washing clothes.

'Ninety per cent of these children will die of bilharzia,' Fischer yells.

'What can be done?' Olofson asks.

'Who wants to see a child die for no reason?' Fischer shouts. 'You have to understand that this is why we're so bitter. If we had been allowed to continue the way we were going, we probably would have got the better of the intestinal parasites as well. But now it's too late. When you abandoned us, you also abandoned the possibility for this continent to create a bearable future.'

Fischer has to slam on the brakes for an African who jumps on to the road and waves his arms, trying to get a ride. Fischer honks the horn angrily and yells something to the man as they pass.

'Three hours, then we'll be there,' Fischer shouts. 'I hope you'll at least think about what I said. Of course I'm a racist. But I'm not a stupid racist. I want the best for this country. I was born here and I hope to be allowed to die here.'

Olofson tries to do as Fischer asks, but his thoughts slip away, lose their hold. It's as if I'm travelling in my own recollections, he thinks. Already this journey seems remote, as if it were a distant memory . . .

Afternoon arrives. The sun shines straight into the car's front windscreen. Fischer comes to a stop and shuts off the engine.

'Is it the distributor again?' asks Olofson.

'We're here,' says Fischer. 'This must be Mutshatsha. The river we just crossed was the Mujimbeji.'

When the dust settles, a cluster of low, grey buildings appears, grouped round an open square with a well. So this is where Harry Johanson ended up, he thinks. This is where Janine headed in her lonely dream . . . From a distance he sees an old white man approaching with slow steps. Children flock round the car, naked or wearing only rags.

The man walking towards him has a pale, sunken face. Olofson senses at once that he is not at all welcome. I'm breaking into a closed world. A matter for the blacks and the missionaries . . . He quickly decides to reveal at least part of the truth.

'I'm following in Harry Johanson's footsteps,' he says. 'I come from his homeland and I'm searching for his memory.'

The pale man looks at him for a long time. Then he nods for Olofson to follow him.

'I'll stay until you tell me to leave,' says Fischer. 'I can't get back before dark anyway.'

Olofson is shown into a room containing a bed with a crucifix hanging above it, and a cracked washbasin. A lizard scurries into a hole in the wall. A sharp smell that he can't identify pricks his nose.

'Father LeMarque is on a trip,' says the pale man with the reticent voice. 'We expect him back tomorrow. I'll send someone over with sheets and to show you where to get some food.'

'My name is Hans Olofson,' he says.

The man nods without introducing himself.

'Welcome to Mutshatsha,' he says in a sombre voice before he leaves.

Silent children stand in the doorway, watching him attentively. Outside a church bell rings. Olofson listens. He feels a creeping fear inside. The smell that he can't identify stings his nose. I'll just leave, he thinks agitatedly. If I take off right now, I never will have been here. At the same moment David Fischer comes in carrying his suitcase.

'I understand you'll be staying,' he says. 'Good luck with whatever it is you're doing. If you want to come back, the missionaries have cars. And you know where I live.'

'How can I thank you?' Olofson says.

'Why do people always have to thank each other?' says Fischer, and leaves.

Olofson watches the car go down the road. The children stand motionless and stare at him.

Suddenly he feels dizzy from the intense heat. He goes inside the cell assigned to him, stretches out on the hard bed and closes his eyes.

The church bells fall silent and everything is still. When he opens his eyes the children are still standing in the doorway watching him. He stretches out his hand and motions to them. In an instant they are gone.

He has to go to the toilet. He walks out through the door and the heat strikes him hard in the face. The big sandy area is deserted, and even the children are gone. He walks around the building in his search for a toilet. At the rear he finds a door. When he pushes the handle the door opens. He steps inside and in the darkness he is blind. The sharp smell makes him feel sick. When he gets used to the dark he realises that he's in a morgue. In the dark he can distinguish two dead Africans lying stretched out on wooden benches. Their naked bodies are scarcely covered by dirty sheets. He recoils and slams the door behind him. The dizziness returns at once.

On the steps outside his door sits an African, looking at him.

'I am Joseph, *Bwana*,' he says. 'I will guard your door.'

'Who told you to sit here?'

'The missionaries, *Bwana*.'

'Why?'

'In case something happens, *Bwana*.'

'What would that be?'

'In the dark many things can happen, *Bwana*.'

'Like what?'

'You'll know it when it happens, *Bwana*.'

'Has anything happened before?'

'There's always a lot happening, *Bwana*.'

'How long are you supposed to sit here?'

'As long as *Bwana* stays here, *Bwana*.'

'When do you sleep?'

'When there is time, *Bwana*.'

'There is only night and day.'

'Now and then other times arise, *Bwana*.'

'What do you do while you're sitting here?'

'I wait for something to happen, *Bwana*.'

'What?'

'You'll know when it happens, *Bwana*.'

Joseph shows him where there is a toilet and where he can

take a shower under an old petrol tank with a dripping hose. After he has changed his clothes, Joseph accompanies him to the mission station's mess hall. An African with one leg shorter than the other walks around the empty tables wiping them with a dirty rag.

'Am I the only one here?' he asks Joseph.

'The missionaries are on a trip, *Bwana*. But tomorrow they may return.'

Joseph waits outside the door. Olofson sits down at a table. The lame African brings a bowl of soup. Olofson eats, swatting at flies that buzz around his mouth. An insect stings him on the back of the neck and when he starts, he spills the soup on the table. The lame man comes at once with his rag.

Something is wrong on this continent, he thinks. When someone cleans up, the dirt is just spread even more.

The brief twilight is almost over as he leaves the mess hall. Joseph is waiting for him outside the door. In the distance fires are gleaming. He notices that Joseph is standing rocking on his feet, that he can hardly keep his balance.

'You're drunk, Joseph,' he says.

'I'm not drunk, *Bwana*.'

'I can see that you're drunk!'

'I'm not drunk, *Bwana*. At least not much. I only drink water, *Bwana*.'

'You can't get drunk on water. What have you been drinking?'

'African whisky, *Bwana*. But it's not allowed. I won't be permitted to stand watch here if any of the *mzunguz* find out about it.'

'What would happen if someone saw that you were drunk?'

'Sometimes in the morning we have to line up and breathe at a *wakakwitau*, *Bwana*. If anyone smells of anything but water he is punished.'

'Punished how?'

'In the worst case he would have to leave Mutshatsha with his family, *Bwana*.'

'I won't say a thing, Joseph. I'm no missionary. I'm only here on a visit. I'd like to buy a little of your African whisky.'

He watches Joseph trying to assess the situation and make a decision.

'I'll pay you well for your whisky,' he says.

He follows Joseph's wobbly figure creeping through the dark, close to the building walls, over towards an area with grass huts. Faces he cannot see laugh in the darkness. A woman scolds an invisible man, children's eyes shine near a fire.

Joseph stops outside one of the grass huts and calls something in a low voice. Two men and three women emerge from the hut, all drunk. Olofson has a hard time distinguishing them in the dark. Joseph makes a sign to him to enter the hut. An ingrained stench of urine and sweat meets him in the darkness within.

I ought to be afraid, he thinks briefly. Yet I feel quite safe in Joseph's company . . .

At the same moment he stumbles over something on the floor, and when he feels with his hand he finds that it's a sleeping child. Shadows dance across the walls, and Joseph motions him to sit down. He sinks down on to a raffia mat and a woman hands him a mug. What he drinks tastes like burnt bread and it's very strong.

'What am I drinking?' he asks Joseph.

'African whisky, *Bwana*.'

'It tastes bad.'

'We're used to it, *Bwana*. We distil *lituku* from maize waste, roots, and sugar water. Then we drink it. When it's gone we make more. Sometimes we drink honey beer too.'

Olofson can feel himself becoming intoxicated.

'Why did the others leave?' he asks.

'They're not used to a *mzungu* coming here, *Bwana*. No *mzungu* has ever been inside this hut before.'

'Tell them to come back. I'm no missionary.'

'But you're white, *Bwana*. A *mzungu*.'

'Tell them anyway.'

Joseph calls out into the darkness, and the three women and two men return and squat down. They are young.

'My sisters and my brothers, *Bwana*. Magdalena, Sara, and Salomo. Abraham and Kennedy.'

'Salomo is a man's name.'

'My sister's name is Salomo, *Bwana*. So it's a woman's name too.'

'I don't want to bother you. Tell them that. Tell them I don't want to bother you.'

Joseph translates and the woman named Sara says something, casting glances at Olofson.

'What does she want?' he asks.

'She wonders why a *wakakwitau* is visiting an African hut, *Bwana*. She wonders why you drink, since all the whites here say it is forbidden.'

'Not for me. Explain to her that I'm not a missionary.'

Joseph translates and an intense discussion breaks out. Olofson watches the women, their dark bodies in relief under their *chitengen*. Maybe Janine will come back to me in a black guise, he thinks . . .

He gets drunk on the drink that tastes like burnt bread and listens to a discussion he doesn't understand.

'Why are you so excited?' he asks Joseph.

'Why don't all the *mzunguz* drink, *Bwana*? Especially the ones who preach about their God? Why don't they understand that the revelation would be much stronger with African whisky? We Africans have understood this since the days of our first forefathers.'

'Tell them I agree. Ask them what they really think about the missionaries.'

When Joseph has translated, there is an embarrassed silence.

'They don't know what to say, *Bwana*. They aren't used to a *mzungu* asking such a question. They're afraid of giving the wrong answer.'

'What would happen?'

'Living at a mission station means food and clothing, *Bwana*. They don't want to lose that by giving the wrong answer.'

'What would happen then?'

'The missionaries might be displeased, *Bwana*. Maybe we would all be chased off.'

'Does that happen? That anyone who doesn't obey is chased off?'

'Missionaries are like other whites, *Bwana*. They demand the same submission.'

'Can't you be more clear? What would happen?'

'*Mzunguz* always think that we blacks are unclear, *Bwana*.'

'You speak in riddles, Joseph.'

'Life is mysterious, *Bwana*.'

'I don't believe a word of what you're saying, Joseph. You won't be chased away by the missionaries!'

'Of course you don't believe me, *Bwana*. I'm just telling you the truth.'

'You're not saying anything.'

Olofson takes a drink.

'The women,' he says. 'They're your sisters?'

'That's right, *Bwana*.'

'Are they married?'

'They would like to marry you, *Bwana*.'

'Why is that?'

'A white man is not black, unfortunately, *Bwana*. But a *bwana* has money.'

'But they've never seen me before.'

'They saw you when you arrived, *Bwana*.'

'They don't know me.'

'If they were married to you they would get to know you, *Bwana*.'

'Why don't they marry the missionaries?'

'Missionaries don't marry blacks, *Bwana*. Missionaries don't like black people.'

'What the hell are you saying?'

'I'm just saying the truth, *Bwana*.'

'Stop calling me *Bwana*.'

'Yes, *Bwana*.'

'Of course the missionaries like you! It's for your sake they're here, isn't it?'

'We blacks believe that the missionaries are here as a penance, *Bwana*. For the man that they nailed to a cross.'

'Why do you stay here then?'

'It's a good life, *Bwana*. We will gladly believe in a foreign god if we get food and clothing.'

'Is that the only reason?'

'Of course, *Bwana*. We have our own real gods, after all. They probably don't like it that we fold our hands several times each day. When we speak to them we beat our drums and dance.'

'Surely you can't do that here.'

'Sometimes we go far out in the bush, *Bwana*. Our gods wait there for us.'

'Don't the missionaries know about this?'

'Of course not, *Bwana*. If they did they would be very upset. That wouldn't be good. Especially not now, when I might get a bicycle.'

Olofson stands up on his unsteady legs. I'm drunk, he thinks. Tomorrow the missionaries will return. I have to sleep.

'Follow me back, Joseph.'

'Yes, *Bwana*.'

'And stop calling me *Bwana!*'

'Yes, *Bwana*. I'll stop calling you *Bwana* after you leave.'

Olofson gives Joseph some money. 'Your sisters are beautiful.'

'They would like to marry you, *Bwana*.'

Olofson crawls into his hard bed. Before he falls asleep he hears Joseph already snoring outside the door.

He wakes up with a start. The pale man is standing over him.

'Father LeMarque has returned,' he says in a toneless voice. 'He would like to meet you.'

Olofson dresses hastily. He feels bad, his head is pounding from the African whisky. In the early dawn he follows the pale man across the red dirt. So the missionaries travel by night, he thinks. What is he going to tell me about why he came here?

He enters one of the grey buildings. At a simple wooden table sits a young man with a bushy beard. He is dressed in a torn undershirt and dirty shorts.

'Our guest,' he says with a smile. 'Welcome.'

Patrice LeMarque comes from Canada, he tells Hans Olofson. The lame man has brought two cups of coffee and they sit at the back of the building in the shade of a tree. At the Mutshatsha mission station there are missionaries and health care personnel from many countries.

'But none from Sweden?' Olofson asks.

'Not at the moment,' replies LeMarque. 'The last one was here about ten years ago. A Swedish nurse who came from a city I think was called Kalmar.'

'The first one came from Röstånga. Harry Johanson.'

'Have you really come all this way to see his grave?'

'I stumbled upon his story when I was quite young. I won't be finished with him until I have seen his grave.'

'Harry Johanson sat in the shade of this very tree,' LeMarque says. 'When he wanted to be alone and meditate, he used to come here, and no one was allowed to bother him. I've also seen a photograph of him sitting in this spot. He was short but he was physically very strong. He also had a keen sense of humour. Some of the older Africans still remember him. When he was angry he could lift a baby elephant over his head. That's not true, of course, but as an illustration of his strength the image is good.'

He sets down his coffee cup. 'I'll show you his grave. Then I must go back to my work. Our pumping station has broken down.'

They walk along a winding path that leads up a hill. Through the dense thickets they glimpse the reflection of the river.

'Don't go there without Joseph,' says LeMarque. 'There are many crocodiles in the river.'

The terrain levels out and forms a mesa on top of the high hill. Olofson finds himself facing a simple wooden cross.

'Harry Johanson's grave,' says LeMarque. 'Every four years we have to put up a new cross because the termites eat them. But he wanted to have a wooden cross on his grave. We comply with his wish.'

'What did he dream about?' asks Olofson.

'I don't think he had much time for dreaming. A mission station in Africa requires constant practical work. One has to be a mechanic, carpenter, farmer, businessman. Harry Johanson was good at all those things.'

'What about religion?'

'Our message is planted in the maize fields. The gospel is an impossibility if it is not involved in daily life. Conversion is a matter of bread and health.'

'But in spite of everything, conversion is the crucial thing? Conversion from what?'

'Superstition, poverty, and sorcery.'

'Superstition I can understand. But how can one convert someone from poverty?'

'The message instils confidence. Wisdom requires the courage to face life.'

Hans Olofson thinks of Janine. 'Was Harry Johanson happy?' he asks.

'Who knows the innermost thoughts of another human being?' says LeMarque.

They head back the way they came.

'I never met Harry Johanson, after all,' says LeMarque. 'But he must have been a colourful and wilful person. The older he got, the less he felt he understood. He accepted that Africa remained a foreign world.'

'Can a person live long in a foreign world without trying to recreate it so that it resembles the world he left behind?'

'We had a young priest from Holland here once. Courageous and strong, self-sacrificing. But one day, with no warning, he got up from the dinner table and walked straight out into the bush. Purposefully, as if he knew where he was going.'

'What happened?'

'He was never seen again. His goal must have been to be swallowed up, never to return. Something in him snapped.'

Olofson thinks of Joseph and his sisters and brothers. 'What do the blacks really think?' he asks.

'They get to know us through the God we give them.'

'Don't they have their own gods? What do you do with them?'

'Let them disappear on their own.'

Wrong, Olofson thinks. But maybe a missionary has to ignore certain things in order to endure.

'I'll find someone who can show you around,' says LeMarque. 'Unfortunately almost everyone who works here is out in the bush right now. They're visiting the remote villages. I'll ask Amanda to show you around.'

Not until evening is Olofson shown the infirmary. The pale man, whose name is Dieter, informs him that Amanda Reinhardt, who LeMarque thought would show him around, is busy and asks his forgiveness.

When he returns from Johanson's grave Joseph is sitting by his door. He notices at once that Joseph is frightened.

'I won't say anything,' he says.

'*Bwana* is a good *bwana*,' says Joseph.

'Stop calling me *Bwana*!'

'Yes, *Bwana*.'

They walk down to the river and search for crocodiles without seeing any. Joseph shows him Mutshatsha's extensive maize cultivation. Everywhere he sees women with hoes in their hands, bent over the earth.

'Where are all the men?' he asks.

'The men are making important decisions, *Bwana*. Maybe they are also busy preparing the African whisky.'

'Important decisions?'

'Important decisions, *Bwana*.'

After eating the food served to him by the lame man, he sits down in the shade of Harry Johanson's tree. He doesn't understand the emptiness that pervades the mission station. He tries to imagine that through him Janine really has accomplished her long journey. The inactivity makes him restless. I have to return home, he thinks. Return to what I'm supposed to do, whatever that might be . . .

In the twilight, Amanda Reinhardt suddenly appears in his doorway. He had been lying on top of his bed and dozed off. She has a kerosene lamp in her hand, and he sees that she is short and chubby. From her broken English he gathers that she is German.

89

'I am sorry you are left alone,' she says. 'But we are so few here just now. There is so much to do.'

'I've been lying here thinking of Harry Johanson's tree,' Olofson says.

'Who?' she asks.

At that moment an excited African appears from the shadows. He exchanges a few sentences with the German woman in the language Olofson doesn't understand.

'A child is about to die,' she says. 'I must go.'

In the doorway she stops short and turns around. 'Come with me,' she says. 'Come with me to Africa.'

He gets up from the bed and they hurry towards the infirmary, which lies at the foot of Johanson's hill. Olofson shrinks back as he steps into a room full of iron beds. A few kerosene lamps cast a dim light over the room. Olofson sees that there are sick people lying everywhere. On the beds, between the beds, under the beds. In several beds lie mothers intertwined with their sick children. Cooking vessels and bundles of clothing make the room almost impassable, and the intense smell of sweat and urine and excrement is stupefying. In a bed made of bent iron pipes tied together with steel wire lies a child of three or four years old. Around the bed women are squatting.

Olofson sees that even a black face can radiate pallor.

Amanda Reinhardt bends over the child, touches his forehead, talking all the while with the women.

The anteroom of death, he thinks. The kerosene lamps are the flames of life . . .

Suddenly a shriek breaks out from all the women squatting around the bed. One of the women, hardly more than eighteen years old, throws herself over the child in the bed, and her wail is so penetrating and shrill that Olofson feels the need to flee. The lamentation, the roars of pain that fill the room, strike him with a paralysing effect. With a giant leap he wants to leave Africa behind.

'So does death look,' says Amanda Reinhardt in his ear. 'The child has died.'

'From what?' asks Olofson.

'Measles,' she replies.

The women's shrieking rises and falls. Never before has he experienced the voice of grief as in this dirty room with its unearthly light. Someone is pounding on his eardrums with sledgehammers.

'They will scream all night,' says Amanda Reinhardt. 'In this heat the burial must take place tomorrow. Then the women will lament for some more days. Maybe they faint from exhaustion, but they continue.'

'I never thought such a wailing existed,' says Olofson. 'This must be the ancient sound of pain.'

'Measles,' says Amanda Reinhardt. 'You have surely had this disease. But here children die of it. They came from a distant village. The mother walked five days and carried her child. Had she come earlier we could have maybe saved him, but she went first to the witch doctor in the village. When it was too late she came here. Actually it is not measles that kills. But the children are malnourished, their resistance is poor. When the child dies it is the end of a long chain of causes.'

Olofson leaves the infirmary alone. He has borrowed her kerosene lamp and tells her he will find his own way. He is followed by the screams of the wailing women. Outside his door sits Joseph by his fire.

This man I will remember, Olofson thinks. This man and his beautiful sisters . . .

The next day he drinks coffee again with Patrice LeMarque.

'What do you think of Harry Johanson now?' he asks.

'I don't know,' says Olofson. 'Mostly I'm thinking about the child who died yesterday.'

'I've already buried him,' replies LeMarque. 'And I've got the pumping station going too.'

'How do I get out of here?' Olofson asks.

'Tomorrow Moses is driving to Kitwe in one of our cars. You can ride along with him.'

'How long will you stay here?' Olofson asks.

'As long as I live,' says LeMarque. 'But I probably won't live as long as Harry Johanson. He must have been very special.'

At dawn Olofson is awakened by Joseph.

'Now I'm travelling home,' he tells him. 'To another part of the world.'

'I will wait at the white men's doors, *Bwana*,' replies Joseph.

'Say hello to your sisters!'

'I already have, *Bwana*. They are sad that you're leaving.'

'Why don't they come and say goodbye then?'

'They are, *Bwana*. They're saying goodbye, but you don't see them.'

'One last question, Joseph. When will you chase the whites out of your country?'

'When the time is ripe, *Bwana*.'

'And when is that?'

'When we decide that it is, *Bwana*. But we won't chase all the *mzunguz* out of the country. Those who want to live with us can stay. We aren't racists like the whites.'

A Jeep drives up to the building. Olofson puts his suitcase in it. The driver, Moses, nods to him.

'Moses is a good driver, *Bwana*,' says Joseph. 'He just drives off the road once in a while.'

Olofson gets into the front seat and they turn on to the road. Now it's over, he thinks. Janine's dream and Harry Johanson's grave . . .

After a few hours they stop to rest. Olofson discovers that the two dead bodies he'd seen in the morgue are packed in the boot of the Jeep. At once he feels sick.

'They're going to the police in Kitwe,' says Moses, noticing his distress. 'All murder victims must be examined by the police.'

'What happened?'

'They are brothers. They were poisoned. Their maize field was probably too big. Their neighbours were jealous. Then they died.'

'How?'

'They ate something. Then they swelled up and their stomachs burst open. It smelled terrible. The evil spirits killed them.'

'Do you really believe in evil spirits?'

'Of course,' says Moses with a laugh. 'We Africans believe in sorcery and evil spirits.'

The journey continues.

Olofson tries to convince himself that he is going to go back to his legal studies. He clings once more to his decision to become the defender of extenuating circumstance. But I've never clarified what it would mean to spend my life in courtrooms, he thinks. Where I'd have to try to distinguish what is a lie from what is truth. Maybe I should do as my father did. Maybe I should go and chop down horizons in a forest of paragraphs. I'm still searching for a way out of the confusion that marks my beginning . . .

The long trip from Mutshatsha is coming to an end. I must decide before I land at Arlanda again, he thinks. That's all the time I have left.

He shows Moses the way to Ruth and Werner's farm.

'First I drive you, then I drive the corpses,' says Moses.

Olofson is glad that he doesn't call him *Bwana*.

'Say hello to Joseph when you return.'

'Joseph is my brother. I'll say hello to him.'

Just before two o'clock in the afternoon they arrive . . .

Chapter Eleven

The sea. A bluish-green wave that moves towards infinity. A frozen wind blows from the Kvarken Straits. A sailboat with an uncertain helmsman is becalmed on the swells with sails flapping. Seaweed and mud blow their musty odour in Hans Olofson's face, and even though the sea isn't as he had imagined it, the reality is overwhelming.

They beat into a stiff wind along a spit of land outside Gävle, Hans and his father. In order to divert his son from the pain of constantly thinking of Sture, Erik Olofson has asked for a week off to take Hans to the sea. One day in the middle of June they depart with the country bus from town, change in Ljusdal, and reach Gävle late in the evening.

Hans finds a worn-out toy boat made of bark that someone has thrown away and stuffs it inside his jacket. His father dreams about the banana boats he once sailed on. The face of a sailor emerges from the woodcutter's, and he realises once again that the sea is his world.

To Hans, the sea is constantly changing its face. It's never possible to completely capture the surface of the water with his gaze. Somewhere there is always an unexpected movement, the interplay of the sun and clouds glitters and changes continuously and tirelessly. He can't get his fill of looking at the sea rolling and grunting, tossing wave-tops back and forth, flattening during a calm, and once again foaming and singing and moaning.

The thought of Sture is there, but it's as if the sea has flooded over it, slowly covering up the last of the pain and the most gnawing grief. The muddled feeling of guilt, of having acted as the invisible hands that heaved Sture off the bridge span, sinks away, leaving only a churning unrest, like a pain that can't decide whether to strike or not.

Already Sture has begun to change from a living person to a memory. With each passing day the contours of his face grow dimmer, and although Hans can't express it, he realises that life, the life that goes on all around him, will always be the most important thing. He senses that he is on his way into something unknown, where new and disquieting powers are beginning to emerge.

I'm waiting for something, he thinks. And while he waits he searches assiduously for flotsam along the beaches. Erik Olofson walks a little to one side, as if he doesn't want to bother him. Erik is tormented by the fact that his own waiting never seems to end. The sea reminds him of his own ruin . . .

They stay at a cheap hotel next to the railway station. When his father has fallen asleep, Hans creeps out of bed and sits on the wide window seat. From there he has a view over the little square in front of the station.

He tries to picture the room in the distant hospital where Sture is lying. An iron lung, he heard. A thick black hose in his throat, an artificial throat that breathes for Sture. His spine is broken, snapped in two, like a perch killed by a fisherman.

He tries to imagine what it would be like not to be able to move, but of course he can't, and suddenly he can't stand the anxiety, but casts it aside.

I don't like it, he thinks. I crawled across the arch of the bridge and I didn't fall off. What the hell was he doing there, all alone, in the morning fog? He should have waited for me . . .

The days by the sea pass quickly. After a week they have to go home. In the rattling bus he suddenly calls to his father.

'What about Mamma?' he shouts. 'Why don't you know where she is?'

'There are lots of things a person can never know,' Erik says defensively, surprised at the unexpected question.

'Pappas disappear,' shouts Hans. 'Not mammas.'

'Now you've seen the sea,' says Erik. 'And this is not a good place to talk. The bus is rattling so damned loudly.'

The next day Erik Olofson goes back to clearing the horizon. Impatiently he hacks with his axe at a single branch that refuses to be separated from the trunk. He puts all his bodily strength behind the blow, hacking furiously at the branch.

I'm hacking at myself, he thinks. Chopping off these damned roots that are binding me here. The boy is almost fourteen. In a few years he can take care of himself. Then I can go back to sea, to the ships, to the cargoes.

He chops with his axe, and with each blow it's as though he's striking his fist against his brow and saying: I must . . .

Hans is running through the bright summer evening of Norrland. Walking takes too long, he's in a hurry now. The soft, waterlogged earth is burning . . .

In a grove in the woods past the abandoned brickworks he builds an altar to Sture. He can't imagine him either alive or dead, he's just gone, but he builds an altar out of pieces of board and moss. He has no idea what he's going to do with it. He thinks of asking Janine, initiating her into his secret, but he refrains. Visiting the altar once each day and seeing that no one has been there will suffice. Even though Sture doesn't know it, they're sharing one more secret.

He dreams that the house where he lives is cast off its moorings and floats down the river, never again to return . . .

He bolts through the summer, runs along the river until he is out of breath and sweaty. When nothing else is left there is always Janine.

One evening when he comes running, she isn't home. For a brief moment he worries that she too is gone. How could he lose another person who supports his world? But he knows that she's at one of the Joyous Fellowships at the church, and so he sits down on her front steps to wait.

When she arrives she's wearing a white coat over a light-blue dress. A breeze passes through his body, a sudden apprehension.

'Why are you blushing?' she asks.

'I'm not blushing,' he replies. 'I never do.'

He feels caught red-handed. Shove it in your nose, he thinks furiously. Shove it in the hole.

That evening Janine starts talking about the trip.

'Where would someone like me go?' says Hans. 'I've been to Gävle. I probably won't go any further. But I could try to stow away on the train to Orsa. Or go to the tailor and ask him to sew on a pair of wings.'

'I'm serious,' says Janine.

'I am too,' says Hans.

'I want to go to Africa,' says Janine.

'Africa?'

For Hans that is an unfathomable dream.

'Africa,' she says again. 'I would go to the countries by the big rivers.'

She begins to tell him. The curtain in the kitchen window flutters gently, and a dog barks in the distance. She tells him about the dark moments. About the anguish that makes her long to go to Africa. There she wouldn't attract attention everywhere she went with her missing nose. There she wouldn't always be surrounded by male loathing and revulsion.

'Leprosy,' she says. 'Bodies that rot away, souls that atrophy in despair. There I would be able to work.'

Hans tries to imagine the Realm of the Noseless, tries to see Janine among the deformed human bodies.

'Are you going to be a missionary?' he asks.

'No, not a missionary. Maybe I would be called one. But I would work to alleviate suffering,' she says. 'It's possible to travel without actually travelling. A departure always begins inside yourself. It was probably the same for Harry Johanson and his wife Emma. For fifteen years they prepared for a journey that they probably never thought would happen.'

'Who is Harry Johanson?' Hans asks.

'He was born in a poor cottage outside Röstånga,' says Janine. 'He was the next-youngest of nine children. When he was ten years old he decided to be a missionary. That was in the late 1870s. But not until twenty years later, in 1898, after he had married and he and Emma had had four children, were they able to set off. Harry had turned thirty and Emma was a few years younger, and they left on a ship from Göteborg. In Sweden there were followers of the Scottish missionary Fred Arnot who tried to build up a network of mission stations along the routes that Livingstone had travelled in Africa. From Glasgow they sailed with an English ship and arrived in Benguella in January of 1899. One of their children died of cholera during the passage, and Emma was so sick that she had to be carried ashore when they reached Africa.

'After a month of waiting, they set off together with three other missionaries and over 100 black bearers on a 1200-mile journey, straight through uncharted country. It took them four years to reach Mutshatsha, where Fred Arnot had determined that the new mission station should be located. They had to wait for a whole year by the Lunga River before the local chieftain gave them permission to pass through his lands.

'The whole time they were plagued with illness, lack of food, impure water. After four years, when Harry finally reached Mutshatsha, he was alone. Emma had died of malaria, and the children had perished from various intestinal diseases. The three other missionaries had also died. Harry himself was dazed by malaria when he arrived along with those of the bearers who hadn't left years before. His loneliness must have been indescribable. And how did he manage to hold on to his faith in God when his entire family had been obliterated on the way to spread God's message?

'Harry lived for almost fifty years in Mutshatsha. By the time he died, an entire community had grown up around the little hut which was the beginning of the mission station. There was an infirmary, an orphanage, a building for older women who had been driven out of their villages because of accusations of witchcraft. When Harry Johanson died he was called *Ndotolu*, the wise man. He was buried on the hill to which he had retired during his last years and built a modest little hut. When he died there were English doctors and another Swedish missionary family in Mutshatsha. Harry Johanson died in 1947.'

'How do you know all this?' Hans asks.

'An old woman who once visited Harry in Mutshatsha told me,' Janine replies. 'She went there as a young woman to work at the mission station, but she got sick and Harry forced her to go back to Sweden. She visited our congregation last year and I had a long talk with her about Harry Johanson.'

'Say it once more,' says Hans. 'The name.'

'Mutshatsha.'

'What was he doing there, anyway?'

'He arrived as a missionary. But he became the wise man. The doctor, the carpenter, the judge.'

'Say it one more time.'

'Mutshatsha.'

'Why don't you go there?'

'I probably don't have what Harry Johanson had. And Emma, although she never made it there.'

What was it that Harry Johanson had? Hans wonders as he walks home in the bright summer evening. He pictures himself dressed in Harry Johanson's clothes; behind him is a long line of bearers. Before the safari crosses the river he sends out scouts to check whether crocodiles are lurking on the sandbanks. When he reaches the house where he lives, four years have passed and the safari has reached Mutshatsha. He's all alone; there are no bearers left, they have all deserted him. As he walks up the steps he decides that the altar he built for Sture in the grove behind the brickworks will be called Mutshatsha . . .

He opens the door and the dream of Harry Johanson and Mutshatsha retreats and leaves him, because in the kitchen sits Erik Olofson, drinking with four of the town's most notorious drunks. *Célestine* has been taken from her case, and one of the drunks is sitting there picking at the meticulously constructed rigging with fumbling fingers. A man who hasn't even taken off his dirty rubber boots is asleep on top of Hans's bed.

The drunks stare at him curiously, and Erik Olofson gets up, wobbling, and says something that is drowned in the crash of a bottle hitting the floor. Usually Hans feels sad and ashamed when his father starts drinking and goes into one of his spells, but now he feels only fury. The sight of the full-rigger on the table, as if it had run aground among glasses and bottles and ashtrays, makes him so outraged with sorrowful anger that he is perfectly calm. He walks over to the table, picks up the ship, and stares into the glazed eyes of the drunk who was picking at it.

'You keep your filthy mitts off her,' he says.

Without waiting for a reply he puts the ship back in its case. Then he goes into his room and kicks at the snoring man lying on his bed.

'Get up! Up, God damn it!' he says, and he doesn't stop until the man wakes up.

His father is holding on to the door frame, with his trousers half falling off, and when he sees his flickering eyes he starts to hate him. Hans chases the dazed drunk into the kitchen and slams the door behind him, right in front of his father. He tears off the bedspread and sits down, and feels his heart pounding in his chest.

Mutshatsha, he thinks.

In the kitchen the chairs scrape, the outer door is opened, voices mutter and then there is silence. At first he thinks that his father has left with the drunks for town. But then he hears a shuffling and a thud from the kitchen. When he opens the door he sees his father crawling around with a rag in his hand, trying to wipe the dirt off the floor. He looks like an animal. His trousers have slipped down so his bottom is bare. A blind animal crawling around and around . . .

'Pull up your trousers,' he says. 'Stop crawling around. I'll clean the damned floor.'

He helps his father up, and when Erik Olofson loses his balance they wind up on the kitchen sofa in an involuntary embrace. When Hans tries to pull himself loose his father holds on to him. At first he thinks his father wants to fight, but then he hears him snuffling and whimpering and hiccuping, and realises he is sobbing violently. He has never seen him do this before.

Sorrow and glistening eyes, a quavering voice that has turned thick, that much he knows. But never this open surrender to tears. What the hell is he going to do now? Hans wonders, with his father's sweaty and unshaven face against his neck.

The elkhounds are skulking restlessly underneath the kitchen table. They have been kicked and stepped on and haven't had any food all day. The kitchen stinks of closed-in sweat, fuming pipes, and spilled beer.

'We have to clean up,' says Hans, tearing himself loose. 'You go and lie down and I'll clean up the mess.'

Erik Olofson slumps down in the corner of the sofa and Hans starts washing the floor.

'Take the dogs out,' mumbles Erik.

'Take them out yourself,' says Hans.

The fact that Shady, the most contemptuous and feared drunk in town, had been allowed to stretch out in the kitchen makes him feel sick. They can stay in their hovels, he thinks, with their old hags and brats and beer bottles . . .

His father is asleep on the sofa. Hans places a quilt over him and takes out the dogs and chains them up near the woodpile. Then he goes to his altar in the woods.

It's already night, the light summer night of Norrland. Outside the People's Hall some youths are talking loudly around a shiny Chevrolet. Hans returns to his safari, counts his bearers, and gives the order to march.

Missionary or not, a certain authority is required so that the bearers won't succumb to idleness and maybe even start stealing supplies. They should be encouraged with glass beads and other trinkets at regular intervals, but also forced to witness punishments for neglect when necessary. He knows that during the many months, perhaps years, that the safari will be under way, he can never permit himself to sleep with more than one eye closed at a time.

As they pass the hospital the bearers begin to shout that they have to rest, but he keeps driving them. Not until they reach the altar in the woods does he let them put down the large bundles they are carrying on their heads . . .

'Mutshatsha,' he says to the altar. 'Together we will travel to Mutshatsha one day, when your spine has healed and you can get up again . . .'

He sends the bearers on ahead so he can have peace and quiet to meditate. Travelling might mean deciding to conquer something, he thinks vaguely. Conquer the doubters who didn't believe he would get away, never even as far as Orsa Finnmark. Or conquer the ones who had travelled even further, vanished even deeper into the wilderness. And conquer his own indolence, cowardice, fear.

I conquered the river bridge, he thinks. I was stronger than my own fear . . .

He strolls homeward through the summer night. There are so many more questions than answers. Erik Olofson, his incomprehensible father. Why is he starting to drink again? After they went to the sea together and saw that it was still there? In the middle of summer, when the snow and cold is gone? Why does he let the drunks in the house, let them get their hands on *Célestine*?

And why did Mamma leave, anyway? Outside the People's Hall he stops and looks at the remnants of the poster for the last movie programme of the spring.

Run for Your Life, he reads. That's it, run for your life. And he runs on silent feet through the warm summer night. Mutshatsha, he thinks. Mutshatsha is my password . . .

Chapter Twelve

ans Olofson says goodbye to Moses and watches the car bearing the dead men vanish in a cloud of dust.

'You stay as long as you like,' says Ruth, who has come out on to the porch. 'I won't ask why you're back so soon. All I'm saying is that you can stay.'

When he enters his old room, Louis is already busy filling the bathtub. Tomorrow, he thinks, tomorrow I will re-examine myself, decide what I'm going back to.

Werner Masterton has gone to Lubumbashi to buy bulls, Ruth tells him as they sit with their whisky glasses on the veranda.

'Such hospitality,' says Olofson.

'Here it's necessary,' says Ruth. 'We can't survive without one another. Forsaking a white person is the only mortal sin we recognise. But no one commits it. It's especially important that the blacks understand this.'

'Perhaps I'm wrong,' says Olofson, 'but I feel there is a state of war here. It isn't visible, but it's here.'

'Not a war,' says Ruth, 'but a difference that is essential to maintain, using force if necessary. Actually it's the whites that are left in this country who are the ultimate guarantee of the new black rulers. They use their newly won power to shape their lives like ours. The district governor borrowed from Werner the plans for this house. Now he's building a copy, with one difference: his house will be bigger.'

'At the mission station in Mutshatsha an African talked about a hunt that was ripening,' says Olofson. 'The hunt for the whites.'

'There's always someone who shouts louder than others,' replies Ruth. 'But the blacks are cowardly. Their method is assassination, never open warfare. The ones who shout aren't the ones you have to worry about. It's the ones who are silent that you have to keep a watchful eye on.'

'You say that the blacks are cowardly,' says Olofson, feeling the beginnings of intoxication. 'To my ears that sounds as if you think it's a racial defect. But I refuse to believe it.'

'Maybe I said too much,' says Ruth. 'But see for yourself. Live in Africa, then return to your own country and tell them what you experienced.'

They eat dinner, alone at the big table. Silent servants bring platters of food. Ruth directs them with glances and specific hand gestures. One of the servants spills gravy on the tablecloth. Ruth tells him to go.

'What will happen to him?' asks Olofson.

'Werner needs workers in the pig sties,' replies Ruth.

I ought to get up and leave, Olofson thinks. But I won't do anything, and then I'll acquit myself by saying that I don't belong, that I'm only a casual passing guest . . .

He has planned to stay for several days with Ruth and Werner. His plane ticket permits him to return no sooner than a week after arriving. But without his noticing, people gather around him, taking up the initial positions for the drama that will keep him in Africa for almost twenty years. He will ask himself many times what actually happened, what powers lured him, wove him into a dependent position, and in the end made it impossible for him to stand up and go.

The curtain goes up three days before Werner is supposed to drive him to Lusaka. By that time he has decided to resume his legal studies, make another try at it.

One evening the leopard shows itself for the first time in Hans Olofson's life. A Brahma calf is found mauled. An old African who works as the tractor foreman is summoned to look at the dead animal, and he instantly identifies the barely visible marks as being from the paws of a leopard.

'A big leopard,' he says. 'A lone male. Bold, probably cunning too.'

'Where is it now?' asks Werner.

'Nearby,' says the old man. 'Maybe it's watching us right now.'

Olofson notices the man's terror. The leopard is feared; its cunning is superior to that of men . . .

A trap is set. The slaughtered calf is hoisted up and lashed to a tree. Fifty metres away, a grass blind is built with an opening for a rifle.

'Maybe it will come back,' says Werner. 'If it does, it will be just before daybreak.'

When they return to the white house, Ruth is sitting with another woman on the veranda.

'One of my good friends,' says Ruth. 'Judith Fillington.'

Olofson says hello to a thin woman with frightened eyes and a pale, harried face. He can't tell her age, but he thinks she must be forty years old. From their conversation he understands that she has a farm that produces only eggs. A farm located north of Kalulushi, towards the copper fields, with the Kafue River as one of its boundaries.

Olofson keeps to the shadows. Fragments of a tragedy slowly emerge. Judith Fillington has come to announce that she has finally succeeded in having her husband declared dead. A bureaucratic obstacle has finally been overcome. A man struck to the ground by his melancholia, Olofson gathers. A man who vanished into the bush. Mental derangement, perhaps an unexpected suicide, perhaps a predator's victim. No body was ever found. Now there is a paper that confirms he is legally dead. Without that seal he has been wandering around like a phantom, Olofson thinks. For the second time I hear about a man who disappeared in the bush . . .

'I'm tired,' Judith says to Ruth. 'Duncan Jones has turned into a drunk. He can't handle the farm any more. If I'm gone for more than a day everything falls apart. The eggs don't get delivered, the lorry breaks down, the chicken feed runs out.'

'You'll never find another Duncan Jones in this country,' says Werner. 'You'll have to advertise in Salisbury or Johannesburg. Maybe in Gaborone too.'

'Who can I get?' asks Judith. 'Who would move here? Some new alcoholic?'

She quickly drains her whisky glass and holds it out for a refill. But when the servant brings the bottle she pulls back her empty glass.

Olofson sits in the shadows and listens. I always choose the chair where it's darkest, he thinks. In the midst of a gathering I look for a hiding place.

At the dinner table they talk about the leopard.

'There's a legend about the leopards that the older workers often tell,' says Werner. 'On Judgement Day, when the humans are already gone, the final test of power will be between a leopard and a crocodile, two animals who have survived to the end thanks to their cunning. The legend has no ending. It stops just at the moment when the two animals attack each other. The Africans imagine that the leopard and the crocodile engage in single combat for eternity, into the final darkness or a rebirth.'

'The mind boggles,' says Judith. 'The absolute final battle on earth, with no witnesses. Only an empty planet and two animals sinking their teeth and claws into each other.'

'Come with us tonight,' says Werner. 'Maybe the leopard will return.'

'I can't sleep anyway,' says Judith. 'Why not? I've never seen a leopard, although I was born here.'

'Few Africans have seen a leopard,' says Werner. 'At daybreak the tracks of its paws are there, right next to the huts and the people. But no one sees a thing.'

'Is there room for one more?' asks Hans. 'I'm good at making myself quiet and invisible.'

'The chieftains often wear leopard skins as a sign of honour and invulnerability,' says Werner. 'The magic essence of the leopard unites various tribes and clans. A Kaunde, a Bemba, a Luvale; all of them respect the leopard's wisdom.'

'Is there room?' Olofson asks again, but without receiving an answer.

Just after nine the group breaks up.

'Who are you taking with you?' asks Ruth.

'Old Musukutwane,' replies Werner. 'He's probably the only one here on the farm who has seen a leopard more than once in his life.'

They park the Jeep a little way off from the leopard trap. Musukutwane, an old African in ragged clothes, bent and thin, steps soundlessly out of the shadows. Silently he guides them through the dark.

'Choose your sitting position carefully,' whispers Werner when they enter the grass blind. 'We'll be here for at least eight hours.'

Olofson sits in a corner, and all he hears is their breathing and the interplay of night-time sounds.

'No cigarettes,' whispers Werner. 'Nothing. Speak softly if you do speak, mouth against ear. But when Musukutwane decides, all of us must be silent.'

'Where is the leopard now?' asks Olofson.

'Only the leopard knows where the leopard is,' replies Musukutwane.

The sweat runs down Olofson's face. He feels someone touch his arm.

'Why are they doing this, anyway?' asks Judith. 'Waiting all night for the leopard, when it probably won't show up?'

'Maybe I'll figure out an answer myself before dawn,' says Olofson.

'Wake me up if I fall asleep,' she says.

'What is required of a foreman on your farm?' he asks.

'Everything,' she replies. 'Fifteen thousand eggs have to be gathered, packed, and delivered each day, including Sundays. Feed has to be found; 200 Africans must be taken by the ear. Every day involves preventing a number of crises from developing into catastrophes.'

'Why not a black foreman?' he asks.

'If only it were that easy. But it isn't.'

'Without Musukutwane there will be no leopard. To me it's inconceivable that an African cannot be promoted to foreman in this country. They have a black president, a black government.'

'Come and work for me,' she says. 'All Swedes are farmers, aren't they?'

'Not exactly,' he replies. 'Maybe in the old days, but not any longer. And I don't know anything about chickens. I don't even know what 15,000 hens eat. Tons of breadcrumbs?'

'Waste from the corn mills,' she says.

'I don't think I have the temperament to take someone by the ear,' he says.

'I must find someone to help me.'

'In two days I'll be leaving on a plane. I can't imagine I'll be coming back.'

Olofson swats at a mosquito singing in front of his face. I could do it, he thinks hastily. At least I could try until she finds someone suitable. Ruth and Werner have opened their house to me and given me a breathing space. Maybe I could do the same for her. What tempts him is the possibility of escaping his sense of emptiness. But at the same time he mistrusts the temptation; it could just be another hiding place.

'Is there a lot of paperwork?' he asks. 'Residence permit, work permit?'

'An unbelievable amount of paperwork is required,' she says. 'But I know a colonel in the Immigration Department in Lusaka. Five hundred eggs delivered to his door will procure the required stamps.'

'But I don't know anything about chickens,' he says again.

'You already know what they eat,' she replies.

A grass blind and a hiring office, he thinks, and he feels as though he has become involved in something very unusual . . .

Cautiously he shifts his position. His legs are aching and a rock is pressing against the small of his back. A night bird screeches a sudden complaint in the dark. The frogs fall silent and he listens to the different people breathing around him. The only one he can't hear is Musukutwane. Werner moves his hand, a faint metallic sound comes from the rifle. Like in the trenches, he thinks. Waiting for the invisible foe . . .

Just before dawn Musukutwane suddenly emits a faint throaty sound.

'Starting now,' whispers Werner. 'Not a sound, not a movement.'

Olofson turns his head cautiously and pokes a little hole in the grass wall. Judith is breathing close to one ear. A faint sound tells them that Werner has taken the safety off his gun. The light of dawn comes softly, like a vague reflection of a distant fire. The cicadas fall silent, the screeching night bird is gone. The night is suddenly soundless.

The leopard, he thinks. When it approaches it is preceded by silence. Through the hole in the wall he tries to make out the tree to which the cadaver is tied.

They wait, but nothing happens. Suddenly it is full daylight; the countryside is revealed. Werner locks the safety on his rifle.

'Now we can go home,' he says. 'No leopard tonight.'

'It has been here,' says Musukutwane. 'It came just before dawn. But it sensed something and disappeared again.'

'Did you see it?' asks Werner suspiciously.

'It was dark,' says Musukutwane. 'But I know he was here. I saw him in my head. But he was suspicious and never climbed up in the tree.'

'If the leopard was here there must be some tracks,' says Werner.

'There are tracks,' says Musukutwane.

They crawl out of the grass blind and walk over to the tree. Flies are buzzing around the dead calf. Musukutwane points at the ground. The leopard's tracks.

He came from a dense thicket just behind the tree, made a circuit to observe the calf from different directions, before he approached the tree. Then he turned and quickly vanished back into the thicket. Musukutwane reads the tracks as if they were written words.

'What scared it off?' asks Judith.

Musukutwane shakes his head and touches the track carefully with his palm.

'He didn't hear anything. But he still knew it was dangerous. It's an old, experienced male. He has lived long because he is smart.'

'Will he come back tonight?' asks Olofson.

'Only the leopard knows that,' replies Musukutwane.

Ruth is waiting for them with breakfast.

'No shots last night,' she says. 'No leopard?'

'No leopard,' says Judith. 'But I may have found myself a foreman.'

'Really?' says Ruth, looking at Hans. 'Are you thinking of staying?'

'A short time,' he replies. 'While she looks for the right person.'

After breakfast he packs his bag and Louis carries it out to the waiting Land Rover.

In surprise he realises that he has no regrets at all. I'm not making any commitment, he tells himself. I'm just allowing myself an adventure.

'Maybe the leopard will come tonight,' he says to Werner when they say goodbye.

'Musukutwane thinks so,' says Werner. 'If the leopard has any weakness it's the same as that of a human being: an unwillingness to lose prey that is already caught.'

Werner promises to cancel Olofson's return trip for him.

'Come back soon,' says Ruth.

Judith pulls a dirty cap over her brown hair and with great difficulty jams the car into first gear.

'We never had children, my husband and I,' she blurts out as they drive through the gates of the farm.

'I couldn't help overhearing,' says Olofson. 'What actually happened?'

'Stewart, my husband, came out to Africa when he was fourteen,' Judith says. 'His parents left England during the Depression in 1932, and their savings were just enough for a one-way trip to Capetown. Stewart's father was a butcher, and he did well. But his mother suddenly began going out in the middle of the night and preaching to the black workers in the shanty towns. She went insane and committed suicide only a few years after they arrived in Capetown. Stewart was always afraid that he would wind up like his mother. Every morning when he woke up he searched for signs that he was starting to lose his mind. He would often ask me if I thought he was doing or saying anything odd. I never thought he had inherited anything from his mother; I think he fell ill from his own fear. After independence here, with all the changes, and the blacks who could now make their own decisions, he lost heart. Still, I was unprepared when he disappeared. He left no message, nothing . . .'

After a little over an hour they arrive. 'Fillington Farm' Olofson reads on a cracked wooden sign nailed to a tree. They turn in through a gate opened by an African in ragged clothes, pass by rows of low incubation buildings, and stop at last outside a house of dark-red brick. A house that was never completed, Olofson can see.

'Stewart was always fixing up the house,' she says. 'He would tear things down and add things on. I don't think he ever liked the house; he probably would rather have pulled it down and started again.'

'A castle out in the African bush,' says Olofson. 'A strange house. I didn't think there were any like this.'

'Welcome,' she says. 'Call me Judith and I'll call you Hans.'

She shows him to a large, bright room with odd angles and a sloping ceiling. Through the window he looks out over a partially overgrown yard with dilapidated garden furniture. German shepherds run restlessly back and forth in a fenced dog run.

'*Bwana*,' says someone behind him.

A Masai, he thinks as he turns around. I've always imagined them like this. Kenyatta's men. This is how they looked, the Mau-Mau warriors, the ones who drove the English out of Kenya.

The African who stands before him is very tall, his face noble.

'My name is Luka, *Bwana*.'

Can one have a servant who is nobler than oneself? Olofson wonders. An African warrior who runs one's bath?

He notices Judith standing in the doorway. 'Luka will take care of us,' she says. 'He reminds me of what I forget.'

Later, when they are sitting in the dilapidated wooden furniture drinking coffee, she tells him about Luka.

'I don't trust him,' she says. 'There's something wily about him, even though I've never caught him stealing or lying. But he does both, naturally.'

'How should I treat him?' asks Olofson.

'Firmly,' says Judith. 'The Africans are always looking for your weak point, those moments when you can be talked into something. Give him nothing; find something to complain about the first time he washes your clothes. Even if there's nothing; then he'll know that you make demands . . .'

Two large tortoises are asleep at Olofson's feet. The heat gives him a churning headache, and when he sets down his coffee cup, he sees that his table is a stuffed elephant foot.

I could live here the rest of my life, he thinks. The impulse is immediate, it overwhelms his consciousness and he can't formulate a single objection. I could put twenty-five years of my life behind me. Never again have to be reminded of what came before. But which of my roots would die if I tried to transplant them here, to this red earth? Why leave the meadowlands of Norrland for the sandy red soil they have here? Why would I want to live on a continent where an inexorable process of eviction is under way? Africa wants the whites out, I've understood that much. But they persevere, build their forts to defend themselves using racism and contempt as their tools. The whites' prisons are comfortable, but they are still prisons, bunkers with bowing servants . . .

His thoughts are interrupted. Judith looks at the coffee cup in her hand.

'The porcelain is a reminder,' she says. 'When Cecil Rhodes received his concessions over what today is called Zambia, he sent his employees into the wilderness to conclude agreements with the local chieftains. Perhaps also to obtain their help in finding unknown ore deposits. But these employees, who sometimes had to travel for years through the bush, were also supposed to be the vanguard of civilisation. Each expedition was like sending out an English manor house with bearers and ox carts. Every evening when they made camp, the porcelain service was unpacked. A table was set up with a white tablecloth, while Cecil Rhodes bathed in his tent and changed into his evening clothes. This service once belonged to one of the men who cleared the way for Cecil Rhodes's dream of an unbroken British territory from the Cape to Cairo.'

'Everyone is occasionally seized by impossible dreams,' says Olofson. 'Only the craziest try to realise them.'

'Not the madmen,' replies Judith. 'There you are mistaken. Not the madmen, but the intelligent and far-sighted ones. Cecil Rhodes's dream was not an impossibility; his problem was that he was all alone, at the mercy of impotent and capricious British politicians.'

'An empire that rests upon the most precarious of all foundations,' says Olofson. 'Oppression, alienation in one's own country. Such an edifice must collapse before it's even completed. There is one truth that's impossible to avoid.'

'And what's that?' asks Judith.

'The blacks were here first,' says Olofson. 'The world is full of various judicial systems, and in Europe it's based on Roman law. In Asia there are other legal forms, in Africa, everywhere. But natural law is always followed, even if the laws are given a political interpretation. The Indians of North America were almost totally wiped out in a couple of hundred years. And yet their natural law was written into the American law . . .'

Judith bursts into laughter. 'My second philosopher,' she says. 'Duncan Jones is also steeped in ephemeral philosophical reflections. I've never understood a word of it, even though I tried to in the beginning. Now he has drunk his brain into mush, his body shakes, and he chews his lips to shreds. Maybe he'll live a few more years before I have to bury him. Once he was a man with dignity and resolve. Now he lives in an eternal twilight zone of alcohol and decay. The Africans think he is being transformed into a holy man. They're afraid of him. He's the best watchdog I could have. And now you arrive, my next philosopher. Maybe Africa tempts some people to start ruminating.'

'Where does Duncan Jones live?' Olofson asks.

'I'll show you tomorrow,' says Judith.

Olofson lies awake for a long time in his irregular room with its sloping roof. A scent that reminds him of winter apples pervades it. Before he puts out the light he gazes at a big spider web, motionless on one of the walls. Somewhere a roof beam is complaining and he feels transported back to the house by the river. He listens to the German shepherds that Luka has let outside. They run restlessly around the house, making one circuit after another.

A short time, he thinks. A temporary visit to lend a helping hand to people with whom he has nothing in common, but who have taken care of him during his journey to Africa. They have abandoned Africa, but not each other, he thinks. That will also turn out to be their ruin . . .

In his dreams the leopard appears, the one he waited for last night in a grass blind. Now it races into the space inside him, searching for a quarry that Olofson left behind. The leopard searches through his internal landscape, and he suddenly sees Sture before him. They are sitting on the boulder by the river and watching a crocodile that has crawled up on a sand bank, right by the huge stone caissons of the river bridge.

Janine is balancing on one of the iron beams with her trombone. He tries to hear what she's playing, but the night wind carries away the tune.

Finally there is only the leopard's watchful eye, observing him from the dream chamber. The dream falls away, and when he awakens in the African dawn he will not remember it.

It is a day in late September of 1969. Hans Olofson will remain in Africa for eighteen years . . .

PART II

THE CHICKEN FARMER
IN KALULUSHI

Chapter Thirteen

When he opens his eyes in the dark, the fever is gone. There is only a wailing and whining sound inside his head.

I'm still alive, he thinks. I'm not dead yet. The malaria has not yet conquered me. I still have time to understand why I have lived before I die . . .

The heavy revolver presses against one cheek. He turns his head and feels the cold barrel against his forehead. A faint smell of gunpowder, like cow manure burned out in a pasture, pricks his nose.

He is very tired. How long was he asleep? A couple of minutes or twenty-four hours? He has no idea. He listens to the darkness, but the only thing he hears is his own breathing. The heat is stifling. The sheet is incapable of absorbing all the sweat he has produced.

Now is my chance, he thinks. Before the next fever attack is upon me. Now is when I have to get hold of Luka, who has betrayed me and left me to the bandits so they can slit my throat. Now is when I can catch him and scare him into running on his silent feet through the night to bring help. They are out there in the dark, with their automatic weapons and pickaxes and knives, and they're waiting for me to get delirious again before they come in here and kill me . . .

And yet he doesn't seem to care whether the malaria kills him or the bandits. He listens to the night. The frogs are croaking. A hippopotamus sighs down by the river.

Is Luka sitting outside the door, on his haunches, waiting? His black face concentrating, turned inward, listening to his forefathers speaking inside him? And the bandits? Where are they waiting? In the dense thickets of hibiscus beyond the gazebo that blew down last year in a violent storm that came after everyone thought the rainy season was over?

One year ago, he thinks. For ten years he has lived here by the Kafue River. Or fifteen years, maybe more. He tries to tally them up but he's too tired. And he was only supposed to stay here two weeks. What actually happened? Even time is betraying me, he thinks.

He can see himself descend from the aeroplane at Lusaka International Airport that day so inconceivably long ago. The concrete was completely white, the heat hung like a mist over the airport, and an African pushing a baggage cart laughed as he stepped on to Africa's burning soil.

He remembers his anxiety, his instant suspicion towards Africa. Back then he left behind the adventure he had imagined ever since childhood. He had always imagined that he would step out into the unknown with a consciousness that was open and utterly free of anxiety.

But Africa crushed that idea. When he stepped out of the aeroplane and found himself surrounded by black people, foreign smells, and a language he didn't understand, he longed to go straight back home.

The trip to Mutshatsha, the dubious pilgrimage to the final goal of Janine's dream – he carried it out under a compulsion he had imposed on himself. He still recalls the humiliating feeling that terror was his only travelling companion; it overshadowed everything else in his mind. The money sticking to him inside his underpants, the terrified creature huddled in the hotel room.

Africa conquered the sense of adventure within him as soon as he took his first breath on the soil of this foreign continent. He began planning his return at once.

Fifteen or ten or eighteen years later, he is still there. His return ticket is somewhere in a drawer full of shoes and broken wristwatches and rusty screws. Many years ago he discovered it when he was looking for something in the drawer; insects had attacked the envelope and made the ticket illegible.

What actually happened?

He listens to the darkness. Suddenly he feels as if he's lying in his bed in the wooden house by the river again. He can't tell if it's winter or summer. His father is snoring in his room and he thinks that soon, soon, the moorings of the wooden house will be cut and the house will drift away down the river, off towards the sea . . .

What was it that happened? Why did he stay in Africa, by this river, on this farm, where he was forced to witness the murder of his friends, where he soon felt he was surrounded only by the dead?

How has he been able to live so long with a revolver under his pillow? It isn't normal for a person who grew up by a river in Norrland – in a town and a time where nobody ever thought of locking the door at night – to check that his revolver is loaded every night, that no one has replaced the cartridges with blanks. It isn't normal to live a life surrounded by hate . . .

Once again he tries to understand. Before the malaria or the bandits have conquered him he wants to know . . .

He can feel that a new attack of fever is on its way. The whining in his head has stopped abruptly. Now he can hear only the frogs and the sighing hippo. He takes a grip on the sheet so he can hold on tight when the fever rolls over him like a storm surge.

I have to hang on, he thinks in despair. As long as I keep my will the fever won't be able to vanquish me. If I put the pillow over my face they won't hear me yell when the hallucinations torment me.

The fever drops its cage around him. He thinks he sees the leopard, which only visits him when he's sick, lying at the foot of the bed. Its cat face is turned towards him. The cold eyes are motionless.

It doesn't exist, he tells himself. It's just racing around in my head. With my will I can conquer the cat as well. When the fever is gone the leopard won't exist any more. Then I'll have control over my thoughts and dreams. Then it won't exist any more . . .

What happened? he wonders again.

The question echoes inside him. Suddenly he no longer knows who he is. The fever drives him away from his consciousness. The leopard watches by the bed, the revolver rests against his cheek.

The fever chases him out on to the endless plains . . .

Chapter Fourteen

One day in late September 1969.

He has promised to stay and help Judith Fillington with her farm, and when he wakes up the first morning in the room with the odd angles, he sees that some overalls with patched knees are lying on his chair.

Luka, he thinks. While I sleep he carries out her orders. Silently he places the overalls on a chair, looks at my face, disappears.

He looks out the window, out over the vast farm. An unexpected elation fills him. For a brief moment he seems to have conquered his fear. He can stay for a few weeks and help her. The trip to Mutshatsha is already a distant memory. Staying on Judith's farm is no longer following in Janine's footsteps . . .

During the hot morning hours Olofson listens to the gospel according to chickens. He and Judith sit in the shade of a tree and she instructs him.

'Fifteen thousand eggs per day,' she says. 'Twenty thousand laying hens, additional colonies of at least 5,000 chicks who replace the hens that no longer lay and then go to slaughter. Every Saturday morning at dawn we sell them. The Africans wait in silent queues all night long. We sell the hens for four *kwacha*, and they resell the hens at the markets for six or seven *kwacha* . . .'

She looks like a bird. A restless bird who keeps expecting the shadow of a falcon or eagle to drop down over her head. He has put on the overalls that lay on the chair when he awoke. Judith is wearing a pair of faded, dirty khaki trousers, a red shirt that is far too big, and a hat with a wide brim. Her eyes are inaccessible in the shadow of the brim.

'Why don't you sell them at the markets yourself?' he asks.

'I concentrate on survival,' she says. 'I'm already close to cracking under the workload.'

She calls to Luka and says something that Olofson doesn't understand. Why do all the whites act impatient, he wonders, as if every black man or woman were insubordinate or stupid?

Luka returns with a dirty map, and Olofson squats down next to Judith. With one finger she shows him on the map where her farm delivers its eggs. He tries to remember the names: Ndola, Mufulira, Solwezi, Kansanshi.

Judith's shirt is open at the neck. When she leans forward he can see her skinny chest. The sun has burned a red triangle down towards her navel. Suddenly she straightens up, as if she were aware that he was no longer looking at the map. Her eyes remain hidden under the hat.

'We deliver to the shops of the state cooperative,' she says. 'We deliver to the mining companies, always big orders. At most a thousand eggs per day go to local buyers. Every employee gets one egg a day.'

'How many people work here?' Olofson asks.

'Two hundred,' she replies. 'I'm trying to learn all their names by paying out the wages myself. I take deductions for drunkenness and for those who miss work without having a good excuse. I give out warnings and fines, I hire and fire, and I rely on my memory to guarantee that no one who is sacked comes back under a false name to be hired again. Of the 200 who work here, twenty are night watchmen. We have two laying houses, each manned by an assistant foreman and ten workers in shifts. In addition we have butchers, carpenters, drivers, and manual labourers. Only men, no women.'

'What will I be doing?' asks Olofson. 'I know what the chickens eat and where the eggs are delivered, but what will I do?'

'Follow me like a shadow. Listen to what I say, check that it gets done. Everything we want done has to be repeated, ordered a second time, and then checked.'

'Something must be wrong,' Olofson says. 'Something the whites have never understood.'

'Love the blacks if you want,' says Judith. 'But take my advice. I've lived among them my whole life. I speak their language, I know how they think. I get doctors for their children when the medicine man fails, I pay for their funerals when they don't have any money. I send the smartest children to school at my expense. When the food runs out I organise transport of sacks of maize to their houses. I do everything for them. But anyone who is caught stealing a single egg I turn over to the police. I fire a man who is drunk, I kick out the night watchmen who fall asleep.'

Olofson slowly begins to realise the scope of the operation. The dominion of a single woman, Africans who subordinate themselves because they have no alternative. Two different types of poverty, face to face at a common meeting point. The terror of the whites, their truncated lives as left-over colonialists in a burned-out empire. The ash heap of loneliness in a new or resurrected black colony.

The poverty of the whites is their vulnerability. Their lack of alternatives becomes apparent when they arrange to meet the Africans. Even a garden like this one, with the barely visible dream of a Victorian park embedded in the greenery, is a fortified bunker. Judith Fillington's last bastion is her hat, which conceals her eyes.

The poverty and vulnerability of the blacks is the poverty of the continent. Broken and destroyed living patterns, their origins lost in the mists of the past, replaced by insane empire builders who changed into their dinner jackets deep in the rainforests and on the plains of elephant grass. This world of stage sets still exists. Here the Africans are trying to shape their future. Perhaps they have endless patience. Perhaps they still have doubts about how the future should look, how these stage sets can be dissolved and obliterated. But what happens when they burst?

Hans Olofson decides he must work out a contingency plan, an escape route. I'm only here for a short visit, he thinks. I'm doing a favour for a strange woman, as if I were helping her up after a fall on the street. But the whole time I remain outside the actual event. I don't get involved, I can't be held responsible . . .

Judith gets up abruptly. 'Work is waiting,' she says. 'Most of your questions you can probably answer yourself. Africa belongs to each individual, it's never shared.'

'You know nothing about me,' he says. 'My background, my life, my dreams. And yet you're prepared to grant me enormous responsibility. From my Swedish point of view it's incomprehensible.'

'I'm alone,' she replies. 'Abandoned by a man I never even had a chance to bury. Living in Africa means always being forced to take full responsibility.'

Much later he will remember his first days at Judith Fillington's farm as an unreal journey into a world he seems to understand less and less, the more his insight grows. Surrounded by the faces of the black workers, he feels that he is in the midst of an ongoing but not yet triggered catastrophe.

During those days he discovers that feelings secrete different odours. He can sense hate in a bitter smell, like manure or vinegar, everywhere; wherever he follows Judith like a shadow the smell is always nearby. When he wakes in the night, the smell is there, a faint current through the malaria net that hangs above his bed.

Something has to happen, he thinks. An outbreak of rage at the impotence and poverty. Not having an alternative is like having nothing at all, he thinks. Not being able to see anything beyond poverty except more poverty . . .

He decides that he has to get away, leave Africa before it's too late. But after a month he is still there. He lies in his room with the sloping ceiling and listens to the dogs restlessly patrolling around the house. Every evening before he goes to bed, he sees Judith check that the doors and windows are locked. He sees how she first turns out the light in each room before she goes in to draw the heavy curtains. She is always listening, stopping suddenly in the midst of a step or a movement. She takes a shotgun and a heavy elephant gun into her bedroom every night. During the day the weapons are locked inside a steel cabinet, and he sees that she always carries the keys with her.

After a month he realises that he has begun to share her fear. With the rapidly falling twilight the strange house is transformed into a bunker of silence. He asks whether she has found a successor, but she shakes her head.

'In Africa anything important takes a long time,' she replies.

He begins to suspect that she hasn't written any classified ads, hasn't made contact with the newspapers that Werner Masterton suggested. But he refrains from giving vent to his suspicion.

Judith fills him with awed respect, perhaps even devotion. Hans follows her from dawn to dusk, follows her unceasing effort, which means that 15,000 eggs leave the farm each day, despite run-down and mistreated lorries, a continual shortage of the maize waste that makes up the primary fodder, and sudden outbreaks of viral diseases which during one night can take the lives of all the hens in one of the oblong, walled-off stone buildings where they are forced into steel cages. One night she wakes him up, pulling open his door and shining a torch into his face, and tells him to get dressed at once.

Outside the house with its locked doors a frightened night watchman is shouting that hunter ants have got into one of the chicken coops, and when they reach the site Olofson sees terrified Africans using burning bundles of twigs to swat at the endless columns of ants. Without hesitation Judith takes the lead, forcing the ants to change direction, and she screams at him when he doesn't understand what she wants him to do.

'Who am I?' he asks her early one morning. 'Who am I to the blacks?'

'A new Duncan Jones,' she replies. 'Two hundred Africans are searching for your weak spot right now.'

Two weeks pass before he meets the man he has come to replace. Each day they go past the house where he sits locked in with his bottles, transforming himself into a holy man. The house is on a hill right by the river, surrounded by a high wall.

A rusty car, maybe a Peugeot, is sometimes parked outside the wall. It's always parked as though it had been abandoned in haste. The boot stands open, and the corner of a filthy blanket hangs out of one door.

He imagines a state of siege, a final battle that will be fought around this hill, between the black workers and the lone white man inside in the dark.

'The night watchmen are afraid,' says Judith. 'They can hear him wailing in the night. They're afraid, but at the same time they feel a sense of security. They think that his metamorphosis to a holy man will mean that the bandits will stay away from this farm.'

'The bandits?' Olofson asks.

'They're everywhere,' she replies. 'In the slums outside Kitwe and

Chingola there are plenty of weapons. Gangs spring up and are destroyed, and new ones appear in their place. White farmers are attacked, cars with whites are stopped on the roads. The police are almost certainly involved, as well as workers on the farms.'

'What if they come here?' he asks.

'I rely on my dogs,' she says. 'Africans are afraid of dogs. And I have Duncan wailing in the night. Superstition can be good if you know how to use it. Maybe the night watchmen believe he's being transformed into a snake.'

Then one morning he meets Duncan Jones for the first time. He is standing supervising the loading of empty feed sacks into a battered lorry when the black workers stop working. Duncan Jones comes walking slowly towards him. He is dressed in dirty trousers and a ripped shirt. Olofson sees a man who has slashed his face with his straight razor. A suntanned face, skin like tanned leather. Heavy eyelids, grey hair that is tangled and filthy.

'Don't ever take a piss before all the sacks are loaded and the back door locked,' says Duncan Jones, coughing. 'If you go to take a piss before that, you have to expect that at least ten sacks will disappear. They sell the sacks for one *kwacha* each.'

He holds out his hand.

'There's just one thing I don't understand,' he says. 'Why has Judith waited so long to find my successor? Everyone has to be put out to pasture eventually. The only ones spared are those who die young. But who are you?'

'I'm a Swede,' says Olofson. 'I'm only here temporarily.'

Duncan Jones opens his face in a smile and Olofson looks straight into a mouth full of black stumps of teeth.

'Why does everyone who comes to Africa have to apologise?' he asks. 'Even those who were born here say that they're only here for a short visit.'

'In my case it's true,' says Olofson.

Jones shrugs his shoulders. 'Judith deserves it,' he says. 'She deserves all the help she can get.'

'She put an ad in the paper,' says Olofson.

'Who can she get?' says Jones. 'Who would move here? Don't abandon her. Never ask me for advice, I don't have any. Maybe I had some once, advice I should have taken myself. But it's all gone now. I'll live for another year. Hardly longer than that . . .'

Suddenly he bellows at the Africans who are silently watching his meeting with Hans Olofson.

'Work!' he yells. 'Work, don't sleep!'

Instantly they grab hold of their sacks.

'They're afraid of me,' says Jones. 'I know they think I'm about to dissolve and be resurrected in the figure of a holy man. I'm about to become a *kashinakashi*. Or maybe a snake. How do I know?'

Then he turns and leaves. Olofson watches him stop and press one hand against the small of his back, as if a pain has suddenly struck him. That evening, as they are eating dinner, Olofson mentions the meeting.

'Maybe he will succeed in reaching some kind of clarity,' she says. 'Africa has set him free from all dreams. For Duncan, life is an undertaking that has been arbitrarily assigned. He is drinking himself consciously and methodically towards the big sleep. Without fear, I think. Maybe we should envy him. Or maybe we should feel pity that he so utterly lacks hope?'

'No wife, no children?' asks Olofson.

'He lies with the black women,' she replies. 'Maybe he has black children. I know that sometimes he mistreats the women he takes to his bed. But I don't know why he does it.'

'It looked as though he was in pain,' says Olofson. 'Maybe it's his kidneys.'

'He would say that Africa is taking him from inside,' she says. 'He would never admit to any other illness.'

Then she asks Olofson to stay a bit longer. He realises that he is listening to a liar when she says that the classified ads in the newspapers in South Africa and Botswana have not yet produced any replies.

'All right, but not for long,' he replies. 'A month at most, no more.'

A week before the time has run out, Judith takes sick one night. He wakes up when she touches his arm and finds her standing in the dark by his bed. What he sees when he manages to light the bedside lamp with a drowsy hand is something he knows he'll never forget.

A dying woman, maybe already dead. Judith is dressed in an old, stained dressing gown. Her hair is uncombed and tangled, her face shiny with sweat, her eyes wide open as if she were looking at something unbearable. In one hand she holds her shotgun.

'I'm sick,' she says. 'I need your help.'

Utterly powerless she sinks down on the edge of the bed. But the mattress is soft. She slides off on to the floor and sits leaning her head against the bed.

'It's malaria,' she says. 'I must have medicine. Take the car, drive to Duncan's place, wake him up, and ask him for medicine. If he doesn't have any you'll have to drive to Werner and Ruth's. You can find your way all right.'

He helps her into the bed.

'Take the shotgun,' she says. 'Lock the house behind you. If Duncan doesn't wake up, fire the gun.'

When he turns the key in the ignition the night is filled with loud rumba music from the radio. This is crazy, he thinks as he forces the stiff gearstick into position. I've never been this scared in my life. Not even when I was a child and crawled across the river bridge.

He drives over the potholed sandy road, much too fast and recklessly, jamming the gears and feeling the barrel of the shotgun against his shoulder.

Outside the hen houses the night watchmen appear in the headlights. A white man in the night, he thinks. It's not *my* night, it belongs to the blacks.

Outside Duncan Jones's house he honks the horn wildly. Then he forces himself out of the car, finds a rock on the ground, and begins slamming it against the gate in the wall. He cracks the skin on his knuckles, listens for sounds from inside the house, but he hears only his own heart. He gets the gun from the car, remembers the safety catch, and then fires a shot at the distant stars. The butt slams against his shoulder and the shot booms in the night.

'Come on!' he yells. 'Wake up from your drunken stupor, bring me the damned medicine!'

At last he hears a scraping sound on the other side of the gate and Olofson shouts his name. Duncan Jones stands naked before him. He has a revolver in his hand.

This is insanity, Olofson thinks again. No one would believe me if I described it; I'll probably hardly even believe my own memories. I have to get her some medicine. Then I'll go back home. This is no life, this is madness.

Jones is so drunk that Olofson has to tell him over and over why he came. Finally he sticks the barrel of the shotgun in his chest.

'Malaria medicine!' he shouts. 'Malaria medicine . . .'

At last Jones understands, and he staggers back to his house. Olofson steps into an indescribable mess of dirty clothes, empty bottles, half-eaten meals, and piles of newspapers.

This is a morgue, he thinks. Here death is busy taking control. He won't be able to find any medicine in this chaos, thinks Olofson, and he prepares to drive the long road to the Mastertons' farm. But then Jones comes wobbling out of what Olofson assumes is his bedroom, and in his hand he has a paper bag. Olofson snatches the bag and leaves the house.

After he returns and has locked all the doors behind him, he realises that he is drenched with sweat.

He carefully shakes Judith from a feverish sleep and forces her to swallow three tablets after reading the instructions. She sinks back on to the pillows and he sits down in a chair to catch his breath. He becomes aware that he is still holding the shotgun. This isn't normal, he thinks. I would never be able to get used to a life like this. I would never survive . . .

He stays awake all night, watching her fever attacks subside and then return. At daybreak he feels her forehead. Her breathing is deep and steady. He goes into the kitchen and unlocks the back door. Luka is standing there waiting.

'Coffee,' says Olofson. 'No food, just coffee. Madame Judith is sick today.'

'I know, *Bwana*,' Luka replies.

Weariness suddenly gets the upper hand in Olofson's mind. He bursts out with a furious question. All these Africans know everything in advance.

'How can you know?'

Luka seems unperturbed by his outburst. 'A car drives much too fast through the night, *Bwana*,' he says. 'All *mzunguz* drive in different ways. *Bwana* stops outside *Bwana* Duncan's house. Fires off his shotgun, yells in the night. Luka wakes up and thinks madame must be sick. Madame is never sick unless she has malaria.'

'Now fix my coffee,' says Olofson. 'It's too early to listen to long explanations.'

Just after six o'clock he gets into the Jeep again and tries to imagine that he is Judith. He does her chores, checks off on a roll call that all the workers have arrived, ensures that the eggs are gathered and leave the farm. He makes an estimate of the feed supply and organises a tractor transport to the mill whose turn it is to deliver maize waste.

At eleven o'clock a rusty car with worn-down shock absorbers pulls up in front of the mud hut where Judith has set up her office. Olofson walks out into the sharp sunshine. A conspicuously well-dressed African comes towards him. Again Olofson finds himself involved in a complicated greeting procedure.

'I'm looking for Madame Fillington,' says the man.

'She's ill,' replies Olofson.

The African looks at him, smiling and appraising him.

'I'm Mr Pihri,' he says.

'I'm Madame Fillington's temporary foreman,' says Olofson.

'I know,' says Mr Pihri. 'It's precisely because you are who you are that I have come here today with some important papers. I'm the Mr Pihri who does small favours for madame now and then. Not large favours. But even small favours are necessary from time to time. To avoid problems that might become bothersome.'

Olofson senses that he has to be careful. 'Papers?' he says.

Mr Pihri at once looks sad.

'Madame Fillington usually offers me tea when I come to visit,' he says.

Olofson has seen a teapot inside the hut, and he calls to one of the Africans bent over the illegible roll call lists to fix tea. Mr Pihri's sorrowful face is then transformed by a large smile. Olofson decides to smile too.

'Our authorities are scrupulous about formalities,' says Mr Pihri. 'We learned that from the British. Perhaps our authorities today exaggerate their scrupulousness. But we must be careful with people who visit our country. All papers must be in order.'

This also applies to me, Olofson thinks. Why did this smiling man have to come today of all days, when Judith is sick?

They drink tea in the dimness of the hut and Olofson sees Mr Pihri dump eight teaspoons of sugar into his cup.

'Madame asked me for help in facilitating the processing of your visa,' says Mr Pihri, as he drinks his tea in slow sips. 'Of course it is important to avoid unnecessary impediments. Madame and I usually exchange services to our mutual benefit. It makes me very sad to hear that she is ill. If she died it would be particularly disadvantageous.'

'Perhaps I can assist you in her stead,' says Olofson.

'That would be excellent,' replies Mr Pihri. From his inside pocket he takes some papers, typed and stamped.

'I'm Mr Pihri,' he says again. 'Police officer and a very good friend of Madame Fillington. I hope she doesn't die.'

'I am of course grateful on her behalf. I would be happy to do you a service in her place.'

Mr Pihri continues to smile. 'My friends and colleagues at the Immigration Department are quite busy at the moment. The workload is extremely heavy. They also deny many applications for temporary residency. Unfortunately they must sometimes reject people who would like to stay in our country. Naturally it is never pleasant to have to leave a country within twenty-four hours. Especially when Madame Fillington is ill. I only hope she doesn't die. But my friends at the Immigration Department showed great understanding. I'm happy to be able to deliver these papers, signed and stamped in due order. One should always avoid trouble. The authorities take a dim view of any individuals who lack the required documents. Unfortunately, sometimes they are also forced to incarcerate people for an indefinite period.'

Mr Pihri looks sad once again.

'The prisons in this country unfortunately suffer from neglect. Especially for Europeans who are used to quite different conditions.'

What the hell does he want? Olofson wonders.

'I am naturally very grateful,' he says. 'I would like to express my appreciation on behalf of Madame Fillington.'

Again Mr Pihri smiles.

'The boot of my car is not very big. But 500 eggs could be fitted into it with no problem.'

'Load 500 eggs into Mr Pihri's car,' Olofson tells one of the crouching office workers.

Mr Pihri hands him the stamped documents.

'I regret that from time to time these stamps must be renewed. It is always good to avoid problems. This is why Madame Fillington and I meet regularly. In this way one can avoid much unpleasantness.'

Olofson escorts Mr Pihri to his car, where the egg cartons are stacked in the boot.

'My car is getting old,' says Mr Pihri in a worried voice. 'Perhaps it will simply stop running one day. Then it would be quite trouble-some for me to visit Madame Fillington.'

'I'll tell her that your car has begun to run poorly,' replies Olofson.

'I would be grateful. Tell her also that just now there is an excellent used Peugeot for sale by one of my friends in Kitwe.'

'I'll mention it to her.'

They repeat the complicated greeting procedure.

'It was very nice we could meet,' says Mr Pihri.

'Naturally we are very grateful,' replies Olofson.

'Trouble should be avoided,' says Mr Pihri as he gets behind the wheel and drives off.

Corruption's Song of Songs, thinks Olofson as he walks back to the dark hut. Like a well-groomed beard. A polite, quiet talk . . .

When he studies the documents that Mr Pihri left, he finds to his astonishment that Judith has applied for and been granted a visa for him as a 'resident' for a period of two years.

He is instantly agitated. I'm not going to stay here, he thinks. I have no intention of letting myself be entrapped by her plans for her own future . . .

When he returns to the house to eat lunch, Judith is awake. She is still lying in his bed. She is pale and tired, and it's a big effort for her to smile. When he starts to speak she shakes her head.

'Later,' she says. 'Not now. I'm too tired. Luka will give me what I need.'

When Olofson returns in the evening she has moved back to her own room. He observes how forlorn she looks in the wide double bed. The illness has diminished her, he thinks. Her skin has shrunk. Only her eyes are unchanged, just as big and restless as ever.

'I'm feeling better,' she says. 'But I'm very tired. Every time I get malaria my powerlessness gets worse. I despise weakness, not being able to do anything.'

'Mr Pihri came to visit,' he tells her. 'He left me some papers with a lot of stamps on them and I gave him what he wanted, 500 eggs.'

'Smiling the whole time,' says Judith. 'He's such a crook, one of the worst. Although he is reliable; playing the corruption game with him always gives results.'

'He wants a new car. He has picked out a used Peugeot.'

'He'll get it when I have a sufficiently difficult matter for him to solve.'

'Why did you apply for a two-year residence visa for me?'

'I don't think they come any shorter than that.'

As sick as she is, she can still lie, he thinks. When she gets well I'll have to ask her why. He listens outside her door and hears her soft snoring.

Then he makes a pilgrimage through the house, counts the

number of rooms, finds his way through deserted guest rooms, and stops outside a door he hadn't noticed before. He's at the end of a winding corridor, and the door is scarcely visible, set into the brown panelling.

The door opens when he touches the handle, and a musty smell of camphor wafts towards him. He slides one hand over the wall to find a light switch. A bare lightbulb in the ceiling comes on. He sees a thigh bone that he surmises is from an elephant or a cape buffalo. A crocodile with the extended ribs of a reptile. Various skulls and horns, some of them broken, lie jumbled together. He imagines that the animals were once locked alive in this room and slowly rotted away, until all that remained were bones and skulls.

Her husband's room, he thinks. A little boy's dream of what a grown man's room would be. In a dusty window niche lies a notebook. He can make out the pencil handwriting passably well and realises he is looking at poems. Quivering poetic fragments, written with a pencil that is so faint it could never have been intended that the text survive . . .

A rucksack full of ants was all that remained, he thinks. That is poetry too, the epitaph of a man who disappeared. Depressed, he leaves the room.

Once again he listens outside Judith's door and then goes into his own room. A faint odour from her body is still between the sheets. The imprint of fever. He places her shotgun next to the bed. I don't want to take over from her, he thinks. Yet one of her weapons stands by my bed.

All at once he is homesick, childishly so; he feels abandoned. Now I have seen Africa, he thinks. What I've seen I haven't understood, but I've still seen it. I'm no explorer; expeditions into the unknown tempt me only in my imagination.

Once I climbed over a bridge span, as if I were riding on the axis of the earth itself. I left something behind up there on that cold iron span. It was the longest journey I ever took in my life . . . It's possible that I'm still up there, with my fingers gripping the cold iron. Maybe I never really came down. I'm still up there, wrapped in my terror.

He gets into bed and turns off the light. The sounds stream forth from the darkness, the padding dogs, the hippo sighing from the river.

Just before he falls asleep he is wide awake for a moment. Someone is laughing out in the dark. One of the dogs barks and then all is quiet again.

In the silence he remembers the brickworks. The ruin where he became aware of his consciousness for the first time. In the laughter that reaches him from the night he thinks he senses a continuation of that moment. The ruin of the brickworks clarified his existence. The fortified bedroom in the house by the Kafue River, surrounded by large dogs, reveals certain conditions. The laughter that penetrates the night describes the world he temporarily happens to inhabit.

This is how it looks, he thinks. Earlier I knew without knowing. Now I see how the world has capsized, I see the poverty and misery that are the real truth. Perched high on the river bridge there were only the stars and the expansive horizon of fir trees. I wanted to get away from there and now I have done so. Being here must mean that I'm in the centre of a time that belongs to me. I have no idea who was laughing. Nor can I determine whether the laugh is a threat or a promise. And yet I know.

Soon he must leave this place. His return ticket is his main insurance. In a place where the world is divided, where the world is fixed, he doesn't have to be involved. He stretches out his hand in the dark and runs his fingers along the cold barrel of the shotgun. The hippo sighs down by the river.

All of a sudden he's in a hurry to get home. Judith will have to look for Duncan Jones's successor without his help. The visa that Mr Pihri extracted from his friends and was paid for with 500 eggs will never be used . . .

But he is wrong; Hans Olofson is wrong. Like so many times before, his assessments turn on their own axis and come back to the starting point as their opposites. The return ticket has already begun to decompose.

Chapter Fifteen

Hans Olofson's dreams are almost always reminders. Through his dreams, his subconscious self ensures that he forgets nothing. Often there is a recurrent prelude, as if his dreams were drawing aside the old worn curtain for the very same music. The music is the winter night, the clear, starry midwinter cold.

He is out there, Hans Olofson, still barely grown. He is standing somewhere by the church wall beneath a street lamp. He is a lonely, sad shadow against all the white of that stern winter night . . .

How could he have known? He couldn't peek into the veiled world of the future when he finally finished his last day of school, flung his school books under the bed and marched away to his first full-time job as the youngest man in the warehouse of the Trade Association. Back then the world was exceedingly knowable and whole. Now he was going to earn his own money, pull his own weight, learn to be a grown-up.

What he would later recall about his time at the Trade Association was the constant hauling of goods up the hill to the train station. The cart he was given was neglected and worn-out, and with a continuous curse inside him he would drag and pull it in a perpetual circuit between the freight office and the warehouse. He quickly learned that swearing didn't make the hill any easier to overcome. Swearing was revenge and helpless rage, and as such possibly a source of strength, but it didn't flatten out the hill.

He decides that the hellhole that is the Trade Association's warehouse can't represent the truth. The Honour of Work and the Community of Work must look different.

And there is a difference in going to work for Under, the horse dealer who needs a helper because one of his stable boys has been badly bitten on the arm by an angry stallion.

Hans Olofson makes his entrance into the strange world of the horse dealer one day in late September, when there is already snow in the air. Winter preparations are in full swing; stalls have to be rebuilt and expanded, the leaky roof has to be fixed, the harnesses checked, the supply of horseshoes and nails inventoried. Late autumn is the time to prepare for hibernation; horses as well as people have to sleep, and Hans stands with a sledgehammer in his hand and knocks out one of the cross-walls in the stable. Under wanders around in his galoshes in the cement dust and dispenses advice. Visselgren, a short man from the south of Sweden, who Under discovered at the Skänninge marketplace, sits in one corner mending a pile of harnesses, and winks at Hans. The immensely strong Holmström twins pull down one of the cross-walls by themselves. Horses couldn't have done it any better. Under saunters contentedly back and forth.

In the world of Under there is a continual switching between absentminded indifference and sound opinions which he passionately defends. The very foundation of his world view is that nothing is initially a given, other than when it comes to horses. Casting modesty aside, he views himself as a member of the elite who carry the world on their shoulders. Without horse dealing, chaos would rule, and wild horses would take over the world as the new barbaric rulers. Hans swings his heavy sledgehammer and is happy to have escaped the worn-out cart. Now this is living!

For one year he is part of this strange community. His assignments are always changing; the days differ sharply but enticingly.

One evening he runs across the river bridge to Janine's house. On this very evening she has adorned herself with the red nose, and she is sitting at the kitchen table polishing her trombone when he stamps the snow off his feet on the steps.

He stopped knocking long ago. Janine's house is a home, a different home from the wooden house by the river, but still his home. A little leather bag hanging above the kitchen table spreads the fragrance of cumin. Janine, who no longer has a sense of smell, still remembers cumin from the time before the botched operation.

He confides almost everything to Janine. Not everything, that would be impossible. Thoughts and feelings that he can scarcely acknowledge to himself, those remain secret. This applies especially to Hans's increasingly agitated and vulnerable discovery of the strange desires that are boiling inside him.

Today she has her red nose on. Usually the hole underneath her eyes is covered by a white handkerchief, stuffed into the hole so that he can see the red scars left by the scalpel, and the sight of naked flesh under her eyes becomes something forbidden, hinting at something quite different.

He imagines her naked, with the trombone at her lips, and then he blushes with excitement. He has no idea whether she senses what he's thinking. He wishes that she would, as often as he wishes the opposite.

She plays a new tune she has learned, 'Wolverine Blues', which she has put on her gramophone. Hans keeps the beat with a darning egg, yawns and only half listens.

When she finishes he can't stay any longer. Nothing is calling him but he's still in a hurry. Ever since he finished school he has been running. Something is urging him on, exciting and enticing him.

The house stands where it always has stood. Light snow covers the potato patch that nobody ever digs in. In one of the lighted windows he sees his father's shadow. Hans suddenly feels sorry for him. He tries to imagine the way his father must have stood on the afterdeck of a ship heading into a warm trade wind. Far off, against the last ribbons of the sunset, glow the faint lights from the next port of call.

But when he walks into the kitchen there's a knot in his stomach, because his father is sitting at the table with glazed eyes and before him stands a half-empty bottle. Hans knows that his father has begun to drink himself into a stupor again.

Why is life so damned hard? he thinks. Bare ice to slip on wherever you turn . . .

This winter even Under finally reveals himself as something other than a well-meaning horse dealer in galoshes. There is malice behind the friendly mask.

Hans learns that the friendliness has a price. Beneath the voluminous overcoat lurks a reptile. Gradually he begins to understand that in the horse dealer's world he is nothing more than a strong pair of arms and obedient legs. When Visselgren is struck by arthritis in the middle of February, the good times are over for him. The horse dealer buys him a one-way ticket back to Skänninge and drives him to the station. Under doesn't even bother to get out of the car and thank him for all his hard work. Back at the stable he rants for a long time about Visselgren's duplicity, as if his shortness should be regarded as a character defect.

New employees come and go, and eventually it's only the Holmström twins and Hans who remain of the old crew. Hans is starting to think the same thoughts as he had as he was pulling the cart between the warehouse and the freight office.

Has he ended up back there again? If so, where is the Honour and Community of Work in the daily drudgery that he thought was the great Goal of life?

A few weeks after Visselgren's departure, the horse dealer comes into the stable late one afternoon with a black box under his arm. The Holmström brothers have already left in their decrepit Saab, and Hans is alone getting the stable ready for the night.

The horse dealer heads towards a seldom used stall where a worn-out Northern Swedish horse is crouched in a corner. He had only just purchased him for a few symbolic notes, and Hans was wondering why the horse hadn't already been sent to the slaughter-house.

From the black box the horse dealer takes out something that most resembles the transformer for an electric train. Then he calls Hans over and tells him to bring him an extension cord. The horse dealer is humming, pulling off his big coat, and Hans does as he is told.

And what is he told to do?

The old horse has to be tied with chains while steel clamps are fastened to his ears. Then the electricity passes through the cables, and the animal convulses under the shocks of the current. Under contentedly turns the little knob on the metre, as if he were directing a toy train, and Hans helplessly promises himself never to forget the horse's tormented eyes. For almost an hour the torture continues, while Under orders Hans to check that the chains are tight so the horse won't get loose.

He hates the damned horse dealer who is tormenting this broken-down horse. He realises that Under must have a prospective buyer in the background even for this worn-out animal. With

145

electricity and steel clamps a trace of vitality is infused back into the horse, a strength based only on fear.

'He'll be practically young again,' says Under, turning up the current a bit.

The horse foams at the mouth, his eyes are popping out of their sockets. Hans wishes he could put the steel clamps on the horse dealer's nose and then turn up the current until he begged for mercy. But of course he doesn't do that. He does as he's told. Then it's all over. The horse stands facing the wall and the horse dealer regards his work. Then he grabs Hans by the shirt as if he had set his teeth in him.

'This is just between us,' he says. 'Between you and me and the horse. Get it?'

From his pocket he draws a crumpled five-krona note and presses it into Hans's hand. Later, as he tears the note to bits outside the church wall he wonders whether the purpose of life will ever be revealed to him. Who needs him – Hans Olofson? And what is he needed for, except to drag a cart or work in a winter stable where helpless horses are tortured?

I have to get away, he thinks. Away from that damned horse dealer. But what will he do instead? Are there really any answers in life? Who can whisper the password in his ear? He walks home in the winter night in February 1959. For a dizzying second life is a breath in the mouth of eternity. Thinking you can cheat time will just drive you crazy. He stops outside the wooden house. The cold glitters in the snow.

The plough, the anchor, the moorings. To be myself and no one else, he thinks. But then what? Onward, and just keep going? He goes upstairs in the silent house, unlaces his ski boots. His father is snoring and sighing in his room. Like restless flocks of birds his thoughts gather in his mind after he gets into bed. He tries to catch them, examine them one by one, but all he sees are the terrified eyes of the horse and the horse dealer cackling like an evil troll. Life is a dizzying second, he thinks before he falls asleep.

In his dream *Célestine* grows out of her case and surges towards the backdrop of a world he doesn't recognise at all, and finally he chops through her moorings.

Chapter Sixteen

Does time have a face?

How can one tell when it's waving and saying goodbye?

One day he realises that he has been with Judith Fillington for a year. The rainy season has passed. Again the motionless heat presses down on him and the African earth.

And the questions he asked himself? They're still there, but one puzzlement has only been exchanged for another. After a year he is no longer surprised that he is where he is, but instead by how the time could have passed so quickly. After her malaria attack Judith had been stricken by a long drawn-out fatigue that lasted half a year. A parasite, identified far too late, bored into her internal organs and made this fatigue even worse. Olofson saw no possibility of leaving. It would have meant abandoning her, the exhausted woman who lay in the bed that was much too large. He considered it mysterious that she dared to turn over the care of the farm, just like that, to his untrained hands.

One day he discovers that he is waking in the mornings with a quite new and unfamiliar happiness. For the first time in his life he feels he has an objective, even if it's only to see the lorries full of eggs pull away in a cloud of red dust. Maybe there's nothing more important than this, he thinks. To produce food and know that someone is always waiting for it.

After a year he also has thoughts that seem frivolous to him. I'll stay, he thinks. As long as Judith is powerless, as long as the successor doesn't show up. I'll teach myself something about all this. About the eggs and the constant feed problem. About leading 200 Africans by the hand. Surely something of this will be meaningful even after I go back home.

After half a year he writes to his father and tells him that he will be staying in Africa for an indefinite period. Of his studies and his ambition to become the defender of mitigating circumstances, he writes only: *I'm still young.* The letter is an epistle of digression, a personal tall tale, in which he twists and distorts the facts.

It's a belated thank you, he thinks. A thank you for all the escapades with the sea charts in the house by the river.

I'm involved in an adventure, he writes. *An adventure that grew from the energy source that is possibly the true essence of adventure: coincidences that became intertwined, in which I was permitted to take part.*

As a worthy cargo to lower down into *Célestine*'s hold, he sends a crocodile tooth.

Here the reptile's teeth protect against danger, he writes. *I'm sending you an amulet that can protect you from misplaced blows of your axe or a falling tree you otherwise wouldn't have escaped.*

One night he can't sleep. When he goes to the kitchen to get a drink of water, he hears Judith crying in her locked room. And maybe this is when the first inkling flits past, as he stands in the warm darkness outside her door. The idea that he will stay in Africa. A door that stands ajar in his mind, a glimpse into a future that was never intended.

A year has passed. The hippo that he never sees sighs down by the river. A shiny cobra coils one morning in the wet grass before his feet. In the night he can see fires burning on the horizon,

149

and the distant sound of drums reaches him like a language that is hard to decipher.

The elephant grass burns and the animals flee. He imagines that he is watching a distant battlefield, a war that has gone on since the mists of prehistoric time.

I, he thinks, I, Hans Olofson, am just as afraid of the unknown as I was when I stepped out of the plane into a world made utterly white by the sun. I realise that I'm surrounded by catastrophe, a temporarily postponed end of time, as two epochs collide. I know that I'm white, one of the candles that is seen much too clearly, one of those who must perish on this continent. And yet I stay.

I've tried to safeguard myself, to remain a nonentity in this test of strength. I stand outside, a temporary visitor, without involvement or guilt. Could it be pointless? The white man's ultimate fancy? Yet I can see quite clearly that my fear is not the same as when I first stood in this white sun.

I no longer believe that every black is whetting his *panga* so he can slit my throat while I sleep. Today my fear is directed: against the murderous gangs that ravage this land, against the hit men who might also be hiding on this farm. But I don't justify my lack of understanding by seeing a murderer in every black I meet. The workers on the farm are no longer nameless, threatening faces that all look the same.

One evening after Judith has begun to get her strength back, Ruth and Werner Masterton come to visit. It's a lengthy dinner, and they sit for a long time behind the locked doors and empty their glasses.

Olofson gets drunk that evening. He doesn't say much, huddling in a corner, feeling like an outsider again. Late that evening Ruth and Werner decide to spend the night. The attacks on solitary cars have increased again, and at night the white man is a hunted quarry.

On his way to bed, Hans meets Judith outside her door. He convinces himself that she is standing there waiting for him; she is tipsy too, with wandering eyes that remind him of his father.

She holds out her hand, grabs him, pulls him into her room, and they perform a love act on the cold stone floor that is equally helpless and violent. As he grasps her skinny body, he thinks of the room upstairs, the dead animals' bone yard.

Afterwards she pulls away as if he had struck her. Not a single word, he thinks. How can one make love without saying a single word?

The next day he has a hangover and feels terrible, and he recalls her body as something harsh and repulsive. In the dawn they say goodbye to Ruth and Werner. She avoids his eye, pressing the broad-brimmed hat down on her brow.

One year has passed.

The nightly web of sound of the cicadas has become familiar. The smells of charcoal, dried fish, sweat, and stinking rubbish heaps surround him as though they had always been there. But the entirety, the black continent, becomes increasingly elusive the more he thinks he understands. He senses that Africa is not actually a unified entity; at least not something that he, with his ingrained notions, can comprehend and penetrate.

There are no simple passwords here. Wooden gods and forefathers speak as distinctly here as the living people. European truth loses its validity on the endless savannah.

He still sees himself as an apprehensive traveller, not as one of those purposeful and well-equipped pathfinders. And yet he is where he is. Beyond the ridges of fir trees, beyond the Finnish forests, on the other side of the river and the bridge.

One day in October, when he has worked for Judith for a year, she comes walking towards him in the overgrown garden. It's Sunday, and there is only an old man busy watering the garden.

Olofson is spending the day trying to fix an attachment to the pump that brings the water from the Kafue to their house.

Against the light he sees her face and is instantly worried. I don't want to hear what she has to say, he thinks. They sit down in the shade of the big tree, and he can tell that she has prepared this conversation, for Luka shows up with coffee.

'There is a point of no return,' she says, 'in every person's life. Something one does not want, something one fears but can't avoid. I have come to the realisation that I can't do this any more: not the farm, not Africa, or this life. That's why I'm making you a proposal now. Something you can think about, you don't have to decide right away. I'll give you three months, and what I tell you will require you to make a decision. Soon I will be leaving here. I'm still sick, the fatigue is suffocating me, and I don't think I'll ever regain my strength. I'm going to Europe, maybe to Italy. Beyond that I have no plans. But my offer is that you take over my farm. It makes a profit, there's no mortgage on it, and there are no indications that it will lose its value. Forty per cent of the profits will be mine for as long as I live. That's the price you have to pay me if you take over the farm. If you should sell the farm within ten years, seventy-five per cent of the profits will go to me. After ten years the amount is reduced to fifty per cent, and after twenty years to nothing. It would be easiest for me, of course, to sell the farm immediately. But something is preventing me: a sense of responsibility, I think, to those who work here. Maybe I can't stand the thought of Duncan being forced off the land that will one day be his grave. For a year I've seen you on my farm. I know that you'll be able to take it over . . .'

She falls silent and Olofson feels that he wants to sign a deed of transfer at once. An absolutely unreserved joy fills him. The voice from the brickworks which he carries inside him begins to speak. To be needed, to be somebody . . .

'This is unexpected,' is all he says.

'I'm afraid of losing the only thing that is irreplaceable,' she says. 'My will to live. The simple power that makes me get out of bed when the sun comes up. Everything else can probably be replaced. But not that.'

'It's still unexpected,' he says. 'I realise you're tired, I see it every day. But at the same time I can tell that your strength is coming back.'

'Each day brings nothing but revulsion,' she replies. 'And you can't see that. Only I can feel it. You must understand that I've been preparing for this moment for a long time. For years I've been putting money into banks in London and Rome. My lawyer in Kitwe has been informed. If you say no, I'll sell the farm. There will be no shortage of prospective buyers.'

'Mr Pihri will miss you,' he says.

'You can take over Mr Pihri,' she says. 'His eldest son will become a policeman too. You can also take over the young Mr Pihri.'

'It's a big decision,' he says. 'I really should have gone home long ago.'

'I haven't seen you leave,' she says. 'I've seen you stay. Your three months begin right now, here in the shadow of this tree.'

'Then you'll come back?' he asks.

'To sell or to pack,' she replies. 'Or both.'

Her preparations have been thorough. Four days after their conversation, Olofson drives her to the airport in Lusaka. He accompanies her to the check-in counter and then stands in the warm night on the roof terrace and watches the big jet plane accelerate with a roar and take off towards the stars.

Their leave-taking was simple. It should have been me, he thinks. In all fairness it should have been me who finally left this place . . . He stays overnight at the hotel he once hid inside. To his surprise he discovers that he has been given the same room, 212. Magic, he thinks. I forget that I'm in Africa.

A restless anxiety sends him down to the bar, and he looks for the black woman who offered herself to him last time. When he isn't noticed quickly enough, he shouts sharply at one of the waiters who is standing idle by the bar.

'What have you got today?' he asks.

'There isn't any whisky,' replies the waiter.

'So there's gin? But is there any tonic?'

'We have tonic today.'

'So you have gin and tonic?'

'There is gin and tonic today.'

He gets drunk and renames the property in his mind: *Olofson Farm*.

Soon a black woman is standing next to his table. In the dim light he has a hard time making out her face.

'Yes,' he says. 'I would like company. Room 212. But not now, not yet.'

He sees her hesitate, wondering if she should wait at his table or not.

'No,' he says. 'When you see me go up the stairs, wait for another hour. Then come.'

After he has eaten, he starts up the stairs, but doesn't see her. She sees me though, he thinks.

When she knocks on the door he discovers that she is very young, hardly more than seventeen. But she is experienced. She walks into the room and demands an immediate agreement.

'Not the whole night,' he says. 'I want you to go.'

'A hundred *kwacha*,' she says. 'Or ten dollars.'

He nods and asks her name.

'Whatever name you want,' she says.

'Maggie,' he suggests.

'My name is Maggie,' she says. 'Tonight my name is Maggie.'

He has sex with her, and feels the meaninglessness. Beyond

the arousal there is nothing, a room that has been empty for far too long. He breathes in the scents from her body, the cheap soap, the perfume that reminds him of something sour. She smells like an apple, he thinks. Her body is like a musty flat I remember from my childhood.

It is over quickly; he gives her the money and she gets dressed in the bathroom.

'I'll be here another time,' she says.

'I like the name Janine,' he says.

'Then my name will be Janine,' she replies.

'No,' he says. 'Never again. Now go.'

When he goes into the bathroom he discovers she has taken the toilet paper and his soap. They steal, he thinks. They would cut out our hearts if only they could.

By twilight of the next day he is back on the farm. He eats the dinner Luka has prepared for him. I'm going to run this farm differently, he thinks. Through my example the constant arguments about the necessity of the whites will disappear. The man I appoint to be my overseer must be black. I will build my own school for the workers' children, I won't offer them help only when they're to be buried.

The truth about this farm today, or Ruth and Werner's farm, is the underpaid labour, the worn-out workers. Judith's money in the European banks is the wages that were never paid.

I'm going to transform this farm, and I'll dedicate the school I'm going to build to Janine. When I leave the farm it will be in commemoration of the moment when the ideas of the white farmers were finally refuted.

But he also realises that even as he starts out he is prosperous. The farm represents a fortune. Even if he doubles the workers' wages the hens will keep laying directly into his own pockets.

Impatiently he waits for daybreak. He walks through the silent rooms and stops in front of the mirrors and looks at his face. He utters a moan that echoes through the empty house.

At dawn he opens the door. Faint bands of mist are drifting over the river. Luka is waiting outside, as well as the gardeners and the woman who washes his clothes. When he sees their silent faces he shudders. Their thoughts are clear enough . . .

Eighteen years later he remembers that morning. As if the memory and the present have merged. He can recall the mist that drifted over the Kafue, Luka's inscrutable face, the shudder that went through his body.

When almost everything is already past, he returns to that moment, October 1970. He remembers wandering through the silent house and the plans he made for the future. In the reflection of that night he looks back on the many years, a lifetime of eighteen years in Africa.

Judith Fillington never came back. In December 1970 he has a visit from her lawyer, to his surprise an African and not a white man, who delivers a letter from Naples, asking for his decision. He gives it to Mr Dobson, who promises to telegraph it to her and return as soon as possible with the papers to be signed. At the New Year, signatures are exchanged between Naples and Kalulushi. At the same time Mr Pihri comes to visit with his son.

'Everything will be the same as always,' says Hans Olofson.

'Trouble should be avoided,' replies Mr Pihri with a smile. 'My son, young Mr Pihri, saw a used motorcycle for sale in Chingola a few days ago.'

'My visa will have to be renewed soon,' says Olofson. 'Of course young Mr Pihri needs a motorcycle.'

In mid-January a long letter arrives from Judith, postmarked Rome. *I have understood something,* she writes. *Something I never dared realise before. During my whole life in Africa, from my earliest childhood, I grew up in a world that depended on the differences between blacks and whites. My parents took pity on the blacks, on their poverty. They saw the necessary development, they taught me to understand that the whites' situation would only prevail for a limited time. Maybe two or three generations. Then an upheaval would take place; the blacks would take over the whites' functions, and the whites would see their imagined importance reduced. Maybe they would even dwindle to an oppressed minority. I learned that the blacks were poor, their lives restricted. But I also learned that they have something we don't have. A dignity that will someday turn out to be the deciding factor. I realise now that I have denied this insight, perhaps especially after my husband disappeared without a trace. I blamed the blacks for his disappearance; I hated them for something they didn't do. Now that Africa is so far away, now that I have decided to live the rest of my life here, I can dare once more to acknowledge the insight I previously denied. I have seen the brute in the African, but not in myself. A point will always come in everyone's life when the most important thing must be turned over to someone else.*

She asks him to write and let her know when Duncan Jones dies, and gives him the address of a bank on the island of Jersey.

Mr Dobson comes with men who pack up Judith's belongings in huge wooden crates. He checks them off meticulously on a list.

'Whatever is left is yours,' he tells Olofson.

They go into the room that is filled with bones.

'She doesn't mention anything about this,' says Mr Dobson. 'So it's yours.'

'What am I going to do with it?' asks Olofson.

'That's hardly a matter for a lawyer,' replies Mr Dobson amiably. 'But I suppose there are two choices. Either you leave it be, or you get rid of it. The crocodile can easily be taken back to the river.'

Together with Luka he carries the remains down to the river and watches as they sink to the bottom. The femur of an elephant glints through the water.

'We Africans will avoid this spot, *Bwana*,' says Luka. 'We see dead animals who still live on the bottom. The crocodile's skeleton may be more dangerous than the living crocodile.'

'What are you thinking?' asks Olofson.

'I think what I think, *Bwana*,' replies Luka.

Olofson stretches taut his eighteen-year arc of time, filled with transforming his farm into a political model.

Early one Saturday morning he gathers all the workers outside the mud hut that is his office, climbs up on a petrol tank, and tells them that now he is the one, not Judith Fillington, who owns the farm. He sees their guarded faces but he is determined to carry out what he has decided to do.

During the years that follow, years of ceaseless work, he tries to implement what he has taken on as his great task. He singles out the most industrious workers as foremen and gives them all more responsible assignments. He introduces drastic wage increases, builds new housing, and overseas the construction of a school for the workers' children. From the start he is met by opposition from the other white farmers.

'You're undermining your own position,' Werner Masterton tells him when they visit one evening.

'You don't have a clue,' says Ruth. 'I hope it isn't too late when you come to your senses.'

'Too late for what?' Olofson asks.

'For everything,' Ruth replies.

Sometimes Duncan Jones stands like a phantom and watches him. Olofson sees how the blacks fear him. One night when he is again awakened by the night watchmen to fight a fierce battle against invading hunter ants, he hears Duncan Jones wailing from his fortified house.

Two years later he is dead. During the rainy season the house begins to smell, and when they break in they find Jones's half-decayed body on the floor among bottles and half-eaten meals. The house is full of insects, and yellow moths swarm over the dead body. In the night he hears the drums pounding. The spirit of the holy man is already hovering over the farm.

Duncan Jones is buried on a little hill by the river. A Catholic priest comes from Kitwe. Other than Olofson there is no white man at the coffin, only the black workers.

He writes a letter care of the bank in Jersey, announcing that Duncan Jones is dead. He never hears a word from Judith.

The house stands empty for a long time before Olofson decides to tear down the wall and set up a health centre for the workers and their families.

With infinite slowness he seems to sense a change. Metre by metre he attempts to eradicate the boundary between himself and the 200 workers.

The first hint that everything has gone totally wrong, that all his good intentions have backfired, comes after a trip he takes to Dar-es-Salaam. The production figures begin to fall inexplicably. Complaints come in about broken eggs or eggs that are never delivered. Spare parts start disappearing, chicken feed and tools vanish unaccountably. He discovers that the foremen are falsifying roll call lists, and during a night check he finds half of the watchmen asleep, some dead drunk. He calls in the foremen and demands an explanation, but all he gets are peculiar excuses.

He had made the trip to Dar-es-Salaam to buy spare parts for the farm's tractor. Then the day after the tractor is repaired, it's gone. He calls the police and fires all the night watchmen, but the tractor remains missing.

This is when he makes a serious mistake. He sends for Mr Pihri and they drink tea in the mud hut.

'My tractor is gone,' says Olofson. 'I made the long journey to Dar-es-Salaam to buy spare parts that are unavailable in this country. I made this long trip so that my tractor would function again. Now it's gone.'

'That is naturally very troublesome,' replies Mr Pihri.

'I don't see why your colleagues can't track down the tractor. In this country there aren't that many tractors. A tractor is hard to hide. It must also be difficult to drive it over the border to Zaire to sell it in Lubumbashi. I don't understand why your colleagues can't find it.'

Mr Pihri all at once becomes very serious. In the dim light Olofson thinks he sees a dangerous glint in his eyes. The silence lasts a long time.

'The reason my colleagues can't find the tractor is because it is no longer a tractor,' replies Mr Pihri at last. 'Perhaps it's already been taken apart? How can one distinguish one screw from another? A gear shift has no face. My colleagues would be very upset if they found out that you are displeased with their work. Very, very upset. It would mean trouble that even I could do nothing about.'

'But I want my tractor back!'

Mr Pihri serves himself more tea before he answers.

'Not everyone is in agreement,' he says.

'In agreement about what?'

'That whites should still own most of the best land without even being citizens of our country. They don't want to exchange their passports, but still they own our best land.'

'I don't understand what that has to do with my tractor.'

'Trouble should be avoided. If my colleagues can't find your tractor, it means that there is no longer a tractor to be found. Naturally it would be quite unfortunate if you were also to upset my colleagues. We have much patience. But it can come to an end.'

He follows Mr Pihri out into the sun. His farewell is unusually brief, and Olofson realises that he has stepped over an invisible boundary. I have to be careful, he thinks. I should never have mentioned the tractor.

In the night he wakes abruptly, and as he lies in the dark listening to the dogs' restless patrolling of his house, he feels that he is ready to give up. Sell the farm, transfer the profits to Judith, and take off. But there is always something that needs to be done first. The drop in production halts after he takes all decisions into his own hands for a while.

He writes to his father, asking him to visit. Only once does he get an answer, and the inarticulate letter tells him that Erik Olofson is drinking more heavily and more often. Maybe someday I'll understand it, he thinks. Maybe when I understand why I'm staying here. He looks at his suntanned face in the mirror. He has changed his appearance, let his beard grow.

One morning he realises that he no longer recognises himself. The face in the mirror belongs to someone else. He gives a start. Luka is standing behind him, and as usual he hasn't heard his bare feet on the stone floor.

'A man has come to visit, *Bwana*,' he says.

'Who?'

'Peter Motombwane, *Bwana*.'

'I don't know anyone by that name.'

'He has still come, *Bwana*.'

'Who is he and what does he want?'

'Only he knows, *Bwana*.'

Olofson turns around and looks at Luka.

'Ask him to have a seat and wait, Luka. I'll be right there.'

Luka leaves. Something is making Olofson nervous. Not until many years later will he understand why.

Chapter Seventeen

Who whispers the password in his ear? Who reveals what his Goal will be? How does he find a direction in life that is not merely a point of the compass?

This year too, 1959, springtime finally breaks through the obstinate barriers of cold, and Hans Olofson has decided that one more leave-taking is necessary. His decision is vague and hesitant, but he knows that he can't escape the admonition that he has given himself.

One Saturday evening in May, when Under comes roaring up in his Buick in a cloud of dust, Hans screws up his courage and goes out to meet him. At first the horse dealer doesn't understand what the boy is muttering about. He tries to brush him off, but Hans is stubborn and doesn't back down before he has delivered his message. When Under grasps that the boy is standing there stammering out his resignation, he flies into a rage. He raises his hand to deal a box on the ear, but the boy is quick to scamper away. The only thing left for Under is to dispense a symbolic humiliation, and he pulls out a wad of money and peels off one of the lowest value, a fiver, and tosses it in the gravel.

'You're being paid according to your services. But it's a damned shame that the authorities don't print notes worth even less. You're being overpaid . . .'

Hans picks up the note and goes into the stable to say goodbye to the horses and the Holmström twins.

'What will you do now?' ask the brothers, who are washing themselves under the cold tap in preparation for Saturday night.

'I don't know,' he replies. 'Something will turn up.'

'We're going to move on next winter too,' the brothers tell him as they change their mucking-out boots for black dancing shoes.

They offer him aquavit.

'That damned horse dealer,' they say, passing around the bottle. 'If you see a Saab, it's us! Don't forget it.'

He runs across the river bridge in the spring night to tell Janine of his decision. Because she hasn't yet returned from one of Hurrapelle's Joyous Spring Fellowships, he strolls about in her garden and thinks about the time he and Sture splashed varnish all over her currant bushes. He shudders at the memory, wishing he hadn't been reminded of that thoughtless act.

Is there anything that can be understood? Isn't life, which is so difficult to manage, nothing but a series of incomprehensible events lurking behind the corners as one passes? Who can ever deal with the dark impulses hidden inside? Secret rooms and wild horses, he thinks. That's what you have to carry around.

He sits down on the steps and wonders about Sture. He's out there somewhere. But is he in a distant hospital or on one of the furthest stars in the universe? Many times he thought of asking Nyman the courthouse caretaker, but it never came to anything. There are many reasons not to find out. He doesn't want to know for sure. He can see the horrifying images far too clearly in his mind. An iron pipe, thick as the pipe on a coffee pot, rammed down his throat. And the iron lung? What can that be? He sees a big black beetle opening up its body and enclosing Sture under its shiny wings.

But not to be able to move? Day after day? For his whole life?

He tries to imagine it by sitting on Janine's porch, completely still, but it doesn't work. He can't comprehend it. That's why it's good that he doesn't know for sure. Then a little door still remains to be pushed open. A little door to the idea that Sture may have recovered, or that the iron bridge and the river and the red jacket were all a dream.

There's a crunching on the gravel, and Janine appears. He has been so deep in thought that he didn't hear her open the gate. Now he jumps up as if he has been caught in the act of doing something forbidden.

Janine stands there in her white coat and light-blue dress. In the dusk the light falls so that her white nose handkerchief under her eyes takes on the same colour as her skin.

Something passes by, a shiver. Something that is more important than all the world's evil horse dealers. How long ago was it? Two months already. One morning, Under had flung a terrified stable girl in among the horses, a girl he had found on a lonely horse farm deep in the forests of Hälsingland. A girl who wanted to get away, who knew about horses, and who he'd stuffed in the back seat of his Buick.

Hans Olofson had loved her boundlessly. For the month she was at the stable he had circled round her like an attentive butterfly, and every evening he had stayed behind just to be alone with her. But one day she was gone. Under had taken her back, cursing her parents for pestering him with calls about how she was doing.

Hans had loved her, and in the twilight when he can't see the nose handkerchief he loves Janine too. But he's afraid of her ability to read his thoughts. So he gets up quickly, spits in the gravel, and asks where the hell she has been.

'We had a spring fellowship,' she says.

She sits down next to him on the steps and they watch a sparrow hopping about in a footprint in the gravel. Her thigh touches his leg. The stable girl, he thinks. Marie, or Rimma as they called her. One time he stayed behind, hiding behind the hay, and watched her take off her clothes and wash naked by the water pump. He was just about to rush forward, force himself on her, and let himself be swallowed up by the inconceivable mystery.

The sparrow crouches in the footprint. Janine hums and touches her leg to his. Doesn't she understand what she's doing? The wild horses are tugging and twitching where they are chained in his secret stalls. What will happen if they break loose? What can he do then?

Suddenly she gets up, as if she understood his thoughts.

'I'm cold,' she says. 'The church is draughty, and today he talked for so long.'

'Hurrapelle?'

She laughs at him. 'He's probably the only one who doesn't know his nickname,' she says. 'He would certainly be upset if he did.'

In the kitchen he tells her about quitting his job with the horse dealer. But what is really the truth? How did it all happen? He hears himself describe how he was excited and shouting, while the horse dealer was puny as a trembling dwarf. But wasn't he the one who squeaked and mumbled, hardly able to make himself understood? Is he the one who's too little, or is it that the world is too big?

'What are you going to do now?' she asks.

'I'll probably have to go to high school and think a little,' he replies.

And that is precisely what he decides to do. He knows his marks are good enough: Headmaster Gottfried told him that, although it might be hard to convince Erik Olofson of the useful-ness of going back to a worn-out school bench.

'Do it,' she says. 'I'm sure you'll do well.'

But he's still feeling defensive. 'If it doesn't work out then I'll leave town,' he says. 'There's always the sea. I'll never go back to the horse dealer. He can get somebody else to torture his horses.'

On the way home from Janine's house he goes down to his boulder. The spring flood is roaring and a huge log has lodged on the point at People's Park. Life is hard, he thinks.

Tonight is as good as any other to tell his father about his decision. He'll sit there until the tram rattles across the river bridge and disappears into the woods. The springtime river dances.

Erik Olofson is sitting polishing his little pearl-handled revolver when Hans comes home. He bought the revolver from a Chinese man he met in Newport; it cost him nine dollars cash and a jacket. Hans sits down across the kitchen table from his father and watches him carefully rub the gleaming handle.

'Will it fire?' he asks.

'Of course it'll fire,' replies his father. 'Do you think I'd buy a weapon I couldn't use?'

'How should I know?'

'No, how would you know?'

'Exactly.'

'What do you mean?'

'Nothing. But I quit that damned horse dealer.'

'You never should have started working for him. What did I tell you?'

'You didn't tell me anything, did you?'

'I told you to stay at the Trade Association!'

'What does that have to do with it?'

'You're not listening to what I'm saying.'

'Well, what does it have to do with anything?'

'Here you come home and say I never tell you anything.'

'I never should have started at that warehouse. And now I'm finished with that damned horse dealer.'

'What did I tell you?'

'You didn't say a thing.'

'Didn't I tell you to stay at the warehouse?'

'You should have told me never to start!'

'Why would I say that?'

'I already told you! Aren't you going to ask what I plan to do instead?'

'Sure.'

'Then ask me!'

'I shouldn't have to ask. If you've got something to say, then say it. This handle will never get clean.'

'I can see it shining.'

'What do you know about mother-of-pearl revolver handles? Do you know what mother-of-pearl is?'

'Not really.'

'See what I mean?'

'I'm going to start at secondary school. I've already applied. And my grades are good enough.'

'All right.'

'Is that all you have to say?'

'What do you want me to say?'

'Do you think it's a good idea?'

'I'm not the one going there.'

'God damn it . . .'

'Don't swear.'

'Why not?'

'You're too young.'

'How old do you have to be to swear?'

'Well . . .'

'So what do you think?'

'I think you should have stayed at the warehouse. That's what I've always said . . .'

The spring, the summer, are so short, so fleeting, and now it's time for the rowan berries, when Hans Olofson will be walking through the gates of the secondary school. What sort of ambition does he have? Not to be the best, but not the worst either. To be somewhere in the middle of the stream, always far from the deep current. He doesn't intend to take the lead and swim on ahead.

Hans will be a pupil that teachers forget. He sometimes seems slow, almost sluggish. A pupil who can usually answer, and be right most of the time. But why doesn't he ever raise his hand, even when he knows the answer? In geography he possesses knowledge about the oddest places. He can talk about Pamplemousse as though he has been there. And Lourenço Marques, wherever that is.

Hans never drowns in the flood of knowledge through which he swims for four long years. He makes himself inaccessible and as invisible as possible in the middle ranks of the class. There he stakes out his territory and arranges his hiding place. It serves as a protective cover against a strange hesitant feeling.

What does he actually hope to get out of these four years? It's not as though he had any plans for the future. The dreams he harbours are so different. With quiet obsession he hopes that each lesson will reveal the Goal to him. He dreams of the decisive moment, when he can close his books, get up and leave, never to return. Attentively he watches the teachers, searching for his signpost.

But life being what it is, many other fires are also burning inside him during those last years he lives by the river. He is entering that age when every person is his own pyromaniac, equipped with a piece of flint in an otherwise incomprehensible world. It's the passions that flare up and die down, that again gather speed to devour him, yet always let him climb out of the ashes alive.

The passions release powers that leave him bewildered. This is the time when he seems to burst the final membranes that bind him to his childhood, to the time that perhaps both began and ended in the ruins of the brickworks, when he discovered that he was precisely himself and no one else, a specific 'I' and no other.

And these passions flame to the insipid music of Kringström's band. They have a bass and drums, clarinet, guitar and accordion. With a sigh they strike up 'Red Sails in the Sunset', weary unto death, after a thousand years of incessant playing in the draughty dance rotunda of the People's Hall. Kringström, who barely remembers his own first name, suffers from chronic bronchitis caused by a lifetime standing in the heat of the smoky stoves and the cross-draught of doors eternally opened and closed. Once, in his lost youth, he had intended to be a composer. Not a heavy-hipped man of gravity who wrote down notes for posterity, but the creator of light and popular tunes – he would be a master of pop songs. But what did he become? What remains of life's wan smile? The melodies were utterly lost, they never appeared on his accordion, no matter how much he prayed for inspiration, how much he practised his fingering. Everything had already been written, and so he put together his band in order to survive. People are now stomping on the boards of the dance rotunda, where they will play until the moment that eternity shoves them off the last precipice. The music that once was a dream has become an affliction.

Kringström coughs and envisions a horrendous death from lung cancer. But he plays on, and when the last note dies out he receives his listless applause. Below the bandstand, as usual, hooting and drunken youngsters hang around, not knowing any dance steps, but all the more willing to hurl jeers if the music isn't to their liking. Long ago Kringström's band stopped throwing pearls before swine; his music falls from the instruments like granite. With ear plugs he mutes the sound as best he can, hearing only enough so he doesn't lose the beat. They take a break as often as they can, and drag it out as long as they dare. In a dreary back room where a single lightbulb dangles from the ceiling and a torn poster depicting a snake charmer is peeling from the wall, they drink coffee laced with schnapps, sitting in silence, and take turns peeking out the door and keeping an eye on the instruments. If any of the drunken youths were to get the idea of staggering up on to the bandstand and sinking their teeth into a clarinet . . .

After 'Red Sails in the Sunset' comes 'Diana', and then they have to speed it up so the audience won't start snarling. And Kringström's band thumps away at something that's supposed to be 'Alligator Rock', and he feels as though an evil being is standing behind him pounding him on the head with a sledgehammer. On the dance floor the young people are jumping and bounding like mad, and Kringström feels that he is spending his life in an insane asylum. After this musical outburst come two slow numbers, and sometimes Kringström takes his revenge on the demanding youth by playing a waltz. Then the dance floor thins out, and the noisy mob crowds through the swinging doors that lead to the café, where it's easy to mix aquavit from hip flasks into lukewarm Loranga soda.

Hans Olofson also enters this world. Most often he comes with the Holmström twins. They still haven't found their chosen crafts and left the horse dealer to his fate. Their patrimony, the future planned out for them, will have to wait another year, and when the autumn evenings start to turn cold they head for the

Saturday dances at the People's Hall. They park their Saab and bump into Hans Olofson, loitering against a wall, unsure as to whether he dares go inside. They take him under their wing, drag him along behind the beauty parlour and offer him some schnapps. The fact that he stood up to the horse dealer and told him that he was quitting has made a deep impression. Most who leave Under's stable are simply kicked out. But Hans Olofson took a stand, and for that he has earned a snort and their protection.

Hans can feel the schnapps warming his blood, and he follows the twins into the crowd. Superintendent Gullberg stands by the ticket cage and watches the hullabaloo with suspicious eyes. He ejects those who are too obviously drunk, which usually results only in lame protests. But he knows that one litre after another of brandy and schnapps is being carried past him in handbags and roomy overcoats. They slip through the eye of the needle, step into the smoky heat, the world of malfunctioning lightbulbs. The Holmström twins are no great dancers, but with sufficient schnapps in their bellies they can offer a fairly well-executed fox trot. At once they run into some ladies they know from some faraway summer lodgings, and Hans finds himself abandoned.

He knows how to dance – Janine taught him that. But she never taught him to dare ask a girl to dance. He has to go through this trial by fire alone, and he steps on his own toes in fury over not being able to ask one of the female flock waiting in desire and dread along the wall of the dance rotunda, which is never called anything but 'the mountain wall'. On the dance floor the Enviable Ones are already gliding past, the Beauties and the Willing, those who are always asked to dance and hardly ever manage to return to 'the mountain wall' before they're swept off again. They dance with the men of sure steps, the men who own cars and have the right looks. Hans sees last year's 'Lucia' glide past in the arms of Julin the driver, who operates one of the Highway Department's big road graders. The sweat stinks, the bodies are steaming, and Hans rages at standing there like an oaf.

Next time, he thinks. Next time I'll cross the water.

But once he has decided on the daughter of the district nurse, taken his bearings and set his feet in the right direction, it's already too late. Like angels to the rescue the Holmström brothers come clamouring, flushed and hot after intense efforts on the dance floor. In the men's room they refresh themselves with some lukewarm schnapps and dirty stories. From one of the locked toilet stalls they hear the loud song of someone throwing up.

Then they head out again, and now Hans is in a hurry. Now it's sink or swim, now he has to conquer the 'mountain wall' to avoid going under from self-loathing. On unsteady legs he pushes across the dance floor just as Kringström starts off an infinitely slow version of 'All of Me'. He stops in front of one of the bridesmaids from the year before. She follows him out into the fray, where they shove their way on to the overcrowded dance floor.

Many years later, in his house on the banks of the Kafue, with a loaded pistol under his pillow, he recalls 'All of Me', the smoking heat of the stove, and the bridesmaid he pushed along the dance floor. When he wakes in the African night, drenched with sweat, afraid of something he dreamed or perhaps something he heard outside in the dark, he returns there. He can see everything, exactly the way it was.

Now Kringström is starting up a new dance. 'La Paloma' or 'Twilight Time', he can't remember which. He has danced with the bridesmaid, had a few more snorts from the Holmström brothers' flask, and now he's going to dance again. But when he stops in front of her on his unsteady legs she shakes her head and turns away. He reaches out his hand to grab hold of her arm, but she pulls away. She grimaces and says something, but the drums are banging and when he leans forward to hear what she's saying, he loses his balance. Without knowing how it happened, he finds himself all at once with his face among feet and shoes. When he tries to get back up, he feels a strong hand on his collar lifting him up. It's Superintendent Gullberg, who vigilantly spotted the intoxicated youth crawling about on the floor and decided that he should be put out in the street at once.

In the African night he can recall the humiliation, and it's just as awful as when it happened.

He staggers away from the People's Hall through the autumn night, knowing that the only person he can turn to in his misery is Janine. She wakes up when he pounds on her door, roughly torn out of a dream in which she was a child again. She opens the door groggily and there's Hans, standing wide-eyed.

She slowly thaws him out, as always waiting patiently. She can see that he's drunk and miserable, but she waits, leaving him alone with his silence. As he sits in her kitchen and the image of his defeat becomes clearer, it assumes grotesque proportions. No one could have been subjected to greater disgrace, whether it was madmen who tried to set fire to themselves or who stood in the winter night determined to tear down the church with a frozen crowbar. There he had lain among the feet and shoes. Tossed out like a cat by the scruff of his neck.

She spreads out a sheet and a blanket in the room with the gramophone and tells him to lie down. Without a word he staggers in and falls on the sofa, out cold. She closes the door and then lies in her own bed, unable to sleep. She tosses restlessly, waiting for something that never happens.

When Hans wakes up in the morning, with temples pounding and mouth parched, he is thinking about a dream: the door opened, Janine came into his room and stood naked looking at him. The dream is like a polished prism, as clear as an image from reality. It penetrates the fog of contrition. It must have happened, he thinks. She must have come in here last night, with no clothes on.

He gets up from the sofa and goes into the kitchen for a drink of water. The door to her room is closed, and when he listens he can hear her snoring softly. The clock on the wall says quarter to five, and he crawls back on to the sofa to fall asleep and dream or forget that he exists.

When he wakes up a few hours later it's already dawn and Janine is sitting in her robe at the kitchen table, knitting. When he sees her he wants to take the knitting out of her hands, untie her robe, and bury himself in her body. The door to this house on the south side of the river will be closed for good; he will never leave this house again.

'What are you thinking?' she asks.

She knows, he thinks. It won't do any good to lie. Nothing will do any good; the difficulties of life are looming before him like enormous icebergs. What is he actually imagining – that he can find a password that will make it possible to control this damned life?

'You're thinking about something,' she says. 'I can tell by your face. Your lips are moving as if you're talking to someone. But I can't hear what you're saying.'

'I'm not thinking,' he says. 'What would I be thinking about? Maybe I'm incapable of thinking!'

'You don't have to talk if you don't want to,' she says.

Again he thinks that he's going to go over to her and undo the sash of her robe. Instead, he borrows a jumper from her and vanishes into the frosty landscape of autumn.

At the People's Hall, Superintendent Gullberg's wife is busy cleaning up. She peevishly opens the back door when he knocks.

His coat is still hanging on its hook like an abandoned skin. He hands her his cloakroom number.

'How can anyone forget his coat?' she asks.

'It's possible,' replies Hans Olofson and leaves. He realises that there is a kind of forgetfulness that is quite vast.

The seasons change, the river freezes over and then one day floods its banks. No matter how much his father chops at them, the fir forests remain motionless on the horizon. The tram clatters across the bridge, and season after season Hans trudges to Janine's house. The river of knowledge on which he floats, year after year, reveals no Goal to him. But he keeps waiting.

He stands outside Janine's house. The notes from her slide trombone trickle out through a half-open window. Every day he stands there and every day he decides to untie the sash of her robe. More and more often he chooses to visit her when he can expect her not to be dressed. Early on Sunday mornings he knocks on her door; other times he stands on her steps long past midnight. The sash tied around her robe glows like fire.

But when it finally happens, when he grabs with fumbling fingers for her sash, there is nothing that reminds him of what he had imagined.

It's a Sunday morning in May, two years after he left the horse dealer. The evening before, he was pushed and shoved on the dance floor. But this time he left early, long before Superintendent Gullberg angrily began flashing the lights and Kringström's band started to pack up their instruments. Suddenly he decided he'd had enough, and so he left. For a long time he roamed around in the light spring night before slipping past Egg-Karlsson's door and crawling into bed.

He wakes early and drinks coffee with his father in the kitchen. Then he goes over to Janine's house. She lets him in and he follows her into the kitchen and loosens her sash. Softly they sink to the floor, like two bodies falling through the sea on their way to a distant bottom. Roughly they unite around each other's desire. This desire had never been completely extinguished for Janine on Hurrapelle's penitential bench. For a long time she feared that it would dry up one day, but her hope never ran out.

At last Hans steps out of himself, out of his introverted powerlessness. For the first time he feels that he holds life in his hands; from behind his forehead Sture lies motionless in his bed and watches what's happening with a smile.

But neither of them has any idea that passion is a faithless master when they fling their limbs around each other on the kitchen floor. Now there is only great relief. Afterwards they drink coffee. Hans steals a glance at her and wishes she would say something.

Is she smiling? And her thoughts? The hands on the wall clock wander their mute circuit. A moment not to forget, he thinks. Possibly life is more than just trouble and suffering after all. Possibly there is also something else. A moment not to forget . . .

Chapter Eighteen

In a black-and-white photograph he is standing next to Peter Motombwane.

Behind them is the white wall of the house, and the picture has been taken in bright sunlight. A lizard sits motionless on the wall beside Peter Motombwane's head. It will wind up being part of their shared portrait.

Both of them are laughing in the picture, at Luka holding Peter's camera. But why did he want to have the picture? Why did Peter suggest that they take the photograph? He can't remember.

One day Hans Olofson invites his foremen to dinner in his house. Mutely they sit at his table, devouring the food as if they hadn't eaten in a very long time, drinking themselves quickly into a stupor. Olofson asks questions and gets one-syllable replies.

Afterwards he asks Luka to explain. Why this reluctance? This sulky silence?

'You are a *mzungu*, Bwana,' says Luka.

'That's no answer,' says Olofson.

'It *is* an answer, Bwana,' says Luka.

One of the workers who cleans the feed supply and hunts rats falls from the stacked-up sacks and lands so badly that he breaks his neck. The dead man leaves behind a wife and four daughters in a wretched mud hut that Judith once had ordered built. Her name is Joyce Lufuma, and Olofson begins going to her house quite often. He gives her a sack of maize, a *chitenge*, or something else she needs.

Sometimes, when he is very tired, he sits down outside her house and watches the four daughters playing in the red dirt. Maybe this is my lasting contribution, he thinks. Aside from all my great plans, to help these five women.

But usually he keeps his weariness under control, and one day he gathers his foremen and tells them that he will give them cement, bricks, and roofing metal so that they can repair their houses, maybe even build new ones. In return he requires that they dig pits for their refuse and build covered toilet pits.

For a short time he seems to see an improvement. Then everything is the same as it was before. Rubbish whirls across the red earth. The old roofing metal suddenly reappears. But where are the new materials he bought? He asks but receives no answer.

He discusses this with Peter Motombwane as they sit on his veranda in the evenings, and he tries to understand. He realises that Peter Motombwane is his first black friend. It has taken four years.

Why Motombwane first came to visit him on the farm he has no idea. He stood in the doorway and said he was a journalist, that he wanted to write about the egg farm. But Olofson never read anything about it in the *Times of Zambia*.

Motombwane returns and never asks Olofson for anything, not even a tray of eggs. Olofson tells him about his grand plan. Motombwane listens with his serious eyes fixed on some point above Olofson's head.

'What sort of answer do you think you'll get?' he asks, when Olofson is finished.

'I don't know. But what I do has to be right.'

'You'll hardly get the answers you're hoping for,' says Motombwane. 'You're in Africa now. And the white man has never understood Africa. Instead of being surprised you're going to be disappointed.'

Their conversations are never concluded, because Peter Motombwane always breaks off unexpectedly. One moment he is sitting in one of the deep soft chairs on the terrace, and the next he has stood up to say goodbye. He has an old car, and only one rear door will open. To get behind the wheel he has to crawl over the seats.

'Why don't you fix the doors?' Olofson asks.

'Other things are more important.'

'Does the one have to exclude the other?'

'Sometimes, yes.'

After Motombwane has visited him he feels restive. Without being able to explain what it is, he feels that he has been reminded of something important, something he always forgets.

But other people come to visit too. He gets to know an Indian merchant from Kitwe named Patel.

On an irregular basis and without any apparent logic, various necessities suddenly vanish in the country. One day there's no salt, another day no newspapers can be printed because there's no paper. He remembers what he thought when he first arrived in Africa: on the black continent everything is in the process of running out.

But through Patel he can get hold of whatever he needs. From hidden storerooms Patel fetches whatever the white colony requires. Along unknown transport routes the scarce goods are brought into the country, and the white colony can get what it needs for a reasonable additional fee. In order not to provoke the wrath of the blacks and risk seeing his shop plundered and burned down, Patel makes personal visits to the various farms to hear whether anything is needed.

He never comes alone. He always has one of his cousins with him, or a friend from Lusaka or Chipata who happens to be visiting. They're all named Patel. If I shouted that name I'd be surrounded by a thousand Indians, thinks Olofson. And they would all ask whether there was anything I needed.

I can understand their caution and fear. They are hated more than the whites, since the difference between them and the Africans is so striking. In the shops they have everything that the blacks so seldom can afford to buy. And everyone knows about the secret storerooms, everyone knows that their great fortunes are smuggled out of the country to distant bank accounts in Bombay or London. I can understand their fear. Just as clearly as I can understand the blacks' hatred.

One day Patel stands outside his door. He's wearing a turban and smells of sweet coffee. At first Hans Olofson doesn't believe in accepting the dubious privilege that Patel offers him. Mr Pihri is enough, he thinks.

But after a year he gives in. He's been without coffee for a long time. He decides to make an exception, and Patel returns to his farm the next day with ten kilos of Brazilian coffee.

'Where do you get hold of it?' Olofson asks. Patel throws out his hands and gives him a sorrowful look.

'So much is in short supply in this country,' he says. 'I'm only trying to relieve the worst of the shortages.'

'But how?'

'Sometimes I don't even know myself how I do it, Mr Olofson.'

Then the government introduces harsh currency restrictions. The value of the *kwacha* drops dramatically when the price of copper falls, and Olofson realises that he will no longer be able to send money to Judith Fillington as required in their contract.

Once again Patel comes to his rescue.

'There's always a way out,' he says. 'Let me handle this. I ask only twenty per cent for the risks I'm taking.'

How Patel arranges it Olofson never knows, but each month he gives him money and a receipt comes regularly from the bank in London, confirming that the money has been transferred.

During this period Olofson also opens his own account in the London bank, and Patel withdraws two thousand Swedish kronor monthly as his fee.

Olofson notices an increasing unrest in the country, and this is confirmed when Mr Pihri and his son begin to pay more frequent visits.

'What's going on?' Olofson asks. 'Indian shops are being burned down or plundered. Now there's talk of the danger of rioting, because there isn't any maize to be had and the blacks have no food. But how can the maize suddenly run out?'

'Unfortunately there are many who smuggle maize to the neighbouring nations,' says Mr Pihri. 'The prices are better there.'

'But aren't we talking about thousands of tonnes?'

'The ones who are smuggling have influential contacts,' replies Mr Pihri.

'Customs officials and politicians?'

They are sitting in the cramped mud hut talking. Mr Pihri lowers his voice.

'It may not be wise to make such statements,' he says. 'The authorities in this country can be quite sensitive. Recently there was a white farmer outside Lusaka who mentioned a politician by name in an unfortunate context. He was deported from the country within twenty-four hours. The farm has now been taken over by a state cooperative.'

'I just want to be left in peace,' says Olofson. 'I'm thinking of those who work here.'

'That's quite as it should be,' says Mr Pihri. 'One should avoid trouble for as long as possible.'

More and more frequently there are forms that have to be filled out and approved, and Mr Pihri seems to be having a harder and harder time fulfilling his self-imposed obligations. Olofson pays him more and more, and he sometimes wonders whether it's really true, what Mr Pihri tells him. But how can he check?

One day Mr Pihri comes to the farm accompanied by his son. He is very solemn.

'Perhaps there is trouble coming,' he says.

'There's always trouble,' says Olofson.

'The politicians keep taking new decisions,' says Mr Pihri. 'Wise decisions, necessary decisions. But unfortunately they can be troublesome.'

'What's happened now?'

'Nothing, Mr Olofson. Nothing.'

'Nothing?'

'Nothing really, not yet, Mr Olofson.'

'But something is going to happen?'

'It's not at all certain, Mr Olofson.'

'Only a possibility?'

'One might put it that way, Mr Olofson.'

'What?'

'The authorities are unfortunately not very pleased with the whites who live in our country, Mr Olofson. The authorities believe that they are sending money out of the country illegally. Of course this also applies to our Indian friends who live here. It is suspected that taxes are not being paid as they should be. The authorities are therefore planning a secret raid.'

'What are you talking about?'

'Many police officers will visit all the white farms at the same time, Mr Olofson. In all secrecy, of course.'

'Do the farmers know about this?'

'Of course, Mr Olofson. That's why I'm here, to inform you that there will be a secret raid.'

'When?'

'Thursday evening next week, Mr Olofson.'

'What shall I do?'

'Nothing, Mr Olofson. Just don't have any papers from foreign banks lying about. And especially no foreign currency. Then it could be quite troublesome. I wouldn't be able to do anything.'

'What would happen?'

'Our prisons are unfortunately still in very poor condition, Mr Olofson.'

'I'm very grateful for the information, Mr Pihri.'

'It's a pleasure to be able to help, Mr Olofson. My wife has been mentioning for a long time that her old sewing machine is causing her a great deal of trouble.'

'That's not good, of course,' says Olofson. 'Isn't it true that there are sewing machines in Chingola at the moment?'

'I've heard it mentioned,' replies Mr Pihri.

'Then she ought to buy one before they're gone,' Olofson says.

'My view precisely,' replies Mr Pihri.

Olofson shoves a number of notes across the table.

'Is the motorcycle all right?' he asks young Mr Pihri, who has been sitting quietly during the conversation.

'An excellent motorcycle,' he replies. 'But next year there's supposed to be a new model coming out.'

His father has taught him well, Olofson thinks. Soon the son will be able to take over my worries. But part of what I will be paying him in future will always fall to the father. They ply me well, their source of income.

Mr Pihri's information is correct. The following Thursday two broken-down Jeeps full of police officers come driving up to the farm just before sundown. Olofson meets them with feigned surprise. An officer with many stars on his epaulettes comes up on to the terrace where Olofson is waiting. He sees that the policeman is very young.

'Mr Fillington,' says the policeman.

'No,' Olofson replies.

Serious confusion results when it turns out that the search warrant is made out in the name of Fillington. At first the young officer refuses to believe what Olofson says, and in an aggressive tone he insists that Hans Olofson's name is Fillington. Olofson shows him the deed of transfer and title registration, and at last the police officer realises that the warrant he is holding in his hand is made out to the wrong person.

'But you are welcome to search the house anyway,' Olofson adds quickly. 'It's easy to make a mistake. I don't want to cause any difficulties.'

The officer looks relieved, and Olofson decides that now he has made another friend, perhaps someone he may find useful in future.

'My name is Kaulu,' says the police officer.

'Please come in,' says Olofson.

After barely half an hour the officer comes out of the house leading his men.

'Might one ask what you are looking for?' asks Olofson.

'Activities inimical to the state are always under way,' says the officer gravely. 'The value of the *kwacha* is continually being undermined by illegal foreign exchange transactions.'

'I understand that you have to intervene,' says Olofson.

'I shall tell my supervisor of your accommodation,' replies the police officer and gives him a salute.

'Please do,' says Olofson. 'You're welcome to visit anytime.'

'I'm quite fond of eggs,' shouts the officer as Olofson watches the dilapidated vehicles drive off in a cloud of dust.

Suddenly he understands something about Africa, an insight into the young Africa, the anguish of the independent states. I ought to laugh at this inadequate search of the premises, he thinks. At the young police officer who surely comprehends nothing. But then I would be making a mistake, because this inadequacy is dangerous. In this country people are hung, young policemen torture people, kill people with whips and truncheons. Laughing at this helplessness would be the same as putting my life at risk.

The arc of time grows, and Hans Olofson continues to live in Africa.

When he has been in Kalulushi for nine years, a letter arrives to inform him that his father has died in a fire. One cold night in January of 1978 the house by the river burned down.

The cause was never clarified. You were sought for the funeral, but your whereabouts was not discovered until now. One other person died in the fire, an elderly widow named Westlund. It is also believed that the fire started in her flat. But of course, this will never be known. Nothing was left; the building burned to the ground. What will happen with the inventory of your father's estate, I am not at liberty to say.

The letter is signed with a name that vaguely reminds him of one of his father's foremen at the lumber company.

Slowly he lets the grief seep in. He sees himself in the kitchen, sitting across the table from his father. The heavy odour of wet wool. *Célestine* stands in her case, but now she is a smoking wreck burned black. There is also the charred sea chart of the approaches to the Strait of Malacca.

He glimpses his father under a sheet on a stretcher. Now I'm alone, he thinks. If I choose not to return, my mother will remain an enigma, in the same way as the fire.

His father's death becomes a burden of guilt, a feeling of

betrayal, of having given up. Now I'm alone, he thinks again. I'll have to bear this loneliness as long as I live.

Without really knowing why, he gets in his car and drives to Joyce Lufuma's mud hut. She is standing there pounding corn, and she laughs and waves when she sees him coming.

'My father is dead,' he says.

At once she senses his grief and begins to moan, casting herself to the ground, wailing out the pain that is actually his.

Other women come over, hear that the white man's father is dead in a distant land, and instantly join the lamenting chorus. Olofson sits down beneath a tree and forces himself to listen to the women's appalling lamentations. His own pain is wordless, an anxiety that digs its nails into his body.

He returns to his car, hears the women shrieking behind him, and thinks that Africa is giving Erik Olofson his tribute. A sailor who drowned in the sea of the Norrland forests.

As if on a pilgrimage he sets off on a journey to the sources of the Zambezi River in the northwest corner of the country. He travels to Mwinilunga and Ikkelenge, sleeps overnight in his car outside the mission infirmary at Kalenje Hill, and then continues along the almost impassable sand track that leads to the long valley where the Zambezi has its source. He walks for a long time through the dense, desolate bush until he reaches it.

A simple stone cairn marks the spot. He squats down and sees how individual drops of water fall from broken blocks of stone. A rivulet no wider than his hand winds through the stones and bush grass. He cups his hand in the rivulet and thus stops the flow of the Zambezi River.

He doesn't leave until late in the afternoon, knowing he must reach his car before it grows dark. By then he has decided to stay in Africa. There is nothing left to return to in Sweden. From his grief he also gathers the strength to be realistic. He will never be able to transform his farm into the political model of his dreams. Even though he once firmly vowed never to lose himself in idealistic labyrinths, he ended up doing just that.

A white man can never help Africans develop their country from a superior position, he thinks. From below, from inside, one can surely contribute to expertise and new working patterns. But never as a *bwana*. Never as someone who holds all power in his hands. Africans see through words and actions – they see the white man as owner, and they gratefully accept the wage increases he gives them, or the school he builds, or the sacks of cement he is willing to forgo. His thoughts of influence and responsibility they regard as irrelevant whims, random gestures which increase the possibility for the individual foreman to make off with some extra eggs or spare parts that he can later sell.

The long colonial history has freed the Africans from all illusions. They know the capriciousness of the whites, their constant exchange of one idea for another, while demanding that the black man be enthusiastic. A white man never asks about traditions, even less about the opinions of their ancestors. The white man works quickly and hard, and haste and impatience are viewed by the black man as a sign of low intelligence. Thinking long and precisely is the black man's wisdom.

At the source of the Zambezi he seeks the way to a new starting point, free of suppositions. I have run my capitalistic farm under the guise of a socialist dream, he thinks. I have occupied myself with an impossibility, incapable of realising even the most fundamental contradictions that exist. The starting point was always mine: my ideas, never the Africans' thoughts, never Africa.

From the profit that the blacks produce, I pass on a share to those workers that is more than Judith Fillington or the other farmers ever did. The school I built, the school uniforms I pay for, are their own achievements, not mine. My most important function is to keep the farm operating and not permit too much pilfering or absenteeism. Nothing more. The only thing I can do is someday turn over the farm to a workers' collective, transferring ownership itself. But this too is an illusion. The time is not ripe for it. The farm would fall into disrepair, some people would get rich, and others would be shoved out into even greater poverty. What I can do is to continue to run the farm as I do today, but without disrupting the great tranquillity with whims and ideas that will never amount to anything for the Africans. Their future is their own creation. I contribute to the production of food, and that is always time well spent. I know nothing about what the Africans think of me. I'll have to ask Peter Motombwane, maybe also ask him to investigate it by talking to my workers. I wonder what Joyce Lufuma and her daughters think.

He returns to Kalulushi with a feeling of calm. He realises that he will never understand the underlying currents of life. Sometimes it's necessary to stop asking certain questions, he thinks. There are some answers that simply don't exist.

As he turns in the gates to the farm, he thinks of Egg-Karlsson, who evidently survived the fire. In my childhood I lived next door to an egg dealer, he thinks. If anyone had told me back then that one day I would be an egg dealer in Africa, I wouldn't have believed it. That would have been unreasonable to believe.

I'm still the same person today. My income is large, my farm is solid. But my life is a quagmire.

One day perhaps Mr Pihri and his son will come and tell me that they can no longer handle my papers. The authorities will declare me an undesirable. I live here with no actual rights; I'm not a citizen with roots legally planted in Africa. I could be deported without notice, the farm confiscated.

A few days after his return from the Zambezi he looks up

Patel in Kitwe and arranges increased transfers of foreign currency to the bank in London.

'It's becoming harder and harder to handle,' says Patel. 'The risks of discovery are increasing all the time.'

'Ten per cent harder?' asks Olofson. 'Or twenty per cent harder?'

'I would say twenty-five per cent harder,' replies Patel in a worried voice.

Olofson nods and leaves the dark back room with its odours of curry and perfume. I'm putting my trust in an increasingly complex tangle of bribes, illegal financial transactions and corruption, he thinks. I scarcely have any choice. It's hard to imagine that the corruption in this country is more widespread than it is in Sweden. The difference lies in the candour of it. Here everything is so obvious. In Sweden the methods are more evolved, a more refined and well-concealed pattern. But that is probably the only difference.

The arc of time is expanding. Hans Olofson loses a tooth, and just afterwards one more.

He turns forty and invites his many white and few black friends to a party. Peter Motombwane declines and never gives an explanation. Olofson gets very drunk during this party. He listens to incomprehensible speeches from people he scarcely knows. Speeches that praise him, pouring out a foundation of veneration for his African farm. They're thanking me because I've started running my farm without extravagant thoughts about its function as a future model, he thinks. Not a true word is being spoken here.

On wobbly legs he stands up at midnight to thank his guests because so many of them came. Suddenly he realises that he has begun speaking in Swedish. He hears his old language, and he hears himself make a raging attack on the racist arrogance that characterises the whites who still live in this African land. He raves on in Swedish with a friendly smile.

'A pack of scoundrels and whores is what you are,' he says, raising his glass.

'How nice,' an elderly woman tells him later. 'Mixing the two languages like that. But of course we're wondering what you said.'

'I hardly recall,' Olofson replies, and steps outside in the dark alone.

Something whimpers at his feet and he discovers the German shepherd puppy he got as a present from Ruth and Werner Masterton.

'Sture,' he says. 'Your name is Sture from now on.'

The puppy whimpers and Olofson calls Luka.

'Take care of the puppy,' he says.

'Yes, *Bwana*,' says Luka.

The party degenerates into a Walpurgis Night. Drunken people lie sprawled in the various rooms, an ill-matched couple has taken over Olofson's own bed, and in the garden someone is shooting a pistol at bottles that a terrified black servant is lining up on a garden table.

Olofson suddenly feels aroused, and he begins to hover about a woman from one of the farms that lies furthest from his own. The woman is fat and swollen, her skirt is hitched up above her knees, and her husband is asleep under a table in the room that was once Judith Fillington's library.

'I'd like to show you something,' says Olofson.

The woman gives a start from her half-doze and follows him up to the second floor of the house, to the room where skeletons once filled all the walls. He lights a lamp and closes the door behind him.

'This is what you wanted to show me?' she says with a laugh. 'An empty room?'

Without replying he presses her against the wall, pulls up her skirt, and forces himself inside her.

'An empty room,' she says again and laughs.

'Imagine that I'm black,' Olofson says.

'Don't say that.'

'Imagine that I'm black,' he says again.

When it's over she clings to him and he smells the sweat from her unwashed body.

'One more time,' she says.

'Never,' says Olofson. 'It's my party, and I decide.' He goes quickly, leaving her alone.

Pistol shots echo from the garden and he suddenly can't stay there any longer. He staggers out into the darkness, deciding that the only person he wants to be near is Joyce Lufuma.

He gets in his car and leaves his house and his party with a screech of tyres. Twice he drives off the road, but manages to avoid flipping over, and finally pulls in front of her house.

The yard is silent and dark. He sees the disrepair in the headlights of his car, and he turns off the motor and sits in the dark. The night is warm and he feels his way to his usual spot under the tree.

We all have a lonesome, abandoned dog sitting and barking inside us, he thinks. Its paws are different colours, its tail may be cut off. But we all have that dog inside us.

He wakes up at dawn when one of Joyce's daughters stands looking at him. He knows she is twelve years old; he can remember when she was born.

I love this child, he thinks. In her I can recognise something of myself, the child's magnanimity, an ever-present readiness to show consideration for others.

Gravely she watches him, and he forces himself to smile.

'I'm not sick,' he says. 'I'm just sitting here resting.'

When he smiles she smiles back at him. I can't abandon this child, he thinks. Joyce and her daughters are my responsibility, no one else's.

He has a headache and feels bad; the hangover is pounding in his chest and he shudders when he recalls the hopeless fornication in the empty room. I might just as well have mounted one of the skeletons, he says to himself. The humiliation I subject myself to seems to have no limits.

He drives back to his house and sees Luka picking up shards of glass in the garden, and he realises he also feels ashamed in front of Luka. Most of the guests have disappeared, only Ruth and Werner Masterton are left. They're sitting on the terrace drinking coffee. The German shepherd puppy he named Sture is playing at their feet.

'You survived,' says Werner with a smile. 'The parties seem to be getting more and more intense, as if a day of judgement were imminent.'

'Who knows?' Olofson says.

Luka walks past below the terrace. He's carrying a pail full of broken bottles. They follow him with their gaze, watch him vanish towards the pit in the ground where he dumps the rubbish.

'Drop by and say hello sometime,' says Ruth as she and Werner get up to return to their farm.

'I will,' Olofson says.

A few weeks after the party he comes down with a severe attack of malaria, worse than any he has had before. The fever dreams hound him.

He imagines that he is being lynched by his workers. They rip off his clothes, pound him bloody with sticks and clubs, and drive him before them towards Joyce Lufuma's house. There he senses his salvation, but she meets him with a rope in her hand, and he awakes just as he realises that she and her daughters are coming to hoist him up in the tree, with the rope fastened in a noose around his neck.

When he recovers and pays his first visit to Joyce, he suddenly remembers the dream. Maybe it's a sign after all, he thinks. They accept my assistance, they are dependent on it. They have every reason to hate me, I forget that far too often. I forget the simplest antagonisms and truths.

The arc of time extends further over his life, the personal river he carries inside him. Often he returns in his thoughts to a frozen winter night, to the remote site he has never visited. He imagines his father's grave. Now that he has been in Africa for eighteen years he ought to start looking for a spot for his own grave.

He walks over to the hill where Duncan Jones has already rested for many years, and he lets his gaze wander. It's late afternoon and the sun is coloured red by the invisible soil that whirls over the African continent. He sees his long white hen houses against the light, workers on their way home from the day's work. It's October, just before the long rain begins to fall. The ground is scorched and dry, only scattered cactuses glow like green patches in the desiccated landscape. The Kafue is almost empty of water. The riverbed is laid dry, except for a narrow trickle in the middle of its furrow. The hippopotamuses have sought out distant water holes, and the crocodiles will not come back until the rain has returned.

He clears the weeds from Duncan Jones's grave and squints towards the sun, seeking his own future gravesite. But he won't make a decision; that would be tempting Death to come to him too soon. But what is the past? Who can make sense of his allotted time?

No one remains unaffected for almost twenty years, surrounded by African superstition, he thinks. An African would never search for his gravesite, not to mention select it. That would be like sending a resounding summons to Death.

I'm really standing on this hill because the view from here is beautiful. Here is the treeless landscape, the endless horizons that my father always looked for. Maybe I think it's so beautiful because I know that it's mine.

Here is the beginning and perhaps the end too, a chance journey and even more chance meetings led me here. He decides to pay another visit to Mutshatsha.

In all haste he sets out. It's the middle of the rainy season and the roads are like liquid mud. Yet he drives fast, as if he were fighting to escape from something. A despair breaks through the barriers. Janine's trombone echoes in his mind.

He never makes it to Mutshatsha. All at once the road is gone. With his front wheels balanced over a precipice, he looks straight down into a ravine that has opened up. The road has collapsed, and there is no longer a road to Mutshatsha. When he tries to turn the car around, it gets stuck in the mud. He breaks branches from bushes and lays them under the wheels, but the tyres can't get a firm purchase. In the brief twilight the rain arrives with a roar, and he sits in his car and waits. Maybe no one will come by, he thinks. While I sleep the car might be invaded by wandering ants and when the rainy season is over only my skeleton, picked clean, will be left, polished like a piece of ivory.

In the morning the rain stops and he gets help with the car from some people in a nearby village. Late in the afternoon he arrives back at the farm.

The arc of time expands but suddenly begins to bend towards the earth again.

In the shadows people are grouping around him, and he doesn't notice what's happening. It is January 1987. He has now been in Africa for eighteen years.

The rainy season this year is intense and drawn out. The Kafue floods over its banks, the torrential rains threaten to drown his hen houses. Transport lorries get stuck in the mud; power poles topple and cause long power cuts. This is a rainy season like none he has ever experienced before.

At the same time there is more unrest in the country. Throngs of people are on the move; hunger riots strike the cities in the copper belt and Lusaka. One of his egg vans is stopped on its way to Mufulira by an excited mob who empties its cargo. Shots are fired in the night and the farmers refrain from leaving their homes.

Early one morning when Olofson goes to his little office, he finds that someone has flung a large rock through a window of the mud hut. He questions the night watchmen but no one has heard or seen anything.

One older worker stands at a distance and watches as Olofson carries out the questioning. Something in the old African's face makes him break off abruptly and send the night watchmen home without any sort of punishment. He senses something menacing but can't say what it is. The work is being done, but a heavy mood rests over the farm.

One morning Luka is gone. When Olofson opens the door to the kitchen at dawn as usual, Luka isn't there. This has never happened before. Mists roll over the farm after the night's rain. He calls for Luka but no one comes. He asks questions, but nobody knows, nobody has seen Luka. When he drives to his house, he finds it open with the door flapping in the wind.

In the evening he cleans the firearms he once took over from Judith Fillington, and the revolver he bought ten years earlier

195

from Werner Masterton, the revolver he always keeps under his pillow. During the night he sleeps restlessly, the dreams are hounding him, and suddenly he wakes up with a start. He thinks he hears footsteps in the house, footsteps upstairs, above his head. In the dark he grabs the revolver and listens. But it's only the wind slithering through the house.

He lies awake, the revolver resting on his chest. In the dark, just before dawn, he hears a car drive up in front of the house and then loud pounding on the front door. With the revolver in his hand he calls through the door and recognises the voice of Robert, Ruth and Werner Masterton's foreman. He opens the door and realises once again that even a black man can look pale.

'Something has happened, *Bwana*,' says Robert, and Olofson sees that he is terrified.

'What happened?' he asks.

'I don't know, *Bwana*,' replies Robert. 'Something. I think it would be good if *Bwana* could come.'

He has lived in Africa long enough to be able to distinguish gravity in an African's enigmatic way of expressing himself.

He dresses quickly, stuffs his revolver in his pocket, and grabs his shotgun. He locks the house carefully, wonders again where Luka is, and then gets into his car and follows Robert. Black rain clouds are scudding across the sky when the two cars turn up towards the Mastertons' house.

I came here once, he thinks, in another time, as a different person. He recognises Louis among the Africans standing outside the house.

'Why are they standing here?' he asks.

'That's just it, *Bwana*,' says Robert. 'The doors are locked. They were locked yesterday too.'

'Maybe they went on a trip,' says Olofson. 'Where's their car?'

'It's gone, *Bwana*,' Robert replies. 'But we don't think that they left.'

He looks at the house, its immovable façade. He walks around the house, calls out to their bedroom. The Africans follow him at a distance, expectantly. All at once he is afraid without knowing why. Something has happened.

He feels a vague fear of what he is about to see, but he asks Robert to fetch a crowbar from the car. When he breaks open the front door the alarm sirens don't go off. As the front door yields he discovers that the telephone line to the house has been cut next to the outer wall.

'I'm going in alone,' he says, taking the safety off his gun and pushing the door aside.

What he finds is worse than he could have imagined. As if in a macabre film, he steps into a slaughterhouse, where human bodies lie hacked up all over the floor.

He never will understand why he didn't pass out at the sight of what he saw.

Chapter Nineteen

And afterwards?

What is left?

The last year before Hans Olofson leaves the heavy fir ridges behind, leaves his father Erik Olofson behind in his mute dream of a distant sea that calls inside him. The last year that Janine is alive.

On an early Saturday morning in March 1962, she takes up position on the corner between the hardware shop and the People's Hall. It's the very heart of town, the one corner that no one can avoid. In the early morning she raises a placard above her head. On it is a text in black letters that she wrote the night before.

Something unheard of is about to happen. A rumour is growing and threatening to boil over. There are a few people who dare acknowledge that Janine and her lonely placard express a sensible opinion that has been lacking for too long. But their voices disappear in the icy March wind.

The right-thinking ones mobilise. A person who doesn't even have a nose? Everyone has assumed that she was resting securely in the embrace of Hurrapelle. But now here she stands, the woman who ought to be living unnoticed and hiding her ugly face. Janine knows what thoughts are spreading like wildfire.

And she has also learned something from Hurrapelle's monotonous exhortations. She knows how to resist when the wind changes and entrenched beliefs fumble for a foothold. She is driving a stake into the slumbering anthill on this early morning. People hurry along the streets, coats flapping, and they read what she has written. Then they hurry on to grab their neighbour by the collar and ask what that crazy woman can possibly mean. Is a noseless shrew going to tell us what to think? Who asked her to raise this unseemly barricade?

The old men come staggering out from the beer tavern to witness the spectacle with their own eyes. They don't care about the fate of the world, but nevertheless they become her mute supporters. Their need for revenge is boundless. Whoever drives a stake into the heart of the anthill deserves all the support imaginable. Blinking at the light they stumble out of the pilsner's dark room. With glee they note that nothing looks the same this morning. They understand at once that Janine needs all the support she can get, and one daring fellow staggers across the street and offers her a beer, which she amiably declines.

At that moment Hurrapelle comes skidding to a stop in his new car, alerted by an agitated member of the congregation who woke him with the shrill ring of his telephone. And he does what he can to stop her. He entreats her, entreats as much as he can. But she only shakes her head; she's going to stay there. When he realises that her decision is unshakeable, he goes to his church to take counsel with his God about this difficult matter.

At the police station they are consulting the legal texts. Somewhere there must be a paragraph that permits an intervention. But it can hardly be called 'reckless endangerment', can it? It's not 'incitement to riot' or 'assault with a deadly weapon' either. The policemen sigh over the gaps in the law books, leafing feverishly through the thick text, while Janine stands at her post on the corner.

Suddenly something reminds them of Rudin, who several years before had set fire to himself. That's where the solution lies! Taking into custody a person who is incapable of taking care of herself. Sweaty fingers leaf further, and finally they are ready to intervene.

But when the police officers come marching and the crowd eagerly waits to see what's going to happen, Janine calmly takes down her placard and walks away. The police gape, disconcerted, the crowd of people grumbles, and the old men from the tavern applaud with satisfaction.

When calm has been restored it is possible to argue about what she had written on her shameless placard: 'No to the atom bomb. Only one Earth.' But who wants a bomb on their head? And what did she mean by 'Only one Earth.'? Are there supposed to be more? If the truth is to be preached, people refuse to have it served up by just anyone who claims to have been warned, and least of all by some woman with no nose.

Janine walks with her head held high even though she usually looks down at the ground. She is thinking of standing on her corner again next Saturday, and no one will be able to stop her. Far from the arenas where the world plays out in earnest, she will make her small contribution in accordance with her abilities. She walks across the river bridge, tosses her hair, and hums 'A Night in Tunisia'. Under her feet dance the first ice floes of the spring thaw. She has proven herself in her own eyes and she has dared to act. She has someone who desires her. If everything is transitory after all, at least she has experienced this outpouring of life, when the pain was completely suppressed.

There is a movement in their life, this last year that Hans Olofson lives in the house by the river. Like a slow displacement of the Earth's axis, a movement so slight that it's not noticeable at first. But even to this isolated town in the sticks, a swell comes rolling in to tell them about a world outside which will no longer tolerate being relegated to endless darkness. The perspective has begun to shift, the quaking from distant wars of liberation and uprisings penetrates through the walls of the fir ridges.

Together they sit in Janine's kitchen and learn the names of the new nations. And they notice the movement, the vibration from distant continents where people are rising up. With amazement, and a certain amount of alarm, they see how the world is changing. An old world in dissolution, where rotten floors are collapsing to reveal indescribable misery, injustice, atrocity. Hans begins to understand that the world he soon intends to enter will be a different one to his father's. Everything will have to be discovered anew, the sea charts revised, the changed names replacing the old ones.

He tries to talk with his father about what he's witnessing. Tries to encourage him to whack his axe into a stump and go back to sea. Usually the conversation ends before it has really begun. Erik Olofson is defensive and doesn't want to be reminded. But then something unexpected happens.

'I'm going to Stockholm,' Erik Olofson says as they're eating dinner.

'Why?' Hans asks.

'I have a matter to take care of in the capital.'

'You don't know anybody in Stockholm, do you?'

'I got an answer to my letter.'

'What letter?'

'The letter I wrote.'

'You don't write letters, do you?'

'If you don't believe me, we won't talk about this any more.'

'What letter?'

'From the Vaxholm Company.'

'The Vaxholm Company?'

'Yes. The Vaxholm Company.'

'What's that?'

'A shipping company. They handle transport throughout the Stockholm archipelago.'

'What do they want with you?'

'I saw an advert somewhere. They need seamen. I thought it might be something for me. Domestic harbours and coastal traffic in the inland waters.'

'Did you apply for a job?'

'Are you listening to me?'

'So what did they say?'

'They want me to come to Stockholm and present myself.'

'How can they tell by looking at you that you're a good sailor?'

'They can't. But they can ask questions.'

'About what?'

'Why I haven't been to sea in so many years, for instance.'

'What are you going to say?'

'That the children are grown and can take care of themselves.'

'The children?'

'I thought it would sound better if I said I had more than one. Seamen are supposed to have a lot of children, that's always been the case.'

'And what are the names of these children?'

'I'll think of something. I just have to come up with some names. Maybe I can borrow a photo from somebody.'

'So you're going to borrow a picture of someone else's children?'

'What's the difference?'

'It makes a hell of a lot of difference!'

'I probably won't even have to prove they're mine. But I know how ship owners are. It's best to be prepared. There was a ship owner in Göteborg one time who demanded that anyone who wanted to go out on his boats had to be able to walk on his hands. The Seamen's Association protested, of course, but he had it his way.'

'Can you walk on your hands?'

'No.'

'What are you telling me, anyway?'

'That I have an appointment in Stockholm.'

'When are you leaving?'

'I haven't decided yet.'

'What do you mean?'

'Maybe I'll say the hell with it.'

'Of course you have to go! You can't keep wandering around in the woods.'

'I don't wander around in the woods.'

'You know what I mean. When I finish school we'll leave this place.'

'And go where?'

'Maybe we can ship out on the same vessel.'

'On a Vaxholm boat?'

'What the hell do I know? But I want to go further. I'm going out in the world.'

'Then I'll wait till you've finished school.'

'Don't wait! You have to go now.'

'That won't work.'

'Why not?'

'It's already too late.'

'Too late?'

'Time ran out.'

'When?'

'About six months ago.'

'Six months ago?'

'Yes.'

'And you're only telling me now? Why didn't you go?'

'I thought I'd talk to you first.'

'Good Lord . . .'

'What is it?'

'We have to get out of here. We can't live here. We have to get out and discover the world again!'

'I'm starting to get too old, I think.'

'You're getting old by stomping around in the woods.'

'I'm not stomping around in the woods! I'm working.'

'I know. But still.'

Maybe there's still time, Hans thinks. Maybe he'll take off again. He carries the sea inside him, I know that now. Hans hurries over to Janine's to tell her. I'll never have to see him crawling around scrubbing the kitchen at night, with water up to his neck.

He stops on the river bridge and looks down in the water where the ice floes rock their way towards the sea. Far off in the distance is the world, the new world that's waiting for the conqueror of the new era. The world which he will discover with Janine.

But somewhere along the way they turn off in different directions. For Hans the change takes the form of a period of waiting for something. His pilgrimage, with or without his father Erik Olofson, will take place in a world that others are putting in order for him.

Janine's thoughts are different. She makes the crucial discovery that incredible poverty is neither a whim of nature nor a law decreed by fate. She sees people who consciously choose a barbaric evil as the tool for their own gain. So they part ways at the centre of the world.

Hans emerges from his period of waiting. Janine discovers that her conscience requires action, more than just the intercessions for sufferers in which she takes part under Hurrapelle's leadership. The question deepens, and never leaves her in her dreams. And she begins to search for a means of expression. A personal crusade, she thinks. A solitary crusade, in order to tell of the world that exists beyond the fir ridges.

Slowly a decision matures, and without saying anything to Hans she decides to take up her post on the street corner. She knows that she must carry out her plan alone. Until she has stood there for the first time she won't share her crusade with anyone.

On that particular Saturday morning in March, Hans spends his time in the forestry officer's garage. Along with one of the officer's sons he has worked in vain to try to revive an old motorcycle. Not until late in the afternoon, when he stops at Pettersson's kiosk, does he hear about what happened. His heart tightens when he hears what Janine has done. He feels that he has been exposed. Surely everyone knows that he sneaks up to her door, even though he tries to avoid being seen when he walks through her gate. He begins at once to hate her, as if her real intention had been to pull him into her own humiliation. He knows that he has to distance himself from her at once, to separate from her.

'No one should care about a woman without a nose,' he says.

They had agreed that he would visit her that evening. But now he spends the evening at the People's Hall instead. He dances with every girl he meets, spitting out the most disparaging remarks about Janine that he can think of when he is crowded and jostled in the men's toilet. When Kringström's band finishes up with 'Twilight Time' he feels that he has presented a sufficient defence. Now nobody will think that he has a secret life with the placard-carrying lunatic. He goes out to the street, wipes the sweat off his brow, and stands in the shadows watching the couples leave. The night is full of shouts and giggles. He rocks back and forth on his feet, dizzy from all the lukewarm aquavit. That damn bitch, he thinks. She would have yelled at me and asked me to help hold her sign if I happened to pass by.

Suddenly he decides to visit her one last time and tell her what he's thinking. So as not to be discovered he sneaks like a criminal across the bridge and waits for a long time outside her gate before he slips into the shadows.

She welcomes him without reproach. He was supposed to come but didn't. No more than that.

'Did you wait for me?' he asks.

'I'm used to waiting,' she replies. 'It doesn't matter.'

He hates her and he desires her. But at the same time he knows that tonight he brings with him the opinion of the town, and he tells her that he will never come back if she stands on the street corner again.

A cold wind blows through her heart. She had thought he would encourage her, agree that what she was doing was right. That's how she had interpreted their conversation about the way the world was cracking under the winds of change. Sorrow sinks like a lead weight on to her head. Now she knows that she will be left alone again. But not yet, because his desire takes over, and once again they are entwined with each other.

Their last time together becomes a long drawn-out agony. Hans returns to the starting point, the chopped-off crow's head that he and Sture put in her letterbox. Now it's her head he's swinging at. He spits and swears at her, breaks arrangements, and paints her black for anyone who will listen.

In the midst of this chaos he passes his secondary school examination. With an intense outburst of concentrated energy he succeeds in getting unexpectedly high marks. Rector Bohlin has seen to it that an application is sent to the college in the county seat. When he puts on the grey graduation cap, he decides to keep studying. Now he doesn't have to wait for his father to fling away the axe of indecision, now he's in charge of his own future. With one single motion he can set himself free.

On the evening after the exam he stands outside Janine's door. She's waiting with flowers for him, but he doesn't want her damned flowers. He's going to leave this place and now he's here for the last time. He hangs his grey cap over the picture of the Virgin Mary sitting in her window. But to the last day, all summer long, he visits her. And yet the secret that will be her last he never will know.

The final break-up, the end, is irresolute and forlorn. One evening in the middle of August he visits her and now it is really for the last time. They meet briefly in her kitchen, with few words, as if it were their first time, when he stood there with his hedge clippers in his hand. He says he'll write, but she tells him it would be better if he didn't. It's best to let everything dissolve, blow away with the wind.

He leaves her house. Behind him he hears the notes of 'Some of These Days'.

The next day his father accompanies him to the train station. Hans looks at his father, grey and indecisive.

'I'll come home sometime,' he says. 'And you can always come to visit.'

Erik Olofson nods. He'll certainly come to visit. 'The sea . . .' he says and falls silent.

But Hans doesn't hear him. He's waiting patiently for the tram to take him away.

For a long time his father stays at the station, and he tells himself that the sea still does exist, after all. If only he . . . Always that 'if only'. Then he goes home to the house by the river, and lets the sea roar out of his radio.

The month of the rowan berries. A Sunday morning in September. A bank of fog lies heavy over the town as it slowly begins to awake. There's a chill in the air and the gravel crunches as a lone man turns off the main road and takes a short cut down the slope to the river. The People's Park on its promontory shines forlornly like a half-razed ruin in the grey morning light. In the horse dealer's pastures the horses are grazing in the fog. Noiselessly they move like ships waiting for the wind.

The man unties a rowboat at the river bank and sits down at the oars. He rows out into the sound between the point of the People's Park and the south bank of the river. There he throws out an anchor that grips the rocks on the river bed. He tosses out a line and waits.

After an hour he decides to try further down towards the point. He lets the anchor drift under the keel of the boat as he rows. But abruptly it catches, and when he finally pulls it loose he sees that an almost rotten piece of cloth has been pierced by his hook. A bit of a woman's blouse, he can see. Pensively he rows back to shore.

The bit of cloth lies on a table at the police station, with Hurrapelle standing looking at it. He nods.

The hastily assembled river-dragging crew doesn't have to search long. On the second pass the two rowboats make through the sound, one of their hooks catches on something at the bottom. From the shore Hurrapelle watches Janine return.

The doctor examines the body one last time before he finishes the autopsy. When he has washed his hands, he stands by the window and looks out over the fir ridges coloured red by the setting sun. He wonders whether he is the only one who knows Janine's secret. Without knowing why, he decides not to include it in the autopsy report. Even though this is not proper procedure, he doesn't think it will change anything. He knows that she drowned. Around her waist there was a thick steel wire and in her clothing were irons and heavy pieces of drainpipe. No crime was committed. So he doesn't need to report that Janine was carrying a child when she died.

In the house by the river Erik Olofson sits poring over a sea chart. He adjusts his glasses and pilots his vessel with his index finger through the Strait of Malacca. He smells the sea, sees the glimmering lanterns from distant vessels on an approaching course. In the background the carrier waves from the shortwave radio hiss through the ether. Maybe it's still possible, he thinks. A little ship that takes goods along the coast? Maybe it's still possible.

And what about Hans? He doesn't remember who told him. But someone heard about it, and Hans learns that Janine is dead. The woman who stood every Saturday with her placard on the corner between the People's Hall and the hardware shop. In the night he leaves the room in his boarding house, which he already detests, and wanders restlessly through the dark town. He tries to convince himself that no one is to blame. Not him, nor anybody else. But still, he knows. Mutshatsha, he thinks. You wanted to go there, Janine, that was your dream. But you never went and now you're dead.

I once lay behind a broken-down kiln in the old brickworks and realised that I was myself and no one else. But since then? Now? He asks himself how he can stand four years in this distant college. Inside him an incessant struggle is going on between belief in the future and resignation. He tries to cheer himself up. Living must be like continually preparing for new expeditions, he thinks. It's either that or I'll become like my father.

All at once he decides. Someday he will go to Mutshatsha. Someday he will make the journey that Janine never made. That thought becomes instantly holy for him. The most fragile of all Goals has revealed itself to him. The dream of another which he is taking over.

Cautiously he tiptoes up the stairs to his room. He recognises the smell of old lady Westlund's flat. Apples, sour drops. On the table the books lie waiting for him. But he is thinking of Janine. Maybe growing up means realising one's loneliness, he thinks. He sits motionless for a long time.

He feels as if he were again sitting on the huge span of the iron bridge. High overhead, the stars.

Below him Janine . . .

PART III

THE LEOPARD'S EYE

Chapter Twenty

In Hans Olofson's dreams the leopard is hunting.

The terrain is a landscape slipping away, the African bush displaced to become his internal space. The perspective is changing constantly. Sometimes he's in front of the leopard, sometimes behind it, and at times he becomes the leopard himself. In the dream it is always dusk. Surrounded by the tall elephant grass he stands far out on a savannah. The horizon frightens him. A threat coming ever closer is the leopard's landscape, which returns night after night in his restless mind.

Sometimes he wakes up abruptly and thinks he understands. He is not being pursued by a lone leopard, but two. In his internal landscape the leopard is breaking with its nature as a lone hunter and joining with another animal. He never manages to discern what kind of weapons he is carrying during his recurrent nocturnal hunts. Is he setting out snares or does he carry a spear with a hand-wrought iron point? Or is he following the leopard empty-handed? The landscape stretches away in his dreams as an endless plain where he senses an indistinct river bed at the distant edge of his vision. He burns the tall elephant grass to drive out the leopard. Sometimes he also thinks he spies the leopard's shadow, like a rapid movement against the moonlit terrain. The rest is silence, his own breathing echoing inside the dream.

The leopard is bringing a message, he thinks when he wakes. A message I haven't yet managed to decipher.

When the malaria attack forces his mind into hallucinations, he sees the leopard's watchful eye.

It's Janine, he thinks in confusion. It's her eye I see; she's looking up at me from the bottom of the river as I'm balancing on the span of the iron bridge. She has drawn a leopard skin over her shoulders so I won't know it's her.

But she's dead, isn't she? When I left Sweden and put all my old horizons behind me, she had already been gone for seven years. Now I've been in Africa for almost eighteen years.

The malaria attack flings him up from his lethargy, and when he awakes he doesn't know where he is. The revolver resting against his cheek makes him remember. He listens to the darkness.

I'm surrounded by bandits, he thinks desperately. It's Luka who lured them here, severed the telephone line, cut off the electricity. They're waiting outside in the dark. Soon they will come to tear open my chest and carry off my still beating heart.

Summoning all his remaining strength, he sits up in bed so that his back is resting against the bedstead. Why don't I hear anything, he wonders. The silence . . .

Why aren't the hippos sighing by the river? Where's that damned Luka? He yells into the dark, but no one answers. He has the pistol in his hands.

He waits.

Chapter Twenty-One

Werner Masterton's severed head lies in a pool of blood on the kitchen floor. Two forks are stuck in his eyes. In the dining room sits Masterton's headless body at the table, the chopped-off hands lie on a tray in front of him, the white tablecloth is drenched in blood.

In the bedroom Olofson finds Ruth Masterton with her throat slit, her head almost detached from her body. She is naked, one of her thighbones smashed by a powerful axe-blow. Flies swarm over her body and he thinks that what he is seeing can't be real.

He notices that he is weeping from terror, and when he comes out of the house he collapses to the ground. The waiting Africans shrink back, and he screams at them not to go in. He calls to Robert to fetch the neighbours, call the police, and suddenly in despair he fires his shotgun into the air.

Late in the afternoon he returns home, paralysed, apathetic. He still can't face the rage that he knows will come. For the whole long day the rumour has spread in the white colony, cars have come and gone, and one opinion is soon discernible. Ruth and Werner Masterton did not fall victim to normal bandits. Even though their car is gone, valuables vanished, this senseless double murder is something more, a dammed-up hatred that has found its release. This is a racial murder, a political murder. Ruth and Werner Masterton have met their fate at the hands of self-appointed black avengers.

At the house of one of the Mastertons' neighbours the white colony quickly gathers for a meeting to discuss broader security measures. But Olofson doesn't attend; he says he can't face it. Someone at the meeting suggests visiting Olofson that evening to report on what has been decided. But he refuses the visit; he has his dogs and his weapons, he knows how to be careful.

When he returns to his house it has started to rain, a torrential pounding rain that cuts visibility almost to zero. He thinks he glimpses a black shadow disappearing behind the house as he turns into the courtyard. For a long time he stays sitting in the car with the windscreen wipers working frantically. I'm afraid, he realises. More afraid than I've ever been before. The ones who murdered Ruth and Werner have also stabbed their knives into me. He takes the safety off his gun and runs through the rain, unlocks the door and slams it hard behind him.

The rain booms on the sheet-metal roof, the German shepherd he was given when he turned forty is sitting strangely motionless on the kitchen floor. Immediately he has the feeling that someone has been inside the house while he was gone. Something in the dog's behaviour troubles him. Usually it meets him with energetic joy, but now it is inexplicably quiet.

He looks at the dog given to him by Ruth and Werner Masterton and realises that real life is turning into a nightmare. He squats down in front of the dog and scratches behind his ear.

'What is it?' he whispers. 'Tell me what it is, show me if something has happened.'

He walks through his house, still with his pistol ready, and the dog follows him quietly. The feeling that someone has been inside the house doesn't leave him, even though he can't see that anything is missing or has been moved. And yet he knows.

He lets the dog out to join the others.

'Keep watch now,' he says.

All night long he sits in a chair with his weapons close by. There is a hatred that is boundless, a hatred for the whites which he only now comprehends. Nothing suggests that he would be spared from being enveloped by this hatred. The price he pays for the good life he has led in Africa is that he now sits awake with his weapons next to him.

At dawn he dozes off in his chair. Dreams take him back to his past. He sees himself laboriously trudging through snow metres deep, a pack on his back and wearing ski boots that are always too big. Somewhere he glimpses Janine's face, *Célestine* in her case.

He wakes up with a jolt and realises that someone is pounding on the kitchen door. He takes the safety off his gun and opens the door. Luka stands outside. Out of nowhere comes the fury and he points his gun at Luka, presses the cold barrel against his chest.

'The best explanation you've ever given me,' he shouts. 'That's what I want. And I want it now. Otherwise you'll never come inside my house again.'

His outburst, the pistol with the safety off, doesn't seem to faze the dignified black man standing before him.

'A white snake cast itself at my breast,' he says. 'Like a flame of fire it bored through my body. In order not to die I was forced to seek out a *kashinakashi*. He lives a long way from here, he's hard to find. I walked without stopping for a day and a night. He welcomed me and freed me of the white snake. I came back at once, *Bwana*.'

'You're lying, you damned Negro,' says Olofson. 'A white snake?

There aren't any white snakes, and there aren't any snakes that can bore through a person's chest. I'm not interested in your superstitions, I want to know the truth.'

'What I'm saying is true, *Bwana*,' says Luka. 'A white snake forced its way through my chest.'

In rage Olofson strikes him with the barrel of his pistol. Blood runs from the torn skin on Luka's cheek, but he still fails to disturb the man's unflappable dignity.

'It's 1987,' Olofson says. 'You're a grown man, you've lived among *mzunguz* your whole life. You know that the African superstition is your own backwardness, ancient notions that you are too weak to free yourself from. This too is something the whites have to help you with. If we weren't here, you would all kill each other with your illusions.'

'Our president is an educated man, *Bwana*,' says Luka.

'Perhaps,' says Olofson. 'He has banned sorcery. A witch doctor can be sent to prison.'

'Our president always has a white handkerchief in his hand, *Bwana*,' Luka goes on, unperturbed. 'He keeps it to make himself invulnerable, to protect himself from sorcery. He knows that he can't prevent what is real just by prohibiting it.'

He's unreachable, Olofson thinks. He's the one I should fear most, since he knows my habits.

'Your brothers have murdered my friends,' he says. 'But you know that, don't you?'

'Everyone knows it, *Bwana*,' says Luka.

'Good people,' Olofson says. 'Hard-working people, innocent people.'

'No one is innocent, *Bwana*,' says Luka. 'It's a sad event, but sad events must happen sometimes.'

'Who killed them?' Olofson asks. 'If you know anything, tell me.'

'Nobody knows anything, *Bwana*,' Luka replies calmly.

'I think you're lying,' says Olofson. 'You always know what's going on, sometimes even before it happens. But now you don't know anything, all of a sudden nothing at all. Maybe it was a white snake that killed them and cut off their heads?'

'Maybe it was, *Bwana*,' says Luka.

'You've worked for me almost twenty years,' Olofson says. 'I've always treated you well, paid you well, given you clothes, a radio, everything you asked for and even things you didn't ask for. And yet I don't trust you. What is there to prevent you from smashing a *panga* into my head one morning instead of serving me my coffee? You people cut the throats of your benefactors, you talk about white snakes, and you turn to witch doctors. What do you think would happen if all the whites left this country? What would you eat?'

'Then we would decide, *Bwana*,' Luka says.

Olofson lowers his pistol. 'One more time,' he says. 'Who killed Ruth and Werner Masterton?'

'Whoever did it knows, *Bwana*,' says Luka. 'No one else.'

'But you have an idea, don't you?' says Olofson. 'What's going on in your head?'

'It's an unsettled time, *Bwana*,' Luka replies. 'People have nothing to eat. Our lorries filled with eggs are hijacked. Hungry people are dangerous just before they become completely powerless. They see where the food is, they hear about the meals the whites eat, they are starving.'

'But why Ruth and Werner?' Olofson asks. 'Why them of all people?'

'Everything must begin somewhere, *Bwana*,' Luka says. 'A direction must always be chosen.'

Of course he's right, Olofson thinks. In the dark a bloody decision is reached, a finger points in an arbitrary direction, and there stands Ruth and Werner Masterton's house. Next time the finger could be pointing at me.

'One thing you should know,' he tells Luka. 'I've never killed anyone. But I won't hesitate. Not even if I have to kill you.'

'I'll keep that in mind, *Bwana*,' says Luka.

A car comes slowly along the muddy, rutted road from the hen houses. Olofson recognises Peter Motombwane's rusty Peugeot.

'Coffee and tea,' he says to Luka. 'Motombwane doesn't like coffee.'

They sit on the terrace.

'You've been expecting me, of course,' Motombwane says, as he stirs his tea.

'Actually, no,' Olofson replies. 'Right now I'm expecting both everything and nothing.'

'You forget that I'm a journalist,' says Motombwane. 'You forget that you're an important person yourself. You were the first to see what happened.'

Without warning Hans Olofson begins to sob; a violent outburst of sorrow and fear is released from inside him. Motombwane waits with his head bowed, his gaze directed at the cracked stone floor of the terrace.

'I'm tired,' Olofson says when the fit has passed. 'I see my friends dead, the first people I met when I came to Africa. I see their maimed bodies, an utterly inconceivable violence.'

'Or perhaps not,' Motombwane says slowly.

'You'll get your details,' Olofson says. 'You'll get all the gore you think your readers can stand. But first you have to explain to me what happened.'

Motombwane throws out his hands. 'I'm no policeman,' he says.

'You're an African,' Olofson says. 'Besides, you're intelligent, you're educated, and you surely don't believe in superstition any longer. You're a journalist. You have the background to explain this to me.'

'Much of what you say is true,' Motombwane replies. 'But you're wrong if you think I'm not superstitious. I am. With my mind I turn away from it, but in my heart it will always be part of me. One can move to a foreign land, as you have done, one can seek his fortune, shape his life. But no one can ever totally leave his origins behind. Something will always remain, as more than a memory, as a living reminder of who you really are. I don't pray to the gods carved from wood, I go to doctors in white coats when I get sick. But I also listen to the voices of my ancestors; I wrap a black band around my wrist as protection before I board an aeroplane.'

'Why Werner and Ruth?' Olofson asks. 'Why this senseless bloodbath?'

'You're on the wrong track,' replies Motombwane. 'You're not thinking logically because you've chosen the wrong starting point. Your white brain is deceiving you. If you want to understand you have to think black thoughts. And that's not something you can do, in the same way that I can't formulate white thoughts. You ask why it should be Werner and Ruth who were killed. You might just as well ask why not. You talk about a senseless double murder. I'm not altogether sure that it was. Decapitation prevents people from haunting, severed hands prevent people from taking revenge. It's perfectly obvious that they were killed by Africans, but it was not as senseless as you imagine.'

'So you think it was a normal robbery-murder,' says Olofson.

Motombwane shakes his head. 'If it had occurred a year ago I would have thought so,' he replies. 'But not now, not with the unrest that is growing in our country with each day that passes. Opposing political forces grow in this unrest. I think that Ruth and Werner fell victim to killers who actually wanted to sink their *pangas* into the heads of the black leaders in this country. There are also black *mzunguz*. You erroneously think that it means *white man*, when it actually means *rich man*. Because it was natural to associate wealth with whites, the original meaning of the word has been lost. Today I think it's important to reclaim the real meaning of the word.'

'Give me an explanation,' Olofson says. 'Draw me a political weather map, a conceivable picture, of what might have happened.'

'The first thing you have to understand is that what I do is dangerous,' says Motombwane. 'The politicians in our country are unscrupulous. They guard their power by letting their dogs run free. There is one single efficient organ in this country, well organised and constantly active, and that is the president's secret police. The opposition is watched by a fine-meshed net of informers. In every town, in every company there is someone who is connected to this secret police. Even on your farm there is at least one man who once a week reports to an unknown superior. That's what I mean when I say it's dangerous. Without your knowing it, Luka could be the man who reports from here.

'No opposition must be permitted to grow. The politicians who rule today regard our land as prey. In Africa it's easy simply to disappear. Journalists who have been too critical and didn't listen to the words of warning have vanished; newspaper editors have been selected for their loyalty to the party, and this means that nothing is printed about the vanished journalists in the papers. I can't make it any plainer than that. There is an undercurrent of events in this country that nobody knows about. Rumours spread, but there is no way to confirm them. People are murdered through arranged suicides. Massacred corpses on railway tracks, soaked with alcohol, become accidents due to drunkenness. Alleged robbers who are shot down during escape attempts may be people who tried to take over the state-controlled labour unions. The examples are endless.

'But the unrest is there all the time. In the dark the discontent whispers. People wonder about the corn meal that is suddenly gone, despite the fact that a succession of record harvests has been going on for several years. The rumour spreads that lorries belonging to the authorities drive across the borders at night to smuggle out corn meal. Why are there no more vaccines and medicines in the hospitals, even though millions of dollars' worth are donated to this country every year? People have travelled to Zaire and been able to buy medicines at a chemist's with the text 'Donation to Zambia' printed on the box. The rumours spread, the discontent grows, but everyone is afraid of the informers.

'The opposition are forced to make detours. Perhaps some people have looked at their despair, their hungry children, and their insight into the betrayal by the politicians, and decided that the only chance of getting to the rulers is by taking a detour: murder white people, create instability and insecurity. Execute whites and thereby warn the black rulers. That may have been how it happened. Because something is going to happen in this country. Soon. For over twenty years we have been an independent nation. Nothing has really improved for the people. It's only the few who took over from the white leaders that have amassed unheard-of fortunes. Maybe we have now reached a breaking point, maybe an uprising is approaching? I don't know anything for sure; we Africans follow impulses that come out of nowhere. Our actions are often spontaneous; we replace the lack of organisation with violence in our wrath. If this is how it happened, then we will never know who murdered Ruth and Werner Masterton. Many people will know their names, but they will be protected. They will be surrounded at once by a superstitious respect and awe, as if our ancestors had returned in their form.

The warriors of the past will return. Maybe the police will drag some insignificant thieves out of the dark, say they're the killers, and shoot them during alleged escape attempts. Faked interrogation records and confessions can be arranged. Only gradually will we find out whether or not what I believe is correct.'

'How?' asks Olofson.

'When the next white family is murdered,' replies Motombwane softly. Luka passes across the terrace; they follow him with their gaze, see him go out to the German shepherds with some meat scraps.

'An informer on my farm,' says Olofson. 'Of course I ought to start wondering who it might be.'

'Let's assume that you succeed in finding out,' says Motombwane. 'What happens then? Someone else will be selected at once. No one can refuse, because payment is also involved. You'll wind up chasing your own shadow. If I were you I'd do something entirely different.'

'What?' asks Olofson.

'Keep a watchful eye on the man who actually manages the work on your farm. There's so much you don't know. You've been here for almost twenty years, but you have no idea what's really going on. You could live here another twenty years and you still wouldn't know anything. You think you have divided up power and responsibility by appointing a foreman. But you don't know that you have a sorcerer on your farm, a witch-master who in reality is the one in control. An insignificant man who never reveals the influence he possesses. You view him as one of many workers who have been on the farm for a long time, one of those who never cause you any problems. But the other workers fear him.'

'Who?' asks Olofson.

'One of your workers who gathers eggs,' says Motombwane. 'Eisenhower Mudenda.'

'I don't believe you,' says Olofson. 'Eisenhower Mudenda came here right after Judith Fillington left. It's just as you say, he has never caused me any problems. He has never missed work because he was drunk, never been reluctant to work overtime if necessary. When I encounter him he bows almost to the ground. Sometimes I've even felt annoyed by his subservience.'

'Where did he come from?' Motombwane asks.

'I can't recall,' Olofson replies.

'Actually you don't know a thing about him,' says Motombwane. 'But what I'm telling you is true. If I were you I'd keep an eye on him. Above all, show him that you're not frightened by what happened to Ruth and Werner Masterton. But never reveal that you now know that he is a sorcerer.'

'We've known each other a long time,' Olofson says. 'And only now you're telling me something you must have known for many years?'

'It wasn't important until now,' Motombwane replies. 'Besides, I'm a cautious man. I'm an African. I know what can happen if I'm too generous with my knowledge, if I forget that I'm an African.'

'If Eisenhower Mudenda knew about what you're telling me,' Olofson asks, 'what would happen then?'

'I would probably die,' says Motombwane. 'I would be poisoned, the sorcery would reach me.'

'There isn't any sorcery,' Olofson says.

'I'm an African,' replies Motombwane.

Again they fall silent as Luka passes by.

'To fall silent is to talk to Luka,' Motombwane says. 'Twice he has passed by and both times we were silent. So he knows we're talking about something he's not supposed to hear.'

'Are you afraid?' Olofson asks.

'Right now it's smart to be afraid,' says Motombwane.

'What about the future?' Olofson asks. 'My close friends have been slaughtered. Next time a finger in the darkness could point at my house. You're an African, you're a radical. Even though I don't believe you could chop people's heads off, you're still a part of the opposition that exists in this country. What do you hope will happen?'

'Once more you're wrong,' says Motombwane. 'Once more you draw the wrong conclusion, a white's conclusion. In a certain situation I could easily raise a *panga* and let it fall over a white man's head.'

'Even over my head?'

'Maybe that's where the boundary lies,' Motombwane replies softly. 'I think I would ask a good friend to chop off your head instead of doing it myself.'

'Only in Africa is this possible,' Olofson says. 'Two friends sit drinking tea or coffee together and discussing the possibility that in a certain situation one might chop off the other's head.'

'That's the way the world is,' Motombwane says. 'The contradictions are greater than ever. The new empire builders are the international arms dealers who fly between wars offering their weapons for sale. The colonisation of the poor peoples by superior powers is just as great today as any time before. Billions in so-called aid flows from the rich countries, but for every pound that comes in, two pounds wander back out. We're living in the midst of a catastrophe, a world that is burning with thousand-degree flames. Friendships can still form in our time. But often we don't see that the common ground we stand on is already undermined. We are friends but we both have a *panga* hidden behind our backs.'

'Take it a step further,' Olofson says. 'You hope for something, you dream about something. Your dream might be my nightmare, if I understand you correctly?'

Peter Motombwane nods.

'You're my friend,' he says, 'at least for the time being. But of course I wish all the whites were out of this country. I'm not a racist, I'm not talking about skin colour. I view violence as necessary; faced with the prolongation of my people's pain there is no other way out. African revolutions are most often appalling bloodbaths; the political struggle is always darkened by our past and our traditions. Possibly, if our despair is great enough, we can unite against a common foe. But then we point our weapons at our brothers by our side, if they are from a different tribe. Africa is a seriously wounded animal; in the bodies of us all hang spears that were cast by our own brothers. And yet I have to believe in a future, another time, an Africa that is not ruled by tyrants who imitate the European men of violence who have always been there. My anxiety and my dream coincide with the anxiety that you are noticing right now in this country. You have to understand that this anxiety is ultimately the expression of a dream. But how does one re-establish a dream that has been beaten out of people by the secret police? By leaders who amass fortunes by stealing vaccines that are supposed to protect our children against the most common diseases?'

'Give me a word of advice,' Olofson says. 'I'm not sure I'll follow it, but I'd still like to hear what you have to say.'

Motombwane looks out across the yard. 'Leave,' he says. 'Leave before it's too late. Maybe I'm wrong, maybe it will be many years before the sun goes down for *mzunguz* of various skin colours on this continent. But if you're still here by then it will be too late.'

Olofson follows him to his car.

'The bloody details,' he says.

'I've already got those,' Motombwane replies. 'I can imagine.'

'Come back,' Olofson says.

'If I didn't come, people on your farm would start to wonder,' says Motombwane. 'I don't want people to wonder for nothing. Especially not in such uneasy times.'

'What's going to happen?'

'In a world on fire, anything can happen,' says Motombwane.

The car with its coughing engine and its worn-out shock absorbers disappears. When Olofson turns around he sees Luka on the terrace. He stands motionless, watching the car drive away.

Two days later Olofson helps carry Ruth and Werner Masterton's coffins to their common grave, right next to the daughter who died many years before. The pallbearers are white. Pale, resolute faces watch the coffins being lowered into the red earth. At a distance stand the black workers. Olofson sees Robert, motionless, alone, his face expressionless. The tension is there, a shared rage that flows through the whites who are gathered to say farewell to Ruth and Werner Masterton. Many of them are openly bearing arms, and Olofson feels that he is in the midst of a funeral procession that could quickly be transformed into a well-equipped army.

The night after the burial the Mastertons' house burns down. In the morning only the smoking walls remain. The only one they trusted, Robert the chauffeur, has vanished. Only the workers are left, expectantly waiting for something, no one knows what.

Olofson builds barricades in his house. Each night he sleeps in a different room, and he barricades the doors with tables and cabinets. In the daytime he tends to his work as usual. In secret he watches Eisenhower Mudenda, and receives his still equally humble greetings.

Yet another egg transport is plundered by people who have built a roadblock on the way to Ndola. Indian shops in Lusaka and Livingstone are stormed and burned down.

After darkness falls, nobody visits their neighbours. No headlights play through the darkness. Pouring rain washes over the isolated houses; everyone is waiting for a finger to point to them out of the darkness. Violent thunderstorms pass over Kalulushi. Olofson lies awake in the dark with his weapons next to him in bed.

One morning soon after Ruth and Werner's funeral, Olofson opens the kitchen door for Luka after yet another sleepless night and sees at once from Luka's face that something has happened. The inscrutable and dignified face is changed. Olofson sees for the first time that even Luka can be frightened.

'*Bwana*,' he says. 'Something has happened.'

'What?!' shouts Olofson and feels the panic rising.

Before Luka can reply, he discovers it for himself. Something is nailed to the mangrove tree that stands facing the drive, a windbreak planted by Judith Fillington and her husband many years earlier. At first he can't see what it is; then he has an idea but doesn't want to believe what he suspects. With his revolver in his hand he slowly approaches the tree.

Lashed fast with barbed wire to the tree trunk is the severed head of a German shepherd. The dog he received from Ruth and Werner, the one he named Sture. The head grins at him, the tongue cut out, the eyes open and staring.

Olofson feels terror well up inside him. The finger has pointed in the dark. Luka's terror – he must know what it means. I'm living among insane savages, he thinks desperately. I can't read them; their barbaric signs are unintelligible.

Luka is sitting on the stone steps to the terrace. Olofson can see that he's so scared he's shaking. The sweat is glinting on his black skin.

'I don't intend to ask you who did this,' Olofson says. 'I know what answer I will get – that you don't know. Nor do I think it was you, since I can see that you're afraid. I don't think you would be trembling over your own actions. Or at least you wouldn't reveal yourself to me. But I want you to tell me what it means. Why would someone chop off the head of my dog and lash it to a tree during the night? Why would someone cut out the tongue of a dog that's already dead and can't bark any more? Whoever did this wants me to understand something. Or is the intention just to frighten me?'

Slowly Luka's answer comes, as if each word he utters were a mine threatening to explode.

'The dog is a gift from dead people, *Bwana*. Now the dog is dead too. Only the owner lives. A German shepherd is what *mzunguz* most often use to protect themselves, since Africans are afraid of dogs. But he who kills a dog shows that he is not afraid. Dead dogs protect no *mzungu*. Cutting out the tongue prevents the dead dog from barking.'

'The people who gave him to me are dead,' Olofson says. 'The gift has had his head cut off. Now only the owner remains. The last link in this chain is still alive, but he is defenceless. Is that what you're telling me?'

'The leopards are hunting at daybreak,' Luka mutters.

Olofson sees his eyes, wide open from something he carries inside him.

'It wasn't a leopard that did this,' he says. 'It was people like you, black people. No *mzungu* would fasten a severed dog's head to a tree.'

'The leopards are hunting,' Luka mumbles again, and Olofson sees that his terror is real.

A thought occurs to him.

'Leopards,' he says softly. 'People who have turned themselves into leopards? Dressed in their skins to make themselves invulnerable? Maybe it was people in leopard skins who came in the night to Ruth and Werner Masterton.'

His words increase Luka's anxiety.

'Leopards see without being seen,' Olofson says. 'Maybe they can hear at long distances too. Maybe they can read people's lips. But they can't see or hear through stone walls.'

He gets up and Luka follows him. We have never been this close to each other, Olofson thinks. Now we are sharing the burden of each other's fear. Luka senses the threat. Perhaps because he works for a white man, has the trust of a white man, and receives many advantages? Maybe a black man who works for a *mzungu* is unreliable in this country. Luka sits down on the edge of a kitchen chair.

'Words travel in the dark, *Bwana*,' he says. 'Words that are hard to understand. But they are there, and they come back. Someone speaks them, and no one knows whose voice it is.'

'What are the words?' Olofson asks.

'They speak of unusual leopards,' says Luka. 'Leopards who have begun to hunt in packs. The leopard is a lone hunter, dangerous in his loneliness. Leopards in packs are many more times as dangerous.'

'Leopards are predators,' Olofson says. 'Leopards are looking for the prey?'

'The words speak of people who gather in the dark,' says Luka. 'People who turn into leopards that will chase all the *mzunguz* out of the country.'

Olofson remembers something that Peter Motombwane told him.

'*Mzunguz*,' he says. 'Rich men. But there are both black and white men that are rich, aren't there?'

'The whites are richer,' says Luka.

One question remains, even though Olofson already knows what Luka's answer will be.

'Am I a rich man?' he asks.

'Yes, *Bwana*,' Luka replies. 'A very rich man.'

And yet I will stay here, he thinks. If I'd had a family I would have sent them away. But I'm alone. I have to stay put or else give up completely. He puts on a pair of gloves, takes down the dog's head, and Luka buries it down by the river.

'Where's the body?' Olofson asks.

Luka shakes his head. 'I don't know, *Bwana*. In a place where we can't see it.'

At night he stands guard. He dozes fitfully in a chair behind barricaded doors. Guns with their safeties off lie across his knee, stacks of extra ammunition are stashed at various spots in the house. He pictures himself making his last stand in the room where the skeletons were once stored.

In the daytime he visits the surrounding farms, telling people Luka's vague story about the pack of leopards. His neighbours supply him with other pieces to the puzzle, even though no one else has received a warning sign.

Before independence, during the 1950s, there was something known as the leopard movement in certain areas of the Copperbelt; an underground movement that mixed politics and religion and threatened to take up arms if the federation was not dissolved and Zambia gained independence. But no one had heard of the leopard movement using violence.

Olofson learns from the farmers who have spent long lives in the country that nothing ever actually dies. For a long-vanished political and religious movement to reappear is not unusual; it only increases the credibility of Luka's words. Olofson declines to take on volunteers as reinforcements in his own house. At twilight he barricades himself in and eats his lonely dinner after he has sent Luka home.

He waits for something to happen. The exhaustion is a drain on him, the fear is eating deep holes in his soul. And yet he is determined to stay. He thinks about Joyce and her daughters.

People who live outside all underground movements, people who each day must fight for their own survival.

The rain is intense, thundering against his sheet-metal roof through the long, lonely nights.

One morning a white man stands outside his house, a man whom he has never seen before. To Olofson's astonishment he addresses him in Swedish.

'I was prepared for that,' says the stranger with a laugh. 'I know you're Swedish. Your name is Hans Olofson.'

He introduces himself as Lars Håkansson, an aid expert, sent out by Sida, the Swedish aid agency, to monitor the development of satellite telecommunications stations paid for by Swedish aid funds. His mission turns out to be more than merely stopping by to say hello to a countryman who happens to live in Kalulushi. There is a hill on Olofson's property that is an ideal location for one of the link stations. A steel tower topped by a satellite dish. A fence, a passable road. A total area of 400 square metres.

'Naturally there is payment involved, if you're prepared to relinquish your property,' Håkansson says. 'We can arrange for you to get your money in real currency, of course: dollars, pounds or D-marks.'

Olofson can think of no reason to refuse. 'Telecommunications,' he says. 'Telephone lines or TV?'

'Both,' says Håkansson. 'The satellite dishes transmit and receive the radio frequency waves desired. TV signals are captured by television receivers, telephone impulses are bounced off a satellite in stationary orbit over the prime meridian, which then sends the signals on to any conceivable telephone in the whole world. Africa will be incorporated into a network.'

Olofson offers his visitor some coffee.

'You've got a nice place here,' Håkansson says.

'There's trouble in the country,' Olofson replies. 'I'm not so sure any more that it's good to live here.'

'I've been abroad for ten years,' Håkansson says. 'I've staked out communications links in Guinea Bissau, Kenya and Tanzania. There's unrest everywhere. As an aid expert you don't notice much of it. You're a holy man because you dispense millions from up your khaki sleeves. Politicians bow, soldiers and police officers salute when you arrive.'

'Soldiers and police officers?' Olofson asks.

Håkansson shrugs his shoulders and grimaces. 'Links and satellite dishes,' he says. 'All types of messages can be sent by the new technology. The police and the army then have greater opportunities to check what's going on in remote border regions. In a crisis situation the men who hold the keys can cut off an unruly section of the country. Swedish aid workers are forbidden by the parliament from getting involved in anything beyond civilian objectives. But who's going to check what these link stations are used for? Swedish politicians have never understood a thing about the actual realities of the world. Swedish businessmen, on the other hand, have understood much more. That's why businessmen never become politicians.'

Lars Håkansson is resolute and determined. Olofson envies his self-assurance.

Here I sit with my eggs, he thinks. The chicken shit is growing under my fingernails. He looks at Lars Håkansson's polished hands, his well-tailored khaki jacket. He imagines that Håkansson is a happy man, about fifty years old.

'I'll be here for two years,' he says. 'I'm based in Lusaka, in an excellent house on Independence Avenue. It's comforting to live where you can see the president pass by almost daily in his well-guarded convoy. I assume that sooner or later I'll be invited to the State House to present this wonderful Swedish gift. To be Swedish in Africa today is better than being Swedish in Sweden. Our foreign aid munificence opens doors and palace gates.'

Olofson gives him selected excerpts from his African life.

'Show me the farm,' Håkansson says. 'I saw something in the papers about a robbery-murder on a farm in this area. Was it nearby?'

'No,' says Olofson. 'Quite far from here.'

'Farmers also get murdered in Småland,' says Håkansson. They climb into his almost brand-new Land Cruiser, and drive around the farm, look at one of the hen houses. Olofson shows him the school.

'Like a mill owner in the olden days,' says Håkansson. 'Do you also sleep with the daughters before they're allowed to get married? Or have you stopped now that all of Africa has AIDS?'

'I've never done it,' Olofson says, registering that Håkansson's remarks upset him.

Outside Joyce Lufuma's house two of the eldest daughters stand and wave. One is sixteen, the other fifteen.

'A family I take special care of,' says Olofson. 'I'd like to send these two girls to school in Lusaka. I just don't know quite how to arrange it.'

'What's the problem?' Håkansson asks.

'Everything,' says Olofson. 'They grew up here on this isolated farm, their father died in an accident. They've barely been to Chingola or Kitwe. How would they get along in a city like Lusaka? They have no relatives there, I've checked. As girls they're vulnerable, especially without family to provide a protective environment. The best thing would be if I could have sent the whole family, the mother and four children. But she doesn't want to go.'

'What would they study?' asks Håkansson. 'Teaching or nursing?'

Olofson nods. 'Nursing. I assume they'd be good at it. The country needs nurses, and both are very dedicated.'

'For an aid expert nothing is impossible,' Håkansson says quickly. 'I can arrange the whole thing for you. My house in Lusaka has two servants' quarters, and only one of them is being used. They can live there, and I'll keep an eye on them.'

'I could hardly put you out like that,' Olofson says.

'In the world of foreign aid we talk about "mutual benefit",' says Håkansson. 'You give Sida and the Zambians your hill in return for a reasonable compensation. I put an unused servants' dwelling at the disposal of two girls eager to learn. It will also contribute to Zambia's development. You can rest easy. I have daughters myself, older of course, but I remember when they were that age. I belong to a generation of men who watch over their daughters.'

'I would support them, naturally,' Olofson says.

'I know that,' says Håkansson.

Once again Olofson finds no reason to refuse an offer from Lars Håkansson. And yet something is bothering him, something he can't put his finger on. There are no simple solutions in Africa, he thinks. Swedish efficiency is unnatural here. But Håkansson is convincing, and his offer is ideal.

They return to the starting point. Håkansson is in a hurry, he has to drive on to another possible location for a link station.

'It'll be harder there,' he says. 'I'll have to deal with a whole town and a local chieftain. It's going to take time. Aid work would be easy if we didn't have to deal with Africans.'

He tells Olofson that he'll be back to Kalulushi in about a week.

'Think about my offer. The daughters are welcome.'

'I'm grateful to you,' Olofson says.

'An absolutely meaningless feeling,' says Håkansson. 'When I solve practical dilemmas, it gives me the sense that life is manageable in spite of everything. One time long ago I was climbing up power poles with spikes on my boots. I fixed telephone lines and connected voices. It was a time when Zambian copper streamed out to the world's telecom industries. Then I studied to be an engineer, divorced my wife, and went out into the world. But whether I'm here or climbing up poles, I solve practical problems. Life is what it is.'

Olofson feels a sudden joy at having met Lars Håkansson. He has encountered Swedes regularly during his years in Africa, most often technicians employed by large international corporations, but the meetings were always brief. Maybe Håkansson is different.

'You're welcome to stay here when you're in the Copperbelt,' Olofson tells him. 'I have plenty of room. I live alone.'

'I'll keep that in mind,' says Håkansson.

They shake hands, Håkansson gets into his car, and Olofson waves as he departs.

His energy has returned. Suddenly he's ready to fight his fear, no longer tempted to surrender to it. He gets into his car and makes a comprehensive inspection of the farm, checking fences, feed supplies, and the quality of the eggs. Together with his drivers he studies maps and plans alternative routes to avoid the hijacking of their lorries. He studies foremen's reports and orders, issues warnings, and fires a night watchman who has come to work drunk on numerous occasions.

I can do this, he thinks. I have 200 people working on the farm, over a thousand people are dependent on the hens laying their eggs. I take responsibility and make the whole thing work. If I let myself be scared off by the meaningless murders of Ruth and Werner and my dog, a thousand people would be thrown into uncertainty, poverty, maybe even starvation.

People who dress like leopards don't know what they're doing.

In the name of political discontent they're pushing their brothers down the precipice.

He shoves the dirty foremen's reports away, puts his feet up on a pile of egg cartons, and lets his mind work on an idea.

I'll start a back fire, he thinks. Even if the Africans are evidently no longer afraid of German shepherds, they have great respect and fear of people who show courage. Maybe Werner Masterton's fate was brought about by the fact that he had softened, turned vague and yielding; an old man who worried about the trouble he was having pissing.

He finds himself thinking a racist thought. The African's instinct is like the hyena's, he tells himself. In Sweden the word 'hyena' is an insult, an expression for contemptuous weakness, for a parasitic person. For the Africans the hyena's hunting methods are natural. Prey left behind or lost by others is something desirable. A wounded and defenceless animal is something to pounce on. Perhaps Werner Masterton appeared a wounded man after all these years in Africa. The blacks could see it and they attacked. Ruth could never have put up any resistance.

He thinks back to his conversation with Peter Motombwane, and makes his decision. He calls in one of the clerks waiting outside the hut.

'Go and fetch me Eisenhower Mudenda,' he says. 'At once.'

The man stands there, uncertain.

'What are you waiting for?' Olofson shouts. 'Eisenhower Mudenda! *Sanksako!* You'll get a kick in the *mataku* if he isn't here in five minutes.'

A few minutes later Eisenhower Mudenda stands inside the dark hut. He's breathing hard and Olofson can tell that the man has been running.

'Sit down,' says Olofson, pointing at a chair. 'But wipe yourself off first. I don't want chicken shit on the chair.'

Mudenda quickly wipes himself off and sits down on the edge of the chair. His disguise is excellent, Olofson thinks. An insignificant old man. But none of the Africans on this farm dares cross him. Even Motombwane is afraid of him.

For a brief moment he hesitates. The risk is too great, he thinks. If I start this back fire, there will be chaos. And yet he knows it is necessary; he has made his decision.

'Someone has killed one of my dogs,' he says. 'His head was nailed to a tree. But you probably know this already, don't you?'

'Yes, *Bwana*,' replies Mudenda.

The lack of expression, Olofson thinks. It says everything.

'Let's speak openly, Eisenhower,' Olofson says. 'You've been here for many years. For thousands of days you have gone to your hen house, and countless eggs have passed through your hands. Of course I know you're a sorcerer, a man who can do *muloji*. All the blacks are afraid of you, and none of them will say a word against you. But I'm a *bwana*, a *mzungu* that your *muloji* won't work on. Now I'm thinking of asking you for something, Eisenhower. You must regard this as an order, in the same way as if I tell you to work on your day off. Someone on this farm killed my dog. I want to know who it was. Maybe you already know. But I want to know too, and I want to know soon. If you don't tell me, I'll have to assume that you were the one who did it. And then you'll be sacked. Not even your *muloji* can prevent that. You'll have to leave your house, and you will never be allowed to show your face on the farm again. If you do, the police will take you away.'

I should have talked to him outside in the sun, thinks Olofson. I can't see his face in here.

'I can give *Bwana* his answer right now,' says Mudenda, and Olofson thinks he can hear something hard in his voice.

'Even better. I'm listening.'

'Nobody on this farm killed a dog, *Bwana*,' Mudenda says.

'People came in the night and then left again. I know who they are, but I can't say anything.'

'Why not?' Olofson asks.

'My knowledge comes to me in visions, *Bwana*,' Mudenda replies. 'Only sometimes can one reveal his visions. A vision can be turned into a poison that will kill my brain.'

'Use your *muloji*,' Olofson says. 'Create a counter-poison, tell me about your vision.'

'No, *Bwana*,' Mudenda says.

'Then you are fired,' says Olofson. 'At this instant your work on my farm is ended. By tomorrow, at dawn, you and your family must be out of your house. Now I'll pay you the wages I owe you.'

He places a pile of notes on the table.

'I will go, *Bwana*,' says Eisenhower Mudenda. 'But I will come back.'

'No,' Olofson says. 'Not if you don't want the police to take you away.'

'The police are black too, *Bwana*,' says Eisenhower Mudenda.

He picks up the stack of bank notes and vanishes into the white sunlight. A test of power between reality and superstition, thinks Olofson. I have to believe that reality is stronger.

That night he barricades himself in his house and again waits for something to happen. He sleeps fitfully on top of the covers of his bed. The dead and dismembered bodies of Werner and Ruth wake him time and time again. Exhausted and pale, he lets Luka in at dawn. Black rain clouds are looming on the horizon.

'Nothing is as it should be, *Bwana*,' Luka says gravely.

'What?' Olofson asks.

'The farm is silent, *Bwana*,' replies Luka.

Olofson gets into his car and drives quickly towards the hen houses. The work stations are abandoned. Not a person in sight.

The eggs are ungathered, the feed chutes empty. Empty egg cartons lean against the wheels of the lorries. The keys are in the ignition.

The test of power, he thinks. The witch doctor and I appear in the arena. In a rage he gets back into his car. With screeching brakes he stops among the low mud houses. The men are sitting in groups at their fires, the women and children in the doorways. Naturally they've been waiting for me, he thinks. He calls over some of the older foremen.

'Nobody is working,' he says. 'Why not?'

The reply is silence, hesitant glances, fear.

'If everyone returns to work at once I won't even ask the reason,' he says. 'No one will be fired, no one will have his wages docked. But everyone has to return to work now.'

'We can't, *Bwana*,' says one of the oldest foremen.

'Why not?' Olofson asks again.

'Eisenhower Mudenda is no longer on the farm, *Bwana*,' the foreman goes on. 'Before he left he called us together and said that every egg that is now laid is a snake egg. If we touch the eggs we will be bitten by poisonous fangs. The farm will be overrun with snakes.'

Olofson thinks for a moment. Words won't help, he realises. He has to do something, something they can see with their own eyes.

He gets into his car and returns to the hen houses and gathers a carton of eggs. When he comes back he assembles the foremen around him. Without a word he crushes egg after egg, letting the whites and the yolks drip to the ground. The men shrink back, but he continues.

'No snakes,' he says. 'Normal eggs. Who sees a snake?'

But the foremen are unreachable.

'When *we* touch the eggs, *Bwana*, there will be snakes.'

Olofson holds out an egg, but no one dares touch it.

'You will lose your jobs,' he says. 'You will lose your houses, everything.'

'We don't believe that, *Bwana*.'

'Do you hear what I'm saying?'

'The hens must have feed, *Bwana*.'

'I'll find other workers. People are queueing up to work on a white farm.'

'Not when they hear about the snakes, *Bwana*.'

'There aren't any snakes.'

'We think there are, *Bwana*. That's why we're not working.'

'You're afraid of Eisenhower Mudenda. You're afraid of his *muloji*.'

'Eisenhower Mudenda is a smart man, *Bwana*.'

'He's no smarter than any of you.'

'He speaks to us through our forefathers, *Bwana*. We're Africans, you're a white *bwana*. You can't understand.'

'I'll sack you all if you don't go back to work.'

'We know that, *Bwana*.'

'I'll get workers from another part of the country.'

'Nobody will work on a farm where the hens lay snake eggs, *Bwana*.'

'I'm telling you, there are no eggs with snakes in them!'

'Only Eisenhower Mudenda can take away the snakes, *Bwana*.'

'I've fired him.'

'He's waiting to come back, *Bwana*.'

I'm losing, Olofson thinks. I'm losing the way the white man always loses in Africa. There's no way to start a back fire against superstition.

'Send for Mudenda,' he says and walks back to his car and drives to his mud hut.

Suddenly Mudenda stands like a silhouette in the doorway against the bright white sunlight.

'I won't ask you to sit down,' says Olofson. 'You have your job back. Actually I ought to force you to show the workers that there aren't any snakes in the eggs. But I won't do that. Tell the workers you have lifted your *muloji*. Go back to work, that's all.'

Eisenhower Mudenda walks out into the sun, and Olofson follows him.

'One more thing you should know. I don't admit that I'm defeated. One day there won't be any more *muloji*, and the blacks will turn against you and crush your head with their wooden clubs. I don't intend to come to your rescue.'

'That will never happen, *Bwana*,' says Eisenhower Mudenda.

'Hens will never lay eggs with snakes inside,' replies Olofson. 'What will you do when someone asks to see one of these snakes?'

The next day a dead cobra is lying on the front seat of Olofson's car. Eggshells are scattered around the dead snake . . .

Chapter Twenty-Two

Africa is still far away. But Hans Olofson is on his way. He still visits new, hostile territories, he has left the house by the river far behind, passed a student examination in the county seat and is now at the university in Uppsala, where he is supposed to be studying law.

To finance his studies he works three afternoons a week at Johannes Wickberg's gun shop in Stockholm. He knows more about the philosophy of skeet shooting than about the Code of Land Laws. He knows much more about the history of superior Italian shotguns, about the viscosity of weapons grease at low temperatures, than he does about Roman Law, which is the foundation of everything.

Now and then big-game hunters come into the gun shop, and they ask different and considerably odder questions than those he has to answer in the introductory law course. Are there black lions? He doesn't think so. But one day a man stands before him who claims to be called Stone, and insists that the black lion exists in the remote Kalahari Desert. Stone has come from Durban to see Wickberg. But Wickberg has gone to the customs house to solve a problem with the import of ammunition from the United States, and Hans Olofson is alone in the shop.

Stone's real name is Stenberg, and even though he has lived in Durban for many years, he comes originally from Tibro. For more than an hour he stays in the shop and tells Hans how he imagines his death. For many years he has suffered from a mysterious itch on his legs that keeps him wide awake at night. He has shown his affliction to doctors and to tall witch doctors, but nothing has helped. When he discovers that most of his internal organs have been severely attacked by parasites, he realises that his time is limited.

In the early 1920s he ventured out into the world as one of the promoters of Swedish ballbearings. He wound up staying in South Africa, dumbfounded by all the night sounds and the endless plains of the Transvaal. Eventually he left ballbearings behind and established an office for big-game hunting, Hunters Unlimited, and changed his name to Stone. But he still buys his guns from Wickberg, and so he travels to Sweden once a year, to Tibro to tend his parents' grave, and to Stockholm to buy weapons. He stands there in the shop telling all this to Hans Olofson. And when he leaves, Hans is certain that black lions do exist.

It's a day in the middle of April, 1969, as Stone stands there telling Hans about his life. For nine months Hans has travelled back and forth between Uppsala and Stockholm, between future studies and making a living. After nine months he still feels that he is in enemy territory, that he came from the north as an illegal immigrant and that one day he will be unmasked and chased back to his origins.

When he left the county seat behind, it was like finally climbing out of his own personal Iron Age. His tools were sharp and cold, and the teachers' questions hung over his head like raised axes. He had experienced the four years of study as if he were living on the dole. The scent of elkhound had never left him, the rented room had eaten its way into him, the flowered wallpaper had been carnivorous. He had made few friends in this scrubbed emptiness. But he had forced himself to persevere, and finally he passed an exam that surprised everyone, including himself. He felt as though his marks did not reflect his knowledge but instead were proof of his determination, as if he were an orienteer or an athlete.

That's also where the idea of studying law originates. Since he has no desire to be a woodcutter, he decides that maybe he can be a lawyer. He has a vague sense that the law might give him the tools to survive. The laws are rules that have been tested and interpreted down through the generations. They clarify the boundaries of decency, specify how the unimpeachable person may act. But perhaps another horizon is also hiding there. Maybe he could become the sworn spokesman of mitigating circumstance?

He once felt as though his whole life ought to be viewed as a mitigating circumstance. From my upbringing I received neither self-knowledge nor a sense of purpose, he thought. Now I try to move through hostile terrain without surrendering to confusion. Maybe the fact that I didn't remain in the place of my birth could be regarded as a mitigating circumstance. But why didn't I stay there? Why didn't I grab a pickaxe and bury the roots, marry one of the bridesmaids?

My inheritance is a dusty full-rigger in a glass case, the smell of wet woollen socks drying over the stove. A mother who couldn't stand it any longer and vanished on a train heading south; a haggard seaman who managed to drift ashore where there wasn't any sea.

As the defender of mitigating circumstance perhaps I can remain unnoticed. I, Hans Olofson, possess an incontrovertible talent. The art of finding the best hiding places.

The summer after his examination he returns to the house by

the river. There is no one to meet him at the station, and when he enters the kitchen it smells newly scrubbed, and his father is sitting at the table regarding him with glazed eyes.

He sees that he is beginning to resemble his father more and more. The face, the tangled hair, the stooping spine. But do I also resemble him inside? If so, where will I drift ashore?

In a surge of responsibility he tries to take care of his father, who is obviously drinking more often and more than before. He sits down across from him at the kitchen table and asks if he isn't going to take off soon. What happened to the boat that sailed along the coast?

He barely receives an answer. His father's head hangs as if his neck were already broken.

One single time Hans crosses the bridge to Janine's house. It's late at night, the bright Norrland night, and he thinks he hears her trombone for a brief dreadful moment. The neglected currant bushes glow. He leaves the place and never returns. He avoids her grave in the churchyard.

One day he bumps into Nyman the courthouse caretaker. On an impulse he asks about Sture. Nyman knows. After ten years Sture is still lying motionless in bed in a hospital for the incurable outside Västervik.

Restlessly he wanders along the river. He walks with his torn-up roots in his hand, searching for a suitable plot of ground to set them down in. But in Uppsala it's all pavement, isn't it? How can he plant them there?

At the beginning of August he can finally take off, and he does so with a great sense of relief. Again circumstances lead him further away. If he hadn't had Ture Wickberg as a classmate he wouldn't have been given the chance to finance his studies by working in Ture's uncle's gun shop in Stockholm.

His father accompanies him to the station, and stands on the platform carefully watching his son's two suitcases. Suddenly Hans feels a great fury. Who would steal his luggage?

The train lurches forward and Erik Olofson raises his hand awkwardly to wave goodbye. Hans sees him moving his mouth but he can't hear what he's saying. As the train rattles across the iron bridge, Hans is standing at the window. The iron beams whirl past, the water of the river runs towards the sea. Then he closes the window, as if he were lowering an iron curtain. He is alone in the gloom of the compartment. He has a fleeting sensation that he is in a hiding place where no one will ever find him.

But the conductors of Swedish Railways do not place philosophical importance on closed, dark compartments. The door flies open and Hans feels caught out in the depths of a great secret, and he hands over his ticket as if begging for mercy. The conductor punches it and tells him how to change trains in the early dawn.

In a wounded and lacerated world there is no room for the scared rabbits of anxiety, he thinks. The feeling refuses to let him go, even when he has commuted back and forth between Uppsala and Stockholm for almost ten months.

Hans finds a place to live with a man who has a passionate love of fungi and works as a lecturer in biology. A lovely attic room in an old wooden building becomes his new hiding place. The building lies in an overgrown garden, and he decides that the lecturer has planted his own private jungle.

Time reigns supreme in the house. Clocks hang on all the walls. Hans imagines the clockwork menagerie, a ticking, rattling, sighing orchestra that calibrates time and the noble insignificance of life. In window niches the sand runs through hourglasses that are constantly turned over. An elderly mother wanders about in the ticking rooms, taking care of the clocks.

The clocks were inherited, he is told. The lecturer's father, an eccentric inventor who in his youth made a fortune on combine harvesters, spent his life passionately collecting timepieces.

The first months of that autumn he will remember as a long drawn-out agony when he seemed to understand nothing. The law seems an unknown cuneiform script for which he completely lacks a personal code. Each day he is prepared to give up, but he mobilises his maximum endurance and finally succeeds, in early November, in cracking the shell and penetrating into the darkness behind the words.

At about the same time he decides to change his appearance. He grows a beard and clips his hair to a downy fringe all over his skull. In photo booths he turns the stool into position, feeds in one-krona coins, and then studies his features. But behind his new look he can still see the face of Erik Olofson.

He imagines dejectedly how his coat of arms might look. A snowdrift, a chained elkhound, against a background of infinite forests. He will never escape it.

One time when he is alone in the ticking house he decides to investigate the secrets of the fungus-loving lecturer and his time-keeping mother. Perhaps I could raise this to a lifelong mission, he thinks. Peeping. I will take on the form of a field mouse and break out of my ingenious system of secret passages. But he finds nothing in the chiffoniers and chests of drawers.

He sits down among the ticking clocks and with an utter seriousness attempts to understand himself. He has wound up here, from the brickworks, via the span of the iron bridge. But after that? Onward, to become a lawyer, the defender of mitigating circumstance, simply because he wouldn't be any good as a woodcutter. I possess neither meekness nor impatience, he thinks. I was born into a time when everything is splitting apart. I have to make a decision. I must make up my mind to continue with what I decided to do. Maybe I will find my mother. My indecision

249

is in itself a hiding place, and there's a risk that I'll never find my way out.

On precisely this day in April when Stone from Tibro has told Hans about his internal parasites and the black lions in the Kalahari, a telegram lies waiting for him when he returns to the house of the clocks. It's from his father, telling him that he's coming to Stockholm on the morning train.

His rage is instant. Why is he coming here? He'd thought that his father was securely chained up beyond the fir ridges. Why is he on his way here? The telegram gives no reason.

Early in the morning he hurries to Stockholm and is waiting on the platform when the Norrland train pulls in. He sees his father cautiously peering out from one of the last cars. In his hand he holds the bag that Hans himself used when he travelled to the county seat. Under his arm he has a package wrapped in brown paper.

'Well now, there you are,' says Erik Olofson when he spies his son. 'I didn't know if the telegram had arrived.'

'What would you have done then? And what are you doing here?'

'It's those Vaxholm boats again. They need seamen now.'

Hans leads him to a cafeteria in the station.

'Do they serve pilsner here?' his father asks.

'No, no pilsner. You'll have coffee. Now tell me!'

'There isn't much to tell. I wrote and got an answer. I have to be at their office at nine o'clock.'

'Where are you going to live?'

'I thought there might be some sort of boarding house.'

'What have you got in the package? It's leaking!'

'A moose steak.'

'A moose steak?'

'Yep.'

'It's not hunting season now, is it?'

'Well, it's a moose steak anyway. I brought it for you.'

'There's blood dripping out of the package. People will think you murdered somebody.'

'Who would that be?'

'Good Lord.'

They find a room at the Central Hotel. Hans watches his father unpack his clothes. He recognises them all, has seen them all before.

'Make sure you give yourself a good shave before you go there. And no pilsners!'

His father hands him a letter and Hans sees that the Vaxholm boats have an office on Strandvägen.

After Erik has shaved they set off.

'I borrowed a picture of Nyman's children. It's so fuzzy you can't really see anything. So it'll do fine.'

'Do you still think you can show pictures of other people's children?'

'Sailors are supposed to have a lot of children. It's expected.'

'Why didn't you tell my mother that?'

'I thought I'd ask around about her. You haven't seen her, by any chance, have you?'

Hans stops dead in his tracks. 'What do you mean by that?'

'Just wondering.'

'Why would I have seen her? Where would I have seen her?'

'There are a lot of people living here. She must be somewhere.'

'I don't understand what you mean.'

'Then we won't talk about it any more.'

'I don't even know what she looks like.'

'You've seen pictures, though.'

'But they're twenty-five years old. People change. Would you recognise her if she came walking down the street?'

'Of course I would.'

'The hell.'

'Then we won't talk about it any more.'

'Why have you never tried to find her?'

'You don't run after people who just up and leave like that.'

'But she was your wife! My mother!'

'She still is.'

'What do you mean?'

'We never got divorced.'

'You're still married?'

'I should think so.'

When they reach Strandvägen and there's still half an hour to go before nine o'clock, Hans takes his father into a café.

'Do they serve pilsner here?'

'No pilsners. You'll have coffee. And now let's take it from the top. I'm twenty-five years old, I've never seen my mother other than in bad photographs. I don't know a thing about her except that she got fed up and left. I've wondered, I've worried, I've missed her and I've hated her. You've never said a word. Not one word.'

'I've been thinking about her too.'

'What?'

'I'm not that good with words.'

'Why did she leave? You must know. You must have brooded about it for as long as I have. You didn't get a divorce, didn't remarry. In some way you've continued to live with her. Deep inside you've been waiting for her to come back. You must have some explanation, don't you?'

'What time is it?'

'You have to answer!'

'She must have been someone else.'

'What do you mean, "someone else"?'

'Someone other than I thought.'

'And what exactly did you think?'

'I don't remember.'

'Good Lord.'

'It won't do any good to worry about it.'

'For twenty-five years you haven't had a woman.'

'What do you know about that?'

'What do you mean?'

'That has nothing to do with it. What time is it? You have to show up on the dot with ship owners.'

'So who?'

'If you really want to know, I've met Nyman's wife from time to time. But you keep your mouth shut about it. Nyman's a nice bloke.'

Hans can't believe his ears. 'Are those my sisters and brothers?'

'Who?'

'Nyman's children. Are they my sisters and brothers?'

'Those are Nyman's children.'

'How can you be sure?'

'We only saw each other when she was pregnant,' Erik says simply. 'You learn these things. There can never be shared paternity.'

'And you expect me to believe this?'

'I don't expect anything. I'm just telling you the truth.'

Hans stays in the café while his father visits the ship owner. My father, he thinks. I evidently never knew a thing about him.

After half an hour Erik comes back.

'How'd it go?'

'Good. But I didn't get a job.'

'So it didn't go so well then.'

'They said they'd let me know.'

'When?'

'When they need seamen.'

'I thought they needed to hire people now?'

'They must have hired someone else.'

'Are you satisfied with that?'

'I've been waiting for years,' says Erik with sudden sharpness. 'I've waited and wished and almost given up. But now at least I've tried.'

'What are we going to do now?'

'I'm going home tonight. But now I want to have a pilsner.'

'What are we going to do for the rest of the day?'

'I thought you were studying at the university.'

'I am. But now you're here in town and we haven't seen each other for a long time.'

'How are your studies?'

'All right.'

'I see.'

'You didn't answer my question.'

'What question?'

'What do you want to do today?'

'I already told you. I want a pilsner. Then I'll go home.'

They spend the day in the hotel room. A pale autumn sun shines through the curtains.

'If I find her,' says Hans, 'what should I say?'

'Nothing from me,' Erik says firmly.

'What was her name before you married?'

'Karlsson.'

'Mary Karlsson or Mary Olofson from Askersund? Anything else?'

'She had a dog named Buffalo when she was a child. I remember she told me that.'

'That dog must have been dead for fifty years by now.'

'Its name was Buffalo anyway.'

'Is that all you know?'

'Yep.'

'A goddamn dog named Buffalo?'

'That's what it was called, I remember that clearly.'

Hans accompanies him to the train. I'm going to look for her, he thinks. I can't have a mother who's a riddle. Either he's lying, hiding something, or else my mother is a strange woman.

'When are you coming home?' his father asks.

'In the summer. Not before. Maybe you'll be a seaman again before that, what do you think?'

'Could be. Could be.'

Hans takes the train with him as far as Uppsala. He has the moose steak under his arm.

'So who's poaching?' he asks.

'Nobody you know,' says Erik.

Hans goes back to the house of the clocks. I can't give up, he thinks. Nothing can really prevent me from becoming the defender of mitigating circumstance. I'll build barricades inside of me.

I can't give up.

Chapter Twenty-Three

He sees the dead snake.

What is it saying? What message does it bring? Sorcerers interpret their ancestors' voices, and the black masses huddle in terrified submission. He knows he should get going, leave the farm, leave Africa.

Suddenly it's incomprehensible to him. Almost twenty years in Africa. An unreal, unbelievable life. What was it I thought I could achieve? Superstition is real, that's what I always forget. I keep deceiving myself with the white point of view. I've never been able to grasp the way the blacks think. I have lived here for almost twenty years without realising on what ground I'm actually standing. Ruth and Werner Masterton died because they refused to understand.

With a feeling that he is no longer able to cope, he gets into his car and drives to Kitwe. So he can get some sleep he checks into the Hotel Edinburgh, pulls the curtains and lies naked on top of the sheet. A violent thunderstorm passes through and the lightning flashes flicker across his face. The torrent pounds like the surf against the window.

Suddenly he longs for home, a melancholy hunger for the clear water of the river, the motionless ridges of firs. Maybe that was what the white snake wanted to tell him. Or was it giving him his last warning?

I ran away from my own life, he thinks. In the beginning there was possibility; growing up with the smell of elkhounds, that may have been meagre but that was still my very own heritage. I could have worked towards realising an ambition, watching over the mitigating circumstance. Chance events that were stronger than I was created my confusion. I accepted Judith Fillington's offer without understanding what it really involved. Now that I've already taken off my shoes in the vestibule of middle age, I'm afraid that my life is shipwrecked. There is always something else I want. Right now to go back, to start over from the beginning if it were possible.

Restlessly he gets dressed and goes down to the hotel bar. He nods to some familiar faces and discovers Peter Motombwane in a corner, bent over a newspaper. He sits down at his table without telling him about the events at the farm.

'What's going on?' he asks. 'New riots? New plundering raids? When I came to Kitwe everything seemed calm.'

'The authorities have released an emergency store of maize,' Motombwane says. 'Sugar is on the way from Zimbabwe, Canadian wheat is in Dar-es-Salaam. The politicians have decided not to have any more riots. Many people have been put in jail, and the president is hiding in the State House. Everything will calm down again, unfortunately. A mountain of sacks of corn meal is enough to delay an African riot for quite a while. The politicians can sleep securely with their fortunes, and you can take down your barricades from the doors and sleep soundly again.'

'How do you know that I build barricades?' Olofson asks.

'Even with no imagination I would guess that,' replies Motombwane.

'But Werner and Ruth Masterton will not get their lives back,' Olofson says.

'At least that's something,' replies Motombwane.

Olofson starts. He feels the rage coming. 'What do you mean?' he asks.

'I was thinking of driving out to see you someday,' Motombwane says unperturbed. 'I'm a journalist, and I've investigated the twilight land that Rustlewood Farm has become. Truths are coming to light, and no one is afraid that the dead will come back to haunt them since their heads were cut off their bodies. The black workers are talking, an unknown world is emerging. I thought I'd drive out to see you someday and tell you about it.'

'Why not now?' Olofson asks.

'I like it on your farm,' replies Motombwane. 'I would have liked to live there. On your terrace one can talk about everything.'

Olofson realises that there is a subtext to Peter Motombwane's words. I don't know him, he thinks. Beyond our conversations, evenings spent in each other's company, the fundamental fact keeps returning that he's black and I'm a white European. The differences between the continents are never so great or blatant as when they are represented by two individuals.

'Two dead, dismembered bodies,' says Motombwane. 'Two Europeans who lived here for many, many years, murdered and cut to bits by unknown blacks. I decided to work backwards, to search for light among the shadows. Perhaps because I might have been wrong, it mightn't have been pure chance that it was the Mastertons who were killed. I start my investigations and an underlying world begins to surface. A farm is always a closed system; the white owners put up both visible and invisible fences around themselves and their workers. I talk with the blacks, put together fleeting rumours into something that suddenly starts to be readable and clear. I stand before an assumption that is slowly confirmed. Werner and Ruth Masterton were hardly murdered by chance. I can never be sure; coincidences and conscious decisions can also be woven together with invisible threads.'

'Tell me,' says Olofson. 'Tell me the story of the shadows.'

'A picture began to emerge,' says Motombwane. 'Two people with an unreasoning hatred of black people. A terror regime with constant threats and punishments. In earlier times we were beaten with whips made from hippopotamus skins. Today that would be an impossibility. The whips are invisible; they leave their marks only in the sensitive skin of the mind and the heart. The blacks who worked at Rustlewood Farm endured a constant barrage of humiliations and threats of dismissal, degrading transfers, fines, and lockouts. A South African territory reveals itself right here, in this country, an utterly unbounded racism. Ruth and Werner Masterton's primary nourishment was the contempt they cultivated.'

'I don't believe it,' says Olofson. 'I knew them. You can't see through the lies you're dragging up out of the shadow world you've been visiting.'

'I'm not asking you to believe me,' says Motombwane. 'What I'm giving you is the black truth.'

'A lie will never be true, no matter how many times you repeat it,' Olofson replies. 'Truths don't follow race; at least they shouldn't do so in a friendly conversation.'

'The various accounts coincided,' Motombwane says. 'Individual details were confirmed. According to what I now know, I have to shrug my shoulders at their fate. I believe it was justified.'

'That conclusion makes our friendship impossible,' says Olofson, getting to his feet.

'Has it ever really been possible?' asks Motombwane, unmoved.

'I thought so,' Olofson says. 'At least it was my sincere hope.'

'I'm not the one who's making something impossible,' says Motombwane. 'You're the one who prefers to deny a truth about dead people when it's right in front of you, instead of choosing a friendship with a living person. What you're doing now is taking a racist position. Actually, it surprises me.'

Olofson feels an urge to hit Motombwane. But he controls himself.

'What would you do without us?' he asks. 'Without the whites this country would fall apart. Those aren't my words, they're yours.'

'And I agree with them. But the collapse wouldn't be as great as you imagine. It would be extensive enough that a necessary transformation would have to be pushed through. A revolt that has been suppressed for far too long might break out. In the best case, we would succeed in ripping away all the European influences that continue to oppress us even though we ourselves are not aware of them. Then perhaps we could finally achieve our African independence.'

'Or else you'll chop each other's heads off,' says Olofson. 'Tribe against tribe, Bemba against Luvale, Kaonde against Luzi.'

'Anyway, that's our own problem,' says Motombwane. 'A problem that wasn't imposed on us by you.'

'Africa is sinking,' Olofson says excitedly. 'The future of this continent is already over. The only thing that remains is a deeper and deeper decay.'

'If you live long enough you'll realise that you're wrong,' replies Motombwane.

'According to all available calculations my life span is superior to yours,' says Olofson. 'No one will shorten it by raising a *panga* over my head, either.'

Theirs is a ragged and weary parting of ways. Olofson merely walks away, leaving Motombwane huddled in the shadows.

When he returns to his room and has slammed the door behind him, he feels sad and forlorn. The lonely dog barks inside him, and he suddenly sees his father's impotent scrubbing. Ending a friendship, he thinks. It's like breaking your own fingers. With Peter Motombwane I lose my most important link to Africa. I will miss our conversations, his clarification of why the black man's thoughts look the way they do. He lies down on the bed to think. Motombwane could be absolutely right, of course. What do I really know about Ruth and Werner? Almost twenty years ago we shared a compartment on the night train between Lusaka and Kitwe; they helped me along, took care of me when I came back from Mutshatsha. They never made a secret of their opposition to the transformation that Africa is undergoing; they always referred to the colonial times as the era that could have led Africa forward. They felt both betrayed and disappointed. But what about the brutality that Motombwane thought he had traced to their daily life?

Maybe he's right, Olofson thinks. Maybe there is a truth that I'm pushing away. He hurries back to the bar to try and reconcile with Peter Motombwane.

But the table is empty; one of the waiters says that he got up and left. Exhausted and sad, Olofson sleeps in his hotel bed.

When he eats breakfast in the morning, he is again reminded of Ruth and Werner. One of their neighbours, an Irishman named Behan, comes into the dining room and stops by his table. A will has been found in the blood-drenched house; a steel safe survived the fire. A law firm in Lusaka is authorised to sell the farm and transfer the remaining profit to the British retirement home in Livingstone.

Behan tells him that the auction of the farm will be held in a fortnight. Many whites are prospective bidders; the farm will not be allowed to fall into black hands.

There's a war going on, Olofson thinks. A war that only occasionally becomes visible. But everywhere the racial hatred is alive – whites against the blacks and blacks against whites.

He returns to his farm. A violent downpour makes visibility through the windscreen nonexistent and forces him to stop on the verge just before the farm. A black woman with two small children crosses the road in front of the car, covered with mud and water. He recognises her as the wife of one of the workers on the farm. She doesn't ask for a ride, he thinks. Nor do I offer her one. Nothing unites us, not even a fierce downpour, when only one of us has an umbrella. People's barbaric behaviour always has a human face, he thinks vaguely to himself. That's what makes the barbarity so inhumane.

The rain drums on the roof of the car; he waits alone for it to ease. I could decide here and now, he thinks. Decide to leave. Sell the farm, go back to Sweden. Exactly how much money Patel has weaseled out of me I have no idea, but I'm not penniless. This egg farm has given me a few years' breathing space. Something about Africa scares me just as much now as the day I stepped out of the plane at Lusaka International Airport. Twenty years' experience of this continent hasn't changed a thing, since I never questioned white assumptions. What would I actually say if someone asked me to explain what is happening on this continent? I have my memories – adventurous, gruesome, exotic. But I don't have any real knowledge.

The rain stops abruptly, a wall of clouds rises and the landscape starts to dry out again. Before he starts the engine he decides to spend an hour each day planning his future.

A perfect calm rests over the farm; nothing seems to have happened. By chance he encounters Eisenhower Mudenda, bowing to the ground. A white man in Africa is someone who takes part in a play he knows nothing about, he thinks. Only the blacks know the next line. Every evening he builds his barricades, checks his weapons, and chooses a different bedroom. Daybreak is always a relief, and he wonders how long he'll be able to endure. I don't even know my own breaking point, he thinks. But it must exist.

Lars Håkansson returns one afternoon, pulling up in his shiny car outside the mud hut. Olofson discovers that he's glad to see him. Håkansson says he'll stay two nights, and Olofson quickly decides to arrange his internal barricades in silence. They sit on the terrace at dusk.

'Why does anyone come to Africa?' Olofson asks. 'Why does anyone force himself out of his own environment? I assume that I'm asking you because I'm so tired of asking myself.'

'I hardly think that an aid expert is the right person to ask,' Håkansson replies. 'At any rate not if you want an honest answer. Behind the slick surface with its idealistic motives there's a landscape of selfish and economic reasons. Signing a contract to work overseas is like getting a chance to become well-to-do while at the same time living a pleasant life. The Swedish welfare state follows you everywhere and is elevated to undreamed-of heights when it comes to well-paid aid experts. If you have children the Swedish state takes care of the best education opportunities; you live in a marginal world where practically anything is possible. Buy a car with duty-free import when you arrive in a country like Zambia, sell it on contract, and then you have money to live on and don't need to touch your salary, which swells and flourishes in a bank account somewhere else in the world. You have a house with a pool and servants, you live as if you had shipped a whole Swedish manor house with you. I've calculated that in one month I earn as much as my maid in the house would make in sixty years. I'm counting what my foreign currency is worth on the black market. Here in Zambia there is probably not a single Swedish expert who goes to a bank and changes his money at the official rate. We don't do as much good as our incomes would lead you to believe. The day the Swedish taxpayers fully realise what their money is going on, the sitting government will be toppled at the next election. The taxpaying Swedish working class has after many years accepted what is called 'aid to under-developed countries'. Sweden, after all, is one of the few countries in the world where the concept of solidarity still holds power. But naturally they want their taxes used in the proper way. And that happens very rarely. The history of Swedish aid is a reef with innumerable shipwrecked projects on it, many scandalous, a few noticed and exposed by journalists, and even more buried and hushed up. Swedish aid smells like a pile of dead fish. I can say this because I feel that my own conscience is clear. After all, helping to develop communications is a way to bring Africa closer to the rest of the world.'

'People used to talk about Sweden as the self-appointed conscience of the world,' says Olofson from his chair in the dark.

'Those days are long gone,' says Håkansson. 'Sweden's role is insignificant; the Swedish prime minister who was murdered was possibly an exception. Swedish money is sought after, of course; political naïveté results in the fact that a huge number of black politicians and businessmen have amassed large private fortunes with Swedish aid funds. In Tanzania I talked with a politician who had retired and was old enough to say what he liked. He owned a castle in France which he had partially financed with Swedish aid money intended for water projects in the poorest parts of the country. He talked about an informal Swedish association among the politicians in the country. A group of men who met regularly and reported on how they most easily had been able to put aid money from Sweden into their own pockets. I don't know if this story is true, but it's possible, of course. That politician wasn't particularly cynical, either. To be an African politician is a legitimate opportunity for developing capital. The fact that it eventually hurts the poorest people in the country is merely an unwritten rule of the game.'

'I have a hard time believing what you're saying,' Olofson says.

'That's precisely why it's possible for it to continue year after year,' says Håkansson. 'The situation is too incredible for anyone to believe, let alone do something about.'

'One question is still unanswered,' says Olofson. 'Why did you come out here yourself?'

'A divorce that was a mental bloodbath. My wife left me in the most banal way. She met a Spanish estate agent in Valencia. My life, which until then I had never questioned, was shattered as if a lorry had driven right into my consciousness. For two years I lived in a state of emotional paralysis. Then I left, went abroad. All my courage to face life had rusted away. I think I intended to go abroad and die. But I'm still alive.'

'What about the two girls?' Olofson asks.

'It's like I said. They're most welcome. I'll watch out for them.'

'It's a while yet before their courses start,' Olofson says. 'But I imagine they'll need time to get settled. I thought I'd drive them down to Lusaka in a few weeks.'

'Please do,' says Håkansson.

What is it that's bothering me? Olofson wonders. An uneasy feeling that scares me. Lars Håkansson is a reassuring Swede, honest enough to tell me that he's taking part in something that could only be described as scandalous. I recognise his Swedish helpfulness. And yet there's something that makes me nervous.

The next day they both go to visit Joyce Lufuma and her daughters. When Olofson tells the eldest daughters, they start dancing with joy. Håkansson stands by, smiling, and Olofson realises that a white man's solicitude is a guarantee for Joyce

Lufuma. I'm worrying for nothing, he thinks. Maybe because I don't have any children of my own. But this too represents a truth about this contradictory continent. For Joyce Lufuma, Lars Håkansson and I are the best conceivable guarantee for her daughters. Not merely because we are *mzunguz*, rich men. She has an utterly unwavering trust in us, because of our skin colour.

Two weeks later Olofson drives the two daughters to Lusaka. Marjorie, the eldest, sits next to him in the front seat, Peggy behind him. Their beauty is blinding, their joy in life brings a lump to his throat. Still, I'm doing something, he thinks, I'm seeing to it that these two young people are not forced to have their lives thwarted for no reason, subjected to far too many childbirths in far too few years, to poverty and privation, to lives that end too soon.

Their reception at Håkansson's house is reassuring. The cottage he puts at the disposal of the two girls is freshly painted and well equipped. Marjorie stands looking at the light switch as if in a dream; for the first time in her life she will have electricity.

Olofson decides that the vague unease he felt means nothing. He is projecting his own anxiety on to other people. He spends the evening at Håkansson's house. Through his bedroom window he can see Marjorie and Peggy, shadows glimpsed behind thin curtains. He remembers arriving in the county seat from his hometown, his first time away, possibly the most crucial journey of all.

The next day he signs a deed of conveyance for his hill, and leaves his English bank account number. Before he leaves Lusaka he stops on a whim outside the Zambia Airways office on Cairo Road and picks up a timetable of the airline's European flights.

The long trip back to Kalulushi is interrupted by thunderstorms that erase all visibility. Not until late that night does he turn in through the gates of his farm. The night watchman comes towards him in the glare of the headlights. He doesn't recognise the man, and has a fleeting thought that it's a bandit dressed in the night watchman's uniform. My guns, he thinks desperately. But the night watchman is the person he says he is, and at close range Olofson knows him.

'Welcome home, *Bwana*,' he says.

I'll never know if he really means it, Olofson thinks. His words could just as well mean that he's welcoming me so that he'll have a chance to cut my heart right out of my body.

'Everything quiet?' he asks.

'Nothing has happened, *Bwana*.'

Luka is waiting for him, and dinner is waiting. He sends Luka home and sits down at the table. The meal might be poisoned – the thought comes out of nowhere. I'll be found dead, a sloppy autopsy will be done, and no poison will ever be detected.

He shoves the tray away, turns out the light, and sits in the dark. From the attic he can hear the scraping of bat wings. A spider hurries across his hand. He suddenly knows that his breaking point is near. Like an attack of dizziness, an approaching whirlwind of unresolved feelings and thoughts.

He sits for a long time in the dark before he grasps that he is about to have an attack of malaria. His joints start to ache, his head is pounding, and the fever shoots up in his body. Quickly he builds his barricades, pulls cupboards in front of the front door, checks the windows, and picks a bedroom where he lies down with his pistol. He takes a quinine pill and slowly drifts off to sleep.

A leopard is chasing him in his dreams. He sees that it is Luka, dressed in a bloody leopard skin. The malaria attack chases him into a chasm. When he wakes in the morning, he realises that the attack was mild. He gets out of bed, dresses quickly, and goes to open the door for Luka. He pushes away a cupboard and realises that he still has his pistol in his hand. He has slept with his finger on the trigger all night. I'm starting to lose control, he thinks. Everywhere I sense threatening shadows, invisible *pangas* constantly at my throat. My Swedish background leaves me unable to handle the fear I keep repressing. My terror is an enslaved emotion that is about to break free once and for all. The day that happens, I will have reached my breaking point. Then Africa will have conquered me, finally, irrevocably.

He forces himself to eat breakfast and then drive to the mud hut. The black clerks, who are hunched over delivery reports and orders, stand up and say good morning to him.

That day Olofson realises that the most simple actions are causing him great difficulty. Each decision causes him abrupt attacks of doubt. He tells himself that he's tired, that he ought to turn over responsibility to one of his trusted foremen and take a trip, give himself some time off.

In the next moment he begins to suspect that Eisenhower Mudenda is slowly poisoning him. The dust on his desk becomes a powder that gives off noxious vapours. Quickly he decides to put an extra padlock on the door of the mud hut at night. An empty egg carton falling from the top of a stack provokes a meaningless outburst of rage. The black workers watch him with inquisitive eyes. A butterfly that lands on his shoulder makes him jump, as if someone had put a hand on him in the dark.

That night he lies awake. Emptiness spreads out its desolate landscape inside him. He starts to cry, and soon he is shouting out loud into the darkness. I'm losing control, he thinks when the weeping has passed. These feelings come out of nowhere, attacking me and distorting my judgement. He looks at his watch and sees it's just past midnight. He gets up, sits in a chair, and begins to read a book taken at random from the collection Judith Fillington left behind. The German shepherds pace back and forth outside the house; he can hear their growling, the cicadas, lone birds calling from the river. He reads page after page without understanding a word, looks at his watch often, and waits for daybreak.

Just before three he falls asleep in the chair, the revolver resting on his chest. He wakes up abruptly and listens into the darkness. The African night is still. A dream, he thinks. Something I dreamed yanked me up to the surface. Nothing happened, everything is quiet. The silence, he thinks. That's what woke me up. Something has happened, the silence is unnatural. He feels the fear coming, his heart is pounding, and he grabs his pistol and listens into the darkness.

The cicadas are chirruping but the German shepherds are quiet. Suddenly he is sure that something is happening outside his house in the dark. He runs through the silence to get his shotgun. With shaking hands he shoves shells into the two barrels and takes off the safety. The whole time he is listening, but the dogs remain quiet. Their growling is gone, the sound of their paws has stopped. There are people outside in the dark, he thinks in desperation. Now they're coming after me. Again he runs through the empty rooms and lifts the telephone receiver. The line is dead. Then he knows, and he's so scared that he almost loses control of his breathing. He runs up the stairs to the top floor, grabs a pile of ammunition lying on a chair in the hallway, and continues into the skeleton room. The single window has no curtains. He peers cautiously into the darkness. The lamps on the terrace cast a pale light across the courtyard. He can't see the dogs anywhere.

The lamps suddenly go out and he hears a faint clinking from one of the glass covers. He stares out into the darkness. For a few brief seconds he's sure he hears footsteps. He forces himself to think. They'll try to get in downstairs, he tells himself. When they realise that I'm up here they'll smoke me out. Again he runs down the hall, down the stairs, and listens at the two outer doors that are blockaded by cabinets.

The dogs, he thinks in despair. What have they done to the dogs? He keeps moving between the doors, imagining that the attack could come from two directions at once. Suddenly it occurs to him that the bathroom window has no steel bars on it. It's a small window, but a thin man could probably squeeze through. Carefully he pushes open the bathroom door; the shotgun is shaking in his hands. I can't hesitate, he tells himself. If I see someone I have to aim and shoot. The bathroom window is untouched and he goes back to the doors.

A scraping sound comes from the terrace. The roof, he thinks. They're trying to climb up to the top floor by going on to the roof of the terrace. Again he runs upstairs. Two guest room windows face the roof of the terrace, both with steel gratings. Two rooms that are almost never used. Cautiously he pushes open the door to the first room, gropes his way over to the window, and runs his fingers over the thin iron bars that are anchored in cement. He leaves the room and pushes open the next door. The scraping noise from the terrace roof is coming closer. He fumbles through the dark and stretches out his hand to feel the steel grating. His fingertips touch the windowpane. The steel grating is gone. Someone has taken it off.

Luka, he thinks. Luka knows that I almost never go into these rooms. I'm going to kill him. I'll shoot him and throw him to the crocodiles. Wound him and let the crocs eat him alive. He retreats to the door, stretches out one hand for a chair that he knows is there, and sits down.

There are six shells in the shotgun; the pistol's clip holds eight. That will have to be enough, he thinks desperately. I'll never be able to reload with my hands shaking like this. The thought of Luka makes him suddenly calmer; the threat out in the dark has taken on a face. He feels a strange need growing inside. A need to point the gun at Luka and pull the trigger. The scraping on the terrace roof stops. Someone starts to shove a tool into the windowsill to prise open the window, probably one of his own tools. Now I'll shoot, he thinks. Now I'll blast both barrels through the window. His head and torso must be just behind the glass.

He stands up in the dark, takes a few steps forward, and raises the gun. His hands are shaking, so much that the barrels of the shotgun are dancing back and forth.

Hold your breath when you pull the trigger, he remembers. Now I'm going to kill a man. Even though I'm defending myself I'm doing it in cold blood. He lifts the gun, aware that he has tears in his eyes, holds his breath and fires, first one barrel, then the other.

The explosions thunder in his ears, splintered glass strikes him in the face. He takes a step back from the recoil and manages to reach the light switch with his shoulder. Instead of turning it off, he roars into the night and rushes up to the window he blasted away. Someone has turned on his car's headlights. He glimpses two black shadows in front of the car, and he thinks one of them is Luka. Quickly he aims and fires towards the two shadows. One of the shadows stumbles and the other disappears. He forgets that he still has two shells left in the shotgun, drops it to the floor, and takes his pistol out of his pocket. He fires four shots at the shadow who stumbled before he realises that it too is gone.

The terrace roof is covered in blood. He bends down for the shotgun, turns off the light, and shuts the door. Then he sits down on the floor in the hallway and starts to reload. His hands are shaking, his heart is thudding in his chest, and he is concentrating with all his might on feeding new ammunition into his guns. What he wants most of all is to be able to sleep.

He sits in the hallway and waits for dawn. In the first morning light he moves aside the cabinet and opens the kitchen door to the outside. The headlights of the car are out, the battery dead. Luka isn't there. Slowly he walks towards the terrace, still holding the shotgun in one hand.

The body is hanging by one foot from a rain gutter with its head in some of the cactuses that Judith Fillington once planted. A bloody leopard skin is draped around the shoulders of the dead African. With the handle of a rake Olofson pokes at the foot, loosening it so the body falls down. Even though almost the whole face has been shot off, he sees at once that it is Peter Motombwane. Flies are already buzzing in the blood. From the terrace he fetches a tablecloth and flings it over the body. By the car there is a pool of blood. A trail of blood leads away into the dense bush. There it suddenly stops.

When he turns around he sees Luka standing below the terrace. Immediately he raises the gun and walks towards him.

'You're still alive,' he says. 'But you won't be much longer. This time I won't miss.'

'What has happened, *Bwana?*' asks Luka.

'You're asking me?'

'Yes, *Bwana*.'

'When did you take off the window grating?'

'What grating, *Bwana?*'

'You know what I mean.'

'No I don't, *Bwana*.'

'Put your hands on your head and walk ahead of me!'

Luka does as he says and Olofson orders him upstairs. He shows him the gaping hole where the window has been shot away.

'You almost pulled it off,' says Olofson. 'But only almost. You knew that I never go in this room. You broke off the steel grating when I was away. I wouldn't have heard when you all sneaked inside. Then you could have crept down the stairs in the dark.'

'The grating is gone, *Bwana*. Someone has taken it off.'

'Not someone, Luka. You took it off.'

Luka looks him in the eyes and shakes his head.

'You were here last night,' Olofson says. 'I saw you and I took a shot at you. Peter Motombwane is dead. But who was the third man?'

'I was sleeping, *Bwana*,' Luka says. 'I woke up to shots from an *uta*. Many shots. Then I lay awake. Not until I was sure that *Bwana* Olofson had come out did I come here.'

Olofson raises the shotgun and takes off the safety.

'I'm going to shoot you,' he says. 'I'll shoot you if you don't tell me who the third man was. I'll kill you if you don't tell me what happened.'

'I was sleeping, *Bwana*,' Luka replies. 'I don't know anything. I see that Peter Motombwane is dead and that he has a leopard skin around his shoulders. I don't know who took off the grating.'

He's telling the truth, Olofson thinks suddenly. I'm sure that I saw him last night. No one else would have had the opportunity to take off the grating, no one else knew that I seldom go into that room. And yet I believe he's telling the truth.

They go back downstairs. The dogs, Olofson thinks. I forgot about the dogs. Just behind the water reservoir he finds them. Six bodies stretched out on the ground. Bits of meat are hanging out of their mouths. A powerful poison, he thinks. One bite and it was over. Peter Motombwane knew what he was doing.

He looks at Luka, who is staring at the dogs in disbelief. Of course there must be a plausible explanation, he tells himself. Peter Motombwane knows my house. Sometimes he waited for me alone. The dogs too. The dogs knew him. It could be as Luka says, that he was sleeping and woke up when I fired the gun. I could have been mistaken. I imagined that Luka would be there, so I convinced myself that I saw him.

'Don't touch anything,' he says. 'Don't go in the house, wait outside until I come back.'

'Yes, *Bwana*,' says Luka.

They push the car to get it started, the diesel engine catches, and Olofson drives to his mud hut. The black workers stand motionless, watching him. How many belong to the leopards? he wonders. How many thought I was dead?

The telephone in the office is working. He calls the police in Kitwe.

'Tell everybody that I'm alive,' he says to the black clerks. 'Tell them all that I killed the leopards. One of them might be only wounded. Tell them that I'll pay a year's wages to anyone who finds the wounded leopard.'

He goes back to his house. A swarm of flies hovers over Peter Motombwane lying under the tablecloth. As he waits for the police he tries to think. Motombwane came to kill me, he tells himself. In the same way that one night he went to Ruth and Werner Masterton. His only mistake was that he came too early. He underestimated my fear, he thought that I had begun to sleep at night again.

Peter Motombwane came to kill me, and that's not something I should ever forget. That is the starting point. He would have chopped off my head, turned me into a slaughtered animal carcass. Motombwane's single-mindedness must have been very great. He knew that I had guns, so he was prepared to sacrifice his life. At the same time I realise now that he tried to warn me, get me to leave here to avoid the inevitable. Perhaps his insight had been transformed to a sorrowful desperation, a conviction that the ultimate sacrifice was required.

The man who crept across my roof was no bandit. He was a dedicated man who gave himself what he thought was a necessary assignment. That too is important for me to remember. When

I killed him, I killed perhaps one of the best people in this wounded land. Someone who possessed more than a dream for the future, someone with a readiness to act. When I killed Peter Motombwane I killed the hope of many people.

He, in turn, viewed my death as crucial. He didn't come here because he thirsted for revenge. I believe that Motombwane ignored such feelings. He crept up on my roof because he was in despair. He knew what was going on in this country, and he saw no other way out than to join the leopards' movement, begin a desperate resistance, and perhaps one day have the chance to experience the necessary revolt. Maybe he was the one who created the leopards' movement. Did he act alone, with a few co-conspirators, or did he recruit a new generation before he took up his own *panga*?

Olofson walks over to the terrace, trying not to look at the body under the tablecloth. Behind some African roses he finds what he is looking for. Motombwane's *panga* is polished to a shine, and the handle has various symbols carved into it. Olofson thinks he sees a leopard head, an eye which is deeply incised in the brown wood. He places the *panga* back among the roses and kicks some dead leaves over it so it can't be seen.

A rusty police car comes along the road, its motor coughing. At the drive it comes to a complete stop; it seems to be out of petrol. What would have happened if I had called them last night, he wonders, if I had asked them to come to my rescue? Would they have informed me that they had no petrol? Or would they have asked me to come and fetch them in my car?

Suddenly he recognises the police officer coming towards him ahead of four constables. The officer who once stood in front of his house with an erroneous search warrant in his hand. Olofson recalls his name: Kaulu.

Olofson shows him the dead body, the dogs, and describes the chain of events. He also says that he knew Peter Motombwane. The officer shakes his head forlornly.

'Journalists can never be trusted,' he says. 'Now it's proven.'

'Peter Motombwane was a good journalist,' says Olofson.

'He was far too interested in things that he shouldn't have stuck his nose into,' says the officer. 'But now we know that he was a bandit.'

'What about the leopard skin?' Olofson asks. 'I've heard vague rumours about some political movement.'

'Let's go inside,' says the officer hastily. 'It's better to speak in the shade.'

Luka serves tea and they sit in silence for a long time.

'Regrettable rumours spread much too easily,' says the police officer. 'There is no leopard movement. The president himself has declared that it doesn't exist. Therefore it doesn't exist. So it would be regrettable if new rumours should arise. Our authorities would not be pleased.'

What is he actually trying to convey? Olofson thinks. A piece of information, a warning? Or a threat?

'Ruth and Werner Masterton,' Olofson says. 'It would have looked like their house here if I hadn't shot him and maybe another man too.'

'There is absolutely no connection,' says the officer.

'Of course there is,' says Olofson.

The police officer slowly stirs his tea.

'Once I came here with a mistakenly issued order,' he says. 'You offered great cooperation on that occasion. It's a great pleasure for me to be able to return the favour now. No leopard movement exists; our president has determined this. Nor is there any reason to see connections where there are none. In addition, it would be extremely unfortunate if rumours should spread that you knew the man who tried to kill you. That would create suspicion among the authorities. People might start to think that it was some type of vendetta. Vague connections between a white farmer and the sources of rumours about the leopard movement. You could very easily land in difficulties. It would be best to write a simple, clear report about a regrettable attack which fortunately ended well.'

There it is, Olofson thinks. After a rambling explanation I'm supposed to realise that it will all be covered up. Peter Motombwane will not be allowed to live on as a desperate resistance fighter; his memory will be that of a bandit.

'The immigration authorities might be concerned,' the officer goes on. 'But I shall repay your previous helpfulness by burying this case as quickly as possible.'

He's unreachable, Olofson thinks. His directive is obvious: no political resistance exists in this country.

'I presume that you have licences for your weapons,' says the officer in a friendly tone.

'No,' Olofson says.

'That might have been troublesome,' says the officer. 'The authorities take a serious view of unlicensed weapons.'

'I never thought about it,' replies Olofson.

'This too it would be my pleasure to ignore,' says the police officer, getting to his feet.

Case closed, Olofson thinks. His argument was better than mine. No one will die in an African prison. When they go outside the body is gone.

'My men have sunk it in the river,' the officer tells him. 'That's the easiest way. We took the liberty of using some scrap iron we found on your farm.'

The policemen are waiting by the car. 'Unfortunately our petrol ran out,' says the officer. 'But one of my men borrowed a few litres from your fuel supply while we drank tea.'

'Of course,' says Olofson. 'You're welcome to stay a while and take some cartons of eggs when you go.'

'Eggs are good,' says the officer, extending his hand. 'It's not often that it's so easy to conclude a crime scene investigation.'

The police car leaves and Olofson tells Luka to burn the bloody tablecloth. He watches him while he burns it. It still might have been him, Olofson thinks. How can I keep living with him near me? How can I keep living here at all?

He gets into his car and stops outside the hen house where Eisenhower Mudenda works. He shows him Peter Motombwane's *panga*.

'Now it's mine,' he says. 'Anyone who attacks my house will be killed with the weapon that could not vanquish me.'

'A very dangerous weapon, *Bwana*,' says Mudenda.

'It's good if everybody knows about it,' says Olofson.

'Everyone will soon know, *Bwana*,' says Mudenda.

'Then we understand each other,' says Olofson and goes back to his car.

He locks himself in his bedroom and pulls the curtains. Outside the window he sees Luka burying the dead dogs. I'm living in an African graveyard, he thinks. On the roof of the terrace is Peter Motombwane's blood. Once he was my friend, my only African friend. The rain will wash away his blood, the crocodiles will tear his body to bits at the bottom of the Kafue. He sits down on the edge of the bed; his body aches with weariness. How will I be able to endure what has happened? he thinks again. How do I move out of this hell?

During the following month Olofson lives with an increasing sense of powerlessness. The rainy season is nearing its end, and he keeps a watchful eye on Luka. The rumour of the attack brings his neighbours to visit him, and he repeats his story about the night Peter Motombwane and his dogs died. The second man was never found; the blood trail ended in thin air. In his imagination the third man becomes even more of a shadow; Luka's face disappears slowly.

He is struck by repeated bouts of malaria and hallucinates again that he is being attacked by bandits. One night he thinks he's going to die. When he wakes up the electricity is off; the fever makes him lose all his internal bearings. He shoots his revolver straight out into the darkness.

When he wakes again the malaria has passed, and Luka waits as usual outside his door in the dawn. New German shepherds are running around his house; his neighbours have brought them as the obvious gifts of the white community.

He attends to the daily work on the farm as usual. Egg lorries are no longer being plundered; quiet has settled over the land. He wonders how he will endure. I could not have avoided killing Peter Motombwane, he thinks. He never would have allowed it. If he could he would have sliced off my head. His despair must have been so strong that he could no longer live with the idea of waiting for the time to be ripe, for the revolt slowly to emerge. He must have thought that this ripening process had to be hastened along, and he took to the only weapon he had. Maybe he was also aware that he would fail.

He compares himself to Motombwane, wandering through his entire life in a long sorrowful procession. My life is built of bad cement, he thinks. The cracks run deep, and someday it will all come crashing down. My ambitions have always been superficial and flawed. My moral gestures are sentimental or impatient. I have almost never made real demands on myself.

I studied to find a way out, a way to get by. I came to Africa because I carried another person's dream. A farm was placed in my hands. When Judith Fillington left here the work was already done. All that was left was to repeat routines that were already in practice. Finally I was assigned the shocking role of killing one or maybe two people, people who were prepared to do what I would never have dared do. I can hardly be blamed for defending my own life. And yet I blame myself.

More and more often he gets drunk in the evenings and staggers around the empty rooms. I have to get away, he thinks. I'll sell the farm, burn it down, take off.

He can think of only one more task he has left to do. Joyce Lufuma's daughters. I can't abandon them, he thinks. Even if Lars Håkansson is there, I have to stay until I'm sure that they're safe enough to complete their education.

After a month he decides to drive to Lusaka and visit them. He doesn't call ahead; he gets into his car and drives off towards Lusaka. He arrives there late one Sunday evening.

As he drives into the city he realises that for the first time in a very long time he feels happy. I should have had children of my own, he thinks. In this respect too, my life is unnatural. But maybe it's not too late.

The night watchman opens the gates for him and he turns into the gravel courtyard in front of the house.

Chapter Twenty-Four

A t the moment of defeat Hans Olofson wishes that he could at least play a flute carved for him of birchwood. But he cannot. He has no flute, he has only his pulled-up roots in his hands.

It is Hans Fredström, son of a pastry chef from Danderyd, who hands down the verdict on Hans Olofson. The students are sitting in a beer café in Stockholm in early September 1969. He doesn't know who came up with the idea that they take the train to Stockholm that Wednesday evening to drink beer, but he follows along anyway; there are five of them, and they met several years before in the introductory law course.

In the spring Hans Olofson had gone home with the embittered feeling that he would never finish his studies. By then he had lived in the house of the clocks and suffered through his lectures and homework long enough to know that he didn't fit in anywhere. The ambition he'd had, to be the defender of mitigating circumstance, had dissolved and vanished like a fleeting mirage. With a growing sense of unreality the clocks went on ticking around him, and finally he realised that the university was just an excuse for the afternoons he spent in Wickberg's gun shop.

The salvation of the summer was the Holmström twins, who

had not yet found their wives-to-be, but were still racing around through the bright summer woods in their old Saab. Hans squeezed into their back seat, shared their schnapps, and watched the forests and lakes glide by. On a distant dance floor he found a bridesmaid and fell immediately and fiercely in love. Her name was Agnes, nicknamed Agge, and she was studying to be a hairdresser at a salon called 'The Wave', which stood between the bookshop and Karl-Otto's used motorcycle shop. Her father was one of the men he had worked with at the Trade Association warehouse. She lived with an older sister in a small flat above the Handelsbank, and after her sister took off with a man and his house trailer to Höga Kusten, they had the flat to themselves. The Holmström brothers showed up there in their Saab, plans were made for the evening, and it was to there that they all returned.

By then he had decided to stay, to get a job and not go back south when autumn arrived. But love was illusory too, just another hiding place, and finally he went back south just to escape. In her eyes he could read his betrayal. But maybe he also went back because he couldn't stand to watch his father fighting with his demons more and more often; now even water couldn't vanquish them. Now he simply boozed, a single-minded genuflection before his inability to return to the sea.

That summer Erik Olofson finally became a woodcutter. He was no longer the seaman who toiled among bark and brushwood to open the horizon and take his bearings. One day *Célestine* fell to the floor, as if she had been shipwrecked in a mighty hurricane. Hans found her while his father was sleeping it off on the sofa. He recalls that moment as a raging helplessness, two opposing forces wrestling with each other.

He returned to Uppsala and now he's sitting in a beer café in Stockholm, and Hans Fredström is dribbling beer on his hand.

Fredström possesses something enviable: he has a calling. He wants to become a prosecutor.

'Hooligans have to be taken by the ears and punished,' he says. 'Being a prosecutor means pursuing purity. The body of society is purged.'

Once Olofson had revealed to him what he planned to be: a spokesman for the weak, thereby instantly winding up in Fredström's disfavour. He mobilises a hostility that Olofson cannot deflect. His conversation is so fiery and prejudiced that it makes Olofson sick. Their discussions always finish just on the verge of a fistfight. Olofson tries to avoid him. If he fights with him he always loses. When Fredström dribbles beer on his hand he pulls it away.

I have to stand up to him, he thinks. The two of us will be defending law and order together for our generation. The thought suddenly seems impossible to him. He ought to be able to do it, he ought to force himself to resist, otherwise Hans Fredström will have free reign to ravage through the courtrooms like a predator, crushing with an elephant foot the mitigating circumstance that may still be there. But he can't do it. He is too alone, too poorly equipped.

Instead he stands up and leaves. Behind him he hears Fredström sniggering. He wanders restlessly through the city, heading down streets at random. His mind is empty, like deserted halls in an abandoned palace. First he thinks there isn't anything at all, only the peeling wallpaper and the echo of his footsteps.

But in one of the rooms lies Sture in his bed, with a rough blackened tube sticking out of his throat. The iron lung folds its shiny wings around him and he hears a wheezing sound, like a locomotive letting off steam. In another room echoes a word, Mutshatsha, Mutshatsha, and perhaps he also hears the faint tones of 'Some of These Days'. He decides to visit Sture, to see him again, dead or alive.

A few days later he is in Västervik. Late in the afternoon he gets off the bus he boarded in Norrköping, which will now continue on to Kalmar. At once he smells the sea, and like an insect driven by its sense of smell he finds his way to Slottsholmen.

An autumn wind blows in off the sea as he walks along the wharves and looks at the boats. A lone yacht runs before the wind into the harbour, and the sail flaps as a woman takes it in.

He can't find a boarding house, and in a fit of recklessness he checks in at the City Hotel. Through the wall of his room he can hear someone talking excitedly and at length. He thinks it might be a man practising for a play. At the front desk a friendly man with a glass eye helps him find the hospital where Sture is presumed to be.

'Fir Ridge,' says the man with the glass eye. 'That's probably it. That's where they take people who weren't lucky enough to die instantly. Traffic accidents, motorcycles, broken backs. That must be it.'

'Fir Ridge' is a deeply misleading name, Olofson realises as he arrives in a taxi the next morning. The forest opens up, he sees a manor house surrounded by a well-tended garden and a glimpse of the sea shining behind one wing of the manor house. Outside the main entrance a man with no legs sits in a wheelchair. He is wrapped in a blanket, sleeping with his mouth open.

Olofson walks in through the tall door; the hospital reminds him of the courthouse where Sture once lived. He is shown to a small office. A lamp glows green and he enters to find a man who introduces himself as Herr Abramovitch. He speaks in a muted, scarcely audible voice, and Olofson imagines that his primary task in life is to preserve the silence.

'Sture von Croona,' whispers Herr Abramovitch. 'He has been with us for ten years or more. But I don't remember you. I assume you're a relative?'

Olofson nods. 'A half-brother.'

'Some people who come to visit for the first time may be a little distressed,' whispers Herr Abramovitch. 'He is pale, naturally, and a little swollen up from constantly lying down. A certain hospital odour is also unavoidable.'

'I would like to visit him,' says Olofson. 'I've come a long way to see him.'

'I'll ask him,' says Herr Abramovitch, getting to his feet. 'What was the name again? Hans Olofson? A half-brother?'

When he returns everything is arranged. Olofson follows him down a long corridor and they stop before a door, on which Herr Abramovitch knocks. A gurgling sound comes in reply.

Nothing is as he imagined in the room he enters. The walls are covered with books, and in the middle of the room, surrounded by pot plants, Sture lies in a blue-painted bed. But there is no tube sticking out of his throat and no giant insect folding its wings around the blue bed.

The door closes silently and they are alone.

'Where the hell have you been?' asks Sture, in a voice that is hoarse but still reveals that he is angry.

Hans's assumptions crumble. He had imagined that a person with a broken spine would be taciturn and softly spoken, not angry like this.

'Have a seat,' says Sture, as if to help him through his embarrassment.

Hans lifts a stack of books from a chair and sits down.

'Ten years you make me wait,' Sture goes on. 'Ten years! First I was disappointed, of course. A couple of years, maybe. Since then I've mostly been damned angry with you.'

'I have no explanation,' says Hans. 'You know how it is.'

'How the hell should I know how it is when I'm lying here?'

Then his face breaks out in a smile. 'Well, you finally came,' he says. 'To this place where things are the way they are. If I want a view they set up a mirror so I can see the garden. The room has been painted twice since I came here. At first they would roll me out to the park. But then I said no. I like it better in here. I've been taking it easy. Nothing to prevent someone like me from surrendering to laziness.'

Hans listens dumbstruck to the will power emanating from Sture as he lies in the bed. He realises that Sture, despite his terrible disadvantage, has developed a power and sense of purpose that he doesn't have.

'Of course, bitterness is my constant companion,' Sture says. 'Every morning when I awake from my dreams, every time I shit myself and it starts to smell, every time I realise that I can't do anything – that's probably the worst thing, not being able to offer any resistance. It's my spine that's severed, that's true. But something was also broken inside my head. It took me many years to realise that. But then I made a plan for my life based on my opportunities, not the lack of them. I decided to live until I turned thirty, about five more years. By then I'll have my philosophy worked out, I'll have clarified my relationship with death. My only problem is that I can't end my own life because I can't move. But I have another five years to figure out a solution.'

'What happened?' asks Hans.

'I don't remember. The memory is completely erased. I can remember things long before and I remember when I woke up here. That's all.'

A stench suddenly spreads in the room and Sture presses his nose to a call button.

'Go out for a while. I have to be cleaned up.'

When he comes back, Sture is lying there drinking beer through a straw.

'I drink schnapps sometimes,' he says. 'But they don't like that.

If I start throwing up there's trouble. And I can get foul-mouthed. My way of getting back at the nurses for everything I can't do.'

'Janine,' says Hans. 'She died.'

Sture lies quiet a long while. 'What happened?'

'She drowned herself in the end.'

'You know what I dreamed of? Undressing her, making love to her. I still kick myself because I never did it. Did you ever think of that?'

Hans shakes his head. He quickly grabs a book to avoid the topic.

'With my upbringing I never would have wound up studying radical philosophy,' says Sture. 'I dreamed of becoming the Leonardo of my time. I was my own constellation in a private cosmos. But now I know that reason is the only thing that gives me consolation. And reason means understanding that one dies alone, irreparably alone – everyone, even you. I try to think about it when I write. I talk on to tape, and someone else types it up.'

'What do you write about?'

'About a broken spine that ventures out into the world. Abramovitch doesn't look too amused when he reads what the girls type up. He doesn't understand what I mean, and it makes him nervous. But in five years he'll be rid of me.'

When Sture asks Hans to tell him about his own life, he doesn't seem to have anything to say.

'Do you remember the horse dealer? He died last summer. He was eaten up by bone cancer.'

'I never met him,' says Sture. 'Did I ever meet anyone other than you and Janine?'

'It's so long ago.'

'Five more years,' says Sture. 'If I haven't found the solution to my final problem, would you help me?'

'If I can.'

'You can't break a promise to someone who's broken his back. If you did I would haunt you until you dropped dead.'

Late in the afternoon they say goodbye. Herr Abramovitch cautiously opens the door a crack and says he can offer Hans a ride into town.

'Come back once a year,' says Sture. 'No more. I don't have time.'

'I can write,' says Hans.

'No, no letters. I just get upset by letters. Letters are too much for me to stand. Go now.'

Hans leaves the town with a feeling of being king of the unworthy. In Sture he saw his own mirror image. He can't escape it. Late in the evening he reaches Uppsala. The clocks tick in the impenetrable jungle of time in which he lives.

Mutshatsha, he thinks. What remains other than you?

The Swedish sky is heavy on that early morning in September 1969 when he leaves all his former horizons behind him and flies out into the world. He has spent his savings and bought the ticket that will fling him out into the upper layers of the air, his dubious pilgrimage to the Mutshatsha of Janine's dreams.

A motionless sky, an endless wall of clouds hangs over his head, as for the first time in his life he boards an aeroplane. When he walks across the tarmac the dampness soaks into his shoes. He turns around as if someone were there after all to wave goodbye to him.

He observes his fellow passengers. None is on his way to Mutshatsha, he thinks. Right now that is the one thing I know for sure. With a slight bow Hans Olofson makes the ascent up into the air. Twenty-seven hours later, precisely according to the timetable, he lands in Lusaka. Africa receives him with intense heat. No one is there to meet him.

Chapter Twenty-Five

A night watchman comes towards him with a cudgel in his hand. Olofson can see that he is very afraid. Two big German shepherds are running restlessly back and forth across the poorly lit courtyard.

Suddenly he feels a raging disgust at being always surrounded by nervous watchdogs and high walls with crushed glass cemented on top. I travel from one white bunker to the next, he thinks. Everywhere this terror.

He knocks on the door of the servants' quarters and Peggy answers. She lets him in, and behind her is Marjorie, and they laugh with joy that he has come. And yet he notices at once that something is wrong. He sits down on a chair and listens to their voices in the tiny kitchen where they are fixing tea for him.

I forget that I'm a *mzungu* even to them, he thinks. Only with Peter Motombwane did I succeed in experiencing a completely natural relationship with an African. He drinks tea and asks how they're getting along in Lusaka.

'It's going well,' replies Marjorie. '*Bwana* Lars is taking care of us.'

He doesn't tell them about the attack in the night, but asks instead whether they are homesick. When they reply that they aren't, he again senses that something is wrong. There's an uncertainty behind their usual happiness. Something is troubling them. He decides to wait until Håkansson comes back.

'Tomorrow I'll be in town all day,' he says. 'We can take the car and drive in to Cairo Road and go shopping.'

As he leaves he can hear them locking the door. In an African village there are no locks, he thinks. It's the first thing we teach them. Locking a door gives a false sense of security.

The night watchman comes towards him again, his cudgel in hand.

'Where is *Bwana* Lars?' Olofson asks.

'In Kabwe, *Bwana*.'

'When is he coming back?'

'Maybe tomorrow, *Bwana*.'

'I'll stay here tonight. Open the door for me.'

The night watchman vanishes in the darkness to fetch the keys. I'm sure he's buried them, Olofson thinks. He strikes one of the German shepherds who sniffs at his leg. Whimpering, it retreats. In this country there are innumerable dogs trained to attack people with black skin, he thinks. How does one train a dog to exhibit racist behaviour?

The night watchman unlocks the house. Olofson takes the keys and locks the door from the inside. First the wrought-iron gate with two padlocks and a crossbar with another lock. Then the outer door with three locks and three deadbolts.

Eight locks, he thinks. Eight locks for my nightly slumber. What was it that was bothering them? A homesickness they're afraid to admit? Or something else? He turns on the lights in Lars Håkansson's big house, walks through the tastefully furnished rooms. Everywhere there is shiny stereo equipment, and he lets the music flow from hidden loudspeakers.

He selects a guest room with a bed made up with clean sheets.

I feel more secure here than on my own farm, he thinks. At least I think I do, because no one knows where I am.

He takes a bath in a shiny bathroom, turns off the music, and climbs into bed. Just as he is about to slip off into sleep, he is suddenly wide awake. He thinks again about Marjorie and Peggy, and his feeling that something is not quite right. He tries to convince himself that Africa has made him far too sensitive in his judgement, that after all these years he thinks he sees terror in everyone's face.

He gets up and goes through the house, opening doors, studying the titles in the bookshelves and a drawing of a link station hanging on a wall in Håkansson's office. Everything is in perfect order. Lars Håkansson has established himself in Africa without a speck of dust, with everything in its place. He pulls out drawers and sees underwear in meticulously arranged piles. One room has been converted to a photography studio; behind another door he finds an exercise bicycle and a table tennis table.

He returns to the big living room. He hasn't found anything that gives a picture of Håkansson's past. Nowhere does he see pictures of children or an ex-wife. He imagines that Håkansson makes use of the fact that Africa is a long way from Sweden. The past is the past; nothing needs to remind him unless he wants it to.

He pulls out a drawer in a chiffonier. It contains stacks of photographs. Only when he aims a lamp on them does he see what they depict. Pornographic pictures of black subjects. Pictures of sexual intercourse, individual poses. Everyone in the photos is very young. Peggy and Marjorie are there. Helplessly vulnerable.

Among the pictures is a letter, written in German. Olofson manages to decipher that it's from a man in Frankfurt thanking Håkansson for the photos he supplied; he wants more and says that three thousand D-marks will be transferred to a bank in Liechtenstein, according to their agreement.

Olofson is scared by his rage. Now I'm capable of anything, he thinks. This fucking man to whom I gave my greatest trust, who has duped or threatened or enticed my black daughters to do this. He doesn't deserve to live. Maybe he also forces himself on them, maybe one or both are already pregnant.

He takes out the pictures of Peggy and Marjorie and stuffs them in his pocket, slams the drawer shut and decides. Through a window that's kept open at night he speaks to the night watchman and finds out that Håkansson is staying at the Department Guest House, near the big military bases in Kabwe, on the southern approach to the city.

Olofson gets dressed and leaves the house. The night watchman is surprised to see him get into his car.

'It's dangerous to drive that far at night, *Bwana*,' he says.

'What's dangerous about it?' Olofson asks.

'Men steal and murder, *Bwana*,' says the night watchman.

'I'm not afraid,' Olofson says.

It's true, too, he thinks as he turns out through the gate. What I'm experiencing now is a feeling that's stronger than all the terror I've lived with for so long.

He leaves the city, forcing himself not to drive too fast; he doesn't want to risk colliding with an African car with no headlights.

I let myself be deceived so easily, he thinks. I meet a Swede and immediately lean on his shoulder. He stood outside my house, asking to buy a hill on my property, and somehow he gained my trust. He was prepared to place a house at the disposal of Peggy and Marjorie much too readily. What did he give them? Money or threats? Or both? There really isn't any punishment for it, he thinks. But I want to know how anyone can behave as he does.

Midway between Lusaka and Kabwe he comes to a military roadblock. He slows down and stops at the checkpoint. Soldiers in camouflage uniforms and helmets walk towards him in the floodlights, automatic weapons raised. He rolls down his window and one of the soldiers bends down and looks inside the car. Olofson notices that the soldier is very young and very drunk. He asks where Olofson is heading.

'Home,' Olofson answers with a smile. 'Kalulushi.'

The soldier orders him to step out of the car. Now I'm going to die, he thinks. He's going to shoot me dead, for no other reason than it's the middle of the night and he's drunk and bored.

'Why are you driving home in the middle of the night?' asks the soldier.

'My mother has taken ill,' replies Olofson.

The soldier looks at him for a long time with glazed eyes; his automatic weapon is pointed at Olofson's chest. Then he waves him on.

'Drive,' he says.

Olofson gets back into his car, and drives slowly away.

African unpredictability, he thinks. I've learned something, at least, after all these years. If it doesn't help to mention my mother, then nothing else will. He picks up speed and wonders if there is any greater loneliness than being white and helpless at a roadblock in the African night.

It's almost four o'clock in the morning when he reaches Kabwe. He drives around for almost an hour before he sees a sign that reads Department Guest House.

The only thing he has decided to do is wake up Lars Håkansson and show him the pictures he has in his pocket. Maybe I'll hit him. Maybe I'll spit in his face.

A night watchman is asleep outside the gates to the guest house. There's a smell of burnt rubber from one of the man's boots that has come too close to the fire. An empty bottle of *lituku* lies next to him. Olofson shakes him but he doesn't wake up. He shoves open the gate himself and drives inside. At once he sees Håkansson's car outside one of the small guest houses. He parks next to the white car, turns off the engine and headlights.

Lars Håkansson, he says to himself. Now I'm coming after you. He knocks on the door three times before he hears Håkansson's voice.

'It's Hans Olofson,' he says. 'I have a matter to discuss.'

He must understand, he thinks. Maybe he's afraid and doesn't dare open the door. But Håkansson opens the door and lets him in.

'You,' he says. 'This is unexpected. In the middle of the night? How did you find me here?'

'Your night watchman,' replies Olofson.

'There's a military commander here who has the idea that his brother is a suitable engineer to build the foundations for the link stations all over the country,' says Håkansson. 'He smelled money and it'll take a little time to convince him that it doesn't really work the way he thinks.'

He puts out a bottle of whisky and two glasses.

'I drove to Lusaka to say hello to Marjorie and Peggy,' says Olofson. 'I suppose I should have called first.'

'They're getting along fine,' says Håkansson. 'Lively girls.'

'Yes,' says Olofson. 'They're the future of this country.'

Håkansson takes a drink and gives him a wry smile.

'That sounds lovely,' he says.

Olofson looks at his silk pyjamas.

'I mean what I'm saying,' he replies.

He takes the pictures out of his pocket and places them on the table, one by one. When he's finished he sees that Håkansson is staring at him with wide eyes.

'Of course I ought to be furious that you're digging through my drawers,' he says. 'But I'll overlook that. Just tell me what you want.'

'This,' says Olofson, 'this.'

'What about it?' Håkansson interrupts him. 'Naked people in pictures, nothing more.'

'Did you threaten them?' he asks. 'Or give them money?'

Håkansson fills his glass and Olofson sees that his hand is steady.

'You tell me you've been in Africa for twenty years,' Håkansson says. 'Then you should know about respect for parents. The bonds of blood are flexible. You have been their father, now that role has partially shifted to me. I just ask them to take off their clothes, to do as I say. They're embarrassed, but respect for father prevails. Why would I make threats? I'm just as concerned as you that they should finish their education. I give them money, of course, just as you do. There is always a dimension of private aid in those of us who venture out.'

'You promised to take responsibility for them,' says Olofson, noticing that his voice is shaking. 'You're turning them into pornographic models and selling their photos in Germany.'

Håkansson bangs down his glass. 'You've been rooting around in my drawers,' he says excitedly. 'I ought to throw you right out, but I won't. I'll be polite and patient and listen to what you have to say. Just don't give me any moral lectures, I can't tolerate it.'

'Do you fuck them too?' asks Olofson.

'Not yet,' Håkansson says. 'I think I'm afraid of AIDS. But they're probably virgins, aren't they?'

I'm going to kill him, Olofson thinks. I'll kill him right here in this room.

'Let's conclude this conversation,' says Håkansson. 'I was asleep, and I have a troublesome, stupid Negro in a uniform to deal with tomorrow. Pornography interests me, but mostly developing it. The nakedness that appears in the developing bath. It can actually be quite arousing. It pays well too. One day I'll buy a yacht and disappear to some remote paradise. Those I take pictures of won't fare badly for it. They get money and the photos are published in countries where nobody knows them. Naturally I know that pornographic pictures are not permitted in this country. But I hold an immunity that is more secure than if I had been the Swedish ambassador. Apart from that idiot of a commander I have here in Kabwe, the military leaders in this country are my friends. I'm building link stations for them, they drink my whisky, now and then they receive some of my dollars. The same with the police, the same with the department. As long as the Swedish state gives out its millions and as long as I'm responsible for it, I'm invulnerable. If you should have the bad idea of going to the police with these pictures, you'd run a great risk of being deported with a simple twenty-four hours' notice in which to pack up your entire eighteen years. So there's really not much more to say. If you're upset I can't do anything about it. If you want to take the girls home I can't prevent you, although it would be a shame, in view of their education. Our dealings can be concluded: I got your hill, you'll get your money. I think it's a shame that it has to end this way. But I can't tolerate people who abuse my trust by digging through my drawers.'

'You're a pig,' says Olofson.

'You have to go now,' says Håkansson.

'Sweden sends people like you out into the world,' Olofson says.

'I'm a good aid expert,' replies Håkansson. 'I'm held in high esteem at Sida.'

'But if they knew about this?' says Olofson.

'Nobody would believe you,' says Håkansson. 'No one would

care. Results count, and everybody has a private life. Raising moral issues lies outside the realm of political reality.'

'A person like you doesn't deserve to live,' says Olofson. 'I ought to kill you here and now.'

'But you won't,' says Håkansson, getting to his feet. 'Now you have to go. Check in at the Elephant's Head and get some sleep. Tomorrow you won't be so upset.'

Olofson snatches the pictures back and leaves; Håkansson follows him.

'I'm going to send some of these pictures to Sida,' Olofson says. 'Somebody will have to take action.'

'The pictures can never be traced to me,' replies Håkansson. 'An embarrassing complaint from a Swedish egg farmer who has lived in Africa too long. The matter will be stamped, filed away and disappear.'

Furious, Olofson gets into his car, turns the key and switches on the headlights. Håkansson is standing in his silk pyjamas, gleaming white in the African night. I can't get to him, thinks Olofson. He puts the car in reverse.

Then he quickly changes his mind, shoves it into first gear, stomps on the accelerator, and speeds straight towards Håkansson. Olofson shuts his eyes as he runs over him. There is only a soft thud and a jolt to the chassis. Without looking back he keeps going towards the gate. The night watchman is asleep, the burnt rubber boot is stinking. Olofson pushes open the gates and leaves Kabwe.

In this country they hang murderers, he thinks in despair. I'll have to say it was an accident and I got so confused that I just drove off without reporting what happened. I was recently subjected to a terrifying attack myself, I'm tired, burned out. He drives towards Kalulushi with a feeling that he should regret what he's done, but he can't. He's sure that Lars Håkansson is dead.

At dawn he drives off the main road and stops; the sun is rising over an endless moorland. He burns the photos of Peggy and Marjorie and lets the ashes drift away on the warm wind.

He has killed two people, maybe even a third. Peter Motombwane was probably the best man in this country, he thinks. Lars Håkansson was a monster. Killing a human being is something incomprehensible. If I'm going to survive I have to tell myself that I atoned for Peter Motombwane by driving my car straight at Håkansson. Something is restored, even though it changes nothing.

For two weeks he waits for the police; anxiety gnaws at him to the point of dissolution. He leaves as much as he can to his foremen and says he's suffering from constant malaria attacks. Patel visits his farm and Olofson asks him for some sleeping pills. Then he sleeps dreamlessly and often wakes up only when Luka has been standing at the kitchen door pounding for a long time.

He thinks that he ought to visit Joyce Lufuma, speak to her, but he doesn't know what to say. I can only wait, he thinks. Wait for the police to come in a broken-down car and get me. Maybe I'll have to give them some petrol so they can take me away.

One morning two weeks later Luka tells him that Peggy and Marjorie have returned on the bus from Lusaka. Terror paralyses him. Now the police are coming, he thinks. Now it's all over.

But the only ones who come are Peggy and Marjorie. They stand in the sunshine outside the dark mud hut where he sits with his papers. He goes out to them and asks why they came back from Lusaka.

'*Mzunguz* came and said that *Bwana* Lars had died,' says Marjorie. 'We couldn't live in our house any more. A man who comes from the same country as you gave us money to come back here. Now we are here.'

He drives them home. 'Nothing is too late,' he says. 'I'll arrange it some other way. You will have the nursing training as we planned.'

We share a secret even though they don't know it, he thinks. Maybe they have a feeling that Håkansson's death has something to do with me and the pictures. Or maybe they don't.

'How did *Bwana* Lars die?' he asks.

'An accident, said the man from your country,' replies Peggy.

'Didn't any police officers come?'

'No police,' says Peggy.

A sleeping night watchman, he thinks. I didn't see any other cars. Maybe Håkansson was the only one at the guest house. The night watchman in Lusaka is afraid of getting involved. Maybe he didn't even say I was there the night it happened. Peggy and Marjorie have certainly not said anything, and nobody has asked them about what happened that night in Kabwe. Maybe there wasn't even any enquiry. An inexplicable accident, a dead Swedish aid expert is flown home in a coffin. An item in the papers, Sida attends the funeral. People wonder, but say to themselves that Africa is the mysterious continent.

Suddenly he realises that no one is going to accuse him of Lars Håkansson's death. A Swedish aid expert dies in strange circumstances. The police investigate, find pornographic photos, and the case is quickly closed. The development of a network of link stations for telecommunications will not be served by disclosing suspicions that a crime has been committed. The link stations have set me free, he thinks. He sits underneath the tree at Joyce Lufuma's mud house. Peggy and Marjorie have gone to collect wood, the youngest daughters fetch water. Joyce is pounding maize with a heavy wooden pole.

The future for Africa depends on the plight of Africa's women, he thinks. While the men out in the villages sit under the shade of a tree, the women are working in the fields, having children, carrying fifty-kilo sacks of maize for miles on their heads. My farm is not the real picture of Africa, with men making up the primary work force. Africa's women carry the continent on their heads. Seeing a woman with a large burden on her head gives an impression of power and self-confidence. No one knows the back problems that result from these loads they carry.

Joyce Lufuma is perhaps thirty-five years old. She has borne four daughters and she still has enough strength to pound the maize with a thick pole. In her life there has never been room for reflection, only work, life-sustaining work. She has perhaps vaguely imagined that at least two of her daughters would be granted the chance to live another life. Whatever dreams she has she invests in them. The pole that pounds the maize thumps like a drum. Africa is a woman pounding maize, he thinks. From this starting point, all ideas of the future for this continent must be derived.

Joyce finishes pounding and begins to sieve her corn meal. Now and then she casts a glance at him, and when their eyes meet she laughs and her white teeth shine. Work and beauty go together, he says to himself. Joyce Lufuma is the most beautiful and dignified woman I have ever met. My love for her is born of respect. The sensual reaches me through her unbroken will to live. There her wealth is so much greater than mine. Her toil to keep her children alive, to be able to give them food and not to see them waste away from malnutrition, not to have to carry them to graveyards out in the bush.

Her wealth is boundless. In comparison with her I am a very poor person. It would be wrong to claim that my money would increase her well-being. It would only make her work easier. She would not have to die at the age of forty, worn out by her labours.

The four daughters return in a row, carrying water buckets and wood. This I must remember, he thinks, and abruptly realises that he has decided to leave Africa. After nineteen years the decision has formulated itself. He sees the daughters coming along a path, their black bodies erect to help their heads balance their burdens; he sees them and thinks about the time he lay behind a dilapidated brickworks outside the town in Sweden.

I came here, he thinks. When I lay behind a rusty brick furnace I wondered what the world looked like. Now I know. Joyce Lufuma and her four daughters. It took me over thirty years to reach this insight.

He shares their meal, eating *nshima* and vegetables. The charcoal fire flares, Peggy and Marjorie tell about Lusaka. They have already forgotten Lars Håkansson and his camera, he thinks. What is past is past. For a long time he sits by their fire, listening, saying little. Now that he has decided to sell his farm, leave, he is no longer in a hurry. He isn't even upset that Africa has conquered him, devoured him to a point where he can no longer go on. The starry sky above his head is perfectly clear. Finally he is sitting alone with Joyce; her daughters are asleep inside the mud house.

'Soon it will be morning again,' he says, and he speaks in her own language, Bemba, which he has learned passably well during all the years he has been in Africa.

'If God wills, one more day,' she replies.

He thinks of all the words that don't exist in her language. Words for happiness, the future, hope. Words that wouldn't be possible because they do not represent the experiences of these people.

'Who am I?' he asks her.

'A *bwana mzungu*,' she replies.

'Nothing more?' he asks.

She looks at him and doesn't understand. 'Is there anything more?' she asks.

Maybe not, he thinks. Maybe that's all I am, a *bwana mzungu*. A strange *bwana* who doesn't have any children, not even a wife. He decides to tell her the absolute truth.

'I will be going away from here, Joyce. Other people will take over the farm. But I will take care of you and your daughters. Maybe it's better if you return with your children to the regions around Luapula where you came from. There you have family, your origins. I will give you money so you can build a house and buy enough *limas* of farmland so that you can live a good life. Before I leave I have to arrange for Peggy and Marjorie to finish their nursing studies. Maybe it would be better if they went to the school in Chipata. It isn't too far from Luapula, and not as big as Lusaka. But I want you to know that I'm leaving, and I want to ask you not to tell anyone yet. The people on the farm might be worried, and I don't want that.'

She listens to him attentively, and he speaks slowly to show her that he is serious.

'I'm going back to my homeland,' he goes on. 'In the same way as you might return to Luapula.'

All at once she smiles at him, as if she has understood the real meaning of his words.

'Your family is waiting for you there,' she says. 'Your wife and your children.'

'Yes,' he says. 'They are waiting there, and they have waited a long time.'

She asks eagerly about his family, and he creates one for her, three sons and two daughters, a wife. She could never understand anyway, he thinks. The white man's life would be incomprehensible to her.

Late in the night he gets up and walks to his car. In the beam of the headlights he sees her close the door to the mud house. Africans are hospitable, he thinks. And yet I have never been inside her house.

The German shepherds come to meet him outside his house. He will never have dogs again, he thinks. I don't want to live surrounded by noisy sirens and animals trained to go for the throat. It's not natural for a Swede to keep a revolver under his pillow, to check every night that it's loaded, that the magazine rotates its cartridges. He walks through the silent house and wonders what there is for him to go back to. Eighteen years might be too long. He has little idea what has happened in Sweden in all these years. He sits down in the room he calls his work room, turns on a lamp and checks that the curtains are drawn.

When I sell the farm I will have stacks of *kwacha* banknotes that I can't take with me or even exchange. Patel can surely help me with some, but he will see the opportunity and demand an exchange fee of at least fifty per cent. I have money in a bank in London, even though I don't really know how much. When I leave I will do so empty-handed.

Again he doubts that his departure is necessary. I could accept the revolver under the pillow, he thinks. The terror that is always present, the uncertainty that I have lived with this long. If I stay here another fifteen years I can retire, maybe move to Livingstone or Sweden. Others besides Patel can help me get the money out to secure my remaining years.

I have nothing to go back to in Sweden. My father is long dead, and hardly anyone in my home town will remember who I am. How will I survive in a winter landscape now that I've grown used to Africa's heat – exchange my sandals for ski boots?

For a moment he toys with the thought of returning to his studies, using his middle years to complete his law degree. For twenty years he has worked at shaping his life, yet he has remained in Africa because of chance events. Going back to Sweden would not be a return. I would have to start all over again. But with what?

He wanders restlessly about his room. A hippo bellows from the Kafue. How many cobras have I seen during my years in Africa? he asks himself. Three or four a year, countless crocodiles, hippos and pythons. In all these years only a single green mamba, which had sneaked into the hen house. I ran over an ape with my car outside Mufulira once, a big male baboon. In Luangwa I saw lions and thousands of elephants, *pocos* and kudus have leaped high through the grass and sometimes crossed my path. But I have never seen a leopard, only sensed its shadow on that night Judith Fillington asked me to help her with her farm.

When I leave here Africa will fade away like an extraordinary dream, stretched out to encompass a decisive part of my life. What am I actually going to take with me? A hen and an egg? That tree branch with inscriptions that I found down by the river one time, a witch doctor's forgotten staff? Or will I take Peter Motombwane's holy *panga* with me, and show people the weapon that sliced up two of my friends and that one night was going to be raised over my own throat? Should I fill my pockets with the red dirt?

I carry Africa inside me, drums pounding distantly in the night. A starry sky whose clarity I have never before experienced. The variations of nature on the seventeenth parallel. The scent of charcoal, the ever-present smell of ingrained sweat from my workers. Joyce Lufuma's daughters walking in a row with bundles on their heads.

I can't leave Africa before I make peace with myself, he thinks. With the fact that I stayed here for almost twenty years. Life is the way it is, and mine became what it became. I probably would have been no happier if I had finished my studies and spent my time in the world of Swedish justice. How many people dream of venturing out? I did it, and one might also say that I succeeded with something. I'll keep brooding over meaningless details if I don't accept my eighteen years in Africa as something I'm grateful for, in spite of everything.

Deep inside I also know that I have to leave. The two men I killed, Africa which is devouring me, make it impossible to stay. Maybe I'll simply flee, maybe that's the most natural leave-taking. I have to start planning my departure right away, tomorrow. Give myself the time required, but no more.

After he goes to bed he reflects that he has absolutely no regrets at having run over Lars Håkansson. His death hardly affects him. But Peter Motombwane's blasted head aches inside him. In his dreams he is watched by a leopard's vigilant eye.

Olofson's final days in Africa stretch out to half a year. He offers his farm to the white colony, but to his astonishment no one bids on it. When he asks why, he realises that the location is too isolated. It's a profitable farm, but nobody dares take it over. After four months he has only two offers, and he realises that the price he will get for it is very poor.

The two bidders are Patel and Mr Pihri and his son. When word gets out that he is leaving his farm, they both come to visit; only chance keeps them from appearing on his terrace at precisely the same moment. Mr Pihri and his son regret his departure. Naturally, Olofson thinks. Their best source of income is disappearing. No used cars, no sewing machines, no back seat stacked full of eggs.

When Mr Pihri enquires about the asking price for the farm, Olofson thinks it's merely the man's eternal curiosity. Only later does he understand to his surprise that Mr Pihri is a bidder. Did I give him that much money over the years? So many bribes that now he can afford to buy my farm? If that's the case, it's a perfect summation of this country, perhaps of Africa itself.

'I have a question,' Olofson says to him. 'And I mean this in a friendly way.'

'Our conversations are always friendly,' says Mr Pihri.

'All those documents,' Olofson says. 'All those documents that had to be stamped so I wouldn't have problems. Were they necessary?'

Mr Pihri thinks for a long time before he replies. 'I don't quite understand.'

Well, that would be the first time, Olofson thinks.

'In all friendliness,' he continues. 'I wonder only whether you and your son have done me such great favours as I have believed.'

Mr Pihri looks distressed; his son lowers his eyes.

'We have avoided trouble,' replies Mr Pihri. 'In Africa our aim is always mutual benefit.'

I'll never know how much he has fooled me, Olofson thinks. How much of my money he in turn has paid to other corrupt civil servants. I'll have to live with that riddle.

The same day Patel drives up to the farm in his rusty car.

'Naturally a farm like this would not be hard to sell,' he says with a smile.

His humility conceals a predator, thinks Olofson. Right now he's calculating percentages, preparing his solemn speech about how dangerous it is to make illegal deposits of currency outside the control of the Zambian National Bank. People like Mr Pihri and Patel are among this continent's most deplorable individuals. Without them nothing functions. The price of corruption is the usual: the impotence of the poor. Olofson mentions his difficulties and the price he had in mind.

'Of course it's a scandalously low price,' he says.

'These are uncertain times,' replies Patel.

Two days later a letter arrives in which Patel informs him that he will be bidding on the farm, but that the price seems a bit high to him, in view of the difficult times. Now I have two bidders, Olofson thinks. Both are ready to talk me down, using my own money.

He writes a letter to the bank in London notifying them that he's selling his farm. The contract that was prepared with the lawyer in Kitwe stipulates that the entire sale price now falls to him. The law firm in Kitwe no longer exists; his lawyer has moved to Harare in Zimbabwe. A reply comes from the bank in London a couple of weeks later, advising him that Judith Fillington died in 1983. Since the bank no longer had any business associated with the old or new owners, it had not deemed it necessary to inform him of her death.

For a long time he sits with the letter in his hand, remembering their helpless act of love. Every life is always a completed whole, he thinks. Afterwards no retouching is permitted, no additions. No matter how hollow it may have been, at the end it is still a completed whole.

One day in late November, a few months before he leaves Africa, Olofson drives Joyce Lufuma and her daughters to Luapula. They load her few possessions into one of the egg lorries. Mattresses, cooking implements, bundles of clothes. Outside Luapula he follows Joyce's instructions, turning down a barely passable bush track, and finally stops by a cluster of mud houses.

Instantly the car is surrounded by dirty, skinny children. Swarms of flies engulf Olofson as he climbs out. After the children come the adults, enclosing Joyce and her children in their community. The African family, Olofson thinks. In some way they are all related to each other, prepared to share even though they possess virtually nothing. With the money I gave Joyce she will be the most well-to-do person in this community. But she will share it all; in the remote villages a sense of solidarity lives on that is otherwise not visible on this continent.

On the outskirts of the village Joyce shows him where she will build her house, keep her goats, and plant her plots of maize and cassava. Until the house is built she will live with her daughters in the house of one of her sisters. Peggy and Marjorie will finish their studies in Chipata. A missionary family that Olofson contacted has promised to take care of them, letting them stay in their house. More I cannot do, he thought. The missionaries will hardly let them be photographed naked and send their pictures to Germany. Maybe they will try to convert the girls, but there's nothing I can do about that.

He has transferred 10,000 *kwacha* into a bank account for Joyce, and taught her how to write her name. He has also transferred 10,000 *kwacha* to the missionaries of Mutshatsha. He knows that 20,000 *kwacha* is what one of his workers earns in an entire lifetime. Everything is unreasonable, he tells himself. Africa is a continent where everything is out of proportion to what I once was accustomed to. It's quite easy to make a rich woman of Joyce Lufuma. I'm sure she doesn't realise how much money I have given her. Maybe it's best that way. With tears in his eyes he says goodbye. Now is when I'm really leaving Africa, he thinks. Whatever binds me to this continent ceases with Joyce and her daughters.

When he gets into the car, the daughters are dancing around him. Joyce beats a drum and the sound follows him away. The outcome of the future depends on these women, he thinks again. I can only pass on a part of the money I still have in abundance. The future is their own.

He assembles his foremen and promises to do what he can so that the new owner will keep them all on. He buys two oxen and prepares for a party. A lorry comes to the farm with 4,000 bottles of beer. The party goes on all night; the fires flare up and drunken Africans dance to a seemingly endless number of drums. Olofson sits with the old men and watches the dark bodies moving around the fires. Tonight nobody hates me, he thinks. Tomorrow the usual reality will resume. This is a night when no knife blades glisten. The whetstones are at rest.

Tomorrow reality is once again as it must be, filled to bursting point with contradictions that one day will explode in a necessary revolt. In the shadows he thinks he sees Peter Motombwane. Which one of these people will carry on his dream? Someone will do it, I'm certain of that.

One Saturday in December he sells off the furniture in the house at an improvised auction. The white colony has come, along with a few blacks. Mr Pihri and his son are an exception, Patel another. None of them places any bids. The books that he once took over from Judith Fillington are purchased by a mining engineer from Luansha. His shotgun goes to one of his neighbours. He decides to keep his revolver. The furniture he once used for barricades is carried off to vehicles which then drive to various farms. He keeps two wicker chairs that sit on the terrace. On this Saturday he receives innumerable invitations to farewell dinners. He accepts them all.

When the auction is over only his empty house remains, and the question of who will take over the farm. Mr Pihri and Patel make identical offers, as if they had entered into a secret pact. But Olofson knows that they are bitter enemies, and he decides once and for all to play them off against each other. He sets a date, 15 December at midday. Whoever gives him the highest bid by that deadline will take over the farm.

With a lawyer he has brought in from Lusaka he waits on the terrace. A few minutes before twelve both Patel and Mr Pihri arrive. Olofson asks them to write down their bids on slips of paper. Mr Pihri excuses himself for not having a pen and has to borrow one from the lawyer. Patel's bid is higher than Mr Pihri's. When Olofson reads the result, he sees the hatred for Patel flash in Mr Pihri's eyes. Patel won't have an easy time of it with him, Olofson thinks. With him or with his son.

'There is one unwritten condition,' Olofson tells Patel when they are alone. 'One condition that I do not hesitate to impose, since you have bought this farm for a shamelessly low price.'

'The times are hard,' says Patel.

'The times are always hard,' Olofson interrupts him. 'If you don't take good care of the employees I will haunt you in your dreams. It's the workers who know how to run this farm, and it's they who have fed me all these years.'

'Of course, everything will remain as it has always been,' Patel replies humbly.

'That's the best way,' says Olofson. 'Otherwise I'll come back and impale your head on a pole.'

Patel blanches and crouches on the stool where he's sitting at Olofson's feet. Papers are signed, the title is transferred. Olofson signs his name quickly to get it over with.

'Mr Pihri kept my pen,' says the lawyer gloomily as he gets up to go.

'You'll never see it again,' says Olofson.

'I know,' says the lawyer. 'But it was a nice pen.'

Now he is alone with Patel. The transfer is dated 1 February 1988. Patel promises to transfer as much money as he can to the bank in London. The difficulties and risks he estimates as equivalent to forty-five per cent.

'Don't you show yourself here before the morning I leave,' says Olofson. 'When you drive me to Lusaka you can have your keys.'

Patel quickly gets to his feet and bows.

'Go now,' says Olofson. 'I'll let you know when you can come to pick me up.'

Olofson uses the time that remains to say goodbye to his neighbours. He visits farm after farm, gets drunk, returns to his empty house.

The waiting period makes him restless. He books his ticket,

sells his car cheap to Behan the Irishman, on the condition that he can use it until he leaves.

When his neighbours ask what he's going to do, he tells them the truth, that he doesn't know. To his astonishment he discovers that many of them envy his leaving. Their terror, he thinks. Their utterly understandable terror. They know that their time is up, just like mine. And yet they aren't able to leave.

A few days before his departure he has a visit from Eisenhower Mudenda, who gives him a stone with blue veins running through it and a brown leather pouch containing a powder.

'Yes,' says Olofson. 'Over me there will be a different starry sky. I'm travelling to a strange world where the sun sometimes shines, even at night.'

Mudenda thinks a long time about what Olofson has said.

'Carry the stone and the pouch in your pocket, *Bwana*,' he says at last.

'Why?' Olofson asks.

'Because I give them to you, *Bwana*,' says Mudenda. 'They will give you a long life. But it also means that our spirits will know when you no longer exist. Then we can dance for you when you return to your forefathers.'

'I shall carry them,' says Olofson.

Mudenda prepares to go.

'My dog,' says Olofson. 'One morning someone chopped off its head and lashed it to a tree with barbed wire.'

'The one who did that is dead, *Bwana*,' says Mudenda.

'Peter Motombwane?' Olofson asks.

Eisenhower Mudenda looks at him for a long time before he replies.

'Peter Motombwane is alive, *Bwana*,' he says.

'I understand,' says Olofson.

Mudenda walks away and Olofson looks at his ragged clothes.

At least I'm not leaving Africa with his curses, he thinks. At least I wasn't one of the worst. And besides, I'm doing what they want, leaving, acknowledging that I'm defeated.

Olofson is alone in his empty house, alone with Luka. The end has come. He gives Luka 1,000 *kwacha*.

'Don't wait until I'm gone,' Olofson says. 'Leave now. But where will you go?'

'My roots are in Malawi, *Bwana*,' replies Luka. 'Beyond the mountains by the long lake. It is a long way to go. But I am strong enough to make the long journey. My feet are ready.'

'Go in the morning. Don't wait by my door at dawn.'

'Yes, *Bwana*. I will go.'

The next day he is gone. I never knew what was in his thoughts, Olofson thinks. I'll never find out whether he was the one I saw the night I killed Peter Motombwane.

On the last night he sits for a long time on the terrace. Insects buzz their farewell around his face. The German shepherds are gone; his neighbours have adopted them. He listens into the darkness, feels the warm wind caress his face. Again it's the rainy season, again the torrents pound on his roof. But on his last evening the sky is clear.

Now, Hans Olofson, he thinks. Now you are leaving here. You will never return. A stone with blue veins, a brown leather pouch, and some crocodile teeth are all you take with you from this place.

He tries to think of what he might do. The only thing that occurs to him is to search for his mother. If I find her I can tell her about Africa, he thinks. About this wounded and lacerated continent. About the superstition and the boundless wisdom. About the poverty and the plague that was created by us, the white men and women. But I can also tell her about the future that is here, which I have seen for myself. Joyce Lufuma and her daughters, the dignified resistance which survives in this most trampled of worlds. There's one thing I understand after all these years: Africa has been sacrificed on a Western altar, robbed of its future for one or two generations. But no more, no longer, I have also understood that.

An owl hoots in the dark. Powerful wings flap past. Invisible cicadas play near his feet. When he at last gets up and goes inside, he leaves the door open behind him.

He awakes at daybreak. It is 2 February 1988, and he is about to leave Africa, a departure that has been postponed for nearly nineteen years.

Through his bedroom window he sees the red sun rise above the horizon. Mists are floating slowly over the Kafue. From one river he is returning to another. From the Kafue and Zambezi he returns to Ljusnan. The sighing hippo he will take with him, and he knows that in his dreams the crocodiles will live in the Norrland river. Two river arteries diverge in my life, he thinks. A Norrland Africa I carry in my heart.

One last time he walks through the silent house. My departure is always empty-handed, he thinks. Maybe that's an advantage after all, something that makes it easier for me.

He opens the door. The ground is wet. Barefoot he walks down to the river. He thinks he can see the elephant's thigh bone on the bottom. He flings his revolver into the water.

He walks back to the house and picks up his bag. In his jacket he has his passport and cash in a plastic case. Patel is sitting on the terrace, waiting. He gets to his feet hastily and bows when Olofson comes out.

'Give me five minutes,' he says. 'Wait in the car.'

Patel hurries down the steps with his trouser legs flapping. Olofson tries to compress almost nineteen years into one last moment. Maybe I'll be able to understand it later, he thinks.

What did all these years in Africa mean? Those years that passed so indescribably fast and which flung me unprepared into my middle age. It's as if I have lived in a weightless vacuum. Only my passport confirms that I still exist.

A bird with wings like a purple cloak flies past. I will remember that, he thinks. He gets into the car where Patel is waiting.

'Drive carefully,' he says.

Patel gives him a worried look. 'I always drive carefully, Mr Olofson.'

'You live a life that makes your hands sweaty all the time,' Olofson says. 'Greed is your inheritance, nothing more. Not your worried, well-meaning, lying face. Drive now, don't say a word!'

That afternoon he steps out of the car at the Ridgeway Hotel. He tosses the keys to his house on to the seat and leaves Patel. He sees that the African holding the door open is wearing shoes in just as bad condition as the workers he'd seen when he arrived almost nineteen years ago.

As he requested, he is given room 212, but he doesn't recognise it. The room has changed, the angles are different. He undresses and spends his waiting time in bed. After many attempts he manages to get his booking confirmed by telephone. A seat is reserved for him under the stars.

Relief and anxiety, he thinks, that's what I experience. Those emotions are my mental shield. They should be included in my epitaph. From the smell of elkhounds and African charcoal fires I take the basic elements of my peculiar life. And yet there is also something else. People like Patel or Lars Håkansson learn to understand the world so they can exploit it. Peter Motombwane understood it in order to change it. He possessed the knowledge but he chose the wrong weapon at the wrong time. Still, we resemble each other. Between Patel and me there is a chasm. And Lars Håkansson is dead. Peter Motombwane and I are the survivors, even though my heart is the only one still beating. That knowledge no one can take away from me.

In the twilight of the hotel room he thinks of Janine and her dream of Mutshatsha. Her lonely vigil on the street corner between the People's Hall and the hardware shop.

Peter Motombwane, he thinks. Peter, Janine and me.

A rusty taxi takes him to the airport. Olofson gives the last of his *kwacha* notes to the driver, who is very young.

At the check-in, almost no one but white people are queueing. This is where Africa ends, he thinks. Europe is already closer than the plains with the tall elephant grass. In the murmur at the counter he listens for the sighing hippo. Behind the pillars he thinks he sees the leopard's eye watching him. Then he walks through the various checkpoints.

Distant drums suddenly begin to rumble inside him. Marjorie and Peggy dance and their black faces glisten. No one met me, he thinks. On the other hand, I met myself. No one is accompanying me to my departure except the man I was back then, the man I now leave behind. He sees his own image in one of the airport's huge windows. Now I'm going home, he thinks. There's nothing remarkable about it, yet it's remarkable enough.

The big aeroplane shines with rainwater and floodlights. Far out on the runway, lit by a yellow lamp, stands a lone African. Utterly motionless, enfolded by a thought. For a long time Olofson looks at him before he boards the aeroplane that will take him away from Africa.

Nothing more, he thinks. Now it's over.

Mutshatsha, farewell . . .

Presented to

Norman Kennedy
for
Bible Class
Attendance
9th June 1985

PICKERING & INGLIS LTD.   PRINTED IN GREAT BRITAIN